The Craftsman

Also by Sharon Bolton

Sacrifice
Awakening
Blood Harvest
Now You See Me
Dead Scared
Lost
A Dark and Twisted Tide
Little Black Lies
Daisy in Chains
Dead Woman Walking

The Craftsman

SHARON BOLTON

Minotaur Books
New York

THE CRAFTSMAN. Copyright © 2018 by Sharon Bolton. All rights reserved. Printed in the United States of America. For information, address St. Martin's Press, 175 Fifth Avenue, New York, N.Y. 10010.

www.minotaurbooks.com

Library of Congress Cataloging-in-Publication Data

Names: Bolton, S. J., author.
Title: The craftsman / Sharon Bolton.
Description: First U.S. edition. | New York : Minotaur Books, 2018.
Identifiers: LCCN 2018020147 | ISBN 9781250300034 (hardcover) | ISBN 9781250300041 (ebook)
Subjects: | GSAFD: Suspense fiction. | Mystery fiction.
Classification: LCC PR6102.O49 C73 2018 | DDC 823/.92—dc23
LC record available at https://lccn.loc.gov/2018020147

Our books may be purchased in bulk for promotional, educational, or business use. Please contact your local bookseller or the Macmillan Corporate and Premium Sales Department at 1-800-221-7945, extension 5442, or by email at MacmillanSpecialMarkets@macmillan.com.

First published in Great Britain by Trapeze, an imprint of The Orion Publishing Group Ltd, an Hachette UK company

First U.S. Edition: October 2018

10 9 8 7 6 5 4 3 2 1

For Carrie

Part One

'I have supped full with horrors.'

Macbeth, William Shakespeare

1

Tuesday, 10 August 1999

On the hottest day of the year, Larry Glassbrook has come home to his native Lancashire for the last time, and the townsfolk have turned out to say goodbye.

Not in a friendly way.

It might be just fancy on my part but the crowd outside the church seems to have grown during the brief, chill funeral service, swelling the numbers that arrived early to claim a good spot, the way people do before a big parade.

Everywhere I look, people stand among headstones, flank the perimeter wall and line the footpaths like some ghastly guard of honour. As we follow the coffin out into sunshine bright enough to cauterise wounds, they watch us, without moving or speaking.

The press are here in force, in spite of the date being kept secret for as long as possible. Uniformed police hold them back, keeping the paths and the porch clear, but the photographers have brought stepladders and huge telescopic lenses. The rounded, fluffy microphones of the news presenters look powerful enough to pick up the scampering of church mice.

I keep my eyes down, push my sunglasses a little higher on my nose, although I know I look very different now. Thirty years is a long time.

A few yards ahead of me, beads of moisture swell and burst on the necks of the pallbearers. These men leave a trail behind them, a smell of aftershave and beer-infused sweat, of suits that aren't dry-cleaned quite often enough.

Standards have slipped since Larry's day. The men who worked for Glassbrook & Greenwood Funeral Directors wore suits as black as newly mined coal. Their shoes and hair gleamed, and they shaved so close as to leave raw, rash-scarred skin behind. Larry's men carried the caskets reverently, like the works of art they were. Larry would never have permitted the cheap laminate coffin I can see in front of me.

Knowing that his own funeral fell short of the standards he'd insisted upon could have been a bitter disappointment to Larry. On the other hand, he might have laughed, loudly and cruelly, the way he did sometimes, when you least expected it, when it was most unnerving. And then he might have run his fingers through his black hair, winked suggestively and resumed dancing to the Elvis Presley tracks that seemed constantly to be playing in his workshop.

After all this time, even thinking about Elvis Presley's music sets my heart racing.

The cheap coffin and its bearers turn like a giant crawling insect and leave the path. As we head south towards the Glassbrook family plot, the heat on our faces is as intense and searching as limelight in a down-at-heel musical hall. In Lancashire, this high on the moors, hot days are scarce, but the sun today seems determined to give Larry a foretaste of the temperatures waiting for him in his next place of confinement.

I wonder what words his headstone might carry: *Loving husband, devoted father, merciless killer.*

As his last minutes above ground tick away, the crowd seems to press forward and hang back simultaneously, like a confused tide that can't quite remember whether it is ebbing or flowing.

Then, out of the corner of my eye, half hidden behind the rim of my sunglasses, I spot the teenagers. A boy and two girls, small, skinny, dressed in garishly coloured polyester. The eyes of the adults flick around the churchyard, resentfully at the mourners, nervously at the police, curiously at the media. The teenagers watch only the chief mourner, the woman who walks immediately behind the vicar, directly in front of me.

She's beautiful in a way that no one would have predicted when she was fifteen. Her hair has become honey-blonde, and her body has filled out. No longer does she resemble a carnival puppet, its head too big for its spindly stick body. Eyes that used to stare like those of a startled bushbaby from a TV wildlife programme are now the right size for her face. The black dress she wears has the crisp texture and clarity of colour of a brand-new purchase.

A muttered whisper suggests the watchers are following. The woman in the new black dress turns her head. I can't help but copy her and see that the three teenagers are coming too.

At the sight of them, the wound on my left hand begins to hurt. I tuck it into my right armpit, using my upper arm to bring gentle pressure against the pain. It helps, a bit, but I can feel sweat trickling down between my shoulder blades. The vicar is no more relaxed than I am. His handkerchief is out, rubbing the back of his neck and dabbing at his forehead, but he begins the burial prayers with the air of a man who knows the end is in sight. At the appointed time, the pallbearers lessen the tension on the ropes they hold and the coffin wobbles lower until we no longer see it.

That's when it hits us. I see my own thought reflected in the eyes of those around me, and a whisper of troubled energy ripples through the crowd.

'Better than you deserve, you bastard,' calls a voice from the back.

This is exactly what Larry did to his young victims. He lowered them into the ground. Only they weren't dead.

One of the teenagers, the youngest, has wandered away from his friends and is half hiding behind a headstone. He peers out at me with a sly curiosity. Stephen, the name comes to me quickly. The skinny kid in the blue shirt is Stephen.

A slick, sweating pallbearer is offering me earth and so I take a handful and approach the grave. There are no flowers on the coffin lid, nor were there any in church. I don't remember ever seeing a church without them before and I have a sudden vision of the women of the parish coming solemnly and silently into the building last night to remove them, because this is not an occasion for flowers.

Close to the church wall, barely visible behind the crowd, is the man who was the sexton in the old days. He is dressed in a black suit now. He doesn't look up, and I don't think my old friend has seen me.

I let the earth fall, conscious that, behind me, it is being offered to the other mourners, who are politely shaking their heads. Taking it was the wrong thing to do, then. The thing that has made me stand out. Again.

The prayers are complete. 'Judge not,' ad-libs the vicar, suddenly brave, 'that ye be not judged.' He bows to no one in particular and scurries off.

The pallbearers fade into the background. I step back too and the woman with honey-blonde hair is alone at the grave.

Not for long. The watchers are egging each other on to become participants. Slowly the mass creeps forward. The teenagers, too, are drawing closer, although they are harder to see than the adults in the bright sunshine.

The watchers come to a standstill. The woman in black looks at them directly, but none will meet her eyes. Then a woman of sixty-something steps forward, until her sandalled feet, toenails grimy with dust, stand on the very edge of the grave. I know this woman. Years ago, she confronted me, when misery and anger got the better of all her decent instincts. I remember her fat finger jabbing at my face, the bitterness of her breath as she leaned in and stabbed me with her threats and accusations. Her name is Duxbury; she is the mother of Larry's first victim, Susan.

Standing on the edge of Larry's grave, she sucks in breath, leans forward and spits. It is possibly the first time in her life that she has done so. The spittle is thin, dribbling. If it makes a sound as it hits the wood, I don't hear it. The next to approach the grave is more practised. A huge, bull-necked, bald-headed man, probably younger than the creases in his skin suggest. He hawks and then phlegm, solid as congealing paint, smacks onto the coffin. One by one the others follow, until the coffin beneath them must be spattered with spittle flowers.

The last of them to approach the graveside is an elderly man, thin and dark-skinned, eyes like stones. He looks round.

'Nowt personal, lass,' he says to the woman in the black dress, as I try to imagine anything more personal than spitting on a grave. 'We never blamed you.' Bow-legged, arthritic, he moves away.

For a minute, maybe more, the woman in the black dress is motionless, staring at something in the middle distance. Then, without looking back, she crosses the grass towards the path, perhaps bracing herself to run the gauntlet of reporters and photographers. They have kept their distance during the service, but they didn't come here for nothing and they won't leave without something.

I follow in her wake, but a sound grabs my attention and I stop. Behind me, at the graveside, I hear the teenagers making high-pitched, sucking noises as they try to copy the adults and spit on Larry's coffin. I suppose they have more excuse than most, but what they are doing seems feeble, and beneath them. I think I might speak to them, tell them it must surely be time to move on, but when I look back, they are nowhere to be seen. Those three kids haven't walked the earth in thirty years and yet I can't help but feel that the woman in the black dress has seen their ghosts too.

2

I have no means of knowing exactly what Patricia Wood suffered in the hours following her disappearance. I suppose I should consider that a blessing.

After we found her, everyone said they couldn't bear to think about it, that it was too terrible even to imagine, that one really shouldn't dwell on such things.

If only I could help myself. Imagination is a valuable tool, vital for any detective worth his or her salt. It's also the heaviest cross we bear.

And so I imagine that Patsy regained consciousness slowly, and that her first lucid thought was that she was struggling to breathe. The fabric that covered her face was satin, light in weight, but in a confined space full of stale air it must have felt stifling.

There would have been an evil taste in her mouth, partly the result of not drinking for several hours. Disorientation would have been the worst of it, though, in those first few minutes, without a clue where she was or how she got there. Any memories she could dredge up would have been half formed, a mass of random pictures and snatches of dialogue. She would have tried opening her eyes, closing them, opening them again and found no difference at all.

I think at this point she would have tried to move. To push herself to a sitting position. That's when panic would really have set in, when she realised that she was entirely boxed in.

It was worse than that, of course. Patsy was deep in the ground. Buried alive.

3

One or two of the older reporters stare as I leave, their eyes narrowing as they search their memories. I made the right decision not wearing uniform today. Given time, they'll place me, but I don't give them time. I push my way out through the gate and head up the hill towards my car. In any event, they are far more interested in the woman in the stylish black dress with the honey-blonde hair. She needs a police escort to get through the crowd, and I catch a glimpse of her as the waiting car pulls away. She looks at me from the passenger seat. In church, she'd given no sign of even knowing I was there. I assumed she'd forgotten me, that to her I was just another curious bystander. That glance through the darkened glass tells me she remembers me perfectly.

I chose to lodge with the Glassbrooks rather than in any of the other boarding houses on offer when I moved to Sabden because I sensed an eccentricity in the family that appealed to me. They were different, somehow, to most of the people I met in town. I thought of them as colourful, exotic birds, surrounded by a flock of small, noisy, dust-covered house sparrows. After just a couple of weeks in Lancashire, I was acutely conscious of how very different I seemed to the people around me. I was looking for birds of a feather, I suppose. Not my only mistake, in this town.

They lived on the outskirts of Sabden, in a large detached house. The narrow gravel drive is choked with weeds now, and dandelion seeds come drifting towards me like an airborne army. Moss covers the low stone wall that holds back the banked garden, and the grass between the fruit trees hasn't been cut in months, maybe years. It is a tiny meadow now. The white clusters of cow parsley reach almost to the low branches of neglected fruit trees, where plums, already rotten, are abuzz with wasps. There are hundreds of apples on the trees, but the fruit is tiny and worm-ridden. A mush at the foot of each suggests that, for years, successive crops have fallen and rotted.

I round the only bend in the drive and see the house. A stone mansion, built for a factory manager or wool merchant at the turn of the twentieth century. Paint has peeled away from the front door, and the huge bay window is dirty and cracked in places. That room was the lodgers' sitting room, where I spent my evenings when I could no longer reasonably stay at work and my room felt too lonely. The two other lodgers were men. Another police constable, called Randall (known as Randy) Butterworth, and a quiet, plump man in his forties called Ron Pickles, who worked with Larry at the funeral business. They and I talked sometimes, occasionally played cards, but mainly we stared at the grainy, dancing screen of a twelve-inch, black-and-white television. There was talk that the family, in the bigger parlour which overlooked the rear garden, had a colour TV, but this remained a rumour.

The tiny television set is still there. So are the PVC-covered armchairs that felt slick and sticky in summer, too cold for comfort in winter. Barring broken light bulbs littering the carpet, the damp stains on the walls and the dirt on the windows, the lodgers' sitting room is exactly as I remember it.

I follow the path to the rear, keeping my eyes fixed on the walls and windows of the house. The curtains are drawn on the family parlour, but I have no real memories of that room anyway. I was never invited in. The back door is open.

I step up and peer into the room they called the back kitchen. It's small, with a huge stone sink and stained wooden worktops. Wall-mounted shelves hold dust-covered crockery, dull glassware and huge copper pans. My own mother would have called this a butler's pantry, but the word 'butler' wasn't part of the lexicon of the people of Sabden back in 1969.

'Hello?' I say.

No one answers. A painful twinge shoots from my left hand towards my elbow as I step inside. A door opposite would take me into the bigger kitchen, where Sally cooked meals for her family and her lodgers. Her lotions and potions, as Larry called them, were made in this room, stored in a walk-in cupboard by the back door. She had a gas cooker, old back in 1969, to boil up herbs and roots. It's still here.

I hear a low-pitched buzzing sound behind me and turn to see that bees have found their way inside somehow. In but not out again, because over a dozen tiny black-and-orange corpses litter the windowsill. Sally kept bees. There were four hives at the bottom of the garden, and during the spring and early summer that I lived here, she'd often go out to feed or inspect them, wrapped up in her heavy white veil and thick gloves. On warm days, she'd sit and watch the predictable trajectory of the worker bees as they zoomed out of the hives heading for blossom.

She had a habit, one I found curious but charming, of making sure the bees were kept informed of any important news in the family. When Cassie, her elder daughter, won a music scholarship, she was sent straight outside to tell the bees. The news of the death of Larry's aunt was told to the bees before some of the family were informed. Calamity would fall on the house, Sally told me, if the bees were kept in the dark.

'Can I help you?' someone says, in a tone that suggests helping me is the last thing on her mind, and I turn to see a stout, grey-haired woman in her seventies standing in the doorway. I fish in my bag and find my Met warrant card. I have no authority in Lancashire, but I doubt she'll know that.

'Assistant Commissioner Florence Lovelady,' I tell her. 'I was looking for the family.'

'Haven't lived here for years,' she says, with her habitual note of triumph when giving bad news.

I know who this woman is. Sally had a 'woman that does' who came in every day to help with the cooking and cleaning. This woman served me breakfast and dinner six days a week for five months and every two weeks brought a clean set of nylon sheets to my room. She never knocked before entering, just announced, 'Sheets,' before dumping them on the bed. I was always expected to change my own bed, but I'm pretty certain she did the job for the men who lodged here. She was the kind of woman happy to wait on men but considered it beneath her to do the same for a woman, especially one younger than herself. In the late 1960s, the worst sex discrimination I had to deal with always came from other women.

I let my gaze move around the dusty surfaces, glance over the dead insects and say, 'I'm surprised they haven't sold it.'

'The girls wanted to. It was Sally who hung on.'

'You're Mary, aren't you? I lived here. In 1969.' I don't add, 'Back when it happened.' It hardly feels necessary.

She squints at me.

'The family called me Flossie,' I say reluctantly. 'My hair was different then. A much brighter shade of red.'

'Ginger,' she says. 'Colour of carrots.'

'How are you, Mary?' I ask her.

'You were covered in freckles.' She takes a step closer, as if to check whether I still have them. I do, although they've faded over time. 'You went bright red when someone showed you up.'

'Where is Sally, do you know?' I ask. 'Is she still alive?'

'Northdean Nursing Home at Barley,' she tells me. 'She won't speak to you.'

I still have my warrant card in my hand. 'Do you mind if I look around?' I ask her.

'Suit yourself,' she tells me. 'I need spuds. Then I'm locking up.'

She leaves me, heading towards the vegetable garden, and I walk further into the house. I don't open the door of the parlour – old habits die hard – and have no interest in the lodgers' sitting room, so instead I walk along the high-ceilinged corridor until I'm almost at the front door, then turn and climb the stairs. My room was the smallest of those given to the lodgers, at the back of the house, overlooking the Hill.

The door sticks and for a moment I'm tempted to see it as a sign that there is nothing to be gained from dredging up old memories. But my stubborn streak always won out against my better instinct and I push hard.

The lilac-and-blue crocheted bedspread that I hated is still here, but its colour has faded from years of being exposed to sunlight. The narrow bed under the window is made up, and I wouldn't be surprised if those are the sheets I slept on all those years ago, that if we were to employ the forensic techniques that weren't available to us in the 1960s, a trace of me could still be found. After all, who else would have lodged here after what happened? The door on the narrow wardrobe is hanging open. One of the drawers in the chest by the bed isn't properly closed and I spot a plastic hairbrush in it that might have been mine once. It is as though no one has been in this room since I left it in a hurry. Randy and I weren't allowed back after Larry Glassbrook's arrest. Our things were collected by other officers and I spent the rest of my time in Lancashire in a hostel on the other side of town.

The three police posters that I taped to the wall are still here.

Missing, reads the first. *Have you see Stephen Shorrock? Missing*, says the second. *Have you seen Susan Duxbury? Missing*, again, on the third. *Help us find Patsy.* I taped the posters directly opposite my bed, in spite of Mary's grumbles that they were morbid and would damage the woodchip wallpaper. They were the first things I saw when I woke up each morning, the last at night.

As I'd approached the house, I'd avoided looking at Larry's workshop, a one-storey brick building a short distance from the back door, but I can't avoid it now. Its flat roof is directly in front of my window.

I reach out and touch the wall for balance, take a deep breath although the air in here is stale and warm.

The workshop is where Larry spent most of his time, where he played his music – no, I do not want those songs in my head – and where he made the coffins and caskets that held the remains of Sabden's dead.

And a few of its very unlucky living.

4

The words 'coffin' and 'casket' are used interchangeably, but the two are quite different. A coffin is a six- or eight-sided box that follows the contours of the body: narrow at the head, widening at the shoulders, tapering in again towards the feet. Think Dracula, rising. A casket is bigger, rectangular, usually with a large, curved lid.

Larry Glassbrook made both, but hardwood caskets were his passion. I lodged with his family for five months in 1969 and once – when he was bored, I think – he invited me into his workshop. He played music as he worked – Elvis Presley, almost certainly – and broke off from time to time to roll his hips or slick back his dark hair. Larry was a handsome man and he made the most of his resemblance to the King of Rock. He was rarely short of female attention but, to be honest, I found him a bit creepy. There was no doubting his skill, though.

He started with the lid, gluing and pressing together long slats of oak in a rounded vice. He used joint fasteners, a sort of heavy-duty staple, to make sure they couldn't move. The box was made in a similar fashion, glued, fastened and joisted to give it strength. Larry liked to boast that his caskets could carry men weighing 300 pounds or more. The lid was fastened to the box with four metal hinges and sixteen screws.

No one was getting out of a Larry Glassbrook casket once they were shut inside. In fairness, very few people tried.

Coffins and caskets weren't hermetically sealed in those days. If they had been, Patsy Wood might have died before she ever regained consciousness. Larry's caskets were closed using a method he invented himself. Immediately below the rim of the lid, directly opposite the outer hinges, were two locking mechanisms hidden beneath decorative trims. When the latch was turned, a small metal strip on the inside of the coffin, concealed behind the fabric lining, slid into place and prevented the lid from being dislodged during interment, or by any clumsy handling. If Patsy had known where to feel, if she'd managed to tear away the satin lining, she might have been able to unlock the casket.

She'd still have needed to deal with the ton of earth above it.

She didn't find the locks. We know that. But I can still imagine her reaching frantically around the tiny space she found herself in. I think she'd have screamed then, her voice loud and scared, but angry too. At fourteen, we don't imagine anything really dreadful can happen to us. At that point, she would have thought she was the victim of a practical joke, horrible but temporary. If she yelled loudly and long enough, they'd get her out of here, wherever 'here' was.

She would have called out the names of those she could last remember, the people she'd been with before it happened. One of the things I wonder, when I think about Patsy's time in the casket, is how quickly she stopped shouting for her friends and began to call for her mother.

I'd put it at less than thirty minutes after she came round, but I imagine time goes slowly when you're trapped beneath the earth.

Caskets are bigger than coffins. She'd have been able to reach up, feel the smooth, pleated satin inches above her head. I think at that point she would have known what contained her. She knew the Glassbrook family. She knew what Larry Glassbrook did for a living. She'd probably been invited into his workshop, or sneaked in with her friends, to see the wooden boxes in various stages of readiness. She'd have known then that she was trapped in a casket, although she'd probably have called it a coffin.

I imagine her falling silent, believing her mates (because of course it was her mates – who else would play such a trick on her?) were just outside the casket, listening to her screams. Patsy would have forced herself to be quiet, thinking they'd be quicker to let her out if they thought she might be in real trouble. Maybe she even gave a gasp or two, as though she were struggling for air.

When that didn't work, because it couldn't work – her friends were nowhere near – I think she'd have screamed again, long, loud and hard this time. I have no idea how long a person can scream before it becomes impossible to go on. I hope I never find out. But at some point, maybe when she'd been conscious for about an hour, Patsy would have fallen silent, if only for a time.

The exertion would have exhausted her. She'd have been panting. Hot. Sweating. It would have occurred to her that air was probably in short supply. I think this is when she would have begun to plan, to think of any possible ways of getting herself out. She'd have started, tentatively and as calmly as she could, to explore her surroundings. And then she'd have discovered something even more terrifying than that she was trapped in a coffin.

She wasn't alone.

5

The sight of Larry's workshop has hit me hard. I sit on the bed to get my breath, positioning myself so that I can't see it and am looking instead at the Hill. Of all the rooms in the house, this one has the best view of it.

The Hill is unchanged, of course. I doubt it ever will change. In the sunshine, in August, it has a wild beauty that might almost make you forget its terrible history, the merciless persecution of helpless women that happened here. The grasses have turned golden, and the heather is blooming all the way up the south face. The bare rocks gleam like jewels in the bright light. It is a huge plateau-topped mass of limestone and clay that has given rise to a thousand legends, all of them dark. It soars above this small town, throwing its shadow over the lives of the people who live at its foot.

This is Pendle. Witch country.

High above the Hill, almost invisible in the cloudless cornflower-blue sky, is the curved outline of a waning moon. In a few more hours it will disappear altogether, before starting to wax again. Long ago, I gave up trying to shake off this constant awareness of the phases of the moon and doubt I ever will now. Every night before I go to bed, I look for the moon. I draw my curtains a little tighter when it is full, and when it's at its darkest, at the end of the waning phase, I know I'll struggle to sleep.

The children were taken during the dark phase of the moon.

I hear a sudden burst of humming, followed by the buffeting of a tiny body against a hard surface. On the window ledge among a scattering of bee carcasses is one desperate to be free. As I reach for the window catch, I avoid looking down at the workshop and see instead the hives at the bottom of the garden.

The last time I saw Larry, he was dying. He sat across from me in the visiting room, coughing repeatedly into a bloodstained handkerchief. Almost seventy, he looked years older. His hair, still thick and slightly too long, had turned snow white, while his face was shrunken, lined and, deep within each wrinkle, there seemed to be a narrow line of prison filth. Long-term prisoners never look clean. His nose had been broken more than once, and an injury to just above his right eye had left his brow in a coarse and puckered zigzag.

'You never ask me anything, Florence,' he said, as his shaking hands reached for another of the cigarettes that were killing him. 'Why is that?'

'I do. All the time.' I tried not to stare at his twisted, arthritic hands. Those hands had once been so clever; now, they could barely hold the cigarette steady.

He curled his lip, Elvis style, an affected habit he'd never lost. 'Stuff about Sally and the girls, about how I am and whether I need anything. I don't mean that.' He leaned a little closer towards me. 'I mean about before. You never ask me anything about that.'

In all the years I visited Larry, I made a point of never talking about the case. I knew all about the power play that went on between convicted killers and their arresting officers, about how a need for information could turn even the smartest officer into an emotional hostage, craving closure he or she was never going to get. There were many gaps in our knowledge of the Glassbrook case, but I could live with that. I wasn't going to beg.

'So I'm wondering' – he had a sly smile on his lips as he ignored my silence – 'whether it's because you've been afraid to learn the truth.'

I faked a heavy sigh. 'Is there something you want to tell me, Larry?'

He seemed to think for a moment although, knowing Larry quite well by this time, I could tell when the thinking was real and when it was staged. Finally, he shook his head. 'Nah,' he said. 'I told it to the bees.'

Something shifts in the house, an old beam, maybe a floorboard, and in my nervous state the abrupt noise sounds like a footstep on the stairs. I spin round, dreading the sight of a small procession of dead teenagers coming up the stairs towards me, maybe even Larry himself. The staircase is empty, of course.

I've spent the better part of thirty years trying to come to terms with my 'ghosts'. I know they're not really there. I don't believe that the dead stay with us, or that we ever genuinely see them again after they've passed. Sometimes, though, I imagine myself having double vision, looking out at two worlds: the one I know to be real, seen by everyone else, and the other, created from the dark places in my own brain.

In the world of my damaged imagination, ghosts are my constant friends.

Needing to get out of this grim house now, I practically run down the stairs. There is no sign of Mary, so I step out into the garden. She's still out of sight. I should tell her I'm leaving, so I skirt round the workshop towards where I remember the vegetable patch to be. I don't find her, but I realise I'm close to the hives.

Tell it to the bees.

A silly idea. Bees don't stay in neglected hives. The four rotting, wooden constructs will have been abandoned years ago. And yet I'm in the mood for rituals, for closure – why else did I come here? – and so I approach warily, the way I always used to, even though the chances of the guard bees rising to ward off an attack are non-existent.

Nothing happens. The hives are empty. Even so I step closer.

Tell it to the bees.

'Larry is dead.' I speak quietly, aware of how foolish I will look if Mary is close. 'He died in prison two weeks ago.'

There is no response from the hive.

'I'm sorry for your loss.' Feeling like an idiot, I'm about to turn away when I see that the upper part of one hive is loose, as though someone has lifted it and not replaced it properly. My love of order doesn't like this, so I step closer and gingerly, because I'm still not a hundred per cent convinced this hive is empty, try to push it back into place.

It won't go. Either the wood has warped or something is in the way. I lift carefully, hold my breath and peer inside. The frames that held the honeycombs are gone, leaving a small, dusty empty space.

Not quite empty.

Empty but for something that is impossible.

I am looking down at what people round here call a 'clay picture', not really a picture at all but a three-dimensional effigy. Around eight inches high and fashioned from clay, it is meant to be female: the hair, breasts, belly and wide hips tell me that. The figure's legs are bent at the knee, and her feet have been trussed, or hog-tied, to her hands behind her back. Worse than that, there are sharp pieces of wood, and I know that it's blackthorn, because it's always blackthorn, impaling each of her eyes and ears, her mouth, head, chest and genitals.

The sounds of the summer day have faded. All I can hear is the steady thudding of my own heartbeat.

This is impossible. The property was searched from front to

back, attic to cellar, hedge to garden wall. This cannot have been here since Larry's arrest.

And yet who could have put it here since?

Tell it to the bees.

My hand is throbbing horribly now. It always does when I'm stressed, but never this bad. I reach out and touch the effigy with just the tip of one finger, tilting it. Some of it crumbles away and I feel physically sick, but I manage to move it enough to see. I've already seen the long, curly hair. I suspected, the second I saw it. Now I know for sure.

Each of Larry's victims was found with one of these effigies. The hog-tying of hands and feet represents the inability to move. They could not move in the caskets. Blackthorn pierced their eyes, ears and mouth because underground they were deaf, dumb and blind. The wounding of the head, chest and genitalia symbolised the draining of life that was inevitable once they were interred.

At least, that's what we assumed. Larry never told his interrogating officers why the clay pictures were important. He might have told me, but I never asked.

I should have asked. I should have asked while I had the chance.

This new effigy has enough detail, especially on the trussed hands, for me to hear its message loud and clear. The right hand has five fingers splayed, the way our hands instinctively spread when we are in pain. The left lies limp, four digits in a soft curl. Only four. The third finger, the finger that would hold a wedding band, is missing.

My own left hand is in agony now. I bring both hands up to my mouth to numb the pain and the third finger of my right hand slips easily into the gap on the left. I wear my wedding band on a chain round my neck because the ring finger of my left hand was sliced off years ago.

The clay effigy is me.

6

People trapped in coffins don't survive for long. Opinions we sought varied, putting survival time anywhere from a few minutes to a couple of days, but on one point all the experts agreed: it depends on the size of the coffin and the person inside. We learned a great deal that summer about cubic litres of air, body volume and a human's oxygen-consumption rate.

Patsy was small; her thin body wouldn't have taken up too much space in the casket: there would have been room for oxygen, had she not been laid on top of a corpse.

Patsy's casket wasn't sealed and had it been left above ground, she'd have had a chance. (Possibly a chance to die of thirst, but a chance all the same.) As it was, the earth piled on top of it formed as effective a seal as anyone could wish for. From the time she was buried, she had a few hours, we decided, eight at most.

At some point, she would have had to make a choice between frantically tearing at her surroundings, trying to fight her way out, and lying still to conserve what oxygen she had, because someone had put her in here and eventually, surely for the love of God, someone would let her out.

How long can a young girl wait, patiently, for a prankster to come back and let her out of a buried coffin? An hour? Let's say two.

We know Patsy's faith wavered because of the state in which we found her – and the casket. Skin had been torn from her hands, several of her fingernails had ripped away, and the satin lining was smeared with her blood. The lining was torn to shreds; she'd wrapped long swathes of it round her fists to protect them against the hard oak of the lid. Even so, several of her knuckles had broken. The casket was unblemished.

When Patsy heard the children playing – faintly, as though through fog, because they were several feet above her and earth insulates against sound in the same way that water does – she would have thought her prayers had been answered and I think then that she would have really let rip with the shouting and the screaming and the pleading, to get her out, for God's sake help her and get her out.

We can time this with some accuracy. She'd been in the ground for four and a half hours when she was given the first real hope of rescue.

She didn't take into account the sheer terror of small children, hearing a voice screaming at them from a newly dug grave.

7

'Mary!' I stand at the back door of the house, yelling for her. 'Mary, I need you back here now.' I sound angry. I only wish I were.

For several seconds nothing happens. I watch a bee bounce from one lavender stem to another, and then Mary appears from round the back of Larry's workshop.

'Where did this come from?' I point to the clay figure, now lying face down on the worktop. 'No, don't touch it. Do you have a clear plastic bag? Or some cling film? It may need to be fingerprinted.'

I am making no sense. I take a deep breath and try again. 'Mary, who comes to this house apart from you? Who have you seen hanging around in the garden?'

She doesn't answer.

'It's important.' I'm close to losing my temper, but I'm not angry. 'We can talk at the local police station, if you like.'

Instead of answering, Mary leans closer to look at the effigy and does something I've never seen before. She snarls. I can think of no better way to describe it. She curls back her lips and glares.

'Have you seen it before?'

She shakes her head. 'Where did you find it?'

'It's me, isn't it? It's got a missing finger.' I hold up my left hand, although Mary knows exactly what happened to me. Everyone in town knew about it.

She digs into her pocket and pulls out a set of keys. As it clatters onto the worktop, more clay dust crumbles from the effigy and I have to stop myself yelling at her to be careful.

'Lock up after yourself,' she tells me, as she steps towards the door. 'Keep the keys. I won't need them.'

She leaves me alone in a house I can't wait to get out of, but somehow I can't move. I'm standing in the kitchen, but in my head I'm looking down into an open drawer in an abandoned bedroom. My hairbrush. I left my hairbrush behind.

I'm not angry. I'm scared.

I wrap the clay picture in an old tea towel and lower it carefully into a supermarket carrier bag before locking the door. I have no idea where I'm going. All I can think is, *They have my hair.*

They have my hair.

8

I'm not thinking as I run down the Glassbrooks' drive, nor am I looking where I'm going. I don't see the tall male figure coming the other way until the two of us have collided. Before I can get a grip of myself, I yelp like a whipped dog.

'What the fuck?' The boy who nearly knocked me off my feet catches hold of my upper arms and takes a half-step back to steady us both. 'Mum, Mum, it's me. No, no, Mum, look at me.'

I can't breathe.

'Come on, look at me and count to ten. One, two . . .'

By the time he reaches ten, I am breathing again and have joined in, mouthing the numbers silently. We have done this before.

'I'm OK.' I'm embarrassed and so I try to look stern instead. 'And what have I told you about swearing?'

'What happened?' My teenage son, three inches taller than me and beautiful as a clear dawn after a long winter's night, ignores the scolding. 'I watched an old dear race down the drive a couple of minutes ago. Then you. What is this place?' He drops my arms and takes a step towards the house.

'Ben, don't . . .'

His head turns back slowly. 'Is this where they lived? You promised Dad you wouldn't.'

'You would have seen Mary. She looks after the place.' My right hand is hurting too now and I glance down to see I'm gripping the house keys. I have no idea why Mary has given them to me. Or what I will do with them.

Ben is staring up the Glassbrooks' drive again. He has a teenage boy's natural fascination with the macabre and would never have stayed in the car had I told him where I was really going.

'I can't believe none of you knew,' he says, almost to himself. 'You lived in the same house all that time and you didn't know.' He glances back, but briefly. 'Did he bring them here? The kids he took?'

'We should go. Aren't you hungry?'

We walk the last few paces down the drive towards the car. I open the car boot and tuck the effigy behind my overnight bag.

'What have you been up to?' I ask.

He sniffs. 'Let down a few tyres. Nicked a pack of fags from that shop down there. Set fire to a garage. Oh, and I might have killed a dog with that thing in your glove compartment.'

'What?' I'm actually looking down the street for a dead dog – 'Please tell me you haven't touched that' – before I see the look on his face.

'How did you even know it was there?' I ask.

'I was looking for matches.' He hands over the car keys, which I left in his safekeeping. 'OK, I was looking for Polos. I found matches in the boot, though. They'd fallen out of your bag. You've brought some weird stuff, Mum.'

'Get in,' I tell him. 'And stay out of the glove compartment. I can't tell you how dangerous that thing is.'

We climb in and the first thing Ben does is open the glove compartment.

'Don't.' I lean over and push it shut.

'What is it?'

'It's a CS gas canister. A Section 1 firearm. I shouldn't even have it with me and if you're found with it we'll both be in big trouble.'

'Is it lethal?'

'No, but painful and incapacitating for several minutes. They're designed to buy enough time to take down and handcuff a violent suspect.'

'And you've got one? Who are you going to use it on? A tea lady who gives you a bit of lip?'

Ben understands perfectly that senior officers within months of retirement are rarely on the front line, but it doesn't stop his sly digs. As we move away from the kerb, he looks longingly at the glove compartment.

'You know, we should just head home,' I say. 'After lunch.'

'We just got here.'

'We can be back by six. Seven at the latest.'

'And what's Dad going to do? Hitch a lift down the M6?'

We reach the bottom of the street. When I lived here before, the road was cobbled and we had to be careful how we drove over it. *Slowly* was the golden rule. It's been Tarmacked over since.

'Mum, did you forget?'

'Of course not. We're picking him up at Terminal 2, after dinner, which means I have to stay sober for the evening.'

I'm not lying. Our family plans had gone out of my head for a second, that's all. I sense Ben watching me. I don't turn to face him, because that would acknowledge what he's thinking. That he and his dad were right all along. I shouldn't have come back.

'And here we are.' I turn off the main road and into the car park behind the hotel where I've booked rooms for the next two nights. When I've switched off the engine and checked my text messages, I see my son is staring up in dismay at the huge, soot-blackened building, with its ornate stonework, its turrets and finials, and its dozens of grimy windows.

'There's a Premier Inn a couple of miles back along the motorway.' I put an apologetic hand on his shoulder. 'We could stay there if you like. It won't be full. Hotels here are never full.'

He slowly shakes his head. 'If it's good enough for the Addams Family.' He lifts both our bags and we walk together towards the front door of the Black Dog.

He lets me go ahead, as always his manners perfect in public, and as I step over the threshold into the dark hallway, I hear the low-pitched growling of a mean dog. At that moment, music starts to play somewhere in the hotel's interior – Elvis Presley's 'Are You Lonesome Tonight?' – and a man, tall and dark-haired, a little younger than me, appears from a back room and leans on the reception counter.

'WPC Lovelady,' he smiles, but in my agitated state it looks more like a sneer. 'Welcome back.'

I think I may be about to faint. This is Larry.

9

I think Patsy would have screamed at the children for a long time after they fled the churchyard. I think hearing signs of life would have given her renewed hope. She'd heard them: they must have heard her too. They'd gone to tell their parents. They'd be back soon, with shovels.

Any second now, she'd hear running footsteps, hear the sliding noise as metal cut through earth. She'd hear the soft thud as dirt went flying. She'd hear voices telling her to hold on, they were coming, they were going to get her out. They'd pull her into day-light, shielding her eyes from the bright sun and pouring orange squash down her throat to quench this dreadful thirst.

She'd have willed herself to be calm, to save her oxygen, because now all she had to do was give them time. They were coming.

No one was coming.

The four children, from three families, told no one what they'd heard. They weren't allowed to play in the churchyard, and they feared a walloping from their dads even more than they feared the monster below ground that they believed they'd unearthed.

10

'Mum?' Ben says.

The man behind the reception desk holds a hand out to my son. 'John Donnelly,' he says. 'I knew your mum years ago. She was quite the heroine round these parts.'

I am breathing again. This is not Larry. Not even much like Larry, now that my eyes are used to the dim interior. A similar height and build, the colouring is right, but his face is broader at the jaw; his nose is wider. This man is not nearly so handsome. This is John Donnelly, all grown up.

We sign in and exchange a few pleasantries, he hands over keys, and Ben and I go upstairs.

'This is a voodoo doll,' says Ben, when I emerge from the bathroom to find him sitting on my bed. He's had the good sense not to remove it from the bag. 'Shit, is it supposed to be you?'

'I thought that,' I say. 'Which is why I was a bit spooked when you saw me. But how could it be? How would anyone know I was going to be there today? And will you please stop swearing?'

He lifts his eyes. 'Maybe you weren't supposed to find it.'

'I'm so glad I brought you with me.'

Ben gives me his wide, close-lipped smile. At primary school, one of his friends called him Goofy because he has a lot of quite large white teeth and he's been self-conscious about them ever since. It's a shame, because when he forgets himself and grins, letting his joy shine out, his smile is dazzling.

'Dad phoned.' He points to my mobile on the bed.

'Everything OK?'

'He's fine, but he may not make it back today.'

'Why?'

'Thunderstorms at Charles de Gaulle. Lots of planes delayed. He may get back to London, but probably not Manchester.'

Nick was supposed to meet us here. We were going to spend the next day and night in Lancashire and drive home together. It was a chance to revisit roots, show my boys the place I earned my spurs. At least, that's what we'd pretended.

'He wants you to call him,' Ben says. 'He thinks we should head home.'

I think we should head home. I've said so already. If Nick is no longer coming to meet us, there is no reason to stay. 'What do you think?' I ask.

There is silence in the room for a few minutes.

'Why are we here?' Ben asks.

'We discussed this. You're still too young to be left on your own.'

He gives me that look of his. Absolutely nothing changes on his face. I swear not an eyelash twitches, and yet the expression becomes completely different. 'Is it a discussion,' he says, 'if only one person is talking?'

'Lots of us attend funerals of people we've put away,' I say. 'It's a form of closure.' I sit down beside him on the narrow bed. 'Maybe because we spend all the time they're in prison dreading the day they come out. When they die, that fear goes away. I was actually a bit surprised to see no one else from the old team in church.'

Ben lies back and puts his feet on my lap. 'It was thirty years ago. They'll be dead.'

'You're a real delight, you know that?'

For a few seconds he stares up at the ceiling and I enjoy the moment of having him close. Then his eyes drift over to the effigy, still on the bedside table, and he sits up again. 'Mum, what happened to your finger?'

In an instant the mood has changed.

'You know what happened to it. I told you.'

'No, I mean what happened to it after, you know? Did you keep it?'

I need a deep breath before I answer that one. I haven't seen my long-lost finger since . . . I'm not even going to think about it. 'No, I didn't keep it,' I say. 'It went into evidence and then . . . I didn't ask, but I suppose it would have gone to the hospital mortuary to be disposed of like other amputated limbs.'

'So it couldn't have fallen into the wrong hands?'

'The wrong hands were cuffed, in the dock,' I say.

A silence that is the very opposite of comfortable falls between us.

They have my hair. They have my hair. I have no idea what I was thinking as I ran from the Glassbrook house. There is no 'they'. There are no 'wrong hands'. Not any more.

Ben jumps to his feet. 'On a scale of one to ten, how pissed off with me are you right now?' he says.

I look him in the eye. 'Had you not said "pissed off", it would have been a six. It's now rising seven.'

He lifts one perfectly shaped dark eyebrow. 'So I've got a couple to play with?'

One thing I've learned about my son in fifteen years: when there's something on his mind, he won't let it go.

'What?' I say.

'Are we here because of the letter?'

I stare back. 'What letter?'

'The one with the postmark "HMP Wormwood Scrubs". The one that arrived two weeks ago, posted the day before he died.'

I say nothing. I have no idea what to say. And then I say the wrong thing.

'You've been reading my letters? Snooping in my bag?'

Ben's face flushes crimson. 'Hell no. You emptied your bag on the kitchen table last night. I saw the envelope when I got up for a drink. I haven't read it.'

'Sorry,' I say. 'Come on, let's go and find some lunch and decide whether we're staying or not. You can read it then. It won't take long.'

11

'This used to be a Kenyon's Bakery,' I say, as Ben joins me, carrying a tray laden with packaged food and drinks containers the size of buckets. I haven't been to the counter in McDonald's since he was seven years old and able to count money. The menus and the various meal combinations are beyond my comprehension.

'The counter ran round those two walls,' I continue. 'The serving ladies wore brown overalls and white pinafores with little white caps, and they made small meat pies that were the most delicious things ever. There were tables at this side of the room, and they were always full.'

Ben isn't listening. He has a McDonald's ritual that involves arranging the various bags of food and sides, adding ketchup and salt and pepper in a pre-set order, putting napkins in the right places. I know I won't get his attention back until it's done. I find my own packet, always what I imagine is the least calorific item available, and start to eat.

'Come on, then,' says Ben, after a few minutes. 'Show me.'

I find the envelope and hand it across. Ben licks his fingers before pulling out the single sheet of pale blue paper.

'Is this it?' he says.

'Told you it wouldn't take long.'

'Did he write it?'

'Yup.'

His eyes dart up. 'Sure?'

'I got a couple of letters a year from him. I know his handwriting.'

'You never told me.'

'When was I supposed to tell you I was on the Christmas-card list of one of Britain's most famous serial killers? When you were five? Your tenth birthday? When you became a teenager, maybe?'

He sits upright, a bit like a meerkat. 'Christmas cards? Can we sell them?'

I lift my coffee and hold his stare through the steam. He looks back down at Larry's last letter to me.

'What does it mean?' he asks.

'I thought you might tell me.'

He ignores my sarcasm. 'Were his others like this?'

'No. His others were what you might expect. If he'd seen something about me in the news, he'd write and comment on it. Congratulate me if something had gone well, commiserate if it hadn't. Mostly, though, he wrote about his family. What Sally and the girls were doing.'

'He and his wife didn't get divorced?'

'You'd be surprised how many couples stay married in similar circumstances. Sonia Sutcliffe stayed married to Peter for thirteen years after he was sentenced.'

'Did you go to see him?'

There is only one sensible answer to that question. Larry Glass-brook buried three kids alive, not to mention everything he tried to do to me. For better or worse, though, I never lie to my son.

'Many times,' I say. 'Larry sent me visiting orders once a year. I nearly always went. I've never really known why.'

Ben is still stuffing food into his mouth, talking between bites. I've lost my appetite. He looks down, reads the letter again, this time aloud. '*I've kept them safe for thirty years. Over to you . . .*' He glances back up. 'You must have some idea what he meant. He knew he was dying. This is a sacred charge, Mum.'

Maybe I haven't wanted to ask myself why.

I smile now at the earnest look on my son's face. 'From a murderer? I can only assume he was talking about Sally and the girls. That he wanted me to keep an eye on them.'

'Must be, I guess.' Ben leans across the table and lowers his voice. 'So what's with the voodoo doll?'

'Clay picture,' I say.

'What?'

'In these parts, they call it a clay picture.'

Ben has a smudge of ketchup on his upper lip. I'm itching to reach out and wipe it away, but I know it will irritate him, so I wait for him to sort it out himself.

'The Pendle witches – you know, the men and women who were hanged for witchcraft in the seventeenth century – they made clay pictures of their enemies as part of their rituals and their spell-casting. To give them extra power, they baked in some essence of the intended victim. You know, hair, fingernails, blood.' I shrug. 'Allegedly.'

'Larry Glassbrook was a witch?' Ben's eyes are wide with glee.

I lower my voice, because I'm pretty certain the people at the next table are listening to us. 'We never really knew what purpose the clay effigies served for Larry.' I stop and think. Ben can find all this out anyway, and knowing my son, he will. 'We found one in each of the caskets, with the victims. He wouldn't say what they were for.'

Ben, too, seems to have lost interest in food. 'And they were young, these kids?'

'They were fourteen, rising fifteen,' I say, as though it's no big deal.

Uncertainty flickers over his face. 'My age?'

For a second the busy, noisy lunchtime restaurant around us falls silent. Or maybe that's only in my head. 'Yes,' I agree. 'Your age.'

His enjoyment in the old stories has faded. Ben is the child of two police officers. He knows that every scintillating story in the papers is very real for someone.

'Bad times,' he says.

'The very worst of times,' I agree, knowing he will pick up on the Dickens reference. He ignores it.

'So why are you smiling?' he says instead.

Part Two

'Now it is the time of night
That the graves, all gaping wide,
Every one lets forth his sprite,
In the church-way paths to glide.'

A Midsummer Night's Dream, William Shakespeare

12

Patsy Wood's family lived in a two-up, two-down, a terraced house of four tiny rooms, in a long, grime-blackened row of mill cottages. There was only one other car in the road when we arrived, a white Hillman Imp, parked a few doors down.

Tom had barely pulled on the handbrake before the kids appeared. Still in school uniform, summoned by the throaty roar of the engine, not to mention the smooth, if too loud, tones of Marvin Gaye's 'I Heard It Through the Grapevine', they emerged from alleys, from behind the strings of beads that hung in doorways, from their football game on the tiny patch of spare land. They stood watching as we climbed out of the car.

Detective Constable Tom Devine, a similar age to me but more senior because he'd joined the force at eighteen, was a flashy dresser who never wore a tie if he could avoid it. His bright paisley-pattern shirt was open at the neck, the collar spread wide over the lapels of his jacket. His dark hair was thick, longer than police regulations permitted, and his sideburns were wide stripes down the side of his face. I'd seen women in the station's typing pool surreptitiously checking their hair and lipstick when they heard Tom's voice in the corridor, but I was used to clean-shaven, short-haired young men who were heading into the City, to officer training at Sandhurst or home to run the family farm. I couldn't look at Tom without thinking, *Dad wouldn't approve.* That said, he was married, so my father's opinion was a moot point.

Posters of the lost children had been strung round lampposts and gazed out from each front-room window. Patsy had been missing less than twenty-four hours, but her face was here too.

We were shown straight through 'to the back' by one of Patsy's siblings. The room was low, dark and cramped. Patsy's mother, Nancy, was bending over the range oven when we entered. She twisted upright, and her face took on that pinched, closed look that was to become so familiar to me in the years that followed. Back then, though, I saw hostility, not fear.

'No news, Nance,' Tom said quickly. Tom had been in charge of the door-to-door questioning that had started early that morning and was back now to update the family and do some follow-up. I'd been told to tag along because the superintendent thought a woman officer might be a nice touch. I was to make Nancy a cup of tea if she was struggling to cope.

'We need to ask you summat,' Tom went on. 'You all right for a minute?'

'I'll just give them their tea.' Nancy carried a metal dish to the table, where four young children sat, and began spooning food onto waiting plates. It was a supper dish I'd seen before in the North-West: an egg for each child, drowned in milk and crumbly local cheese, and then baked until the whole thing set.

'Looks champion, that, kids.' Tom nodded at the wide-eyed, pale-faced children, who hadn't taken their eyes off us. 'You lot all right?'

Nancy added slices of white bread to each plate before wiping her hands on her pinny and giving us her attention.

'Florence here has been to Patsy's school today,' Tom said. 'Have you met Florence? WPC Lovelady? She's from down South, but you'll understand her right enough in time.'

Nancy's eyes flickered in my direction.

'She's been talking to the teachers, headmaster, all the other staff, even the dinner ladies and caretaker,' Tom went on.

'Mainly the children, though,' I added. 'Children always know the most about what's going on among themselves, don't you think, Mrs Wood?'

'I dare say.' Again she barely gave me a glance. 'Folks down at Pilkington's have been saying as how you got the wrong 'uns with those Moors Murders. That whoever took those kids is still out there, and that he's got our Patsy.'

The children in the room were following every word, even as they shovelled food into their mouths.

'Bloody rubbish, excuse my French,' Tom said. 'This is nothing to do with what happened in Manchester. Take my word for it, Nance.'

'Several of Patsy's classmates claim she spoke about Manchester a lot, though.' I tried not to react to the hard look Nancy turned on me. 'She talked about her cousins there, gave the impression she was quite close to them. We wondered whether she might have got on a train or a bus, thinking that perhaps she might stay with them for a while. Maybe after an argument at home?'

Nancy's stare hardened.

'Nobody's saying Patsy had an argument with you or her dad,' Tom said quickly. 'But we do need to know if you have family in Manchester.'

A brief nod. 'Stan's brother lives in Deansgate. Patsy wouldn't know how to find it, though. She's only been once.'

'Children can be rather cunning,' I said. 'She may have found out the address without your knowing. And the public library would have street maps of Manchester.'

'Our Patsy did not go sneaking around,' said Nancy.

'I tell you what, Nance – you give me the address and we'll

have the Manchester force pop round,' Tom said. 'So we can close off that line of enquiry, so to speak.'

Nancy gave a reluctant nod and turned to a nearby dresser.

'One of the theories we're working on is that the three missing children are together somewhere,' I said, as Nancy pulled a tatty address book out of a drawer. 'That they made plans as a group and absconded.'

'Our Patsy had nothing to do with that Shorrock lad. Susan Duxbury neither.'

'Quite frankly, Mrs Wood, that's the best scenario right now,' I told her. 'Because if the three children are together, they'll be looking out for each other. They're still in a lot of danger, though, if they're living rough.'

'Right, we'll leave you in peace.' Tom slipped the address into his pocket. 'Thanks for that, Nance. We'll let you know what we find.'

The door slammed behind us. Tom leaned back against the wall and took out his cigarettes. 'You've a great future behind a desk, WPC Lovelady.'

'I don't know what you're talking about.'

I knew exactly what he was talking about. I knew I hadn't performed well in the Wood house.

'You used words she didn't understand, you let your sentences ramble on into the middle of next week, and you emphasised your poncey Southern accent.'

'I did no such thing.'

I'd done exactly that. I was always doing it. My stomach got tied up in knots when I had to deal with actual real people and all sorts of rubbish came out of my mouth.

He set off towards the car, kicking an abandoned space hopper out of the way. 'You're always doing it. You think it shows how superior you are. Well, it doesn't. It makes you sound like a stuck-up cow, and nobody round here will have any of it.'

Tom drove a Ford Cortina 1600E, sprayed metallic gold with a black vinyl roof. He opened the driver's door and climbed in. 'Oh, and you didn't take any notice of her kids, and you didn't offer to make her a brew.'

'I'm a police officer, not a maid of all work.' I walked round and joined Tom in the hot car.

'Listen to me, our Flossie. You don't mind if I call you that?'

I hated the ridiculous name my new colleagues had given me. It was undignified and demeaning. 'Yes, I mind a lot. My name is Florence.'

Tom sighed. 'You're not popular down the nick, love. You're too smart not to know it.'

I knew it. I got evidence of it on an hourly basis.

'It's not personal,' Tom went on. 'We all know you're clever and you're not afraid of a bit of hard graft, but you've got to stop acting like you're better than the rest of us.'

I didn't think I was better. Better educated, perhaps. But not better, not in an absolute sense.

Did I?

'Everyone at the station has an unreasonable prejudice about anywhere south of Manchester. And half of them don't think women should be police officers anyway.'

Tom gave a short laugh. 'True. But we outnumber you. We're always going to win.'

'I can't change the way I speak. Or my sex.'

'No one wants you to, love. Just remember you're here to help people.'

I turned to look at him then. His dark blue eyes were a tiny bit bloodshot, as though he'd drunk too much the night before, or not slept enough, and in the confines of the car, his aftershave smelled cheap. The women in the typing pool were easily impressed.

'I'm here to fight crime,' I told him.

He shook his head. 'No, love, you're really not.' He sighed again as he switched on the engine and we pulled away. It wasn't until we'd turned onto the main road and were heading back towards the station that I spoke again.

'That thing she said, about the Moors Murders. I heard it earlier today at Patsy's school.' I had to raise my voice. Tom always had the radio on loud and I was competing with Simon & Garfunkel's 'Mrs Robinson'.

'You'll be hearing it a lot more.'

'Surely nobody thinks Hindley and Brady were innocent? That the real killer of those children is still at large?'

'Nobody who's thinking straight,' he said. 'But people don't think straight when they're scared.'

He overtook a slow-moving Triumph and pressed his foot down. I took hold of the door handle.

'It'll be a long time before folk round here get over what them two did,' Tom said. 'Maybe they never will. Something like that happens, it taints a place. People feel responsible when they can't keep their kids safe, even if it's a neighbour's kids or kids from the other side of town. Kids die, it's everyone's fault, and people round here can't cope with it again. Not this soon.'

'Is that why we're pretending the three of them have run away from home?' I said in a small voice.

'I'm going to pretend I didn't hear that.'

I said nothing.

Tom gave a heavy sigh. 'We're not daft, love – we know what's going on. But just think about it. If we have to start calming everyone down and holding everyone's hand and attending public meetings and putting out fires left, right and centre, who the bloody hell will be out looking for the kids?'

I hadn't thought of that.

Tom said, 'God help us if there's another child killer on the loose, Florence. We'll have blood on the streets.'

We pulled into the station and he swung into a parking space. For several seconds he sat still, as the music continued to blare out. Then he turned the radio off and looked at me.

'Sorry to have a go, love. It's not your fault you're posher than the queen. This case is getting to all of us.'

He smiled at me as he switched off the engine and I had a feeling people would forgive Tom for a whole lot more than a bit of plain speaking.

'Tom,' I said. 'Tell me if you think I'm stepping out of line, but there's, well, this idea I've had.'

13

Sabden nick back then bore no resemblance to any police service facility one might come across today. CID was on the second floor, its various rooms marked by flimsy partitions that gave the illusion of privacy but did nothing to block out sound. Each pane of mottled internal glass was hung with venetian blinds, their strings grubby with the grease of a thousand sweaty palms and their blades caked in dust. They rattled as Tom and I pushed open the door.

We made our way along the line of metal filing cabinets that ran down the centre of the room. Each drawer was full to the brim. Paper was king back in 1969 and the station overflowed with it. Box files formed stalagmite towers around the room, and when they tumbled over, they remained in a cascade of paper and cardboard until someone got tired and kicked them out of the way.

The window ledges were similarly piled high with files and the occasional textbook. The windows themselves were rarely opened, for fear of falling objects hitting shoppers in the street below, and yet the collection of dead flies seemed to grow daily. Cleaners never came into CID. They didn't have the nerve.

Most of the detectives smoked and I couldn't spend any time in this room without my eyes stinging.

Before computers stored data, we pinned our information

around us. Every wall was full of notices, instructions, memos, maps, missing persons' photographs, 'wanted' posters. Nothing was ever taken down, just papered over as new information took precedence. Were we to remove all the paper from the walls, the sound insulation would take a dive. Or the walls might fall down.

CID was a hazy mass of ever-moving paper, dust and smoke.

At the far end of the room was a corner office. Tom knocked and pushed open the door at the answering grunt.

Superintendent Stanley Rushton, a tall, thick-set man of around forty, slammed down the phone and stared back at us through a thick cloud of cigarette smoke.

'Fucking twat,' he said to us.

Tom said, 'Earnshaw again, boss?'

'How the devil do you know that?'

No one ever sat down in the super's office. There weren't any chairs other than his, and I'd have liked to see anyone dare take that.

'Lads have been talking,' Tom said. 'Get used to it, boss. Council elections coming up.'

I'd never met John Earnshaw but knew him to be the chairman of the town council. Owner of several mills in town, he was a wealthy and influential man.

'He's called a town meeting for Wednesday evening,' Rushton said. 'Wants me there to explain why we haven't found the kids yet. He also wants me to send officers to the Big Smoke because there are rumours they've been seen on trains south. I need my men here. The fact that he donates a few hundred quid a year to the benevolent fund does not give him the right to tell me how to do my job.'

'No, boss,' Tom said.

Rushton glared. 'What the bugger do you two want?'

'Florence has an idea, boss. We want to run it past you.'

I could feel my face glowing. I blushed easily back then, and the heat wasn't helping.

'I was thinking that we could—' I broke off and tried again. 'Well, I've been speaking to the other kids at her school – Patsy, I mean Patsy Wood – and you can tell they're not really thinking. I ask them if they remember anything and they say, "No," and that's the end of it.'

The super glanced down at his watch. 'One would hope,' he said.

'Boss, you know how you're on *Look North* tomorrow night, doing that appeal thing?' Tom said. 'What Florence has in mind is contacting the producer to see if they'll run a short film beforehand that we help them make.'

The super folded his arms and looked me up and down. 'In the pictures business now, are we?'

'Sir, I'm thinking that we find a girl who looks like Patsy – same build, colouring, as similar as possible – and then we dress her in Patsy's clothes.'

Rushton's eyebrows shot up, but he said nothing.

'Then we get this girl, this new Patsy if you like, and the friends she was with last night and we ask them to do exactly what they did during her last few minutes. You know, set off walking home from the park, down Snape Street, along Argyle Street, then down Livesey Fold. They say their goodbyes at the corner and then Patsy walks off down Nelson Street.'

The super opened his mouth.

'Boss, I've lost count of the number of times I've been interviewing witnesses and they claim to remember nowt,' Tom jumped in. 'Then when you give them something to, I don't know, jog their memories, like, um, "The Clarets were coming out," they go, "Oh yeah, I remember now. The coalman had pulled away and I saw the bloke on the motorbike. Dodgy-looking bugger – I thought so at the time."'

'People think in pictures,' I said. 'Sometimes if you jog their memories with one picture, it helps to release others. People remember more than they think, but their memories are stored deep and you need to find a way to bring them to the surface.'

The super's stare hardened.

'Everyone in town will be watching you on *Look North*,' said Tom. 'If we show them Patsy's last movements, actually show them, not just tell them, it could help them remember. Obviously we have the phone number in big letters at the bottom of the screen.'

'Obviously,' said Rushton. 'You don't seriously think Patsy's parents will agree to this? Not to mention the other kids' folks.'

'Tom has a really good rapport with Patsy's mum,' I said. 'And I know Luna Glassbrook, one of her friends. I'm sure she'd be keen.' What I didn't add, but believed, was that Luna Glassbrook would do anything for attention.

'You're talking about a reconstruction of events,' said the super.

'Exactly,' I said. 'A reconstruction. That's a great name for it, sir.'

'If it works, it could be groundbreaking,' Tom said. 'If it doesn't, well, at least we'll know we tried everything.'

We waited. Rushton had young children himself. There was a picture on the desk of his son, Brian, in a plastic policeman's helmet.

'And that could be important if . . . well, if we don't find them safe and sound,' Tom said.

'Or if another one vanishes,' I added.

Heavy silence. I'd done it again. I could feel Tom's glare on the back of my head.

'Florence could get on the blower to *Look North*, see what they think,' Tom said. 'She's got a posh voice: she'll get on with them nobs.'

There was a pause while Rushton stared at us. 'I suppose a phone call can't hurt.'

Tom and I looked at each other.

'If I come out of this smelling of anything other than laven-der, I will string you two up by parts the sun doesn't see. Do I make myself clear?' Rushton glared at us. 'Now fuck off. You've reminded me I need to organise a haircut.'

14

Look North were surprisingly keen on the reconstruction idea. Unsurprisingly, my colleagues were not. The kinder, less judge-mental ones considered it a waste of time; the rest – and I'm quoting now – a daft idea that would show us up as pillocks in front of the entire country and who did her ruddy ladyship think she was? The super was as good as his word, though, and I was relieved from Tuesday-morning beat to get ready.

I spent it at the school and out on the streets, planning the route. I got back to the station, hungry and hot, at just after two o'clock, to a sense that something had happened in my absence. I caught a muffled 'Here she is' as I passed down a crowded corri-dor towards the canteen.

Tom was sitting alone at one of the tables. I bought a ham sandwich, poured a glass of water and knew that several pairs of eyes were watching me cross the room.

'Ears burning?' Tom asked when I sat down.

I glanced around. Two people looked down quickly. Another continued to stare. 'What's happening?' I asked.

Tom wiped a piece of white bread and margarine round the edge of his plate. 'Boss has two members of the town council, the head of the Rotary Club and a school governor giving him earache as we speak. And John Earnshaw was in first thing.'

'About the reconstruction?'

Tom affected a trembling, elderly voice. 'It will cause unnecessary panic, focus attention in the wrong direction entirely, be bad for business and bring down the seven plagues of Egypt upon our pleasant Northern town.'

'Ten,' I said miserably.

'Huh?'

'Ten plagues of Egypt. You might be thinking about the seven deadly sins. So it's not happening?'

'Oh, it's happening all right.' He turned to his jacket, hanging over the next chair, and began to search through the pockets. 'Rushton is one of the few nobs in town who hasn't succumbed to the lure of the lodge.'

'I have no idea what you're talking about. And your cigarettes are in your shirt pocket.'

He clapped a hand to his chest. 'Freemasons. This town is run by 'em, and Rushton won't join. Why do you think the powers that be can't stand him?'

'So he's really going out on a limb for me?'

'He likes you.' Tom lit up and blew smoke at me. 'Can't understand it myself.'

I spent the next hour waiting to hear the reconstruction was off. I even wandered up to the CID room to find out what was going on. Raised voices could be heard from Rushton's office, but when the door opened, he just walked through the room, jacket fastened, cap on his head, and muttered, 'Good luck tonight, lads,' as he left.

When the time came, we met in Sunnyhurst Park, where Patsy and her friends had spent Sunday evening. It was a little after three o'clock, before the end of the school day, but the cameraman assured me that a filter over the lens would give the impression of twilight.

The six teenagers emerged from the park gates looking as

natural as I could have hoped. A girl called Maureen had been chosen to play Patsy. The clothes our missing girl had been wearing had vanished with her, but I'd searched through second-hand shops in the town centre and found a red cardigan and flower-print dress that even her mother agreed was a good match.

I was waiting with the producer on the first corner as the kids came past. Luna, her eyes bigger than ever thanks to the make-up she'd sneaked into school, was walking alongside Maureen. Behind them was John Donnelly, towering above the others. His father owned the biggest pub in town, a soot-stained, Gothic construction called the Black Dog. At fifteen, he'd had his adolescent growth spurt early and seemed the natural leader of the group.

John had an odd, timeless look about him. His clothes seemed dated, made from natural fabrics rather than the garishly patterned nylon worn by the others, and his dark hair was cut shorter than was fashionable. He was a handsome boy, though, with slanted dark eyes, pale skin and long, graceful limbs.

Tammy Taylor, at his side, was pretty with long, dark hair and a thick fringe. Like Luna, she seemed overdressed for hanging around in the park. Behind her walked Dale Atherton, a small, skinny lad with hair the same colour as mine and even more freckles. Finally, tagging along at the back, was Richie Haworth. He was shorter and squatter than the others, with a cap of blond hair obscuring most of his face. As the children approached the film crew, he was the one who couldn't resist a self-conscious wiggle of his backside.

'We can edit it out,' murmured the producer.

As they walked away from the camera along Argyle Street, Luna dropped back to walk beside John and he slung an arm around her shoulders. It seemed an unusual display of affection for self-conscious teenagers. On the other hand, children here did seem to date young. Only that day at Patsy's school, another of her classmates had told me that Luna had been 'going with' John for two months, that Patsy had wanted to 'go' with him, but he'd turned her down.

We'd expected to have an audience for the reconstruction and, sure enough, people – mainly women – were watching us from doorways and street corners, but as the children reached the corner, I spotted a group of four suited men beside a parked Daimler. One of them seemed to be watching me, but as the first female police officer in Sabden, I was used to being noticed.

At the street corner, the children split up, as they'd done on Sunday night. Maureen carried on alone, her red cardigan sharp as blood against the blackened stone of the houses she passed. She walked past the corner shop, which would have been closed when Patsy walked this way, and the White Lion pub, which would have been open. She passed the bookmaker's and the house that doubled as a hairdresser, with a salon in the front room. When she reached the ginnel, she stopped.

Ginnels – wide, cobbled alleyways that ran between two back-to-back rows of terraced houses – were common in the industrial North-West. Every house had a backyard that led out into a ginnel. People used them a lot to avoid getting the front steps and hallways dirty.

Patsy would have been expected to go home via the ginnel. It was the quickest way and she was late. The door to the Woods' backyard was never locked.

On warm days, Northern housewives strung their washing on lines across ginnels and, on a June evening, it would have been out until late. At four o'clock in the afternoon, it was impossible to stand at one end of the ginnel and see any distance down it. Anyone could get lost amid the hanging rows of towels, shirts and sheets. Anyone could slip behind a large sheet and – poof! Gone.

At a signal from the producer, Maureen stepped into the ginnel, pushed aside the first sheet and was gone.

15

'In the small Lancashire town of Sabden, at the foot of Pendle Hill, fears are growing tonight for the safety of fourteen-year-old Patsy Wood, who vanished from near her home on Sunday evening. She is the third child to go missing in the town in recent months.'

As the anchorman cleared his throat, the television picture vanished, to be replaced by a flickering mass of grey dots. A collective groan went up. Those of us who'd been assigned to take telephone calls were gathered round the station's only TV set, apart from PC Butterworth, who was standing behind it, holding the aerial up high to improve the signal.

The picture flickered back as the camera panned left to show enlarged photographs of Susan Duxbury and Stephen Shorrock. Susan was plump, with dark brown hair that needed washing, bad acne and NHS spectacles. Stephen was smaller, thinner, with mousey hair and a pinched look around the eyes. Neither was particularly attractive, but I guess few are treated kindly by teenage years.

'Susan Duxbury stayed late at school on the afternoon of Monday, 17 March to help a teacher tidy up the classroom,' the anchorman read. 'She left alone and was last seen in the town centre, some distance from her home. Stephen Shorrock was playing football with friends on Wednesday, 16 April. After the group split up, he is believed to have walked home along Sabden's main road but never reached his house.'

The anchorman glanced up briefly from his notepad. 'Sightings of both children near the rail and bus stations gave rise to initial speculation that they might have left Sabden voluntarily, possibly running away from home,' he said. 'But with the disappearance of a third child, questions are being asked of the town's police.'

He spun to face the man on his right and the camera panned back.

'Superintendent Rushton, this is the third child to go missing on your patch in as many months. What are you doing wrong?'

'The question you need to be asking, Frank, is why the people who know something aren't coming forward,' Rushton countered. 'Teenagers don't just disappear. We're working on the theory that the children, all of whom knew each other, may be together somewhere. If that's the case, someone will know something.'

'The three children all went to the same school. Do you consider that significant?'

'There is only one secondary school in Sabden. What I would like to say at this stage is—'

'You're averaging a disappearance a month, superintendent. Are you expecting another child to vanish in a couple of weeks?'

'That isn't true at all. No child was reported missing in May.'

The anchorman's eyebrows sprang upwards. 'Well, I'm sure we can all be very thankful for that. So are you expecting July to be a good month? Can the parents of Sabden relax for a few weeks?'

Had Rushton been in the station, a missile would have been thrown. As it was, he simply stopped blinking. 'We're concentrating on finding Patsy, Stephen and Susan at this stage. Speculative scaremongering would be counterproductive.'

'So if you're not going to warn them to take care, what would you like to say to the people of Patsy Wood's home town?' asked the anchorman.

After the super had made his carefully worded appeal for

witnesses, the station played the reconstruction.

It gave me goosebumps. Even though I'd seen the filming a matter of hours before, the distance created by the television screen made it more real somehow, as though we were actually watching Patsy's last movements. When Patsy (I mean Maureen, of course) turned into the ginnel behind Nelson Street, I heard someone in the room behind me give a low gasp.

When it was over, I held my breath, braced for a repeat of the disparaging comments I'd been forced to listen to all day. The room was uncharacteristically silent. I felt something nudge me in the back and turned to see Tom wink at me.

The calls came streaming in. More than one caller was sure they'd seen Patsy heading towards the centre of town. Others reported seeing her at the bus station, at the train station, back in the park, even on a ferry leaving Liverpool dock.

Visitors arrived for Rushton and reluctantly agreed to see one of the inspectors when they were told the super wasn't available. I only caught a glimpse, but I was pretty certain they were the same four men I'd seen watching the reconstruction earlier that day.

Amid every call that came in, the one that mattered was directed to me, because no one thought that it did matter. 'Loony on the line,' the sergeant called. 'Come and deal with it, Flossie.'

I bit my tongue, picked up the phone and heard the story of a voice calling out for help. From a newly dug grave.

16

The churchyard of St Wilfred's Roman Catholic Church was so close to the Hill that it was difficult to tell where the one ended and the other began. Maybe an outlying stone, tumbled from the boundary wall, marked the spot, or perhaps a clump of heather stealing its way in from wild to tended land. Either way, there came a point at which the ferns, bracken and dry moorland grass had definitely given way to headstones and urns, when the steep rise had levelled out, and it was here, in the sheltered spot between the crumbling wall and the oldest stones, that the local children played.

The sun was low in the sky when we swung the gate. Shadows were lengthening, and the golden glow of minutes earlier had faded to a dull, flat light. Darkness was creeping over the Hill, turning it from green and yellow to turquoise, its crevices deeper, almost black. It was the time of day that locals called the daylight gate, neither day nor night but something in between, when the normal rules of both seemed suspended. A time when anything could happen. I'd lived in Lancashire for only a few months, but I'd already learned that the daylight gate was a time when the housewives closed their windows and latched their yard doors, when younger children were called in from the street.

When the unusual phone call had come in, about children hearing strange noises in the churchyard, the sergeant had given the job of following it up to me. Nervy kids, long-shot call, visit to the edge of town – it had WPC Lovelady written all over it. To the sergeant's annoyance, though, he'd had to send a driver with me, so PC Randy Butterworth and I had gone together to the children's house.

What I'd heard from the kids had been enough for me to borrow the family's phone and call Tom, who'd driven out immediately. He'd sounded sceptical, but he'd come all the same, and he led the way over the grass path towards the grave. The kids' father followed close behind. I went next.

PC Butterworth lingered by the gate.

The grave in question rose from the ground like a newly baked loaf, smooth and perfect, a rounded oval shape. The top layer of earth had dried in the sun and a fine sprinkling of soil, like wholemeal flour, danced a little dust storm above it.

The children, brothers aged six and nine, hadn't come out with us, but I could see them peering from an upper window of their house. Nor were they the only ones. Word had got round and every window that overlooked the churchyard had faces in it. People were gathering at the gate too. Randy stood guard, his back to us, keeping them out.

'This one,' the father said.

The grave was close to the wall. Wreaths, still fresh, lay in a row along its crest. The children's den, a makeshift shelter of corrugated steel, was close by.

'Jimmy ran first,' the older of the two boys had told me earlier. 'I would of stayed, but when we heard the scream, he took off, like, and I had to goes with him.'

We looked down at the grave, none of us quite sure what to do. Then Tom took off his jacket and handed it to me before dropping flat and pressing his ear to the ground.

'They heard banging first,' the father said. 'And scrabbling. They thought it might be a rat.'

'Hush up a bit, mate,' said Tom.

'Then the screaming,' said the dad. 'They both swore they heard it. I spoke to Ray and Elaine next door and their Micky heard it as well. I wouldn't have called you out if it had only been our two.'

'Did you hear any words?' I'd asked the younger boy, whom I'd spoken to alone. 'Just screaming, or words?'

He'd beckoned me close and whispered, 'Help me.'

'They're good lads,' their father was saying now. 'They're not liars. Not normally, anyway.'

Tom's face creased in concentration.

'Maybe we should wait by the gate—' I began.

'Here's Dwane,' said the father.

I heard the gate clang shut and turned to see a peculiar figure had talked his way past PC Butterworth. The size of a ten-year-old child, he had the shoulders, arms and legs of a grown man. His hair was thick and dark brown, his jaw covered in stubble, and his heavy, suntanned features suggested a man of around thirty. His eyes seemed overly large in a head that was itself large. Dressed in dull grey and brown working clothes, he had a large shovel slung over one shoulder.

'Church sexton,' the father added. 'It's his job to look after the graves.'

'Anything?' I asked Tom.

'If you'd all pipe down a second, I might stand a chance,' he snapped back.

I held up one hand and pressed the other to my lips as the small man drew near. The wind rustled the trees above our heads and a bird screeched. In the distance, I could hear voices and the occasional roar of a car engine. When I looked away, I saw that our audience, the people gathered round the periphery of the churchyard, had increased.

Unable to resist any longer, I joined Tom and lay on the other side of the grave. The soil smelled of ash, chopped wood and something sweetly floral. I glanced up to see freesias not six inches away and, beyond them, the horizontal face of Tom Devine. For a second we looked into each other's eyes and I felt an inexplicable but acute sense of embarrassment. Then he pulled a face at me and got up.

'Patsy,' I said, too quietly for it to have any hope of reaching below ground. I wanted to yell it, but even I knew what a spectacle I'd make, screaming a missing girl's name into a fresh grave. 'Patsy,' I repeated, as loud as I dared.

'On your feet, Lovelady,' said a new voice, and I looked up to see the DI standing over us with two of his sergeants.

Detective Inspector Jack Sharples must have been five foot ten, because that was the minimum height for a male officer in Lancashire back then, but he was so thin and frail that he looked smaller. He was a taciturn man but had the ability to see through all the extraneous detail and get right to the heart of any issue. He was known as 'No Shit Sharples'. He was also something of a legend on the force because he'd worked on the Moors Murders. Rumour had it he'd left Manchester because he couldn't face another bad case involving dead kids.

I scrambled up. WPCs in the 1960s wore fitted black skirts. They were pleated at the back to allow us to run, but they were no respecters of modesty when it came to clambering to our feet in the presence of senior officers. Also, I noticed with dismay, the priest. And another man. Early forties, portly, sandy-coloured hair, wearing a suit. I knew his face, if not his name. He'd been one of the occupants of the Daimler watching the filming yesterday, and had come into the station this evening.

'Anything?' The look on Sharples's face left me in no doubt how he expected us to answer.

'Nothing. But Florence may have keener ears than me,' Tom said.

I shook my head.

'That grave's not been touched,' said a high-pitched, sexless voice. Dwane, the sexton, had taken up position at the head of the mound. He nodded down. 'That's how I left it.'

Beneath the wreaths, the grave looked like nothing other than a pile of earth to me.

'How can you be sure of that?' I asked him.

'That's how I smooth it.' He looked at me as though noticing me for the first time. 'People think grave-digging's easy – just dig it up and put it back. You can't do that. If someone else had dug up my grave, I'd know about it.'

'Dwane's always very thorough,' said the priest. 'And very neat.'

The sandy-haired man in the suit was looking back at the people by the church gate. 'I really don't like the attention this is attracting,' he said.

'Come on, folks.' The DI turned to leave. 'We've work to be doing. Sorry to drag you out at this hour, Father, Mr Bannister.'

'Sir!' The word had left my mouth before I could think what was to follow it. The DI looked back over his shoulder. Tom hadn't moved, but his eyes were on his shoes.

'We have four witnesses who claim they heard noises coming from this grave.'

'Four kids,' Sharples corrected me. 'How old were that lot?'

'Aged between six and ten,' Tom jumped in before I could open my mouth. He saw me glaring at him. 'Smart kids, though,' he mumbled. 'Not daft.'

'Been watching The Addams Family, have they?' asked the man called Bannister.

'Their mother puts her foot down on that,' said the father. 'They do like *Doctor Who*, though.'

'Well, there you go.' Sharples looked me up and down. 'Tidy yourself up before you come back, Lovelady.'

I glanced down to see my tights had ripped, and there were grass stains on my black skirt.

'Sir, I think we need to be sure.' Again I stopped him as he was about to turn away. The other man, Bannister, looked at me and shook his head.

I ignored him. 'It's not impossible, sir,' I said.

'No one's touched that grave,' said Dwane.

'Florence, I'm not sure we'd hear her anyway,' said Tom. 'I really don't think sound travels through the ground.'

'Certainly not from a wooden box six feet under,' said Bannister with a nasty smile.

'Four and a half,' said Dwane. 'The grave is six foot deep; the coffin is eighteen inches high. Four and a half feet of earth on top of that.'

'Even one foot might be too much,' said Tom.

'How do you know?' I said. 'How does anyone know? Who's tried it out?'

Bannister said, 'Sharples, this is getting out of hand. Can you control your officer?'

The DI took a step towards me. 'Lovelady, I have three missing kids, and in case it's escaped your notice, we have a bloody audience here. I do not want to set folk talking about them being buried alive.'

'I spoke to those boys, sir. I don't think they were lying.'

The DI glanced at the boys' father. 'I'm sure they weren't, but kids are very imaginative. Playing in a graveyard, it's going to put all sorts of ideas in their heads.'

'They're not supposed to play in here,' said the father. 'If we've told them once, we've told them a dozen times. Some of these old stones are dangerous. I've reported them, but you might as well not waste your breath.'

'Maintaining the churchyard is the council's responsibility, not the church's,' said Bannister. 'Just as controlling wayward children is the responsibility of the parents.'

The kids' dad squared his shoulders.

'Cutbacks,' said Sharples. 'We're all having to deal with them. Oh champion, we've the ruddy undertakers here now.'

We all looked to see Larry Glassbrook striding up the path towards us. His jacket was pale brown corduroy, edged in lilac, and his black hair was swept up and back off his forehead. His blue shirt was open at the neck. He could not have looked less like an undertaker. His partner, Roy Greenwood, an older, taller, thinner man, discreetly dressed in a black suit, was at his side.

'Anything I should know about?' Larry spoke to the DI but nodded at me. 'Flossie,' he said. 'You look hot. Been running?'

Sharples made an inarticulate grunt. 'WPC Lovelady thinks our missing teenager could be hiding out in one of your coffins, Larry,' he said.

'Casket,' Larry corrected. 'Cedar with silver-gilt furniture. Lovely piece. Lined in yellow. I prefer blue and red with the silver and dark wood, but yellow was the old guy's favourite colour.'

'Mr Simmonds,' said Roy Greenwood, with just a hint of reproof. 'Mr Douglas Simmonds, aged seventy-three, passed away peacefully at home last Wednesday.'

'Nobody's touched that grave,' said the sexton.

'Is there any possibility, Mr Glassbrook?' said Tom. 'Can you talk us through what happens to a coffin when it's closed? To put Florence's mind at rest.'

Bannister audibly exhaled. The priest looked troubled.

'Anything for Florence,' said Larry. 'The old boy's been in that casket for four days now, since we carried out the embalming on Friday. The funeral was early yesterday morning, so we didn't have a last viewing.'

'We never do if the service is before eleven o'clock,' his partner said. 'It makes the whole business of getting the coffin into the hearse a bit rushed, and it unsettles the family too.'

I opened my mouth. Tom held up a finger to tell me to shut it again.

'So no one's looked in that coffin – I mean casket – since . . . since when exactly?' Tom asked.

'Since Sunday evening at five,' Larry told us. 'His widow came to see him with one of his sons. They spent about ten minutes and left.'

'And then you nailed it shut?'

Larry winced, and then proceeded to explain to Tom and the others exactly how his caskets were sealed.

'So nobody could have accessed it since then?' Bannister seemed to think that settled the matter.

'Patsy went missing on Sunday night,' I said. 'It was perfectly possible for someone to open it again after you closed it.'

'Must have happened that way.' Dwane.

'They'd have to know how the mechanism worked.' Larry ignored Dwane.

'Or be smart enough to work it out,' I said.

'And they'd have to access our chapel of rest,' said Greenwood, who was possibly the thinnest man I'd ever seen. His upper body seemed to curve forwards, as though his core wasn't strong enough to keep him vertical all the way up. He had a way of leaning over people when he spoke to them.

'I expect you keep your doors locked,' Bannister said.

'Always,' Greenwood confirmed, in his low, toneless voice. 'Unless we're expecting to take delivery of remains. It wouldn't do for someone to walk in unawares when we're carrying out embalming procedures. And certainly the building and the yard are locked at night.'

'If the kids really did hear screaming, that would mean Patsy was alive,' Tom said to me. 'How do you get a living kid into a coffin without her yelling blue murder?'

'I didn't hear a thing when I was filling it in,' said Dwane.

'Drug her,' I answered back. 'Hit her over the head with something. Trick her into thinking it was a joke.'

'I told Rushton he'd regret hiring a woman,' Bannister said. 'Hysterics.'

'She'll be dead by now,' said Dwane. 'She might have hung on a few hours, from funeral to when t' kids heard her, but not overnight. Might as well leave her where she is. No point disturbing a perfectly good mound.'

'Right, I'm going back,' the DI announced. 'Lovelady, you and Butterworth can take up guard at both entrances to the churchyard for the next hour. No, make it two. Our being here will have set tongues wagging and I do not want sightseers and ghost-spotters hanging around upsetting the family.'

'And I'm the one who has to clear up the mess,' said Dwane.

Sharples set off back along the path. Bannister and the priest followed, then Larry and Roy Greenwood. As Larry turned to go, I caught a whiff of the aftershave he always wore. Old Spice. I'd seen new, boxed bottles of it at the bottom of the stairs, waiting to be carried up to the family's bathroom.

'Sir.' I dodged round the other men to get close to Sharples. 'We have to be sure. What if she's down there and we just leave her? We can't.'

Bannister muttered something unintelligible as Sharples heaved a heavy sigh. 'I cannot carry out an exhumation without a Home Office licence. Isn't that right, Father?'

'I don't see why we're having to justify ourselves to the office junior,' Bannister replied.

'Sir, I'm not talking about an exhumation. Just moving a bit of earth and asking Larry to open the casket. We can have it exactly as it was in an hour.'

'Who's paying my overtime?' asked Dwane.

'I'm not listening.' The DI carried on walking.

'Sir, if we have reason to believe that life is in danger, the normal rules of access don't apply.'

'I'll speak to you back at the station, Lovelady,' Sharples snapped.

'Boss, she has a point,' said Tom. 'We can rig up a tent. Wait till dark.'

'No, we can't wait,' I said. 'How much air is she likely to have left?'

'None,' said Dwane. 'The lass is dead.'

'Tom, how many calls that came in tonight reported seeing Patsy at the railway station?' asked the DI.

'Over a dozen,' Tom had to admit.

'Exactly. She left town on a train, and sooner or later we'll find out where. Fannying around with the TV was bad enough, Lovelady. Don't push it.'

'Let it go, Florence,' Tom said, as the others drove away. He took out his cigarettes, thought better of it and put them away again.

I looked down. Four and a half feet of loose, crumbly, damp soil. Dwane could dig it up in an hour.

'I'll walk you to the gate.'

Tom wasn't suggesting we take a stroll together. He wanted me away from the grave. I moved slowly, fighting the gentle pressure on my arm that was pushing me along.

'Who was that man with the priest?' I asked.

'Reg Bannister, a churchwarden. Member of the Rotary.'

'And of the lodge?'

'Who knows? Probably. Look, love, you need to keep your head down and your nose clean for a few days.'

We'd reached the path. People who'd watched the drama from the gate were starting to drift away and I wondered what Sharples had said to them.

'There's a lot of reporters in town,' Tom went on. 'You can't get a room in the Black Dog, and that place hasn't been full since the old Queen died. This reconstruction of yours – I'm not saying it was a bad idea, mind – it's got them wound up.'

'Publicity will help us find the kids,' I said.

Tom stopped, so I did too. He still had hold of my arm. He turned to face me on the path.

'Not everyone will see it that way. That meeting at the town hall tomorrow night is going ahead. After tonight, it'll be packed. Well-meaning busybodies and trouble-making twats will be asking why the police aren't doing enough to find the missing kids and the super will have no answers. So in twenty-four hours, we've gone from an uneasy calm, with most folk accepting that the kids have run away from home, to believing there's a monster on the loose and the boys in blue are clueless. And when it all goes tits up, you'll get the blame.'

'That's not fair.'

'I didn't say it was. You're a soft target, Flossie – sorry, it just slipped out – because you're new and young and just a lass. But you're also smart and you're not afraid to speak your mind. So those who might otherwise hold back will still go for you because no one wants to be shown up by a girl. Do you get what I'm saying?'

I did. I hadn't just put my head above the parapet; I was tap-dancing on it.

'Is that how you feel?' I asked.

'No, but I'm cleverer than most.'

I pulled a face. Tom was many things: good-looking, funny, charming when he wanted to be, but clever?

He took my arm again. 'Let me give you a tip, Florence – it does no harm to let people think you're a soft touch. You might want to give it a go.'

We'd reached the gate. He took his car keys out of his pocket and nodded to Randy, but before he turned away, he leaned close to me one last time. 'The super's under a lot of pressure, and you've just added to it. Promise me you won't do anything stupid.'

I promised. I had to. He wasn't going to leave until I did.

17

I was walking up the drive, a little after ten o'clock, when I heard a car engine.

'Flossie.' Sally Glassbrook smiled as she climbed out, but it was a tired smile, and her canvas midwifery bag was stuffed with bloodstained linen. 'Any news?'

'Nothing concrete, I'm afraid.'

'Come on round.' She pulled her heavier equipment bag from the car too. 'I'll make you a cuppa.'

I wanted nothing more than to get to bed, but I knew Sally was anxious, and so I followed her to the kitchen door, through the outer pantry and into the kitchen, to see Luna Glassbrook at the table, frowning at an exercise book.

From somewhere in the house came the sound of piano music. I thought I recognised Mozart, but the same short piece was being played repeatedly and it was hard to be sure.

'Love, what are you doing still up?'

Luna ignored her mother. 'Flossie, did you see it? Was it all right? I thought it looked stupid when we stopped at Snape Street. Richie's brother—'

'It was super,' I said. 'Everyone was really pleased with it. We had a good response.'

For a split second her face lit up; then her brows darted towards each other. 'Did it work?' She dropped her voice. 'Did you find her?'

'Not yet, I'm afraid. But we took a lot of phone calls. It will take time to follow them up.'

'Richie's uncle said you'd been called out to St Wilfred's, that some kids had heard voices and that you'd been digging up graves. She's not in a grave, is she?'

'No, that was completely unrelated.' I didn't like lying to Luna, to anyone, but it was the response we'd agreed down at the station. The visit to St Wilfred's was in connection with suspected vandalism. Nothing to do with the missing children. How long the lie would hold was anyone's guess.

Luna's face twisted and her eyes filled with tears that I thought might, possibly, be genuine. You could never tell with Luna. 'I can't think of anything worse,' she said.

In the adjacent room, Sally had emptied her bag of bloody cloths and towels into the twin tub. She reached up to the bundles of dried herbs hanging from the ceiling beams and pulled out several handfuls. Lavender, I guessed, for its perfume and rosemary for its disinfecting qualities. I'd learned a lot about herbs in the time I'd been living here.

'Don't pester Flossie.' As the washing machine began its mechanical sloshing, Sally crossed to the kettle. 'You know she can't tell us anything.'

'Let me do it,' I told Sally. 'You must be shattered.'

'Easy one tonight.' She used a match to light the hob. 'Fourth babies practically walk out by themselves. Fifty minutes from waters breaking to delivering the placenta.'

'Mu-um,' Luna moaned.

'What happens to the placenta?'

We all turned to see Cassie, the silver-haired, grey-eyed, older daughter, leaning against the doorframe. She had a way of moving around in total silence. I'd lived with the family for five months but I still found it unnerving. She had a habit of sleepwalking too, which was even creepier because none of the bedrooms in the house came with lockable doors. Shortly after I moved in, I'd woken one night to find her standing in the open doorway of my room. My yell of alarm hadn't woken her, she'd simply turned and walked back along the corridor.

'Gross,' her sister muttered.

'Most mothers eat them.' Sally was spooning loose tea into a pot. She winked at me as she replaced the lid.

'You're kidding?' Luna had abandoned her homework and was staring at her mother with those huge wide eyes that always – I know it's cruel – made me think of a tree frog.

'Some mums are a bit squeamish,' Sally went on. 'Especially the first-timers. Planting under a tree is becoming quite common. A lot give them to the midwives to take home. How was your tea tonight?'

'Did you find her?' Cassie asked me, as Luna mimed vomiting.

I shook my head. 'We had a lot of calls; we've got a few leads; we'll keep looking.'

'She's dead, isn't she?'

Luna's head shot up. 'That's my friend you're talking about.'

'Since when?' Cassie was several inches taller than Luna and could sneer rather well. 'You hadn't the time of day for her when she was alive.'

'Excuse me, nobody's said she's dead yet. Flossie, you don't think she's dead, do you?'

'Bed.' Sally raised her arm to point towards the door. 'Both of you.'

'Dead as a doornail, just like Susan and Stephen, and only a matter of time before he gets another one.' Cassie had a mean smile on her face. 'One by one he steals them away, and nobody knows when he's going to pounce next. Check under the bed tonight, Luna.'

I couldn't help myself. 'Cassie, you're frightening your sister.'

The elder girl turned and flounced from the room. Luna followed.

'Is that what you think?' Sally poured boiling water into the teapot. Quite a bit of it missed and splashed down the pot's sides. 'Is someone doing this?'

'Too early to say.' I was trying not to think of the fresh grave less than a mile away.

'Do I need to tighten up the house rules for the girls? Have a curfew time, maybe? Make sure they never go out by themselves.'

'We've no reason to believe Patsy and the others have come to any harm . . .' I started to say.

Sally looked at me with the tiny, polite smile that was her habitual expression and blinked suddenly, as her grey eyes moistened.

'I would,' I said. 'Yes, definitely. Keep them safe.'

18

Tired as I was, it took me a long time to get to sleep. The reconstruction had seemed such a good idea, but if it led to nothing concrete, all we'd done was draw even more attention to our failure to solve three disappearances. The super would carry the blame nationally, but Tom was right: here in Sabden, it would be down to me.

When I did drop off, I slept badly, waking continually before sinking back into vivid and frightening dreams. Predictably, I dreamed I was trapped in a dark, enclosed space. Tom and Dwane were above me, banging on the lid, trying to get a response, but I was unable to speak.

When I found my voice, Tom and Dwane had gone, and I was screaming for my mother.

I started awake, wrapped tight in damp nylon sheets, afraid for a moment that I'd been calling out loud. When no sounds came from the house – my screams had been silent after all – I sat up and pulled open the curtains. I couldn't see the moon, the starlight was soft and muted, and the Hill was only a vague shape, blacker than its surroundings.

I didn't think I would sleep again that night.

My mother. Thinking of her hurt so much, so most of the time I tried not to do it. Every so often, though, she'd catch me unawares, sneak up on me in a dream, or a random memory.

And she always came for a purpose.

That night, I found myself thinking about a time when I was twelve years old and out driving with her. It had been just the two of us in the car – my brothers were at home with the nanny – and the rare treat of her undivided attention had made me chattier, more confiding than usual. I can't recall what I said to her, but I remember her stopping the car at the side of the road and suggesting we get out to stretch our legs. We climbed a stile, crossed the upper edge of a poppy field and then up onto another stile, where we balanced and looked towards a large village about half a mile distant. I learned later it was called Bletchley. At its centre was a huge Victorian mansion of tall red-brick gables and archways with a domed lead roof on a circular corner window.

'One day, Florence,' she said, 'you'll hear your name being called.'

It was on the tip of my tongue to say I heard that all the time. With three young brothers, there was always something the grown-ups needed help with, but I sensed that wasn't what she meant at all.

She was staring towards the red-brick mansion. 'When it happens, you can't hide away and pretend you didn't hear it. You have to put your hand up and say, "Yes, I'm here."'

Over the following years I gathered, because I wasn't told outright, that my mother had been involved in the war. Something had brought her from her native Hampshire to Buckinghamshire, where she'd met and married my father. She never spoke about it, and I hadn't thought about that day in years, but it came back to me as I sat on my bed, staring out at Pendle Hill.

Somewhere in the darkness, Patsy Wood was calling my name.

Outside, the Hill was a shadow on the horizon. I turned my back on it and unlocked the garden shed with a key I'd borrowed from the kitchen. I pushed the door open gingerly, knowing it creaked. The shed was windowless and for a second or two I couldn't see a thing. I was on the point of risking my torch when I heard the low, throaty growl.

In a corner of the shed, on a nest it had made for itself out of sacking, lay a black dog. Small and skinny, with slick, short fur, the dog blinked as the torch beam shone in its face. Its nose was long, its ears enormous and bat-like. A male. I had never seen it before. The Glassbrooks kept no dog that I knew of.

The whippet – I think it was – growled again. It didn't move, though, and I didn't believe it to be an immediate danger. In fact, the biggest threat it posed was that it would start barking and wake the house.

So I ignored it, spotted the heavy-duty spade I'd come for and grabbed it. I closed the door and turned the key. I'd deal with the dog later.

Getting to the churchyard via the roads would take me forty minutes or more, so I went across country, climbing the wall at the top of the Glassbrooks' garden and then following the upper line of properties at the foot of the Hill. At first it was easy – there was a well-beaten trail to follow, and the spade doubled as a walking stick – but after ten minutes or so, the scrubland gave way to open moor and I had to fight my way through thick fields of bracken.

At one point, I stumbled and when I gave myself a moment to get my breath back, I saw lights on the Hill.

I rubbed my eyes and looked again. Definitely lights, torches or lanterns, about halfway up, and a bigger one that might be a bonfire. There were people on the Hill in the middle of the night, and just the sight of those lights, darting and dancing about, went against all my police instincts of what was normal, rational behaviour.

And now that I was still, that was drumming that I could hear.

Distant, at times hardly audible, carried to me on the wind, and almost certainly not heard by anyone in town, the steady, rhythmic beat continued. Not the simple, repetitive rhythm of a marching band: this sounded altogether more primitive. I was pretty certain it was coming from the Hill, from the point where I could see the lights.

I should call it in. The nearest police box was a ten-minute walk from St Wilfred's. The station officer could have a car investigate.

And I'd have to explain what I was doing out at two o'clock in the morning, armed with a spade.

I turned my back on the lights, walked quickly so that the sound of my treading steps drowned out the drums, but my confidence was faltering. For the latter half of the journey to the churchyard, I was acutely conscious of the night around me, of the wind rushing through treetops and smothering other sound, of bracken moving at odds with the wind. It was almost a relief to swing over the wall and be among the dead.

The grave was exactly as I'd left it, likewise the children's den. I stood at its foot, knowing that in a couple of hours people would start getting up for the early factory shifts and that I had a decision to make. So far, I'd done nothing wrong. Once I started digging, I was committing a serious crime. Were I to be caught, it would be the end of my police career and might even see me charged.

And for what? Even if Patsy were beneath my feet, she'd be dead by this time. I should turn round and go home. And yet . . .

Help me, the six-year-old boy had heard, coming from the ground. I could almost hear it myself, a desperate voice pleading not to be left to her fate.

I didn't really have a choice. Dead or alive, she wasn't staying down there, abandoned by everyone who was supposed to take care of her. I lifted the wreaths one by one and laid them alongside the grave. Then I started digging.

In, lift, throw. In, lift, throw.

After twenty minutes, I gave up any hope of being able to return the grave to a pristine condition. I'd have to do my best and flee, get away before first light.

In, lift, throw. Repeat over and over again. Despite the cool night air, I was soon sweating. After a while, I stopped looking round every few seconds to make sure I was alone. I was too exhausted to care. In, lift, throw. The floral tributes were soon buried under loose earth. The hole became too deep for me to stay on top of the grave, so I gave in to the inevitable and climbed down.

I carried on digging. I was hot, tired, and my hands were sore, but I was getting lower in the ground with every minute that went past.

Thud. My spade struck wood. I carried on. Not digging now but loosening and scraping, sliding my spade along the casket top.

Then I heard something. Something that wasn't the wind, or the sliding back of dislodged earth. Something like . . . A moan?

I pulled myself together and carried on. The dead did not wake up. Not even when someone was banging with a spade on their front door. My hands on the spade were shaking, so I dug faster.

The wind picked up, and the sound of the trees rustling made me think of whispered threats. By the time I could see most of the casket lid, the sky had lost its unrelenting darkness and I could no longer ignore the sense that something had changed. The disquiet I'd been pushing to the back of my mind since I'd entered the churchyard had become a deep unease. I was no longer hot, in fact quite the reverse.

I did not believe in the supernatural. I did not believe the dead have any power over the living, but as I froze in the grave, I was finally able to crystallise the uneasy dread that had been creeping over me. It was simple, really. I was no longer alone.

No sooner had I admitted that to myself than I became aware of a shadow on the ground. Someone – or something – was standing right behind me on the rim of the grave.

19

'You all right there, Florence?' Tom Devine said. 'Need a hand with anything?'

I turned slowly, not wanting to show how shaken I was. In jeans and a denim jacket, Tom was standing at the side of the grave.

'How long have you been there?'

'Do you want the full embarrassing story, or do you want to get this over with?' He reached down. 'Get the hell out. We can't open it with your weight on it.'

I gave Tom my hand because there was nothing else to be done. Despite what he'd said about my weight, he pulled me up easily.

'Don't suppose you remember what that undertaker bloke said about the fastenings?' he said.

My resolve had crumbled. 'Tom, you can't be serious. We'll be in so much trouble.'

'Less of the "we", Florence. If we find nothing, I'm out of here. You're on your own.'

Well, he couldn't say fairer than that. Without exchanging another word, we dropped to our knees and lay flat. We both reached down and found the concealed locks. I talked him through the twisting and pulling that would release the mechanism and the casket lid bounced an inch open.

The smell hit us hard. I'd expected it to be bad but not nearly so intense. It was as though something tangible had rushed from the open casket and slapped me full in the face.

'Florence, on your feet and take a couple of steps back.' Tom didn't look up. 'Actually, I need you to run down the road and call the station. Get someone out here.'

'We need to be sure first.' I took a gulp of fresh air and leaned back in. 'Come on. I'm OK.' I was trying to talk without breathing. I was hoping to suspend breathing until this was over with.

'Florence, that isn't an embalmed corpse we can smell.'

I risked another breath. I had no real idea what an embalmed corpse smelled like, but I supposed there would be strong chemicals overriding the decaying flesh. Not vomit. Not excrement and urine. Not putrefying meat. Not the disgusting cocktail that was tainting the air around us right now.

'I think you were right, Florence.' It was still quite dark, but when I looked across, I thought Tom's face was noticeably paler. 'I think she's in here, I think she's dead, and I don't think this is something you need to see.'

When I thought about his gallantry later, I wasn't sure whether I felt more touched or patronised. At the time, I reached out and took hold of the casket lid. Tom did the same. The lid wouldn't stay up by itself, so I held it and Tom shone his torch down onto Patsy Wood's pitiful dead face.

While we waited for the others to arrive, we made a cordon round the grave with tape from Tom's car and some willow twigs. All the time we were working, I tried not to let him see my face. Which was a waste of time, as it turned out.

'If it helps, I feel like crying too,' he said, when we'd done everything we could and were leaning on the churchyard wall. 'But I'd get it out of the way before the others arrive.'

I was not going to cry, not properly. I couldn't stop the tears trickling down, but—

'How long were you . . . ?' I began. 'When did you . . . ? How?'

'I knew you were planning something stupid,' Tom said, as we caught the first flicker of blue lights in the distance. 'I came out here to teach you the error of your ways. By midnight, you hadn't shown, and it was starting to drizzle, so I crawled inside that kids' den.' He nodded over to the shelter we'd seen earlier. 'Fell asleep,' he admitted.

'You were asleep? All the time I was digging?'

He pulled out cigarettes. 'What can I say? I'm a sound sleeper. And I'd had a couple of pints in the Star. I only woke up when your spade clanged against the lid. The damage was done by then.'

I asked the question I really didn't want to hear answered. 'Do you think she was alive? When we were here earlier?'

His cigarette glowed warm in the chill dawn air. 'No,' he said. 'Definitely not. You saw her just now. She's been dead for more than a few hours.' He took a great long drag on his cigarette.

The tears were coming back. I didn't think I'd be able to hold them off this time. 'Tom, what she must have been through . . .'

He turned to me. 'No. Cut that out. Her family will torture themselves with that. So will her friends. We have a job to do. We have to find the bastard who put her in there.'

The first of the patrol cars had arrived. The flickering lights died and a uniformed officer climbed out.

'I'm so glad you're here,' I said to Tom.

'I'm glad you brought that up,' he said. 'We need to get our stories straight. You couldn't sleep, you came back here to pay your respects to whoever is legitimately down there – you might want to check who it is – and you heard noises from below ground. You had no choice but to dig it up, with a spade that had been conveniently left lying around. When you saw it was Patsy after all, you called me for advice. I came out here, checked and we called it in. Happy with that?'

Two uniformed officers were now heading towards us. Behind them, another car was pulling up.

Pay my respects? A spade left lying around? 'They'll never believe that.'

'Doesn't matter. It's credible enough for them to pretend to. And you, Flossie, had better be more humble than Uriah Heep for the next few days. Nobody likes a smart-arse.'

20

Back at the Glassbrook house, I rinsed the spade under the outside tap and returned it to the shed. I was puzzled and a little spooked to see that the small black dog had vanished, even though the shed had remained locked, but as I walked back towards the house, I could see a pale face watching me from the kitchen window. Cassie Glassbrook was up unusually early.

Two of the station's civilian staff were in the ladies' toilets when I got to work, Elaine from the typing pool and Brenda who worked the switchboard. I envied the civilian women their freedom to wear dresses in the hot weather, and Elaine's was obviously new from the way she was examining herself in the mirrors, twisting round to see the back view. It was short, sleeveless, a multi-coloured confusion of weird, swirling shapes. I didn't like it, but in my half-blues and thick tights, I was already hot. I'd have swapped.

'Good morning.'

I didn't notice immediately that neither of them replied because my locker door was ajar. I pulled it open carefully and caught the same foul smell that hovers around public toilets in the summer and dark alleys close to pubs. My jacket looked untouched, but my cap wasn't where I left it. I knew it would be wet even before I picked it up. Someone had pissed in my cap.

'Know anything about this?' The two women were pretending

not to watch me as I carried my cap to the sink, but they were rubbish at acting.

''Bout what?' Elaine tapped cigarette ash into the sink.

'Problem?' Brenda inspected her nails.

The two of them hadn't worked out that mirrors reflect facial expressions, or maybe they just didn't care that I could see their twisted smiles.

I rinsed my cap and tried my best to dry it with the thin revolving towel, hoping the wetting – two wettings – wouldn't damage it, because I'd be fined.

By this time, I was late on parade. Only a matter of seconds, but it was just my luck for Rushton to be in the parade room and for the shift officers to be standing to attention as I slipped inside.

'Good of you to join us, Flossie,' the sergeant said, as I took my place at the end of the line, feeling my face burning. The constable next to me sniffed and moved a step away. Elsewhere in the room, I heard a snigger, turned quickly into a cough.

'Morning, lads, lass.' The super stepped forward. 'You've all heard the rumours about what happened in the early hours and I'm here to tell you the gossip stops now.'

Rushton seemed to be making eye contact with everyone in the room, nine constables, apart from me.

'The vermin of Fleet Street have descended in force,' he went on. 'Some of 'em were here before the sun came up, but I guess they're not naturally drawn to the hours of daylight. My point is, if I hear of anyone talking to them about the Patsy Wood case, I will have that man' – he looked pointedly in my direction – 'or woman scrubbing the station lavvies until they draw their pension. Do I make myself clear?'

A chorus of 'Yes, sir's' rang out around the room.

'And the same goes for the general populous. We talk to no

one. I will be making an official statement later today. Have a good day, lads.'

In the doorway, Rushton paused for a word with the sergeant. I couldn't hear what they said, but the sergeant glanced my way.

I was given Two Beat, alone, and as soon as we were dismissed, I made for the door, eager to get away from the sideways glances and pointed avoidance of the other constables, not to mention the grumbles about the gauntlet of reporters we all had to run to leave the building.

As I was about to step into Reception, I felt a nudge on my shoulder and looked back to see one of the older constables, a man called Colin, who was known as 'the foreigner' because he'd moved here from Yorkshire ten years earlier.

I guess that made me the Martian.

'I've to drop you off down road.' Without waiting for a response, he turned and made for the yard where the vehicles were kept.

'Why?' I followed him out, catching the back door as it swung towards me. I had my answer as we shot out of the station past the gathered crowd of journalists. I caught my name when they spotted me in the passenger seat of Colin's car. One even started jogging after us.

Colin sniffed. 'Wind window down,' he said, without looking at me.

'Thank you,' I said, when he pulled over two hundred yards down the road. He was staring straight ahead through the windscreen and maybe I wasn't supposed to hear what he said next.

'Don't hurry back.'

For a second – a wise and sensible second – I almost quietly closed the door and walked away. But then I thought of that little girl, interred alive in the most terrifying place imaginable, and of the other two, who'd probably shared her fate. And I thought about their killer, who was almost certainly somewhere in town, walking the streets, watching the children, waiting for his next chance.

The second passed and I bent down until I could see the side of his head.

'What was I supposed to do? Leave her down there?'

He turned then and, angry though I was, I was alarmed by the look on his face. 'Fuck off,' he told me.

So I did.

21

The 'beats' are the defined areas of town that a police officer is expected to patrol, within set times, when on duty. I knew Two Beat well: it was one of the quieter ones during the daytime, considered suitable for a lone WPC. Mainly residential streets and a few corner shops, there was a primary school and an old cotton mill, which had closed its doors for the last time a few years earlier. Having a look around the mill, checking everything was in order, was my first task.

As I turned into the street, I heard Tom Jones bitterly querying the motivation of a woman called Delilah. Tom's voice was replaced by the sound of a baby crying, a woman shouting at her children to hurry up, the high-pitched trilling of someone playing a recorder. All the front windows seemed to be open. Some of the women were already out, housecoats and aprons over their clothes, their hair tied up in scarves, scrubbing their doorsteps. It was almost a ritual in the North-West: the family left for the day; the woman of the house scrubbed the doorstep clean for their return. Most used large wooden brushes, but some still had the traditional donkey stones. A few wished me good morning; others watched me walk past.

Usually quiet during the day, the Perseverance Mill was nevertheless notorious at the station. Barely a week went by without reports of some night-time disturbance or other. In the early hours of that very morning, while I was making my way across the moor, two of our constables had been called out to investigate a possible break-in. They'd found nothing, but the sergeant wanted it checked again in daylight.

The mill lay at the end of a short residential road called Jubilee Street. Its front gates were solid iron, bolted and wrapped with a chain and padlock, the only relief in a high and dirty, broken-glass-topped brick wall that surrounded the mill and its yards. A pair of buzzards had nested in the chimney and I could see them circling as I approached.

Parked in the street, just a few yards down from the mill gates, was a black Daimler. I took a quick glance around, annoyed with myself for not making a note of the registration of the one I'd seen yesterday afternoon. Prestige cars weren't exactly rare in Sabden – the mills and factories and surrounding farms had made some men very wealthy – but they weren't ten a penny either.

I was just tall enough to see over the wall into the mill pond. Rubbish lay on its surface, while the narrow strip of land that circled it was chocked with brambles, nettles and elder. The tall, stately flowers of the sweet bay willowherb rimmed its edges, and pale yellow iris poked their heads up through the water. Buddleia bushes grew around it too, the purple blooms browning as the flowers died. Their scent was strong and sickly in the already-warm morning air.

I made my way towards the rear of the mill, where the second set of gates were not so high, and my attention was caught by graffiti in greasy white paint

Put on the whole armour of God, that you may be able to stand against the schemes of the Devil.

There was a symbol too, a sort of diamond shape. The graffiti was fresh. As I drew close, I could smell the chemicals in the paint.

Religious graffiti. Who'd heard of that? And why, on the whole of this disused building, was this the only sign of vandalism?

From the rear gates I could see across the yard and the entire back of the building. Huge metal loading doors allowed access to the basement. The lower windows were barred, several of them broken. Outbuildings were tucked against the wall. It was surprisingly neat, for an abandoned building. All seemed in order.

And then it didn't. There was someone in the mill. For a second, maybe two, a human-shaped shadow appeared in one of the lower windows, and that presented me with a choice. I could jog back to the nearest police call box and report it or investigate myself. I didn't relish the thought of scaling the gate, but any of my male colleagues would do it, no question.

I looked around – no one watching – and put my foot on the lowest crossbar. I swung a leg over, taking care of my skirt, and then dropped down.

It was all very different on this side of the wall. The mill seemed bigger and the yard darker. The high-pitched cry of one of the buzzards now seemed to be aimed directly at me. Maybe it was. Buzzards were known to be territorial.

I set off across the yard to the window where I'd seen the figure, but the glass was glazed and dirty, impossible to see through. I moved on to the next, and the next. No movement inside that I could see.

I had not imagined that shadow.

'What the bloody hell do you think you're doing?'

I turned to see two men had appeared from round the corner. One of them was a man called Terry Parker, a known offender. A wiry, rodent-faced character, he'd been interviewed when Stephen vanished, partly because of his history, partly because he lived very close to the Shorrock family. He hung back now behind the younger, bigger man.

The man I had a feeling I'd seen before but couldn't place had a large ring of keys in one hand. He was in his mid-forties, with short brown hair and a heavy face. He wore a business suit, but his stomach hung over his waistband, and his shirt collar dug into the folds of his neck.

'We had reports of a disturbance last night, sir,' I said. 'May I ask your name and the nature of your business here?'

I counted four seconds before he answered.

'Mr Earnshaw, property owner. And now can I ask yours?'

'WPC Lovelady, sir.' I looked past him to where Terry seemed to be trying to slink away. 'To save me checking with my sergeant, can you vouch for Mr Earnshaw, Terry?'

Terry twitched and continued to edge backwards. I took his silence as assent.

'I know who you are,' the bigger man said. 'You're Stan Rushton's new poodle. Haven't they got any cells need scrubbing out?'

'Have you been inside the mill this morning, Mr Earnshaw?'

He stepped closer until I could smell stale alcohol and cigarette smoke on his breath. 'I hardly think I have to account for myself on my own property.'

'Nevertheless, sir, we've had reports of a break-in. Have you seen any signs of a disturbance?'

He leaned closer and I had to fight the instinct to back away. Then he raised a finger and tapped the air, inches from my jacket pocket. 'Listen, love, I did not call you lot out last night, and neither did Terry here. We are the only people who have keys and the only ones authorised to report disturbances. So unless you hear from one of us in future, I suggest you stay in the station and concentrate on making tea for the senior officers.'

I nodded at the mill. 'Do you mind if I look around inside?'

'Aye, I do. Now push off before I have a word with Stan Rushton about your behaviour.'

Without a warrant or his permission, I could do nothing more.

I wished them both a good morning and walked away. It crossed my mind to ask them to open the gates, but I had a feeling that request, too, would be denied. So I climbed back over, conscious of them watching. When I landed on the other side, I heard Earnshaw say, 'Get that shit off the wall, Terry. I don't pay you to let the place be vandalised.'

I made my report to the station officer. As I was locking the police box, I felt an unsettling sense of being watched and looked across the road to see Tom leaning against his car. For a second we stared at each other and I thought I could see something in his eyes that didn't look entirely like the Tom I knew. I crossed the road. He didn't speak.

'Where've you been?' I hadn't seen him since I'd left St Wilfred's.

'The Wood house. Then the infirmary. I took Patsy's dad to ID the body.'

'You broke the news?'

'Me and the super. They'd take it best from me, he said.'

'Are they—' I stopped.

'Are they OK? No, Florence, they're a very long way from being OK.'

'Are you?'

He opened the car door. 'Super sent me to get you,' he said. 'Look sharp.'

I got in the car. 'Where are we going?' I asked, as we pulled away from the kerb. Unusually, the radio wasn't switched on.

'Nowhere you'll like,' he told me.

22

'Is this a punishment?' I asked, as Tom and I walked down the tiled corridor on the ground floor of Blackburn Royal Infirmary. I'd never been to a post-mortem and I didn't want to start with Patsy's. Nor did I relish the thought of everyone at the station laughing at tales of me throwing up, or even fainting.

'You really don't know Rushton yet, do you?' Tom spotted a 'no smoking' sign and looked for somewhere to leave his cigarette. Seeing nothing, he dropped it.

At the end of the corridor, through a set of double doors, we found Superintendent Rushton with three of CID's most senior detectives: DI Sharples, who didn't even look my way, and the two detective sergeants working directly under him, Bob Green and Garry Brown. Green, nicknamed Gusty, was in his early thirties, with long, fine hair that flew from his scalp at all angles, as though he were permanently caught in wind. I'd thought, at first, that his unusual hairstyle accounted for his nickname, but soon found out it was for another reason entirely. Brown, a decade older than Green, was called Woodsmoke, for no reason I'd managed to discover. All the men smelled of smoke back then. He smoked a pipe, rather than cigarettes, but it was made from a polished black lacquer, not wood.

A couple of seconds after Tom and I arrived, the pathologist appeared. His eyes settled on me. 'Is the young lady coming with us?' he asked.

'She is,' said Rushton.

Pursing his lips, the pathologist led the way.

The large, hexagonal mortuary had the look of the public baths in Sabden, which I visited at least weekly to supplement my hot-water ration at the boarding house. Everything functional, and yet elaborate too, with the intricate, showy design the Victorians loved. Sound bounced around off the tiled walls before disappearing into the high ceiling.

Arched windows surrounded us. The larger ones, set low in the walls, had been blacked out for privacy, but those higher up still let in natural daylight. Through one, I could see the leafy branches of a sycamore tree. Ignoring the thin, shrouded body on the marble table, I fixed my eyes on the swaying leaves. The pathologist, a Dr Dodds, said, 'Everybody ready, then?' and pulled back the sheet.

Silence fell. I lowered my eyes and looked at Patsy.

Her features had been composed, for which I was grateful. The snarling expression, so dreadful in the torchlight, making me think of a rodent in a trap, had been relaxed into something akin to sleep. In the early hours, though, I hadn't appreciated the dreadful wounds to her hands and lower arms. She hadn't been washed yet and they were covered in dried blood.

Her lips had lost all colour and were horribly cracked. They'd been bleeding too. There were three deep scratches on her left cheek, where she'd raked her own face.

'We're looking at the remains of an adolescent female,' said the pathologist. 'Caucasian. Weighing about a hundred pounds and with a height of around five foot two inches.'

Patsy wasn't wearing clothes. I knew it to be normal, but couldn't help feeling sad for her. She would have had a teenager's extreme sensitivity about her body and could probably imagine little worse than lying naked in front of six men.

I had to stop thinking of her as alive.

'Bit on the thin side,' the pathologist said, 'but otherwise she looks to have been in good health prior to her demise.'

'Cause of death?' Rushton was, of all of us, the furthest away from the table. I wasn't sure he was even looking directly at Patsy, but rather at some undefined spot several inches above her. He'd shaved since the early hours, but badly. He'd cut himself twice, and missed patches of stubble altogether.

'Given the airtight enclosure you found her in, the oxygen-poor environment, I'm looking at asphyxia as the cause of death,' said the pathologist. 'Certainly nothing I can see immediately suggests any different. The wounds to her hands and fingers' – he raised Patsy's left hand and shone his torch on the two middle fingers, both missing nails – 'suggest that she was alive when she was put in the coffin.'

Rushton's whole body trembled.

'Her clothes were stained with urine and faecal matter,' said Brown, who'd been tasked with collating the evidence from the casket that wasn't Patsy herself. 'Also vomit. Again suggesting that she was interred alive.'

I was looking at the sycamore tree again.

'We know she was alive,' Tom said. 'She'd half wrecked the coffin trying to claw her way out.'

I think everyone in the room, except the pathologist, reacted to that. We'd all seen the casket in the early hours of the morning. We'd all seen the torn, blood-stained satin, the vomit in the hair of the dead man whose peaceful resting place it was supposed to have been. Poor Patsy had been laid directly on top of a corpse. She would have been terrified. He'd deserved better too. I tried to remember his name. Douglas, I thought. Douglas Simmonds.

The pathologist frowned. 'What's a little more puzzling is that I can't see any sign of her being restrained.'

'How do you mean?' Rushton asked.

'No obvious bruises around her shoulders or neck.' The pathologist crossed to a nearby worktop and re-angled a lamp to shine more brightly on Patsy's upper body. 'We know her wrists and ankles weren't bound. So the question you gentlemen should be asking is how someone managed to get her in there.'

'Might she have been drugged?' I suggested. 'Chloroform maybe? Any of the anaesthetising drugs?'

One of the others, Sharples I think, exhaled.

Dodds waited a good five seconds before responding. 'The tissue analysis may tell us that. Although the anaesthetising drugs are not commonly available.'

'When did she die?' Rushton asked. 'Can you give us a time of death, doctor?'

My eyes were back up on the sycamore tree.

'Hmmn, rigor mortis has passed; livor mortis has had chance to develop on her back and buttocks. I'd say death occurred sometime in the hours of Monday night through to Tuesday morning.' He looked up at us. 'Some time before you were called out to the churchyard yesterday evening.'

I heard several sighs of relief in the room. One of them, I'm sure, being my own. Rushton, though, merely closed his eyes again. We gave him the moment he seemed to need, and watched threads of colour sneaking back into his face. Meanwhile, Dodds had opened Patsy's mouth with a metal instrument and was shining a small torch inside.

'Interesting,' he said.

The rest of us looked at each other. Waited.

'She appears to have had a tooth removed recently,' Dodds said. 'Top right canine. Bit of a clumsy extraction. You might want to check with her dentist.'

Brown seemed to start. He shot a glance at the boss and opened his mouth.

'Any sign she'd been interfered with?' Sharples asked.

Brown frowned and closed his mouth again as Dodds moved down Patsy's body.

I wasn't about to watch this bit. I kept my eyes down, this time, on the floor tiles, which were the colour of buttermilk, on the grime-stained grouting between them, on the large central drain. I heard the sound of dead flesh being slid over marble, of instruments plonking down onto hard surfaces. No one spoke.

'Hard to say at this stage,' Dodds said.

I glanced up and then straight back down again. Dodds had pulled some sort of upside-down stirrups from beneath the table and Patsy's thin white legs were pinned in each of them.

'I can't see any sign of bleeding here specifically,' Dodds went on. 'And no obvious bruising or tearing.' He grunted, in the way people do as they're bending over or getting up from a low seat. 'Hymen doesn't seem to be intact,' he said, 'but that in itself doesn't prove anything, given what kids are these days. Examining her clothes might give you more idea, but for now I'd say not likely.'

Several more sighs sounded around the room as Dodds removed the stirrups and lowered Patsy's legs.

'Well, I'm about to start the internal examination,' the pathologist said. 'Which you're welcome to stay around for, if you'd like?' He crossed to the worktop and picked up a scalpel.

We didn't like. We thanked him and left the room. Thirty minutes later, the men were in the meeting room next to Rushton's office. I was in the kitchen. Making tea.

23

Rushton had a secretary who usually made tea for her boss's meetings, but she didn't look up as I carried the laden tray past her desk. Nor did she help me open the door to the meeting room. Inside, the men were on their feet.

'I'll get a couple of the lads talking to the funeral directors in the area,' Green was saying. 'Get a list of burials since Susan went missing. We can visit the graves discreetly, see if any look likely.'

'I think you need to go back a bit further,' said Brown. 'If someone's hiding corpses in graves, they won't necessarily go for the most recent ones.'

'But ground hardens up after a while,' I said. 'The newer graves will be easier to dig.'

Silence. I put down the tray.

'We bow to your greater experience,' said the super. 'Maybe go back to the start of the year, Gusty. There can't be that many. We haven't had a pestilence.'

I stayed where I was, leaning awkwardly over the table, unsure whether I was expected to serve the tea or leave. Tom gave me a tight-lipped smile.

'Right.' Rushton pulled out a chair at the head of the table. 'Sit down, gents. I've something to say to WPC Lovelady.' The super was looking directly at me; I could feel my face glowing purple. The noise of scraping chairs subsided.

'I'm glad you did it, Florence,' he said. 'It showed a lot of neck, and it gave us a result, if not the one we wanted.'

A couple of the others muttered agreement. Sharples looked at me with a cold, flinty stare.

'On the other hand, next time you pull a stunt like that, you could find yourself up shit creek, and I won't be handing out paddles.' Rushton leaned across the table towards me. 'I want my officers sticking to the rules and putting themselves first, not going out on a limb following hunches that could get them, and me, in the doo-doo. Do I make myself clear, love?'

'Perfectly, sir. I'm sorry,' I said.

Rushton leaned back in his chair and looked up at the ceiling. 'And while I'm on the subject,' he went on, 'I could have something to say to officers who should know better being led by a pretty face into reckless midnight shenanigans. But I'll leave that to your individual consciences.'

Silence round the table. Making an effort not to look at Tom, I took a step backwards towards the door.

'The second thing, Flossie,' said Rushton, 'is I want you off the beat and moving upstairs for the foreseeable. I'll have someone bring up a desk for you.'

'Do you mind me asking why, boss?' Sharples looked like he'd sucked on an unripe lemon. 'We need bobbies on the beat right now. Even if they're . . . well.'

'I want a small team at the centre of this investigation and Flossie has barged her way into it,' Rushton said. 'Besides, we're going to need a lot of stuff typing up quickly and I don't want it going through the typing pool. Better switch to plain clothes too, Flossie. There might be times in the next few weeks when I don't want it blindingly obvious that you're a police officer.'

'Yes, sir,' I managed, with an uncomfortable feeling that I hadn't exactly earned this co-option to the team, that Rushton just wanted to keep an eye on me. There was also the problem that I couldn't actually—

'And we're going to need a regular supply of tea,' Brown said. 'Milk, two sugars, please, Flossie.'

I picked up the pot, keeping my eyes down. If I kept quiet and made myself useful, they might not kick me out.

'Right, now we've got Flossie sorted, this is even more important,' said Rushton. 'I want no mention of the words "buried alive" outside this group. In fact, I don't even want any of you saying them out loud, not until we know what we're dealing with.'

I looked up. 'But, sir, we can't—' I stopped. Me and my big mouth. Sharples was openly sneering.

'What's on your mind, Florence?' the super said.

'It will have to come out at the inquest,' I said.

'It will, but that will be days away, if not a couple of weeks. We've got some breathing space.'

'The case has a lot of attention, though,' said Green. 'Thanks to Flossie's TV reconstruction. People can hardly get through the front door this morning for hacks and local do-gooders. We're going to have a lot of tough questions.'

'We issue a statement this morning,' Rushton said. 'Flossie, you're good with words: you can type it out. Patsy Wood was found in a newly dug grave that showed signs of having been interfered with. Don't mention you did the interfering. No other comment will be made until after the inquest. Blah de blah, blah. You can make something up, sound impressive.'

I couldn't type. I'd been to university, not secretarial school.

'We still have two missing teenagers,' Rushton went on, 'and if it gets out they might have been buried alive, we'll have a mob with pitchforks on every street corner and every grave from here to Burnley desecrated. We need to find them first. What is it now, Flossie?'

I'd been handing Detective Sergeant Brown his tea when something had occurred to me. Hiding my thoughts was obviously something I had to work on.

'Sorry, sir,' I said. 'It's just that when the pathologist told us about Patsy's missing tooth, DS Brown looked as though he was about to say something.'

Brown didn't look thrilled at my singling him out.

'Anything to share, Woodsmoke?' Rushton asked.

'Not really,' Brown said. 'But I was brought up in these parts and my gran was always a one for the old stories. Scared us half to death at times. Witches were her favourites. She used to talk about spells they did, black magic, that sort of thing. Said they dug up graves to get body parts.'

Sharples said, 'I don't quite—'

'And she were right about that,' Brown interrupted. 'It was documented at the Pendle witch trial back in 16 – whenever. Local magistrate was called out one Sunday because graves had been dug up in one of the churches in the forest. Recent graves and all. People arrived at church to see dead family members littered about.' He looked around at us. 'I'm not telling ghost stories; this is history.'

'Sounds like a pretty nasty piece of intimidation to me,' Rushton said.

'Except, according to Gran, it wasn't only about upsetting people,' said Brown. 'She said the witches needed body parts to make their spells work.'

'Lovely,' said Sharples. 'That's enough milk, Lovelady. I haven't got a calcium deficiency.'

'Hair and fingernails are good, but blood, teeth and bone are better,' Brown went on. 'You can look as sceptical as you like, boss, but my gran always made sure she threw nail clippings and stray hair on the fire so they wouldn't fall into witches' hands. A lot of her generation did.'

There was a knock on the door and the super's secretary poked her head into the room. 'Evidence want a word, sir,' she told the super. 'Urgent.'

'We also need to go back over the first two disappearances.' Rushton got up. 'Talk to their school again, their friends, find out what we missed. Flossie, you're the closest thing we've got to a schoolkid: you're in charge of that. We probably need to sort out use of a car for you.'

The door closed behind the super.

'Can you actually drive, Lovelady?' asked Sharples.

'Yes, sir,' I said. 'I got my licence when I was seventeen.'

The super came back. He'd lost colour.

'Come on,' he said. 'The lot of you. Evidence want us right away. They've found something in the coffin.'

24

The small female figure that had been found in the casket along with Patsy was grotesque. Just over six inches long, made from some sort of reddish-brown clay, its feet and hands were bound together behind its back. Thin slivers of wood, thirteen of them – I counted quickly – pierced the hands and feet, eyes, ears and mouth, genitals and anus, top of the head and middle of the chest.

'Bloody Norah,' Sharples said.

It was revolting, but none of us could look away. Hair fell to its shoulders and was held back by a thin band. The facial features were tiny but perfectly formed. The face had even been made thin around the temples with a high forehead. There was something slightly strange about its mouth, but other than that—

'It looks like Patsy.' I moved away, further round the table. I didn't want to be anywhere near the thing.

'Where'd you find it?' Rushton asked.

The two officers in charge of evidence handling had stepped back to let the six of us get to the examination table. 'Tucked under the satin,' one of them said. 'We only found it when we cut it all loose.'

The casket we'd found Patsy in was here too, taking up too much space in this small, cramped room. I had no idea where the body of Douglas Simmonds had been taken and it didn't seem like the moment to ask.

'It's a voodoo doll,' said Brown.

'Those aren't pins,' Green said quickly. 'They look like bits of wood to me. Voodoo dolls have pins.'

Brown squatted down to bring himself on a level with the tabletop. 'There's something in its mouth. Stuck in, I mean, like when it was – what do they call it, fired? It looks like a tooth, boss.'

Tom and Green joined him.

Patsy's missing canine. We were all thinking it.

'Woodsmoke,' said the super, whose colour had left him again. 'Can you check with Patsy's dentist, soon as you can? See if he took her tooth out. I'm not liking this, I'm really not.'

We all started at the knock on the door. Sharples threw a cloth over the figure a second before one of the secretaries opened the door and asked for Rushton.

After he left, no one uncovered the figure. None of us seemed to know what to say. I walked to the other end of the table, where Patsy's clothes were laid out: red cardigan, flower-print dress, socks, knickers, vest and shoes.

'Do these look unusually clean to anyone?' I said.

'No,' answered Brown, before giving a quick sideways glance at the others. They were still gathered round the hidden figure.

'I'm not talking about the blood and vomit,' I said. 'I'm talking about what's not here. I can't see any soil stains. If she was put in the grave after the official burial, there'd be traces of soil at least. Her clothes shouldn't be this clean.'

I stopped talking, because no one was listening to me. The door opened and the super was back. 'We've Roy Greenwood and Larry Glassbrook downstairs,' he said. 'Wanting to make a statement.'

Sharples seemed to brace himself before reaching down and uncovering the clay figure. 'Good,' he said. 'We can ask them if they've seen this before.'

The figure, the likeness of Patsy, lay naked on the wooden table, her sightless eyes staring at me.

25

'Florence can interview them,' said the super.

'All due respect, sir, we can't send a fresh WPC to interview suspects,' said Sharples. 'I should do it.'

'They're not suspects,' said Rushton. 'They've come in voluntarily to make a statement and you'll scare 'em. Butter 'em up, Flossie. They won't be on their guard with you. Go in with her, Tom. Act a bit daft. You know, your usual approach.'

The two undertakers were shown into the interview room, the one with the two-way mirror, and Tom joined them first to thank them for coming. I followed a couple of minutes later, with another tea tray, a pencil and a notepad. When I opened the door, the smell of men's toiletries came flooding out. Tom wore Brut 33, rather more of it than I cared for, and I was familiar with Larry's Old Spice. The other scent in the air, a cloying, greasy smell, I guessed was the oil on Greenwood's hair.

'We're here to express our concern about what happened at St Wilfred's in the early hours of this morning,' said Roy Greenwood, after Tom had asked what he could do for 'you two gents'.

Roy Greenwood's teeth were perfect, with the startling whiteness of dentures, but he had a habit of pulling his upper lip over them when he wasn't speaking, as though they didn't fit too well. His eyes, deep set in his head, were a dull brown, while his face and hands had a pallor that seemed to sit well with his profession. Beside him, Larry looked like a rock star.

'We want to say that it's shocked us as much as anyone,' Greenwood went on, 'and that we will do whatever we can to help the police investigation.'

'Good of you,' Tom said, as I poured tea into three cups.

'We've been serving this town for nearly twenty years,' Greenwood said, 'and we are disquieted that our respectable establishment should have become embroiled in so heinous a crime.'

I didn't think I'd ever heard the word 'heinous' used in real life before.

'Anything you want to add, Mr Glassbrook?' Tom asked Larry.

Larry shook his head. 'Roy does the talking for both of us.' He waggled his fingers. 'I talk with my hands.'

'Who has keys to the funeral parlour?' Tom asked, once I'd added milk and offered both visitors sugar.

'The two of us,' Greenwood replied.

'And Sally,' Larry added.

Greenwood's head turned sideways. 'Sally has keys? To the parlour?'

Larry shrugged. 'In case I lose mine.'

Greenwood's nostrils twitched.

'I'll make a note to check that Mrs Glassbrook hasn't mislaid her keys.' I took a seat at the far end of the table. 'Would either of you like a biscuit?'

'I think you said yesterday that the parlour was locked once you left for the evening on Sunday?' Tom said.

'I locked it myself,' Greenwood said. 'There are human remains in our parlour. We cannot allow them to be interfered with.' He smiled at Tom, a smile so wide and uncalled for I had to suppress a shudder.

If Tom was rattled, he didn't show it. 'Could anyone access the yard at the back?'

'They would have to scale the wall and unfasten the gate from the inside,' said Greenwood. 'They still couldn't get through the back door, though. It's deadlocked, like the front.'

'Sir,' I said, and it took Tom a second to realise I meant him. 'You told me to remind you to ask about the dimensions of the casket.' I glanced at Larry. 'The casket we exhumed early this morning, the polished cedar one with the silver trim – beautiful piece, by the way – looked jolly big to me.'

Larry's eyes narrowed as he looked at me. 'Caskets are deliberately made substantial,' he said. 'They're the choice of prestige.'

'So plenty of room for a friend,' said Tom.

Greenwood sucked in his cheeks so hard I saw the outline of his jaw.

'We have put more than one body in a casket,' Larry said. 'Although it's not usual. Husband and wife die together. Mother dies in childbirth and the baby's stillborn. It happens.'

'Very unusual,' Greenwood added.

'But I remember you telling me, Mr Glassbrook, when you showed me how caskets are made,' I said, 'that there's a sort of lift inside, to raise the dead person up.'

'A simple, hand-operated mechanism,' Larry agreed. 'Depending on how large a person he or she is, we can adjust the height.'

'So someone could have lowered the body to the base of the casket, leaving room on top,' I said. 'Patsy could have been laid on top of the deceased but beneath the satin covering.' I glanced at Tom. 'Sorry, sir, I didn't mean to interrupt. I got a bit carried away.'

'No problem, love,' he told me. 'All contributions accepted. Any more tea in that pot?'

'Well, it's possible in theory,' Larry began, 'but—'

'It's absurd,' Greenwood repeated. 'No one interferes with our caskets. And besides, the extra weight would be apparent when the pall bearers begin their procession.'

I topped up their cups, forgetting to use the strainer when I poured Tom's.

'One of my colleagues would like to come and see you later today,' Tom said, lifting his cup. 'He needs details of other burials you've carried out this year.'

'Those details are confidential,' Greenwood protested, as Tom pulled a face and looked suspiciously down into his cup.

'No, they're not,' I said. 'Death is a matter of public record.'

Both men looked surprised at my dropping the 'dumb secretary' routine. I lowered my eyes and bit my tongue.

Tom cleared his throat. 'Before we wrap up, can I ask you to confirm that neither of you opened the coffin anytime on Monday morning?' he said.

'Casket,' Larry corrected him.

Tom waited.

'Neither of us did,' Greenwood said. 'I opened up the parlour that morning, and I didn't leave it until the casket was transferred to the hearse. I promise you she was not in it then.'

26

A plate crashed to the floor as I entered the dining room of Sabden Secondary Modern and the children roared applause. A male teacher yelled that they should 'Shut it!' and the clumsy child was sent running for a broom and mop. A calm-faced woman in blue overalls – of West Indian origin, I thought – pushed a trolley towards the mess. She seemed separate, somehow, from her surroundings and no one seemed to notice her.

They noticed me, though.

Silence fell. All heads turned. The children stared; the adults frowned and whispered to each other. At the staff table, a tall, thin man with long hair and a straggly beard got to his feet. 'You're early,' he said. I wasn't, but I said nothing.

He didn't offer to shake hands. 'I'm on yard duty,' he said. 'We can talk outside.'

'Rozzers,' a child hissed, and a giggle raced round the room like a wild creature that had been set free.

As I followed him out, I saw the dinner lady move gracefully to the staff table and clear his place. The dropped plate and its detritus had already vanished. The black woman had a gentle smile on her face, and two things struck me. The first that it was her habitual expression, and the second that it probably didn't reflect her thoughts.

I followed Mr Milner, geography and woodwork teacher, and head of the fourth form, out into the yard behind the school building. It was irregularly shaped, Tarmacked and surrounded by high walls, more like a prison exercise yard than the vast playing fields, lined with swaying lime trees, that I remembered from my own school. A football game was taking place, with satchels serving as goalposts. The girls hung around the edges, wary of being kicked by a misjudged ball.

'Shoot,' said Milner.

At the far side of the yard, I saw John Donnelly in the midst of a group of boys. He was easy to spot because he towered above the others.

'Can I confirm that you're the form head for Patsy Wood, Stephen Shorrock and Susan Duxbury?'

Donnelly had spotted me too.

'Guilty.' Milner gave me a sideways glance. 'They're saying she was buried alive. Care to comment?'

How did he know that? I sensed kids drawing closer, trying to eavesdrop, and wondered if I could insist we go indoors and talk privately.

'I haven't been given any details, I'm afraid,' I said. 'Would you say the three children knew each other quite well?'

The group surrounding Donnelly broke up. He ran forward and joined the game of football. He seemed to be going through the motions, though – looking round every few seconds, staying on the outskirts.

Milner took a deep breath. 'Smith! Put him down – you don't know where he's been. Now, Smith, or I'll have you in detention.'

'Sir, were the three children friends?'

Donnelly left the game and wandered over to a group of girls, in the midst of which I spotted Luna's bright red hair. His head bent down towards hers, and although neither looked round, I knew they were talking about me.

Milner sighed. 'Listen, love.' His eyes washed over me again.

'What did you say your name was?'

'WPC Lovelady, sir. Were they in the same class?'

'If you'll give me chance to open my mouth, constable, you might find listening skills are as valuable as asking questions. They were in the same year, but so are over a hundred other kids. They're grouped into four forms, roughly twenty-five in each. Patsy was in 4C, Stephen in 4M, and Susan . . . I think Susan was in 4M too.'

'Were they in any of the same clubs that you know of?'

'What do you mean? Youth club? Girl Guides? I really wouldn't know.'

'Is there any member of staff here who would know the three children better than you do? School nurse, maybe? School counsellor?'

'They only go to the nurse when they're ill. And a school what?' He strode away from me suddenly, producing a whistle from his pocket and letting out a loud screeching sound. When I caught up with him again, he was halfway across the yard and we were in imminent danger of being struck by a fast-moving football.

I sighed. 'Sir, can you please find someone else to take over your yard duty? You and I need to sit down while I ask you questions about the three children.'

He opened his mouth to object.

'I want to know which subjects they studied, who they sat next to in each class, what sports they played, who they were friends with, which teachers they got on with and which found them difficult, who they walked home with and who they'd fallen out with in the last few months. And then I want to talk about their home lives. How supportive their parents were, whether any of them had part-time jobs, whether any of them was particularly unhappy at home.'

He looked at his watch. 'I haven't got time. Lunch finishes in fifteen minutes.'

'Sir, this is a murder enquiry.'

He took a step away. 'Talk to the headmaster's secretary. She puts plasters on the kids' scrapes when they fall over. She knows them as well as anyone.'

27

The headmaster's secretary wasn't any friendlier than Milner, but I got what I came for: a lot of information on fourth-form dynamics and the lives of the three who'd gone missing. One thing that interested me was that two of the missing children had fathers who were active in the local trade-union movement. Jim Shorrock, Stephen's father, was shop steward of Pilkinton's Mill in the town centre, while Stan Wood was the secretary of the local branch of the TUC.

'Is there much union activity in town?' I asked her.

'Not so much this year. Last year it was quite bad. A few strikes; some went on for a while. Kids were coming to school hungry.'

'What about Susan's father?'

She pulled a face. 'That waste of space? Not out of prison long enough. And no one will employ him any more. Been caught thieving from work more times than I've had perms.' She smiled a little at her own wit.

I'd also got a piece of information that had made the hot day feel a whole lot cooler. The secretary confirmed that children needed permission to leave school for medical appointments and that Patsy's last visit to the dentist had been two months earlier. The extraction the pathologist had spotted was more recent than that.

I was heading for the main door when I had to step to one side to let a group of chattering youngsters rush past.

The children were carrying greenery – twigs, leaves, grasses – and were being followed by the same quiet woman I'd seen in the dining hall. She'd changed her blue overalls for a plastic apron that was stained brown. Most of the children were wearing similar aprons. Potter's aprons.

Acting on instinct, I followed them along the corridor, keeping my distance. At the end, they began climbing stairs, the woman in the apron bringing up the rear. At the first floor, they continued climbing. The woman didn't look back, but I had a feeling she was aware of my coming up steadily behind. She was on the slim side. Her hair was a mass of black corkscrew curls, but she'd swept them up away from her face and allowed them to spread out around the back of her head like a halo. She was maybe thirty, possibly a little older. As we climbed higher, I saw that she had long, thick fingernails painted scarlet red.

We carried on up to the second floor and then up again. As the children poured into a circular, glass-walled room on the third floor, the woman paused at the door, letting me go in first. As she did so, I caught sight of a name badge she wore: Mrs Labaddee.

Through the huge windows that formed an almost complete circle, I could see the moors, the nearby villages, the trees of the municipal park, the numerous factory chimneys. Light came flooding in, and so did the heat. Most of the windows were open to let in the breeze, but the room felt almost unbearably hot to me in my woollen uniform. It was the art room. A worktop ran round its perimeter, cluttered with paint, brushes, pencils and two potter's wheels.

The teacher was a young woman with spectacles and light brown hair. Her apron was canvas, even more stained than those of the children. Her hands were stained brown too.

'Come on, get on with it,' she told the class, once I'd explained who I was and begged a moment of her time. 'I want all your plates finished this period. Marlene, I think Shelley needs some help with her acorns.'

As the black woman – Marlene Labaddee – moved to one of the girls, the art teacher and I stepped towards the door.

'This might seem a bit odd, but I want to ask you about potter's clay,' I said. 'What do you use, and where do you get it from?'

'We mainly use a brown stoneware clay from a school supplier's in Bury,' she told me.

The children were spread around the room now, using the foliage they'd collected to make patterns in the wet clay plates on the worktop.

'What colour is that clay when it's dried?' I asked.

The teacher pointed to a shelf that held several fired but unpainted shapes. All were a dark brownish grey.

'I've recently come across a figure that was much redder in colour,' I said. 'Are there different sorts of clay that you can buy?'

'Loads,' the teacher said. 'Although, the school supplier is quite limited. We have some basic earthenware for when the children are learning. And some white stoneware for the more advanced students. There are lots of sub-categories, though. Depends what you want to achieve.'

We watched Marlene glide over and take a plate from one of the boys who'd been struggling. She pressed it into a ball and began to reshape it, pouring water from a jug until it glistened in her hands. Her fingernails darted in and out of the muddy substance like dancing bugs.

'There's clay available locally,' the teacher said. 'The town museum has quite a lot of pieces. I wouldn't recommend working with it now, though. It takes for ever to set, and it's full of impurities.'

'You sound as though you know what you're talking about.'

'I've never worked with it, but Mr Milner, the geography teacher, wanted to know about local clay for one of his classes,' she said. 'He was teaching local geology, I think. I gave him a brief lesson in how to use it. I'm not sure how much success he had.'

'No, you cannot mix Japanese maple and blackthorn.' The West Indian woman spoke for the first time in my hearing. Her voice was pitched low, both warm and rich. 'One is an imported specimen tree, the other a native English. The two leaves will fight with each other and will look wrong.'

'Mrs Labaddee seems competent,' I said. 'Did I see her in the dining hall a few minutes ago, or does she have a twin?'

'No, only one, more's the pity,' said the art teacher. 'We sometimes wonder what we'd do without Marlene. She's a florist too. The Flower Pot on the main road is her shop.'

'I know it,' I said, thinking of a small, green-fronted shop. 'Busy lady.'

'Was there anything else?' the art teacher asked me. 'Because I really have to get this class wound up before the bell goes.'

Sharples was waiting for me when I got back to CID. 'Lovelady, have you been wandering around the school without permission, going uninvited into classrooms?'

Everyone looked up. Conversations ceased. A woman from the canteen who'd been collecting cups stopped what she was doing.

At his desk in the centre of the room, Tom picked up the phone. 'Afternoon Brenda.' His voice was loud, even by Tom's standards. 'I'm struggling to get a number in Manchester. Can you have a go? Thanks, love, appreciate it.' He reeled off the number.

'Just one classroom, sir,' I told Sharples. 'A pottery class. It seemed too good an opportunity to miss. The school already knew I was on the premises. I'd made an appointment, and I checked in with the office when I arrived.'

'Yeah, well, now we've had a complaint that we're upsetting the kids,' Sharples said.

'Hang on, Doreen – I hadn't finished that.' Tom got to his feet, leaving his phone dangling and knocking over his chair. He strode across the room and looked at the top shelf of the trolley. 'Oh, my mistake, I had. Let me get the door for you, love. ''Scuse me, Florence.'

Tom stepped round me, opened the door and beckoned to the canteen lady. Scowling, she rattled the trolley towards him.

'The kids should be upset,' I said to Sharples. 'Three of their number have gone missing, and one of them died a horrible death.' I moved out of the doorway. I wasn't entirely sure what Tom and the canteen lady were doing, but it sounded like they were fighting for control of the trolley.

'Owt nice for tea later?' I heard him say.

'Tom, fucking shut it!' Sharples snapped. 'Lovelady, I don't care if the boss has taken a shine to you – if you step out of line one more time, I will have you on report.'

I think, behind me, I heard Tom start to say my name.

'With the greatest of respect, sir, we should be warning these children. I'm fed up of hearing Stephen and Susan might have run away from home. We should be telling them not to go out alone, to let their parents know where they are, to be home well before dark. Patsy wasn't the first child to come to harm, and she won't be the last unless we start facing facts.'

As Sharples stepped towards me, the door to Rushton's office opened.

'Flossie, have a run up to St Wilfred's, will you?' he said. 'I've had Father Edward giving me earache, wanting to know what's going on. Soothe his ruffled feathers, will you, lass? You don't need Flossie for anything, do you, Jack?'

Sharples didn't take his eyes off me. 'Nothing at all, boss,' he said.

28

The nave of St Wilfred's was wonderfully cool after my cycle ride up to the north side of town. It was coming up for two o'clock by this time and the day was showing no sign of cooling down.

I found the priest in the vestry. Father Edward was small and plump, with a shock of thick white hair. He'd make an excellent Father Christmas, if it wouldn't be beneath his dignity.

'You?' He didn't get up. 'I was expecting Superintendent Rushton.'

I opened my mouth to remind him that we were dealing with a murder inquiry and that my colleagues at the station were a little busy when the strangest thing happened. It was as though I saw Tom, in his shirt-sleeves, leaning against the window ledge, his eyebrows as high as they would go. And I remembered that Father Edward had been roused from his bed in the early hours to be informed about an unofficial exhumation at his church. And that he was actually quite an elderly man.

'Mr Rushton asked me to thank you,' I said. 'For your discretion and your patience. We appreciate this is a terrible time for St Wilfred's.'

Father Edward puffed air out through his nose with a sound akin to a bike tyre being let down and indicated a chair. Over at the window, phantom Tom inclined his head in approval. I positioned the chair so I couldn't see him.

'I've been with the family most of the morning.' Father Edward raised his hands in a surprisingly feminine gesture. 'What do you say? They don't want to hear that their child's in a better place. Who would?'

'They're fortunate to have you to console them, Father,' I said. 'I've been asked to tell you that we can't release the body until after the inquest, and that could be a couple of weeks away. We'll be informing the family, of course, but the superintendent wanted you to know first.'

He waved a hand towards the window. 'What about all the goings-on outside? The disturbed grave? I have another bereaved family to deal with out there. Not to mention the rest of the parishioners.'

'As soon as I get back, I'll get an estimate of how much longer we'll be.'

I smiled at the old priest. I'd done what I'd been sent to do. Another couple of minutes of polite conversation and I could go.

Or I could do my job.

'Father, I'm afraid I need to ask you something,' I said. 'I'm sorry to cause you more distress, but . . .'

He sighed. 'Whatever you need, my dear. I suppose you're looking for those other two children in . . . similar places?'

'We have to be open to all possibilities,' I said. 'So I need to ask if you've noticed any disturbance in the churchyard in recent months.'

Father Edward looked at me for several long seconds and then got up. He walked to the window, forcing me to turn my chair round.

Phantom Tom had obviously decided I could take it from here. He'd gone.

A whole minute must have passed before the priest spoke.

'Twenty years ago, I was here late one night,' he said. 'I'd been with a parishioner, administering last rites. He was a young man, married with children, and it was very distressing. On my way home, there was something – I can't remember what – that I needed from the church. I didn't put the lights on: I knew if I did, someone in the streets nearby would notice and come to find out what was going on. Some of the dear ladies of the parish, well, they mean for the best. I didn't want to talk to anyone that night.'

He glanced round at me. 'While I was inside, the rain became very heavy and I thought I'd give it time to ease off,' he said. 'I was standing here, at this window, looking at the porch and re-membering that old legend about All Souls' Day. Did I mention it was All Souls' Day?'

'I don't think so.' I sneaked a glance at my watch.

'Well, the story goes that if you sit in the church porch on the night before All Souls' Day, you'll see the ghosts of everyone doomed to die in the coming year pass into the churchyard. I was wondering if I'd ever have the nerve to do it, and why anyone would want to, and remembering the old story about the priest who did and who saw his own ghost, and then I saw movement in the grounds. Come and stand beside me – I'll point out the place.'

I joined him at the window and tried not to start when he put an arm around my waist. With his other hand, he pointed to a place near the corner.

'I saw movement there,' he said. 'What looked like two people, dressed in dark clothes. It was hard to tell, though, because they seemed to be kneeling down.'

'Kneeling at a grave?'

'That's what it looked like. But they weren't still. They weren't praying. They were doing something. And this was three o'clock in the morning.'

'What did you do?'

'I stayed here. Actually, I think I turned round and made sure the vestry door was locked. I don't mind telling you there was something quite chilling about it.'

'You didn't telephone for help?'

He gave a soft laugh. 'It was 1947, dear. There were barely any telephones in town, let alone in the church. The thing to do would have been to rouse the sexton, Dwane's father, as it happens, but I didn't have the courage to go out into the night. I've never been a brave man.' He turned back to the room. 'So I sat down in that chair, that very same chair, and waited for dawn.'

I moved away, ostensibly to look at the shabby armchair by his desk, but really to be out of reach of his arm.

'And what did you find, at dawn?' I asked.

'The grave had been interfered with, no question about it,' he said.

'What happened?'

'Nothing. I reported it to the police, but they concluded it had been the work of foxes.'

'But you'd seen people.'

He walked back to his armchair. 'I saw something, but it was dark. I was tired. And upset. I knew there was nothing to be gained from pushing the point.'

The old priest dropped his head, so that his temples came to rest against his fingertips. 'There are people in this town, important people, who don't take kindly to anyone rocking the boat.' He was talking to the flagged floor now. 'It was about that time that I started having difficulties with the bishop. Groundless accusations, but mud sticks.' His eyes closed.

'Father, that sounds as though someone tried to shut you up.'

He shivered, looked up and gave me a weak smile. 'Nonsense, my dear. People, understandably, get very upset at the thought of graves being desecrated. What you did last night – oh, I know you had your reasons – will not be well received by the parish.'

The parish could take a running jump. I opened my mouth and, I kid you not, there was Tom again, right next to the old priest.

'Has it happened since?' I asked.

His eyes left mine and drifted away somewhere over my left shoulder. 'Let's just say being so close to the Hill means we have a problem with wildlife.'

'So it has? Did you see it happen? Did you see people again?'

'I think that was the last time I was ever in this church at night.' He looked at his watch. 'You'll excuse me now, dear. I have a parishioner waiting and I need to leave myself.'

I stood at the bottom of three steep stone steps, wondering if this would count as stepping out of line. Probably, in DI Sharples's eyes. All the same, a report of grave-robbing, even twenty years ago, that was something worth following up, wasn't it? Especially if, as Father Edward believed, pressure had been brought to bear to prevent it being properly investigated.

The steps had not been cleaned or scoured, and the front door ahead of me hadn't been painted in years. The wood was rotting in the corners, and the hinges were covered in rust. Several of the nails were missing.

'Oh, hello,' I said, as the door opened.

The middle-aged woman with the greying hair and the lined face was one I knew. 'You work at the station, don't you?' I went on. 'In the canteen?'

She didn't reply, and after several awkward seconds, my smile faded. 'Can I speak to Mr Dwane Ogilvy, please?' I held up my ID.

'What about?' she asked, although she managed to do it without using the letter 'T'.

I had a feeling that if I looked back, I'd see Tom at the bottom of the path. So I didn't. 'An ongoing enquiry of a serious nature,' I replied. 'Is he here?'

'Through t'back,' she told me, turning on her heel.

I followed her down a dark hallway so narrow that were I to stretch out my elbows, they would have brushed the walls and into the room that served as kitchen, dining and living room for the family.

A couple of children, tiny and disproportionately formed, too old for the nappies they were wearing, sat on a rug in front of the hearth and squabbled over some coloured bobbins. Another child, normal-sized but with a vacant air, stared at a blank television screen.

There was a mangle on the draining board with the grey sleeve of a work shirt hanging from between the rollers. Mrs Ogilvy went back to it and nodded towards the rear door. 'Out back,' she said.

I pushed the door open and stepped into the Ogilvys' backyard. A washing line, suspended from both boundary walls, zigzagged across the space in between and held up sheets, shirts, pillowcases, dresses and nightwear. The starch in the air burned my nostrils as I ducked behind the first line and found myself trapped in laundry.

'Dwane?' I tried.

No answer, but I heard a regular, rhythmic scraping, like wood being sawn. The garden was narrow and long, and I ducked under line after line of washing, making for the scratching sound.

I'd pushed aside five lines of it before I found Dwane. He was sitting on a long, narrow upturned box, filing down a piece of wood. Behind him was a large wooden shed with a central door and glass windows either side.

Dwane looked up and his eyes, beneath his prominent brow, opened very wide.

'I'm WPC Lovelady,' I told him. 'I met you yesterday, at the church. Do you remember?'

'You dug her up.'

I neither agreed nor corrected him.

'Made a right bloody mess of it. I suppose you've come to ask me to fill it in again.' He stood up. He had a metal file in one hand, a substantial piece of wood in the other. He was a good foot smaller than I but, I admit, I took a step back. He nodded at the box he'd vacated.

'You can sit thee sen down,' he told me.

Sitting down while he stood over me with a file was the last thing I wanted to do, but I had a sense he was acting out of courtesy, so I perched on the edge of the box.

'You should have used one of them,' he said, indicating the box I was sitting on. 'You put it next to the grave and the earth goes in the box. Then when you're ready to backfill, it's all there, not spread all over t'shop.'

'I want to ask you how sure you are that the grave hadn't been interfered with,' I said. 'One of the theories we're working on is that the young girl's body was put in the casket after the funeral.'

'No one touched that grave,' Dwane said. 'Were you not listening? You think anyone can dig a grave?'

He turned and strode towards the far wall. He had a peculiar, swinging way of walking, swaying a little from side to side with each step, as though his legs had to work extra hard to carry his oversized body around.

Heavy tools were lined up against the wall. I saw a small-bladed, sturdy spade, a much bigger shovel, a pick, a fork. And a large wooden outline of a rectangle, which I realised immediately was a template for a grave.

'First you have to move the turf,' he said, picking up the smaller spade. 'You cut it neat, and you keep each piece in its right place so you can put it back.' He pointed to the opposite wall. I turned and saw a sheet of plywood. 'That's my turf sheet. Then you break up the ground.' He pointed to the pick and the fork. 'It can take hours if you don't know what you're doing,' he went on. 'I can dig a grave in virgin ground in three hours. How long did it take you?'

Pretty much three hours, but I wasn't going to tell him that. Besides, I'd been working with soft ground.

'Suppose someone watched you work,' I said. 'Suppose they knew about storing the turf and putting the earth in a box. Those tools of yours can be found in any hardware store. Isn't it at least possible that someone could have learned from you? They weren't working with fresh earth, remember? You'd made the job easy for them.'

He thought about this for a second, and his thick, wet lips spread apart. He shook his head. 'No one touched it. Want to know how I know?'

'Yes, please.'

'I shape it.' He started weaving the spade around, as though moulding earth with it. 'Special to me. I make a shape that only I know how to do. I can show you, if you like.'

'So when we were at the grave yesterday afternoon, was it shaped the way you say?'

He nodded slowly, his lips pressed together. If he was telling the truth, if he had some particular way of finishing off a grave, like a cake-icer's signature flourish, then Patsy must have been in the casket when it was interred. Which meant someone had accessed the funeral parlour.

'Mr Ogilvy, I need to ask you where you were on Sunday evening between nine o'clock and eleven o'clock.'

It was the time period when Patsy had gone missing. If he realised the significance of the question, he didn't let it show. 'Here,' he told me. 'Watching telly.'

'How about Wednesday, 16 April, a little earlier?'

'Here, watching telly.'

'Are you sure? You can check a diary if you want. A calendar, maybe?'

He stared at me.

'What about Monday, 17 March?' I asked him. 'Early evening?'

'Black Dog,' he said.

'Excuse me?'

'Black Dog,' he repeated. 'Pub on Riley Street.'

'You seem very certain,' I said. 'It was three months ago.'

'Friday night and Saturday night I goes to t'pub. Seven o'clock till eleven o'clock. Sundays Mam won't let us go. Mondays I go, and Tuesdays. Wednesday and Thursday I'm usually skint. I get paid Friday.'

'I see. So the landlord will vouch for you?'

'Landlord's three sheets t'wind by half nine.'

'Do you mean drunk?'

He nodded. 'Ted Donnelly's always been a big drinker. His missus too. Mind you, it doesn't stop her—' He stopped, looking troubled. 'I have my own stool,' he finished.

'I was speaking to Father Edward before I came here,' I said. 'He told me the churchyard gets disturbed from time to time.'

Dwane's eyes fell to the ground. 'Churchyards get bothered. It happens.'

'He implied it was animals – foxes, maybe badgers, possibly even dogs – that were responsible.'

'I like the way you talk,' Dwane said.

'Thank you. So what do you think? Do you think it's a wildlife problem?'

He shrugged, but still didn't look at me. 'What else? Do you like small things?'

'Excuse me?'

'Small things, do you like them?'

Did he mean himself? 'I suppose,' I said, a little nervously. 'What sort of small things?'

He gestured that I should get up and follow him to the shed. It was only three paces for him, one for me. He pulled open the door and indicated that I should go in first.

The table in the centre of the shed was an old snooker table. I recognised the thick, carved legs and saw a sliver of green felt beneath the plywood sheet covering it.

On the plywood surface sat a miniature town. A model of Sabden. I couldn't count the different streets, but I recognised the town centre, the war memorial, the park and the bandstand. Every shop along the main road had been reproduced perfectly. I saw Glassbrook & Greenwood, Kenyon's Bakery, the record shop, Sherwin's butcher's, the Flower Pot. I saw the covered market and the town hall, the large, open area where the buses and trams stopped. I found the Black Dog with its pub sign swinging outside, and the great cellar doors open to the street. Beer barrels were being unloaded from a Thwaites brewery wagon.

The long rows of terraced houses fanning out onto the moors on the edges of town had been painted dark grey to resemble soot-blackened stone. The roads weren't smooth. I put a finger down, hesitantly, but Dwane didn't stop me, so I touched the surface of a cobbled street and felt the bumps. They were actual stone. He'd made the streets from tiny chips of pebbles.

It must have taken him years. There was washing strung across the ginnels, tiny squares of white fabric hanging from cotton thread. There were fences made out of matchsticks and tiny tin cars.

Getting my bearings, I followed the route I'd taken up from the station – the station was there, with a tiny helmeted constable on the steps – towards the church. St Wilfred's was perfect. The wall round it, the trees, the headstones were all there.

It was an exact reproduction of the town. I walked round the table, following the outer boundary as it rose up the Hill, to the Glassbrook house.

'That's my bedroom window,' I said. 'But the curtains aren't right. My curtains are blue; these are lilac.'

I stopped, worried I'd said the wrong thing, but he didn't seem upset. He was watching me the way cats watch birds.

'It's exquisite,' I said quickly. 'I've never seen anything like it. You're quite the craftsman.' I'd been about to say that he was wasted digging graves, but something in his face had changed. No one could describe Dwane as a handsome man, but at that moment there was something decidedly unpleasant in his expression. The set of his eyes seemed to deepen; his brows contracted until they became one thick line across his protruding forehead. His mouth had fallen open, and his lips gleamed red and wet.

'Why would you say that?'

He'd actually taken a step away from me. He was looking at me in a way that was making me feel distinctly uncomfortable and yet he almost seemed to be the one afraid of me.

'I have to get back to the station now,' I said. 'Thank you very much for your time.'

He backed out, not taking his eyes off me. I walked ahead of him, through the house, pausing briefly to thank Mrs Ogilvy and step over a sprawled child. I was down the steps and walking towards my bike when Dwane called.

'You should have come for me,' he said. 'I'd have dug her up for you.'

29

'"I'd have dug her up for you"? I've got to hand it to you, Flossie, as chat-up lines go . . .' Detective Sergeant Green put down the glass paperweight he'd been admiring, a gift from my grandparents in the shape of a police box.

'Sarge, what do you make of this business of graves being disturbed? I'm sure Father Edward and Dwane knew more than they were letting on.'

'You aware of any reports of grave-robbing, Tom?' Green called over the top of the filing cabinets.

Green, Tom and I were the only people in the room. Rushton, Sharples and a couple of the constables were out at the town meeting, due back anytime. The rest of the division were on the streets, in the pubs and factories, continuing enquiries. CID, I was learning, worked until the job was done.

Tom's head appeared over the top of the cabinets. 'Can't say as I have, Sarge,' he said.

'Any road, where's the connection?' Green said. 'Whoever put Patsy in that casket was donating to a grave, if you get my drift, not robbing it.'

'Father Edward also talked about important people in town who didn't take kindly to anyone rocking the boat. Those were his exact words. I think he was hushed up.'

The two men did that annoying silent exchange, the one I was starting to think of as 'What's she on about now?' I think Tom was about to speak when we heard footsteps, the door burst open, and DS Brown came in.

'Fifty burials in Sabden this year,' he announced. 'A few more in the villages.'

Tom was still a disembodied head floating above the filing cabinets. 'That's a lot of graves to dig up,' he said.

'Hope you're feeling fit, Flossie,' Green said.

Brown swung round to face me. 'How's that press statement coming on?'

Tom beat me to it. 'Drafted up and approved by the super, but I'll have Elaine type it up in the morning. There's some sort of special style that would take too long to explain to Florence.'

I'd spent over an hour battling with an old typewriter before Tom rescued me. I gave him a grateful smile.

Brown said, 'That meeting finished yet?'

As if on cue, the door opened and Sharples came in.

'How'd it go?' Green asked the DI.

'Usual bollocks.' Sharples sniffed. 'Everyone wanting answers. Earnshaw shooting his mouth off. Boss took a bit of a pasting. Luckily no mention of Patsy being . . . you know.'

'Buried alive?' Tom said, unnecessarily.

Sharples glared at him. 'How'd you get on at the infirmary?'

Tom's head vanished. He appeared round our side of the cabinets a couple of seconds later. 'I spoke to one of the head anaesthetists, asked if it was possible to keep a kid that size unconscious and subdued for up to ten hours.'

'And?'

'Possible but tricky, he said, especially if you want her to wake up at the end of it.' Tom was flicking through his notebook. 'He thought the best way to do it would be with a benzodiazepine, such as diazepam, possibly combined with alcohol, maybe morphine.'

Sharples pulled his thinking face, a sort of contraction of the muscles around his eyes.

'It would be risky, though.' Tom leaned back against the cabinets and something fell down on the other side. 'He said that several times. Unless someone really knew what he was doing, he'd be more likely to kill her.'

'Maybe that was the plan,' I said. 'Maybe she was never expected to wake up.'

'Seems a lot of trouble when you could put a pillow over her face,' said Sharples. 'And where would your average bloke get hold of . . . What was it again?'

'Benzodiazepine,' I said, when Tom struggled to find the place in his book. 'It's a common sedative. Sir, if you've got a minute, I made this.'

I pulled a rolled-up sheet of light card out of my desk drawer. 'Sorry, it's still very rough, but it's a chart of the three children.'

The others gathered round, Sharples a split second behind the rest.

'I've put their names along the top,' I said, as I tried to get the thing to lie flat. 'And then down the vertical axis, I've listed subjects they studied, their friends, their enemies, the clubs they belonged to, outside interests. I need a lot more information, but—'

'What's the point?' asked Green, as it sprang back into a roll.

'It'll show us what they had in common.' Tom helped me straighten it. 'And that will point us towards who took them.'

'There is one thing that's come up already,' I said. 'Stephen Shorrock and Patsy Wood are both children of prominent trade-union officials. Susan Duxbury's father is a known thief.'

I waited. No one spoke.

'They're all children of trouble-making parents,' I said.

'Three different mills, though,' said Tom.

The door opened again and the station officer leaned in. He

was out of breath. 'Trouble at Perseverance Mill,' he said. 'We might have a man down. I can't get anyone out there in less than fifteen.'

All four men strode back to their desks and grabbed car keys, wallets, warrant cards.

I said, 'Do you want me to come?'

Sharples frowned. 'I don't think so.'

Tom stopped in the doorway. 'Boss, the Shorrock family live by that mill. And Linda Shorrock has been a butty short of a picnic since Stephen went. If they're involved, we might need someone to talk her down, make her a brew.'

Sharples gave a brief, curt nod. I grabbed my hat and jacket, and ran out after them.

'I've been waiting for this,' Green said, as Tom sped out of the car park. Sharples was in the passenger seat. I was squeezed in the back between the two sergeants.

'Torch and pitchforks,' muttered Brown.

'Do we know who's injured?' I asked.

No one answered. Sharples was talking directly to Control on the radio. 'How many cars can you get out there? . . . Well, find some more. And let the boss know. He said he was heading home.'

We saw the start of the trouble while we were still a hundred yards away. People were in the middle of the main road, on the corner with Jubilee Street, looking towards the mill building. Some of them scarpered when they saw us, but most ran towards the mill, not away from it.

'That's Randy,' said Tom.

The uniformed constable leaning against the corner wall was missing his helmet, his hand pressed to his temple. Tom pulled up and the men piled out.

'Flossie, I think you should stay where you are,' Green called back. Ignoring him, I ran to Randy as the others walked towards the corner. Randy had blood running down from his temple and looked ghastly pale in the lamplight.

'Come and sit down.' Sliding my arm under his shoulders, I tried to steer him towards the car. 'What happened?'

He resisted. 'Some bastard threw a brick at me. I'm fine, though.'

Randy and I walked to the corner and joined the others. Jubilee Street was not much more than a hundred yards long, culminating in the mill.

'Terry Parker's in the mill, sir,' Randy said. 'Doors are locked. That lot can't get in for the moment, but there's plenty of them trying.'

There were no streetlights on the street and none around the mill. What little light that was left in the sky wasn't reaching this neglected corner of town. Even so, I could see around fifty people at the mill gates. Mainly men. The women and children were still in their houses. I could see them too, anxious faces lining every window, some of the bolder ones on doorsteps.

'Terry Parker's had a couple of cautions for hanging around kids' playgrounds,' Randy said, to no one in particular. 'Years ago, but folk have long memories.'

We'd been spotted. I could see people nudging each other, looking our way. A kid set off running towards the mill.

'Doing your job for you!' someone yelled at us from a doorway.

'Bloody perverts, should be strung up!' shouted another.

'Why now?' Sharples said to Randy. 'Why's it kicking off now?'

'The bin men found Stephen's shoe in Terry's backyard,' Randy replied. 'One of them took it to the pub to find Jim Shorrock half cut and surrounded by his mates. They all charged over to Terry's house, but he slipped out the back and into the mill. He's locked himself in, but it's only a matter of time before this lot break down the door.'

'He used to be the caretaker, didn't he?' Brown said. 'Must have hung on to some keys.'

At that moment, there came a loud crash as the padlock broke and the mill gates were flung open. The crowd pressed forward.

Sharples said, 'Randy, get back to the car and get on to Control. We need back-up now, and we need the fire brigade and a couple of ambulances. Lovelady, go with him.'

'Sir, I could go round the back—'

He didn't give me a chance. 'I'm not having a woman injured on my watch. Get back in the car.'

'With respect, sir, I know this mill and—'

He darted close. 'Enough!' Tiny drops of spit hit my face. 'This will be dangerous enough without a jumped-up swanker of a schoolgirl hanging on to our coat-tails. Now move. Randy, make sure she stays with you. You three, let's go.'

Tom gave me his keys and then the four men ran forward, shouting, 'Police! Everyone stay where you are!' Randy dragged me back towards the car. I glanced over my shoulder to see my four colleagues trying to push and shove their way through the crowd. They were surrounded in seconds.

'Urgent assistance required. Repeat, urgent assistance. Four officers in jeopardy.' Randy looked on the verge of fainting, but he relayed the message as required. I thought for a moment, then reached beneath the driver's seat and pulled it forward.

'What are you doing?' said Randy, as I turned on the ignition.

'He told us to stay in the car. He didn't tell us to stay in a parked car.'

The street ahead was empty. Most of the crowd had gone into the mill yard, and those who'd hung back stayed on their doorsteps as we drove past, lights on full beam. At the bottom of the street, we passed an old warehouse that had been converted to a church, but the doors were closed and the building was in darkness. I drove in through the mill gates and to the edge of the crowd. Some moved out of our way. Not all. When I couldn't go any further, I pulled on the handbrake and the people closed in.

'Please tell me what this achieved,' said Randy, as we sat, engine running, surrounded by drunk, angry men. A stone landed on the roof and I flinched for Tom's paintwork.

Jumped-up swanker of a schoolgirl. Was that really what they all thought of me?

A few yards ahead of us, Sharples and the others were standing in front of the mill doors, facing the crowd. Tom's headlights were powerful, lighting up much of the dim yard, and I took a quick glance around. A high stone wall, a few outbuildings. From this angle, we couldn't see the rear gates I'd climbed over that morning.

The four detectives looked uninjured but not unscathed. The lapel of Tom's jacket had been torn. Gusty looked like he'd run into a hurricane.

'They can see what they're doing now,' I said.

'Yeah, all targets have become a lot easier to hit,' Randy said.

Not waiting to consider whether he might be right, I got out of the car. As I made my way towards the mill, the men circling the car let me through, but grudgingly.

'Go home, lass – there's nowt for you here,' I heard a voice say.

I pushed my way through the crowd of men towards the mill doors, sensing Randy behind me, as Sharples opened his mouth.

'This 'ere door's three inches of solid oak with cast-iron fittings,' he yelled. 'Same around the back. I know that because my dad worked here up until the day it closed. Nobody is getting through it without a key, and I'm willing to bet nobody here has one. So why don't you all turn round, go back to the pub, or your nice warm beds, and let us do our jobs?'

'You're not doing your bloody jobs, are you? Not with animals like Parker on the loose!'

Randy and I reached the front and turned to face the crowd, taking our place next to the others. I heard Sharples swear under his breath.

The headlights of Tom's car shone on us, and much of the mill building, but cast the faces before us into shadow. We could barely see the men threatening us, only their eyes, gleaming. There were eyes everywhere, it seemed. In the crowd, in the windows of the nearby houses, everywhere the glint of watching eyes.

He's here. The thought came out of nowhere, but there was no dismissing it. Somewhere in this crowd of angry, frightened men was the cold heart of a killer. He was here. He was enjoying this, taking pride in his work.

Someone at the back started to chant, quietly but insistently, 'Bring him out. Bring him out.'

'He's a filthy, rotten pervert!' someone shouted.

'Happen he is,' Sharples yelled back. 'But he's my filthy, rotten pervert to deal with how I see fit. Now turn round and go home before I arrest the whole sodding lot of you.'

The crowd seemed to be getting bigger all the time as more and more people slipped in through the gates. I was searching faces, looking for the gleam in a pair of eyes that seemed different. Amid all these blazing eyes, I was looking for ice.

'Bring him out. Bring him out.' More voices had joined in. It was like a drumbeat, soft but menacing, and growing in volume. Soon it would reach the point where nothing could be heard above it and then we'd have lost what little control we had.

'Jim Shorrock!' Sharples shouted at the crowd. 'I know you're at the bottom of this. Where are you, man?'

The line at the front broke apart and a man stepped forward.

I'd seen him at the station after Stephen vanished. A thin, wiry man in his late thirties. His hair was blond and slightly too long. His nose was a little narrow, and a little crooked; his mouth twisted when he talked. He was the grown-up image of Stephen. He stepped forward, directly in front of Sharples, until the two men were only inches apart. They faced each other like a pair of prizefighters. Sharples was older, smaller and thinner, but he wasn't going to back down.

Then Shorrock's face took on a look I can only describe as disgust. He said, 'Do you have any bloody idea what this is doing to me?'

Sharples opened his mouth, but I beat him to it.

'Yes,' I said, and I think both men were so surprised to hear me speak that it gained me an extra few seconds. 'You're heartbroken.'

Shorrock's head turned. His pale eyes glared down at me. His upper lip curled.

I stepped a little closer to him. The same surprise that had temporarily silenced the two men had struck me too now – what was I thinking? – but I knew I couldn't back down. 'Your heart is breaking because you miss your son so much,' I said. 'And you can't bear to see your wife grieving. You're furious with us because we haven't found him yet, and you're angry with yourself too, because you think you could have done something different, although you couldn't – you weren't to blame in any way.'

Shorrock's eyes narrowed, and he seemed to lean towards me.

'And you're scared,' I went on quickly. 'Because you want more than anything to help him and you don't know how. We feel all that too, Mr Shorrock. Not as much as you, I know, but we do. Don't we, sir?'

A second's silence.

'Aye, Florence, we do,' Sharples said, and I realised that the chanting had stopped.

'Is that the shoe?' I spotted something in Jim Shorrock's pocket and reached out my hand. 'May I?' When he didn't object, I took the small, slim plimsoll and held it up. 'It's navy blue, like Stephen's,' I said. 'And it does have white laces.' I turned it over and checked the number on the underside. 'But I don't think this is Stephen's shoe, Mr Shorrock. This is a size eight, and Stephen takes a size seven.' I glanced sideways at Sharples. 'I read the file a few times, sir. I have a good memory for things like that. I'm sure Stephen's plimsoll was a size seven.'

Shorrock took a deep breath that was only a whisper away from a sob and I saw his whole body tremble. I passed the shoe to one side and felt someone take it from me as I took Shorrock's arm.

'Come on, now. You need to be at home.' I turned him round to face the gate. 'Your wife needs you, and your other children do too. You should be with your family. I'll put the kettle on, make you a nice cup of tea. Gentlemen, can you let us through, please?'

The crowd fell away as Shorrock and I, arm in arm, set off towards the gate, moving to one side to get round Tom's car. Behind, I heard Sharples say, 'Randy, go with her.' As we passed through the yard gates, I could hear clattering footsteps, the sound of heavy, steel-capped boots on cobbles, as the men of Jubilee Street followed us out.

I didn't look back. Like Orpheus fleeing the underworld, I had a feeling that if I turned round, it would all go wrong, that the crowd would fire up again and that we'd finish the night with a lynching. So we kept going, and before I knew it, we were in the back room of the Shorrock house, halfway down the street.

By this time, I was shaking too. *Jumped-up swanker of a schoolgirl?* I'd just proved him right. I was going to be in so much trouble.

Linda Shorrock was sitting in front of the stove, staring through its open door to the embers within. She barely looked up. Jim sank onto the other chair, while Randy went upstairs to check on the kids. I found the kettle, put tea directly into oversized mugs and poured the boiling water onto it, the way I'd seen people at the station make their tea. I added sugar and milk, and then crouched to press a mug into Linda's hand. She grabbed at me, spilling hot tea over both of us.

'He comes to me in my sleep,' she said, and her eyes were wide and desperate. 'Pawing at me. Tugging at my hair, saying, "Help me, Mam. I want to come home."'

It was all I could do not to cry out – the tea was scalding hot – but more had gone on her hands and she'd hardly noticed. I put the mug down and she grasped both my wrists.

'I'm so sorry we haven't found him yet,' I said. 'But we won't stop looking.' I glanced over at Jim, but he barely seemed conscious. 'We'll never stop,' I added, as Randy appeared from upstairs and gave me a nod.

'He's close, I can feel it.' Linda was still holding on to me. 'He hasn't run away. He's somewhere close and all he wants to do is come home.'

I caught Randy's eye and knew what he was thinking. When these people found out what had happened to Patsy, their misery would know no limits.

'Let the girl go.' Jim turned to his wife. 'Go on now, lass – you've got a job to do. We'll be OK.'

I looked at Randy again and he nodded. There was nothing more we could do for the Shorrock family, except find their son.

Randy and I walked back down an empty street. People were still up and out, but they watched us from doorways, from the pavement.

'We brought Terry in when Stephen went missing,' Randy said. 'Known nonce, lived in Stephen's street – why wouldn't we? He had alibis for that evening. We ruled him out.'

Tom appeared through the mill doors as we entered the yard. There was a graze on his right cheek, and he'd bitten his lower lip. A thin trickle of blood had dried on his chin. His jacket lapel hung down and looked beyond repair. Tom liked his clothes. He liked his car too and I was glad it was dark, that any damage wasn't immediately visible.

'Found him?' Randy asked.

Tom shook his head. 'Not yet. Christ knows it shouldn't be hard. There's only one floor. A few enclosed rooms. Unless the bugger's scaling the chimney, I haven't the foggiest where he's got to.'

'He isn't in there.' I set off towards the outbuilding I'd spotted earlier. It was tucked into the far corner of the yard, built of stone like the wall, its door all but hidden behind a trailing buddleia bush. I'd seen a gleam in the window that I'd been sure had been a pair of eyes.

I reached the door and it opened easily. Behind me, Tom and Randy shone torches over my shoulder. Huddled in the corner, on the floor, half hidden by sacking, was the small, shaking figure of Terry Parker.

We gave Terry a cup of tea, a blanket and put him in a cell for the night. For his own protection.

He told us the shoe was his own, and he even managed to produce a receipt. With nothing else at all against him, we knew we'd have to let him go in the morning, although he showed no enthusiasm for the idea.

Midnight found us in the Square & Compass, a pub in the town centre. Last orders had come and gone, the landlord had locked the door, and we'd carried on drinking.

This was my first time in the Square & Compass and I was surprised to find it beautiful. Columns decorated in a repetitive pattern like fish scales held up a plaster ceiling carved in over-lapping circles and the red rose of Lancashire. The floor was a curious arrangement of black and white tiles, while the windows were all etched glass. Some of them were round, like portholes on a ship.

'These won't be cheap to replace.' I'd stopped just inside the door to admire the glasswork, thinking of drunken brawls on a Saturday night.

'Nobody throws a brick at these windows.' Brown put his hands on my shoulders to hurry me along. 'Nobody would dare.'

In the Square & Compass, tables weren't scattered around the bar as was usually the case but enclosed within a line of carved wood-panelled stalls that ran along each outside wall. The pattern that kept repeating itself, in the glass, on the wooden panels, along the top of the bar, was of two interlocked triangles that together formed a diamond shape. I didn't think I'd seen it before, but there was something about it that kept drawing my attention. It took me a few minutes to realise the upper of the two triangles was a draughtsman's compass, the lower a square rule.

It wasn't a working man's pub. Most of the other drinkers wore suits; a couple were in the sort of leisure clothes men might wear at the golf club. We'd found a stall in the corner and were reasonably confident that no one could overhear us. I was the only woman in the place – even the bar staff were men – and the stares continued long after we arrived.

'You all right with that, Flossie?' Sharples asked me for the fourth time, looking down at the Britvic orange I'd made last an hour.

The music changed to the latest Andy Williams hit. He was my favourite singer back then and I loved his new song, 'Can't Take My Eyes Off You'.

'I'm fine, boss. Thank you.' I took another sip to show willing.

Even after I'd forced half of it down, the combination of concentrated sugar and artificial orange flavour was burning my tastebuds.

Across the table, Tom was mouthing the words to the song and staring at me.

'I think you're onto something with that chart of yours, Flossie, but you're going to need some help,' Sharples said. 'Woodsmoke, can you have your people feed her information?'

'Sir,' I said, 'I'm not promising anything, but if I can have a look at the funeral details that Sergeant Brown finds, I might be able to spot something.'

'What sort of something? And what sort of details?' Brown looked as though I'd asked for his trouser size.

'Name, sex and age of deceased. Time, date and place of burial. Casket or coffin. Cost of funeral. Anything. I don't really know till I see it.'

'What good will that do?'

'I can spot patterns,' I said. 'I was good at maths and I can . . . Oh, it's hard to explain it. I look at information and if there's a pattern, or even a break in a pattern, an anomaly, I can see it.'

Another silence. Brown dropped his cigarette end and ground it out beneath his foot. I could practically see the words 'jumped-up schoolgirl' running through all their heads.

'Can't hurt,' said Tom. 'Can it?'

'It's not a small job,' said Brown. 'That's a lot of information. Is that really the best use of Flossie's time?'

'She does have plenty to be going on with,' said Sharples. 'She's spending tomorrow morning in the library. Lunchtime in the museum.'

'What's she doing in the library and museum, boss?' Green asked.

'We need as much information on this voodoo doll as we can

get,' Sharples said. 'This talk about grave-robbing is worrying me as well. Even if it was twenty years ago. I think we're going to need an in-house expert on black magic, witchcraft and devil worship, and as Florence keeps reminding us, she's been to university.'

He drained his pint, stood up and pushed open the stall door. 'I'm done,' he said. 'Don't stay too long, lads. We've a lot on to-morrow. And someone make sure Florence gets home. She's not much older than them kids, and it might be a tad embarrassing if anything happened to her.'

He nodded at me, muttered something I didn't catch, then left.

'What did he say?' I asked, not sure I really wanted to know.

'He said, "Nice one,"' Brown told me.

They were all staring at me.

'What?' I said.

'From No Shit Sharples, that's a marriage proposal,' Tom said.

30

We left the pub at one in the morning. At my insistence. I'd got bored watching the three of them get steadily drunk, and by the time their eyes had lost focus and their speech had started to slur, they didn't seem to mind being told what to do. Gusty, who was never allowed inside a vehicle after a few pints, walked to his house in the town centre. I dropped Woodsmoke off along the main road and then, finally, Tom. He was still singing the Andy Williams song when I pulled up. What little of it he knew.

His house was bigger than I'd expected, a new semi-detached bungalow with dormer windows in the roof.

'Why d'you leave me till last?' He leaned against the passenger door and showed no sign of climbing out.

'You're closest to the station,' I said. 'I'll leave your car there overnight.'

His face fell. 'You don't need to do that. Take it home. I trust you. You're a good driver. For a girl.'

I'd been driving since I was twelve. I'd learned on a private estate near to my family home and had done some rally-driving with one of my brothers while we were both at university. I could probably outdrive everyone at the station.

'It's a bigger engine than I'm used to,' I said. 'And I could use some fresh air. It's been quite a day.'

Silence.

'Sleep well,' I said.

'You too, Florence. You sleep well too.'

'You will probably sleep better if you leave the car and go inside your house to bed,' I told him.

Still he didn't move. 'It's been nice,' he said, 'having a drink with you. Thanks for coming.'

'Thanks for asking me.'

It's possible my tone was a little more pointed than I planned. Or maybe I just hadn't expected him to pick up on it. He looked me directly in the eyes. 'It's not that we don't want you to come,' he said. 'We'd be more than happy for you to join us; you're one of us now.'

It really didn't feel that way to me. But Tom was a nice guy. A nice, drunk guy.

'It's not that you're a lass, or a poncey Southerner, or cleverer than the rest of us put together; we're OK with all that. It's that you don't drink.'

'What?'

'You've got to see it from our point of view. We all get wasted – we need to in this job – and we start talking and acting like pillocks, and you sit there sipping your Britvic orange and judging us.'

'I do not.'

He looked at me.

OK, I had done, but not in a mean way. I'd thought it hilarious the way their eyes lost clarity and the stuff that came out of their mouths became increasingly bizarre as the night wore on.

'You're welcome to come, Florence. Come out with us any-time and welcome, but you're going to have to hold your nose and swallow back a couple of Babychams.'

'Tom, get out. Go to bed.'

Finally, he leaned away from the door, opened it and practically fell into the road. He pulled himself up, weaved his way round the front of the car and, after a few fumbles, managed to unlock his front door.

I saw a curtain twitch in one of the upstairs windows.

The station felt deserted. Apart from the station officer, I saw no one when I made my way in through the back and climbed to the first floor. I left Tom's car keys in his desk drawer just as a phone started ringing.

It made me jump. The building was so quiet. It wasn't even my phone, which would have made some sense, but the one on DS Brown's desk.

It stopped. I think I breathed a sigh of relief.

Another started ringing. Opposite side of the room, out of sight behind the row of filing cabinets, unnaturally loud.

It's him. He knows I'm here. He'll ring every phone in the room until he finds me.

After four rings, it stopped.

I was being absurd. The telephone system was programmed to search the room. If a phone wasn't answered in four rings, the call automatically moved on to the next in the group.

It started again. Tom's desk, and I was not afraid of a telephone. I set off towards it. I reached it on the fourth ring but heard nothing except dead air down the line. I put the phone down, looking around, trying to predict where it was going to go next. I'd get it this time.

Nothing. As though the caller had given up.

Detective Sergeant Green's phone started ringing. It was close enough to catch. I ran across and grabbed it.

'Hello,' I said. 'Sabden Police Station, CID room.'

Silence on the line, but not dead silence. Someone was there.

It's him.

'Sabden CID, WPC Lovelady speaking.'

'That girl you found.'

Silence again.

'Who's calling, please?'

'Where is she? Where did you put her?'

'Which girl do you mean? Can I take your name, please?'

'The dead girl. The one you found in the grave. Where is she?'

'I can't give out that information, I'm afraid. Who is this?'

'She has to be cremated.'

'Well, that will be up to her parents. I can't discuss this any more unless you tell—'

'You must not put her back in the ground. She will not rest.'

I think I stiffened. I know I looked over my shoulder. 'What do you mean?'

'Burn her. Do you hear me? You have to burn her.'

The line went dead. I got my bag and switched out the lights. I like to think of myself as not easily ruffled, but I was conscious of my footsteps down the stairs being quicker than they might otherwise have been.

'Sarge,' I said, before I'd even got to the front desk, 'did you put a call through a couple of minutes ago?'

He was away from the desk, sharing a pot of tea with one of the uniformed constables, who'd popped in for a break.

'I wasn't sure what desk you're using,' he told me. 'Did it find you?'

'It did, thanks. Did the caller give her name to you?'

He pulled a face. 'To be honest, love, I thought it was a bloke. No name, though. Problem?'

I shook my head and wished them both good night. As I left the building, I felt a moment of regret that I'd left Tom's car keys upstairs.

I cycled quickly that night, not even stopping for traffic lights, but got back to the Glassbrook house without further incident. That is, until I was trying to unlock the big front door without waking the house.

I fell over something in the porch.

Stepping back, more jumpy than I'd have cared to admit, I found my torch and shone it on the tiled porch floor. Flowers. Not any old flowers but red roses, fat and long-stemmed, wrapped in paper. I bent to pick them up and caught sight of my name written in pencil on the wrapping. They were for me.

I crept inside, the roses – thornless and scentless like florist-bought roses usually are – tucked beneath one arm. In the kitchen, I found a jug and ran water. It was only when I was un-wrapping the flowers that the card fell out. From the Flower Pot in town, Marlene's shop, the message on it was three letters long.

RIP.

31

In the grand Victorian style that dominated so many of its municipal buildings, Sabden Public Library boasted great bay windows on the ground floor, ornate fake balconies on the upper. The roof was an undulating line of gable ends and carved finials; in its centre a round tower, topped with a polished copper dome.

Not for the first time, I wondered about Sabden's wealth. It wasn't a huge town, and ninety-five per cent of its population seemed to live very modest lives, but a walk around the town centre and its impressive, perfectly maintained public buildings made it clear there was money here.

Important people, who didn't take kindly to anyone rocking the boat?

Revolving doors took me into the library's central hall, where the domed ceiling seemed a long way above my head. Sunlight streamed in through skylights, and dust sparkled like particles of gold all around me.

I coughed, although there was nothing in my throat, and then sniffed loudly. There was something about the place that made me want to make a noise.

The children's room was off to my right, the adults' shelves arranged around the outer walls. Great wooden tables and chairs for reading were scattered over the area. The reception desk was a gigantic ring of oak, in the centre of which worked three women, each dressed in various shades of brown and grey. Two were middle-aged. The third looked quite elderly and was engrossed in her task, writing in a large ledger-type book.

I called out a cheery 'Good morning' and then walked across the central atrium to the reference room. The notice on the door told me that silence was expected – nay, demanded – once I crossed the threshold. I let the door slam hard behind me.

I was tired. For the second night in a row I'd barely slept. *RIP*? What was that about? Another small-minded prank, or something more sinister?

The sense of something dark on the loose in Sabden was growing. If I spent any time alone, I could almost see a shadow ahead of me, slipping out of sight, and if I stopped moving, even for a few seconds, the silence around started to feel ominous. When I woke in the night, I found myself listening for sounds beyond my room.

There was nowhere, I realised, that I felt safe. Not at the Glassbrook house, where I couldn't even lock my bedroom door; not at the station, where everyone resented me; and certainly not around town, because every pair of eyes I looked into could be the last ones that Patsy Wood saw.

I wanted to be back at work, in the midst of things, not stuck here in a public library. Especially as I couldn't help feeling Sharples had sent me here to get me out of the way.

And I wasn't always talking about going to university.

I found the section I was looking for, pulled out a few books and sat down. Immediately I could feel my eyelids starting to droop.

'I think you might struggle with that one,' a voice behind me said. 'It's written in old Scots.'

'So I'm discovering.' I looked up, rubbing my eyes.

The librarian who'd approached me wore no make-up, and her huge unruly eyebrows suggested she didn't waste much time in front of mirrors. When she moved her head in a certain way, though, I caught a glimpse of ruby earrings. She had fat, masculine fingers, but her fingernails were perfectly shaped and painted scarlet. Her name badge said, *Mrs D. Reece.*

'I can make it out, but it's heavy-going.' I tried and failed to stifle a yawn. A glance at my watch told me over an hour had passed.

Mrs Reece pulled out a chair and sat beside me. 'Is there anything I can help you with? You seem a little overwhelmed.'

My corner of the big reading table was covered in books. While small in real terms, the library had proven well stocked when it came to material on the occult.

'You can tell me what possessed the King of England to write a book about witchcraft.' I closed the book so that we could both see the front cover: *Daemonologie, in the form of a dialogue, written by the high and mighty prince, James by the grace of God, King of England, Scotland, France and Ireland.* 'Actually, forget that. I don't care. Tell me how so many women throughout history could be executed for something we now know to be utter nonsense.'

If Mrs Reece registered my anger, she didn't show it. 'Different time,' she said. 'Religious faith went unquestioned. People believed in the Devil and all things evil.' She lifted a hand to scratch behind her ear, showing off the beautiful ruby earring again. 'When people, usually women, were seen acting in an unorthodox manner – especially if they enjoyed some unexplained success – accusing them of having supernatural powers was easy.' Her grey eyes glittered as though about to shed tears. 'And, we mustn't forget, most of them confessed.'

The book's cover scraped across the tabletop as I pushed it away. I really didn't want to read it any more. Or the other one I'd pulled down, *The Wonderful Discovery of Witches in the County of Lancashire* by Thomas Potts.

This one told the story of the events leading up to the trial at Lancaster Assizes in 1612 of twenty people, most of them women, over half from Pendle, who had stood accused of witchcraft. Most were found guilty and hanged. *The Wonderful Discovery of Witches* had been written to glorify mass murder, as far as I was concerned.

'There is no such thing as witchcraft,' I said. 'Not now, not then. What was behind it really?'

'Mainly, I'd say, it was about poverty,' Mrs Reece said. 'In those times, women with no property and no man to take care of them found it almost impossible to make a living. Very few jobs were open to them, and even begging was illegal much of the time.'

That, at least, made some sense. 'So it was just about making a living?'

'A lot of people would consider the Pendle witches con-artists,' she said. 'They fooled their communities into believing they could perform spells, heal the sick, help the crops, that sort of thing. Mother Demdike, the most famous of them, was known as a "blesser". Farmers would pay her to "bless" the crops, or a sick animal. Sometimes a sick person. She'd turn up, mutter a few prayers, maybe leave behind some herbs and she and her family would eat that night.'

'But when it went wrong, when the sick person died, they were blamed?' I asked.

'In many ways, they were their own worst enemies,' Mrs Reece said. 'They let people believe they had powers that could harm as well as help. Demdike had this habit of telling people who'd crossed her that she would pray for them. "I will pray for you long and still," she'd say. And then she'd stand like a statue and mutter to herself. Not surprisingly people thought they were being cursed.'

I will pray for you long and still. It was a bit creepy. 'But were they?' I said. 'Were they actually witches, do you think?'

'Almost certainly,' said Mrs Reece. 'But guilty of the charge for which they were hanged, that of murder by witchcraft? That's another question entirely.'

'It's absurd,' I said. 'They couldn't possibly have had that sort of power. Nobody does.'

'Very few,' she said.

I'd had enough. I picked up the King James book and carried it back to the shelf. 'I don't believe King James believed in witchcraft,' I said. 'I don't believe any of them did. These women were terrified and they were tortured. Even hundreds of years ago, I don't believe people were so stupid as to think confessions under torture had any validity.'

Mrs Reece got to her feet too, and seemed to lean a little closer, although she was already very near to me. 'Something has frightened you,' she said. 'What?'

'I'm glad we live in more enlightened times.' I reached for my bag. Coming here had been a waste of time. There was something in the air in the library, an odd sort of smell, stuffy and herbal at the same time, that was making my head ache and dulling my concentration. I couldn't even properly remember what I was doing here. 'No more misogynistic vendettas, no more witch hunts, no more witches.'

I tried to walk away and found myself held by Mrs Reece's intense stare.

'Oh, my dear,' she said. 'There will always be witch hunts. I rather think you're on one yourself right now.'

I found her self-assurance a little annoying. 'I don't believe in witches,' I said.

She gave an odd, tight-lipped smile. 'The last witchcraft act was repealed in 1951. What a complete waste of parliamentary time, if there are no witches.'

I opened my mouth to say something, I'm not sure what, and found myself gaping at her, drawn in by those glittering grey eyes. I was actually finding it hard to blink.

And then she smiled, showing big yellow teeth. 'Don't look so worried, dear. We don't turn people into toads any more.'

She stepped away and the atmosphere seemed to lighten, as though someone had opened a door and a rush of sweet-smelling air had swept in. 'Is there anything else I can help you with?' she asked. 'It's getting a little close to the time when we close for lunch.'

That's why I'd come. 'I'm a police officer.' I watched her eyebrows twitch as she read my warrant card.

'How very nice to meet you, WPC Lovelady.'

'I'm investigating a case. A case that might have links to witchcraft. It's possible you can help me.'

'Is it something to do with the child murders?'

'Why do you ask that?'

'It's all people are talking about. Poor Patsy was found in a graveyard, and people invariably, and wrongly, make the link between unorthodox graveyard activity and witchcraft.'

'Mrs Reece, I'd like to show you something. I would really appreciate it remaining confidential.'

'Of course.'

From my bag I pulled out a Polaroid photograph of the clay effigy. She hooked her reading glasses onto her nose and stared at it.

'Good Lord,' she said, as her eyes darted up towards mine. 'Where did you come across this?'

'I can't say, I'm afraid. I'm sorry. Can you tell me anything?'

She was staring down at the Polaroid again. 'It's a clay picture.'

'A what?'

'You would probably call it an "effigy" these days, but "picture" is what it was called in the old days. The Lancashire witches were accused of making pictures of their enemies.' She frowned and bent closer to the photograph. 'What's piercing the figure? Those don't look like pins.'

'Thin slivers of wood,' I said.

Her head bounced slowly. 'Blackthorn,' she said. 'Long associated with witchcraft. Witches' wands and staffs were supposedly made from blackthorn wood.' She looked at me. 'Is this supposed to be Patsy?'

I said nothing.

'You can't tell me – I understand,' she said. 'Do you know what, I think I've seen this before. Bear with me.'

She crossed the room, bent down in front of another drawer, pulled out a book with a battered brown leather cover and flicked through it.

'I knew it,' she said, putting it in front of me. 'It's a copy of the Louvre Doll.'

I sat back down and looked. The black-and-white photograph was almost exactly the same as the one I'd brought in myself. It showed a clay effigy of a female, hands and feet bound, thirteen pins or sharp twigs piercing her body. It was far, far too similar to be coincidence.

I stood up. 'Mrs Reece, I need you to put that book down on the table. Stop touching it, please.'

Frowning, she did as she was told.

'We're going to leave the room now, and then I'm going to ask you to stand outside the door while I borrow your phone to call the station,' I said.

She looked bewildered, even a little frightened. 'What on earth . . . ?'

'You may have to close the reference library for a couple of hours,' I told her. 'That book, in fact the whole room, will need to be fingerprinted.'

'Nice work, Flossie,' said Green, an hour later.

The reference library was closed temporarily, and the fingerprints team was dusting everything down. Mrs Reece was peering through the glass partition, rapping on it every time they went near a book she considered valuable.

DI Sharples, DS Green, Tom and I were seated at one of the heavy oak tables.

'Now, what can you tell us about the Loo Doll?' Sharples said.

'The Louvre Doll,' I said. 'After the museum in Paris where it's housed.'

The book was in the process of being printed, bagged and taken away, but we had Polaroids of the page in question, and I'd made notes.

'It's an artefact from fourth-century Egypt,' I said. 'A clay figure, impaled with thirteen bronze needles. It was found in a terracotta vase alongside a lead curse tablet engraved with a binding spell.'

'What's a binding spell?' asked Tom.

'It's a type of curse in which someone asks the gods to do harm to someone else. This is a really creepy one, though. I've written it down,' I said. 'Shall I?'

'Go on,' said Sharples.

My handwriting was rushed and I had to concentrate. '*Lead Ptolemais, whom Aias bore, the daughter of Horigenes, to me,*' I read. '*Prevent her from eating and drinking until she comes to me, Sarapammon, whom Area bore, and do not allow her to have experience with another man, except me alone. Drag her by her hair, by her guts, until she does not stand aloof from me . . . and until I hold her obedient for the whole time of my life, loving me, desiring me, and telling me what she is thinking.*'

'That's a love spell.' A hint of a grin was breaking out on Tom's face. 'He wants her to be his bird.'

'Do you think so?' I said. 'I think he wants her to be his slave.'

32

'I tell you what puzzles me, Mrs Reece, about this, er' – Detective Sergeant Brown glanced down – 'this Louvre Doll.' He pronounced it 'Loo-ver'. 'There must be, how many books in Sabden Public Library? Ten thousand? Twenty thousand?'

He glanced at Randy, sitting at his side, who shrugged.

'Thirty-six thousand five hundred and forty-two,' said Mrs Reece, who we'd learned was called Daphne, and I couldn't help feeling it was a figure she'd plucked out of the air that second.

Brown inclined his head. 'And have you read them all?' he asked.

'Don't be a simpleton.'

At my side, Tom sniggered and Sharples glared. The two-way mirror we were standing behind wasn't soundproof. There were signs all over the tiny room warning us to keep quiet during interviews.

'And yet within seconds of WPC Lovelady showing you a Polaroid of a similar figure, you find the exact book with this photograph in it.'

'I'm very familiar with those books in the occult section,' Daphne said. 'The Louvre Doll is quite striking. Few would forget it, having seen it once.'

'Do you know much about its history?'

'Only what it says in the book.'

'Mrs Reece,' said Randy, 'would you happen to know who

might have looked at that book in the last few months?'

Daphne pulled a regretful face. 'One of our staff members keeps a record of all books taken out of the library,' she said. 'She doesn't trust the ticketing system. She tries to keep on top of activity in the reference library too, but she can't always leave the front desk. I've already checked. There's no record of anyone consulting that book in the last three years. Not before today.'

'And the original doll was found with some sort of spell, I understand,' said Brown.

'Yes, a love spell.'

Tom nudged me. When I looked at him, he was making a 'told you so' face. I glared back.

'So how does it work?' Brown said.

'Love spells are very old magic,' Daphne said. She looked up at the mirror and I had a feeling she knew we were behind it. 'The figure will have been formed to closely resemble the subject. The closer the resemblance, the more powerful the magic. And it should contain something very personal.'

'What kind of personal?' Randy asked.

'Something from her body. Hair or fingernails are good. Blood, teeth or bone are more powerful but harder to come by. Clothing or a personal possession would be better than nothing. Whatever it is, that essence of the person must be incorporated into the figure.' She glanced up at the mirror again. 'If the effigy you found is anything to do with that poor child, there will be a phys- ical trace of her in its make-up.'

All three of us in the back room looked at each other. *Patsy's tooth.*

'The spell, the wording on the tablet in the case of the Louvre Doll, says what you want to happen.' Daphne was on a roll now. 'You have to be very clear in magic. The last thing you want is for the energy to become confused and head off in the wrong direction.'

She finished. Brown and Randy both waited.

'That's it?' Brown said, after a moment.

'No, there will need to be a casting of the spell, to tie it all together.'

'How is that done?' asked Randy.

'There are various ways. I have no idea what this man in fourth-century Egypt did.'

'WPC Lovelady has a theory about you, Mrs Reece,' said Brown. 'It's a bit daft, but she's a young lass. She thinks you might be something of a witch yourself.'

Daphne's eyes flashed. 'She's a very smart young woman.'

Brown and Randy shared a look.

'You admit to being a witch?' Brown said.

'I'm proud of being a witch.'

Another look between the men. A heavy sigh from Daphne. Also, I think, her eyes met mine through the mirror.

'Have you ever done a love spell?' Randy asked.

Daphne found something to interest her on one of her bright red fingernails. 'Certainly not,' she said. 'I find the idea of forced affection abhorrent. I have nothing to do with dark magic.'

'And what do you do, exactly, when you're being a witch?' said Brown. 'If not love spells, what?'

'Our rites are private. I can't discuss them with just anyone.'

'I'm not just anyone, Mrs Reece,' said Brown. 'I'm a detective sergeant conducting a murder investigation.'

'And I am not under arrest.' She folded her arms and let them rest on the tabletop. I had to hand it to her: Daphne Reece was as cool as a Fox's Glacier Mint.

Brown said, 'You said "our" rites. So there are more of you? More witches?'

'Yes, a full coven.'

Encouraged, Brown leaned forward. 'And how many in a coven?'

'Thirteen is usual, although some work with a smaller number.'

'And, if I may ask, what does a coven do?'

Daphne gave a big smile and I thought I saw both men recoil a little at the sight of her teeth. 'It's a forum for shared experiences and mutual encouragement,' she said. 'We are a group of like-minded people, mainly women, who believe in the power of working together for the common good.'

'Thank goodness for that. I don't know about you, Randy, but I thought Mrs Reece was going to claim to perform magic.'

'Oh, we do that as well. Is it something you're interested in, Detective Sergeant Brown? Our coven is full at the moment, but we could think about a waiting—'

This time, Tom's snort must have been heard at the end of the corridor. Sharples glared round at us. I had to bite my bottom lip.

Brown picked up his pen. 'Can you give me their names, please?'

A slow but firm shake of her head. 'Not without their permission.'

Poor Woodsmoke.

'Mrs Reece, where were you on the evening of Sunday, 15 June?'

She didn't even think about it. 'Rehearsing.'

'Rehearsing what?'

'*Macbeth*.'

No, she was going too far this time. I looked at Tom but got a blank stare in return.

'I'm sorry, what?' said Brown.

'Shakespeare,' she said. 'One of the tragedies. Not his best, in my view, but I don't get to choose the play. Of course, a lot of the cast won't even say the word "*Macbeth*", calling it "the Scottish

Play" instead, but I've always considered that a load of superstitious nonsense.'

Brown ran a hand through his hair. 'Are we talking about amateur dramatics?'

'Of course. Sabden Library Players' autumn production. We've been rehearsing since the end of May. Opening night is on Friday, 31 October and it runs for three nights.'

'She's having us on,' I whispered. Tom shushed me.

'I'm playing Duncan,' Daphne went on. 'We're short of men. And to save time, because if you don't mind my saying so, Detective Sergeant, you don't seem quite on the ball, we meet at seven and rehearse until nine. After that, we go to the Eagle and Child on Snape Street. That night, I got home at eleven, dropped off by another player, and went straight to bed. Not alone. All told, I can probably give you around a dozen alibis.'

'Thank you,' said Brown weakly. 'What about Wednesday, 16 April?'

'The day Stephen Shorrock disappeared? Don't look so excited – I've been following the case. I was out of the country. The Swiss Alps, to be precise, on a walking holiday with the North of England Library Ramblers Association. I got back on Sunday of that week.'

'Monday, 17 March?' Brown sounded resigned. 'When Susan Duxbury was last seen?'

'Can't say for sure, but I usually spend Monday evenings with friends.'

'The coven?' Brown asked, in a last-ditch attempt.

'Only on a full moon,' said Daphne.

33

Terry Parker was released the next day, Friday. We had no reason to hold him and in spite of his reluctance to be let out into the world again, we returned his belongings and sent him on his way. I went back to the public library and, with Daphne's help, found and checked out every available book on the occult, folklore and witchcraft. I was to have very interesting dreams in the coming days.

Detective Sergeant Brown went to see Patsy's dentist, who told him that while Patsy had visited him recently, she hadn't had an extraction in over a year.

'Some families deal with dental problems themselves, though,' Brown told us when he got back. 'Piece of cotton thread round the tooth, the other end round the handle on an open door. Slam the door shut and Bob's your uncle. We can't assume Patsy's missing tooth was pulled out by her killer. Unless it does turn out to be her tooth in that voodoo doll thing. Then we probably can assume it. What a bloody mess.' Shaking his head, Woodsmoke left the room. I saw him a few minutes later, in the car park, smoking, staring down at the Tarmac.

Once again, I told Sharples we should be visiting schools and warning children to take care. Once again, I was told to shut it and get on with my work.

That same day, while the senior staff and detectives began the process of re-interviewing all known offenders in town, the more junior among us started our systematic search of the town's churchyards. We were looking for graves, particularly the more recent ones, that might have been interfered with. Most of us weren't in uniform, and we travelled on bikes or unmarked cars, to keep a low profile. We kept our enquiries discreet, asking about vandalism, trespass late at night, problems with wildlife, but on my last stop of the day, a man in cream trousers and a sports jacket approached as I left the churchyard.

He ignored Randy, who'd driven us there, and spoke to me. 'Florence, were you expecting to find Stephen and Susan here?'

I stepped round him. I had no idea how he knew my name.

'Are you exhuming any more graves, Florence?' The reporter followed us down the street to the waiting unmarked car.

'All enquiries to the station, mate,' Randy told him.

'How did you know where to find Patsy, Florence?' He grabbed the car door as I was getting in and I had to tug it from him.

'Friend of yours?' Randy said, as we headed back towards the station.

'I've never seen or spoken to him in my life before.'

I didn't get a reply.

The newsagents' headline boards that evening read, *Patsy: Police Search Graveyards*, and someone left a copy of the *Manchester Evening News* on my desk. On the inside front page was a photograph of me, standing at a graveside, making notes.

We worked late and, when the others headed for the pub, I cycled home. There seemed to be more people on the streets than usual, and twice I heard abuse called after me. I went straight to bed, pushed a chair under my door handle, and slept badly.

The Saturday morning headlines asked, *Stephen and Susan: Still Here Somewhere?* The accompanying story in the *Lancashire Morning Post* told us that detectives were continuing to interview known offenders but had no real leads. There was speculation that the TV reconstruction had delayed the investigation by throwing up too many false trails and red herrings and, yes, that story was left on my desk too.

Just before lunch, I got up, left the room and locked myself in a cubicle in the ladies' toilets. I cried for ten minutes, for no reason I could put my finger on.

Daphne was interviewed again, this time with her solicitor; a tall, thin woman with dark, frizzy hair. She declined, yet again, to name the other members of her coven. Sharples was furious, but her alibis were watertight and there was no way we could charge her in connection with the disappearances. Sharples muttered about obstructing a police investigation, but Rushton wouldn't give permission to arrest and charge her. In her interview, she asked after 'that nice young WPC Lovelady'.

I was given the keys to a station pool car, a pale blue Vauxhall Viva. My excitement lasted for the time it took to drive out of the station car park and spot a poster of Patsy on a lamppost.

Sharples sent a member of the team to make enquiries at the local pottery class, but he came back with the news that no one had shown a particular interest in making human figures, or working with local clay. When I got home that night, I asked Sally's permission to dig some up from their garden and try my own hand at modelling.

At nine o'clock, when I was alone in my room, I was called down to the front door by Cassie. The same journalist who'd spoken to me in the churchyard was there. His hair was dark and limp with the heat.

'Hi, Florence,' he said. 'I wondered if you fancied a drink?'

'No, thank you.'

He reached out, to give my arm a nudge. 'Come on, love. Quick port and lemon in the Star – what have you got to lose?'

'Apart from my job,' I almost said, but didn't. I told him to contact the station in the morning if he had an enquiry and closed the door.

Nobody seemed to sleep well that night. I heard several people walking about the house and someone, Luna, I think, crying out in her sleep.

Early the next morning, I made a ball and a fish out of clay from the garden. 'Don't give up the day job, Flossie,' Larry said.

When I arrived at work, it was to find someone had pinned a Crown Paints colour chart above my desk. Ten deepening shades from pale pink to dark red. Someone had crossed out the official paint names – *Blush, Poppy, Crimson Sky, Scarlet Letter, Cherry Jam, Robin's Breast* and so on – and written, *Grave-Robbing, Centre of Attention, Bollocking From Boss, Run Upstairs, Chasing Suspects, Sexual Arousal.* When I dropped it in the bin, every pair of eyes in the room was looking the other way. I had no idea what colour my face was at that moment, but *Completely and Utterly Mortified* wouldn't have been far wrong.

The lab we'd sent the clay effigy to told us that yes, the foreign body in the figure's mouth was the tooth of a young adult human. Dr Dodds confirmed that it could be the canine missing from Patsy's mouth. Detective Sergeant Brown was uncharacteristically silent for some time afterwards.

Daphne Reece made an official complaint about continued police presence outside her house. Avril Cunningham, her solicitor, reported that her car had been vandalised while parked outside the same property.

By Sunday evening, we could no longer deny that the men of the town had decided our presence on the streets wasn't enough to keep their children safe. Groups had taken to meeting on corners and patrolling the streets until dark. Invariably, the patrols ended in the pub. There were two large-scale fights in the late hours of Sunday, and five men nursing hangovers and black eyes in the cells on Monday morning. That day's headline: *Sabden – Have the Police Lost Control?*

CID spent Monday interviewing the families and wider social circles of the three victims. Stories were examined, and alibis were checked. In the middle of the afternoon, I heard a rumour that something was happening in the interview room. I thought about slipping down, but before I could pluck up the courage, Sharples and Tom appeared.

'Larry Glassbrook has just admitted lying about his alibi,' the DI announced.

'Which one?' Brown looked up from his desk.

'All three of them.' Tom gave me a nervous glance as the room fell silent. 'He wasn't at home on the nights the three kids went missing, even though he previously told us he was, and even though his wife backed him up.'

More than one person was glancing my way. They all knew I lodged with the Glassbrooks.

'Where, then?' Woodsmoke asked.

'Black Dog, so he claims now,' said Tom.

'Why lie?'

'Because he wasn't in the bar with all the other punters, who could confirm his new alibi – he was upstairs having extra-maritals with Beryl Donnelly.'

There was silence in the room. Beryl Donnelly was married to Ted Donnelly, the pub owner, and was the mother of John Donnelly, Luna's friend.

'Could be true,' someone said. 'Larry's always been a shagger.'

'It could be true,' Sharples replied, 'but we question Beryl Donnelly very carefully, and we keep an eye on our friend Mr Glassbrook.'

If that wasn't enough excitement for one day, the evening papers came out and the *Manchester Evening News* led with a major scoop for them. And a serious problem for us. *Patsy: Buried Alive?*

'Who the fuck has been talking to the press?'

I'd never seen Rushton so mad. The glass in his office door trembled as he slammed it. More than one person glanced my way.

Rushton seemed to take in the entire room without moving his head. 'Anyone? Has anyone at all spoken to any journalist since we found Patsy?'

'Florence?' said Sharples.

I got to my feet. 'Two occasions, sir,' I said, knowing my face was at *Centre of Attention*, deepening rapidly to *Bollocking From Boss*. 'The same man approached me. I told him nothing and I reported it both times.'

Rushton nodded, but eyes lingered on me as he turned away.

There were even more people on the street that evening, more call-outs to settle trouble and another full set of cells on Tuesday morning. As I drove into work, the news headlines said, *Sabden: Police Say All Children At Risk*, and also, *Stephen and Susan: Have We Failed Them?*

Everyone was tense and short-tempered. People swore more than usual, snapped at colleagues, and I don't think it was the heat.

I was told to put my uniform back on and start visiting schools, including the primaries. I wasn't a good public speaker, too apt to stutter, speak quickly and blush – *Reluctant Public Speaker* – but I wrote out a speech and practised at home. I made more clay figures and learned how to fire them in Sally's oven.

On Wednesday morning, when the headlines said, *Police: Still No Clues*, I took five of my clay models into work and arranged them on the window ledge. A fish, a rabbit, a bird, a cat and, in my imagination at any rate, a human figure.

'Fuck's this, *Blue Peter?*' Detective Sergeant Green said, but they took my point. Whoever had made the clay picture we found with Patsy had some skill as a potter. That same day, the tissue analysis from Patsy's post-mortem came back negative for benzo-diazepine and morphine but positive for alcohol. The toxicologist had tested for several other sedative drugs, but all were negative. As it was highly unlikely that alcohol alone could have kept Patsy unconscious for the length of time she'd have had to lie in the casket before and during the funeral, the toxicologist's findings strengthened the theory that she'd been put in it after burial.

But the unsoiled state of her clothes was still bothering me. As was Dwane's insistence that the grave hadn't been touched. Glassbrook and Greenwood carried out two funerals that week. I made an excuse at the station and slipped out to watch them both, from the time the cortèges left the parlour to the interments in nearby churchyards. I watched everything the funeral directors and staff did, and I thought long and hard.

The super introduced compulsory overtime and put me back on the beat. 'You've done a good job, lass,' he said, to my surprise. 'And Jack will still want to use you, but for the next few days, I want as many visible bobbies as I can get.'

So I went back to walking the streets, noticing that children didn't seem to play on corners so much, and that even the adults seemed to be hurrying home, glancing nervously around.

Focus had shifted, I realised, from a need to find Patsy's killer to the fear that another child was going to be taken.

34

Saturday 28 June 1969

On my first morning off in thirteen days, I slept in. Breakfast was served later at weekends in the Glassbrook house, but I'd missed it all the same.

The kitchen was empty but for Cassie. She was sitting at the central table, her pale hair falling over her face, polishing what looked like jewellery.

'Pretty dress,' I said, although I really thought the white cheese-cloth creation made her look like a cut-price, hippy bride. 'What are you up to?'

'Cleaning my crystals,' she told me.

While I waited for the kettle to boil, I watched her. It wasn't jewellery on the table in front of her but stones, of a pale, gleaming luminescence. Four of them were a silvery white, the other a soft pink.

'What do you clean them with?' I asked, more to make conversation than because I was remotely interested. I'd always found Cassie's vague dreaminess a bit annoying.

'Silk and moonlight,' she told me.

I made a point of peering out of the window. No moon that I could see.

'I leave them outside my window tonight,' she said. 'And to-morrow night too. It's the full moon.'

'I haven't seen your dog for a while,' I said. 'Were you minding it for someone?'

'What dog?' Her eyes were wide, her mouth clasped in a tiny pout. She started to twirl a strand of pale hair round one finger.

'The one I found locked in your shed a couple of weeks ago.'

'Was that the night you dug up the grave?'

I turned away, ostensibly to make tea.

'Or do you often steal my father's keys and let yourself into his private shed?' she asked the back of my head.

I turned back round, not liking the sly smile that was hovering around her mouth.

'If I come across it again, I will have to tell your parents,' I told her. 'You can't keep a dog locked up in a shed. It's cruel.'

'They won't believe you.' She stared at me without blinking for several seconds. I remembered her sleepwalking habit, and that it is supposed to be a sign of emotional strain in children.

'Cassie,' I said, 'is there anything worrying you?'

Her silver-grey eyes narrowed. 'Yes, Flossie,' she said. 'Children my age are being kidnapped and murdered, and the police haven't a clue what to do about it.'

'I meant anything at home. Anything you might feel uncomfortable telling your parents.'

'I tell my parents everything. I'll tell them what you just asked me.'

I stirred the teapot and poured a mug. I found milk in a jug and added it, annoyed to feel my hand shaking. Even more annoyed that I jumped when she spoke again.

'It's considered very unlucky around here to see a black dog. Are you sure it was a real dog, not a grim?'

I'd spent much of the last couple of weeks reading up on all aspects of the supernatural and I knew about the legend of the ghostly black dog that was supposed to be a harbinger of death.

I wasn't going to admit as much to Cassie, though.

'I've no idea what you're talking about.' I carried the spoon to the sink and rinsed it, put the milk jug back in the fridge.

'Or a familiar? Seriously, Flossie, did you actually touch it?'

'Cassie, you're being tiresome.'

I took my tea out into the garden. Even so early in the day, the sun was warm. From Larry's workshop I could hear the shrill buzzing of a power tool, which sounded like a trapped insect. I wandered over to the furthest corner, unfolded Sally's deckchair and sat down.

I drank tea, felt the sun hot on my face and watched the bees zipping in and out of the hives, filling the air with their low-pitched purring, just as the peach-coloured roses that hung over the nearby apple tree filled it with scent. The insects danced as they came back in, shimmering their tiny, plump bodies, clustering round each other as though in deep conversation.

I felt my eyelids start to droop. I hadn't finished my tea, but it seemed a good idea to put it down.

I woke to find myself in shadow. Something told me I'd only nodded off momentarily, but I was no longer alone. Six people surrounded me, one of them, the tallest, was between me and the sun.

One of them had a hand-held transistor radio. The Lulu hit 'Boom Bang-a-Bang', which had won the Eurovision Song Contest a few months earlier, was playing, albeit tinny and distorted.

'What are you doing, Luna?' I'd recognised her red hair out of the corner of my eye. The boy in front of me, blocking out the sun, was John Donnelly. I glanced round to see Richie Haworth, Tammy Taylor, Dale Atherton and a black girl whom I didn't know. These were Patsy's friends, the last people to see her alive, apart from her killer.

John's eyes dropped to his boots. They were old and scuffed, the leather splitting in places. 'We were wondering whether you could tell us anything about Patsy.'

'We had a lot of information come into the station after you did your reconstruction,' I said. 'It will take time to go through it all.'

The children exchanged glances.

'Are we in danger?' said Luna, and I knew she wanted me to say yes.

I wanted to say yes.

'Not if you're sensible,' I said instead. 'Not if you stay in groups.'

'My mum saw Patsy's nan in town this morning,' said Tammy. 'Patsy's body is going to be moved to the chapel of rest in Burnley this afternoon.'

I bent down to retrieve my mug. 'You know more than I do,' I said. 'I hadn't heard that.'

'We're going to go and see her,' said Richie Haworth. 'We're going on the bus this afternoon.'

'Really?' I looked at John, who seemed the most sensible of the group. 'Well, that's up to you. But I'd think carefully if I were you. Dead bodies are never pleasant to look at.' I pushed myself up and got to my feet. 'Enjoy your Saturday,' I told them. 'Whatever you plan to do with it.'

'Miss Lovelady!'

I'd barely gone ten yards when John Donnelly came striding after me. 'You've been at the school a lot,' he said.

I waited.

'Asking lots of questions, about Patsy and the other two. And about all their friends.'

'Yes, that's right. I have.'

'So I was wondering whether you think anyone at the school is responsible.'

'No, of course not. But if Patsy, Stephen and Susan were all taken by the same person – and we don't know that for sure, but if they were – then there will be something that links them. Do you know what I mean by a common denominator?'

He gave a half-nod. 'It's a mathematical term,' he said.

'It also means a feature shared by all members of a group. Patsy and the others will have had something in common. And whatever it is will point to who took them.'

'Have you found anything?'

I hadn't. I'd spent hours gleaning every last bit of information on the children's lives that I could find. I'd spent more hours inputting it onto my various charts and far, far more staring at it, waiting for something to strike me. 'Not yet,' I said. 'But if something's there, I'll find it. I'll see you, John. Take care.'

I went inside and he went back to his friends. They formed a tight circle by the hives, heads together, occasionally glancing over to the house.

'They're up to something.'

Cassie had crept up on me. She was peering over my shoulder, uncomfortably close.

'They're kids,' I said. 'Kids are always up to something.'

'I heard Luna on the phone last night.'

Over Cassie's shoulder I could see the children again. They were climbing over the wall onto the open moor.

Cassie said, 'I heard her say "Patsy" three times. She was talking to Unique Labaddee, that black girl. Her family are well weird.'

'Unique Labaddee? Is her mother called Marlene?'

'I think so. Runs a flower shop on the main road.'

'Anything else?' I hated myself for asking.

She shook her head. 'No, but it was all very cloak and dagger.'

I rinsed my mug and left Cassie in the back kitchen. I didn't like her. I didn't like her habit of sneaking around, and I was sure the teenagers were up to nothing more sinister than a gruesome bit of thrill-seeking at their dead friend's expense. Even so, when I got to my room, I looked out of the window. The children were some distance away, heading not into town but towards open countryside. They seemed to be making for the Hill.

There'd been six of them in the garden. I wasn't sure, but I thought I could only see five now. They were too far away, though, for me to make out who might have left the group.

I remembered the lights I'd seen the night I found Patsy. It couldn't have been the kids: they'd all be in bed. So why were they heading up there now?

The Well Head Road, single-track in most places, ran round Pendle Hill, taking in Sabden on the south, Barley to the east, moving north to run through Downton and then Pendleton on the west. Halfway between Sabden and Barley, a public footpath called Lych Way led up towards one of the steepest but shortest elevations. If the children were heading up the Hill, that was the most likely way they'd gone. It would also, I was reasonably confident, take them past the place where I'd seen lights.

By the time I got to Lych Way, there was no sign of them. I'd walked quickly, but it had taken time to find my boots and a sweater, and they were all young and naturally fit. I followed the sycamore-lined track past pigs and chickens, and a noisy, but restrained, collie dog. After half a mile or so, the path forked at a point where a great, flat stone seemed to be embedded in the earth. Lych Way went on, no longer a track accessible by vehicles, across a field and through a gap in the next stone wall.

Lych Way was ringing a bell. I had a feeling I'd read some reference to it, but it was eluding me.

I couldn't see the children but was pretty certain they were still ahead of me. I turned the other way and started to climb. The way up was easy to follow, much of it lined with stones, but very steep. It was a bit like scaling an endless flight of stairs.

The grass around me was yellow after the recent heatwave, and some of it had scorched where hill fires had broken out. I passed bilberry bushes and heather of several shades coming into bloom. Sheep were everywhere.

When I judged I was about halfway up, the path turned and I stopped to get my breath. From this vantage point, I could see Lych Way again, a darker track of grass following the stone wall of field after field, perfectly straight, leading through stiles, and even over a slender stream. After half a mile or so, it led into a copse of trees through which I thought I could see a vague outline of a building.

Lych Way? Lych Way? No, it wouldn't come.

I set off again, and when I rounded the bend, the track widened into a flat area. A space had either been cut into the Hill or formed from a natural plateau. Stone slabs were visible beneath the grass and bracken. Walls, built from great pieces of blackened stone, disappeared into the bushes. A narrow stream ran close, pooling into a small pond, and then a waterfall, tipping over the escarpment.

People had lived here. On a hill too exposed to suffer any real trees to thrive, there were three good-sized beeches, growing in the shelter of the small cliff. There was even a rose bush, wild but offering the echo of a garden.

In the centre of the space, a large, blackened ring of earth was filled with ash and charred fragments of wood. I'd got the place right, at least, but the children were nowhere to be seen. My foot slid sideways and when I looked down, I saw the stub of a wax candle.

Who brings candles on a hike?

And who had lit a fire, halfway up a moor?

Suddenly, acutely conscious that I was entirely alone and a long way from town, I walked to the edge of the plateau. Still no sign of the children. The ground fell away steeply. This was not a place to lose your footing. I stared down, and it must have been the fact that I hadn't eaten that day that was making me feel dizzy and afraid.

35

Larry was in the garden when I got back, lounging against the wall of his workshop. His hair had been swept up off his forehead with Brylcreem, and his shirt was open several buttons at the neck. As I crossed the grass, he watched me with his eyes half closed.

I was about to give him a tight-lipped smile and walk past when I thought of something. 'Larry, you must spend a lot of your time in graveyards. I mean, some of it at least, in churchyards and cemeteries.'

He blew a smoke ring. 'Some of my favourite places. Lots of quiet corners, not much chance of being disturbed.'

I knew I had to tread carefully. I had not been ordered to interview Larry. 'So hypothetically, if there were reports of graves being disturbed from time to time, you'd hear about it?'

'Nowt hypothetical about it, Flossie. It happens.'

I took a step closer. He removed his cigarette.

'I've looked through files at the station. I can't find any reports of it.'

'Well, you won't.'

'Why not?'

He put his cigarette back in his mouth. 'You interrogating me, Flossie? What if I don't cooperate?'

'Father Edward told me there are important people who don't like anyone rocking the boat. He's scared of them.'

Larry didn't reply.

'Are you scared of them?'

His lip curled. 'Know anything about the masons, Flossie?'

I shook my head. 'Stonemasons?'

'Freemasons. And that's all I have to say on the subject. Look 'em up.'

Freemasons. Tom had mentioned the Freemasons, that Rushton wouldn't join, and that it had made him some powerful enemies.

'Thank you.' I turned away again.

'Fancy a drink tonight?'

I stopped walking. It was a mistake, because suddenly he was right behind me. 'We could have a drive out.' He spoke softly in my ear. 'Barley Mow's not too busy on a Saturday.'

'I'm working.' I could feel him watching me as I walked to the back door of the house. By this time, my blood sugar had plummeted and I was actually a bit shaky as I climbed the stairs back to my room.

I opened the door. For a second I stared, not quite taking it in.

A dog, the same black whippet I'd seen in the shed, was lying on my bed.

In the daylight, immediately below a window, I could see it properly. It looked like an old dog, skinny in the flanks, a little grey around the muzzle. The rims of its black eyes were red, as though it were suffering some minor infection.

'Cassie!' I had little doubt she was behind her bedroom door, listening for my reaction. 'Cassie, get out here now.'

No sound of movement. No doors opened.

'Cassie, get this dog out of my room!'

The dog growled, unnerved by the noise I was making. Without taking its eyes off me, it got to its feet, its ears pinned back, its teeth visible.

'Shoo! Go on, git!' I stood to one side in the doorway so that it had a clear exit. 'Cassie! Sally!'

Nothing. I might be alone in the house but for this black creature.

Are you sure it was a real dog, not a grim?

'Go on, get out of here.'

I wasn't going to touch it. From what I knew of whippets, they were gentle dogs, but this one looked mean. I could see old scars around its head, even the trace of blood below its mouth.

'Yah! Go on.'

Finally, it relaxed and stretched out. Without another glance at me, it leaped from the bed and trotted out of the room. I went to follow it, to make sure it left the house, but it could move quickly and had already reached the bottom of the stairs. When I got to the ground floor, there was no sign of it.

The unusual silence in the Glassbrook house was starting to feel weird. I reached Larry's workshop and banged on the door.

'Larry! You need to come out now.'

He appeared a few seconds later. 'What the fuck?' he said to me. I hadn't heard him swear before.

'There was a dog in my bedroom.'

'A what?'

'Cassie is keeping one, probably a stray, probably without your knowledge. I found it in the shed a couple of weeks ago, and it's been on my bed.'

'Show me.' He pushed past and set off back towards the house.

'Well, it's not there now. It ran out.'

He ignored that, striding ahead, into the house. When we were halfway up the stairs, Cassie appeared from her room.

She yawned and stretched her arms to the ceiling. 'What's going on?' she slurred.

'Florence says there's a dog in her bedroom,' said Larry. He reached the top of the stairs and stood on the threshold of my room. 'Where is it?'

'It ran out – I told you. It was there, lying on the bed, when I got in just now.'

Larry stepped closer to the bed. 'No sign of a dog that I can see,' he said. 'No dog hairs. No mud.' He looked over my shoulder. 'Know anything about a dog, Cass?'

'We haven't got a dog, Daddy,' she replied, opening her grey eyes wider.

'Happy?' Larry said to me.

'No, anything but. I'm not having your children coming into my room and playing stupid practical jokes. This might be your house, but I have a right to privacy and security.' I put my hand on the lock of the door. 'I want a key for this door, today.'

'This is our home. We don't lock our doors.' I turned to see that Sally had crept up the stairs while we'd been arguing. I'd always liked Sally. She'd been nice to me, but she stood now on the top step and I could see that she and Cassie were very alike. The same oval faces and pale grey eyes.

'You heard what my wife said.' Larry leaned against the door frame. 'If you don't like it here, you can find somewhere else.'

Sally didn't demur. When I glanced at Cassie, she had the same sly smile I often saw on Luna's face.

They want me out of here, I realised. They've done this deliberately.

It was a ridiculous thought. The dog had been a mean teenage prank, nothing more, and it was stupid to think Sally and Larry had been complicit, but standing there, faced with their hostile stares, it didn't feel ridiculous.

'I'll leave next Saturday,' I said. 'Unless you want to refund my rent. In which case, I'll go now.' Even as I was speaking, I was thinking, *What am I doing? How can I find another room in even a week?*

'Suit yourself,' said Larry. 'You're a stuck-up cow anyway.'

They all walked away. They hadn't offered to refund my rent. I had a week.

36

Larry Glassbrook was hardly my favourite person by this time. I remembered what he'd said, and after an hour rummaging around in the filing room, I found an old file on the Freemasons of Lancashire. I had only the vaguest idea what the Freemasons were all about. 'Misogynist tomfoolery,' my grandmother had said about them once. 'They do a lot for charity,' Dad had replied. Some sort of nationwide network of an all-male club was the best I could do.

The file didn't help much. Some reports of vandalism and a break-in at the lodge in the western part of town, a newspaper cutting of the superintendent at the time, years before Rushton, attending a black-tie dinner where some of the men wore white gloves, and wide, ceremonial sashes.

There was a map too, showing the location of all the masonic lodges in East Lancashire. I was surprised at their sheer number, and more so at their distribution. The northern area, which encompassed the Pendle Forest, the Hill and the towns of Burnley and Blackburn, contained twelve lodges. The southern and eastern areas, both as big geographically, contained five and four respectively.

Whoever the Freemasons were, there were a lot of them in this part of Lancashire.

When I got back to the CID room, I found Sharples at my desk, staring down at my chart of the missing children. Brown was the only other person in the room.

'I need to add a few things to it,' I said. 'I was working on the duplicate at home last night.'

Sharples nodded absently as Brown wandered over.

'Sir,' I said, 'three different people have told me, or strongly hinted, that graveyards in town get interfered with, but complaints are never investigated because—' I stopped.

'Because what?' Sharples prompted.

'Because there are important people who know that weird stuff happens and who turn a blind eye. Maybe they're the ones who are doing it. And then Larry – yes, I know he's a person of interest, but even so – Larry told me I should look at the Freemasons.'

Sharples and Brown exchanged a look.

'And I did. At least, I tried to. There isn't anything. Except there does seem to be a lot of them round here.'

Both men looked at me without speaking.

They're Freemasons, I thought. *These two are Freemasons.*

Brown stuck out his hand and I flinched, but he was only holding out a pound note. 'Get a receipt,' he said.

'Daphne Reece meets her friends in the Turkish baths most Saturday afternoons,' Sharples told me. 'Get yourself down there. See what you can find out.'

'You want me to interview Daphne Reece in the Turkish baths?' My mind was still reeling from what I'd just learned – guessed – about these two. Was I being ridiculous?

'No, not interview, Lovelady,' Sharples said. 'Don't be simple. Just have a chat. You know, all girls together. I'm not convinced she's told us everything, and I don't like that smart-arse of a solicitor of hers either. You might have more success. She took a shine to you.'

'Turkish baths?'

'Nothing to it,' Brown said. 'You sit around butt-naked and get hot. I go most Wednesday nights. Saturday is ladies' day.'

'You want me to find out if these friends she meets are members of the mysterious coven?'

'It's really not like you to be slow, Lovelady,' Sharples said. 'If you're not up to it, forget it. There's some vomit needs cleaning up in cell three.'

Sabden Public Baths was a large building, with wide stone steps and Roman columns, on the western edge of the town centre. Armed with a ticket, I made for the sign reading, *Turkish Baths, Sauna, Steam Room.* I went a bit nervously, I'd never been in this part of the building before. The door at the corridor's end opened into a large room smelling of female cosmetics and filled with lounge beds.

Only three of the beds were occupied, and I didn't recognise any of the women. One of them was painting her toenails a vivid red; another was winding curlers into her hair; a third was dozing. Just women, or witches?

I'd become a witch-hunter. Had it not been for the events of the morning, I might have laughed.

The sauna was empty, as was the shower room. The scented air of the steam room hit me as I went in, clutching a towel that felt far too small. I could see practically nothing. Even a hand in front of my face would have been blurry, a suggestion of a form in the hot mist. I sank onto the nearest bench.

'And relax,' said a voice from the steam, a deep, melodic voice. 'Breathe in, breathe out.'

There came a sliding noise, an annoyed gasp, then, 'What?' the voice said. 'The woman's obviously stressed. I'm trying to help.'

'I don't know why you imagine everyone wants your help,' said another voice. Daphne's. I'd found her.

'Are you talking to me?' I could barely make out two figures on the bench opposite, about three feet away. I had a sense, though, that there were more than three of us in the steam room.

'Shove some more of the menthol on, will you, Em,' Daphne said.

There was movement on the highest bench, a hissing sound; then the air was full of sharp, piercing menthol, which stung the inside of my nose and forced my eyes shut. I tried to breathe deeply, to relax into the heat, and within seconds an odd lethargy was stealing over me. I leaned back against the warm, damp wall and felt my eyes closing.

'Yes, I was talking to you,' the first voice resumed. It had no hint of an accent, North, South or in between, that I could detect. 'Your distress was quite apparent when you came in.'

'Sorry,' I said, my eyes still shut. 'Difficult day.'

'Not a problem at work, I hope,' said Daphne. 'We need the men and women in blue to be at their best in these troubled times.'

I wondered whether it might be possible to lie down. I didn't think so. I still had the feeling there were several women in the room, some of whom I hadn't yet heard from. I opened my eyes and tried to peer through the steam, but it had thickened, if anything. 'Work is fine,' I said. 'Thank you.' I considered briefly pretending I didn't know who she was, but thought she might see through it. 'Good afternoon, Mrs Reece,' I said. 'How did you know it was me?'

'I caught a glimpse of your hair as you came in,' said Daphne. 'And your voice is quite distinctive, as I've just discovered mine is.'

'I've been telling you that for ten years,' said the first voice.

'This is Avril Cunningham,' said Daphne. 'Darling, this is the charming WPC Lovelady that I was telling you about.'

Avril Cunningham was Daphne's solicitor. We hadn't met. I'd just watched her from behind the mirror.

'Florence,' I corrected her.

'Absolutely. Formalities seem a little forced without clothes,' said Avril. 'So what's troubling you, Florence, dear?'

Sensing an opportunity, I told them about the row at the boarding house, about the annoying teenager, Cassie. When I mentioned the dog, there was a hissing and a muttering from the back of the room, a sense of subdued excitement.

Are you sure it was a real dog, not a grim?

I finished by telling them that I was going to be homeless in a week.

'Well, that won't be a problem,' said Avril. 'There must be any number of houses in town only too happy to rent to a polite young policewoman.'

The steam thickened again and the smell of eucalyptus intensified. It struck me how easy it would be to fall asleep in here, and how dangerous. It really was very hot. It occurred to me the pranksters at work could add *Sweating Like a Pig in a Steam Room* to their colour chart.

'Can we hope for any good news on the murder investigation?' asked Avril.

The correct thing to say, of course, was that we were pursuing several lines of enquiry and that the chief constable or one of his deputies would make an announcement in due course. But I'd been sent here to gain their confidence.

'No,' I said. 'We're at a loss.' I think I even managed to put a tremor into my voice.

'Oh dear, that is worrying,' said Avril. 'We've been doing our best,' she went on, 'but with trouble of this magnitude . . .'

We've been doing our best?

I decided to go for it. 'I hope you don't mind my asking, but are you a member of Daphne's coven?'

'Of course,' Avril replied. 'Although, I wouldn't describe it as "Daphne's coven". Ouch, stop it.'

There was a scuffle, a fumbling in the steam. Avril Cunningham, the solicitor. I had to remember that.

'By any chance do you meet on Pendle Hill? About halfway up the south side, in a clearing where there used to be a building of some sort?'

'Oh, you clever girl!' Daphne said.

'How did you work that out?' asked Avril. 'None of our group would have told you, I'm sure.'

'Not me,' said a third voice, from the back of the room, the mysterious Em, who put menthol on the steam but who hardly spoke. So I'd learned who two of the witches were. Gosh, I was good at this detecting lark.

'I saw lights up there a couple of weeks ago,' I said. 'In the middle of the night. And what looked like a fire. And I was up there today and found the stub of a candle.'

'That's what comes of making friends with a detective,' Daphne said. 'They find out all your secrets.'

'Why do you meet there?' I said. 'It's quite a climb, and in the dark surely it's dangerous? And why do you have to meet in the dark? Why outside? And what on earth is it that you do?'

'That's a lot of questions,' said Avril. 'Have they taught you interview technique yet?'

She meant it as a joke – I could tell from her tone – but it hit home. 'No. I'm not a real detective, just a police constable,' I said. 'I've been sort of co-opted to the team, but I think that might be coming to an end very soon.'

'Nonsense. You're clearly brilliant,' said Daphne. 'And you're right, it is a big climb. We don't meet there every time, just when we have some important work to do. It's a very auspicious place. Almost certainly the site of Malkin Tower. You know what that was, of course?'

I did.

'The home of Old Mother Demdike and her family,' I said, referring to one of the most notorious of the Lancashire witches. 'But nobody is supposed to know where the tower was.'

'Nobody does for sure,' said Avril. 'But those of us who study witch-lore have a shortlist of likely sites and that one stands out for most people. Malkin Tower was almost certainly built for defensive purposes originally, and that site has an excellent vantage point. When it fell into disrepair, who'd want to live halfway up that hill but the poorest of families?'

'And on certain nights, from that spot we get a very clear view of the moon,' said Daphne.

'We're a moon coven,' said Avril. 'We can work at other times, of course, and we have met at noon, sunrise, the daylight gate, but we always have more success when we work with the moon.'

'You keep saying "work",' I said. 'What sort of work do you mean?'

'Magic, of course,' said the voice of Em, and there was something about the way it floated out of the steam that was unnerving.

I was trying to remember what Daphne had told me about witchcraft in the reference library, what I'd read over the past couple of weeks. 'And this magic, this work is done by . . . Sorry, I can't—'

'We use rituals and symbols to provide focus, but generation of energy is key,' said Avril. 'We do that by dancing, chanting and drumming.' No, it was Daphne who was speaking. For a moment she'd sounded so much like Avril. I wondered if they'd swapped places in the steam. I was actually starting to feel a little disorientated.

'Some covens use the sex act to generate energy, but not us. Did you hear drums that night?'

I had. They'd chilled me. 'Very clearly. I think the wind was against you.'

'At the moment of casting, the energy is released,' said one of them. I really wasn't sure which. 'We visualise it floating off to where it is needed.'

'And this works?' I asked.

'Of course it does. You found the poor child that night, didn't you?' said Avril. I think it was Avril. 'Although, we had no means of knowing that it was towards you, Florence, that we were directing our energy.'

It had to be the heat. My head was starting to spin.

'Do you think the proximity would have made a difference?' said Daphne, and I could tell from the lower pitch of her voice that she was talking to the other two now, not to me. 'The fact that Florence was actually at the foot of the Hill, with no physical barriers between us?'

'Interesting question,' said Avril. 'It shouldn't, but we've never had quite such a remarkable success before.'

'Not so quickly, that's for sure,' said Daphne.

'Maybe Florence is a conduit,' said Em.

I had the sense of several women moving closer towards me. And yet there could only be three of them. I'd heard no one else.

'You think the magic you performed on the Hill is the reason I found Patsy that night?' I said.

'Of course,' they replied in unison.

'So why haven't you found Stephen Shorrock and Susan Duxbury?' I didn't mean to sound judgemental, but the idea that I'd acted under the control of these women was ludicrous.

'We've certainly tried,' said Avril. 'All the work we've done since the first child went missing has been to try to trace them.'

'Oh! Oh! I've had a brilliant idea,' said Daphne.

'Law of averages,' said Avril. 'It was bound to happen some-time.'

'I have to get out of here,' said Em. 'I'm burning up.'

I sensed, rather than saw, movement in the room, and then I felt someone's flesh pressing towards mine. I tucked in my legs as a dark shape climbed down from the upper shelf and moved towards the door. As she passed me, I caught a whiff of a woody, earthy perfume I remembered from university. Patchouli. And I saw that she was a West Indian woman. Not Em, then, as in short for Emma or Emily, but the letter 'M'. Short for Marlene.

I'd learned something else too. I now knew who had phoned the station the night of the near-riot at the Perseverance Mill, telling me Patsy's body needed to be burned.

37

'I can't do it,' I said. 'It would be completely unethical . . . Thank you. That looks delicious . . . Besides, you found Patsy without any of her possessions. Can't you do that again?'

Several hours later, I was in Daphne and Avril's house. They lived on the opposite side of town to the Glassbrooks, but in a house of similar size and age. It was stone-built, with high-ceilinged rooms, decorated plasterwork and huge bay windows of old crinkled glass. Their furniture was shabby but comfortable. Books were everywhere, piled high on shelves, tottering on every side-table, even forming strange structural columns on the hardwood floors.

One of the two women was a painter. Landscapes in oils hung on every wall, and there was a smell of turpentine in the house.

Avril, whom I'd met properly in the shower room (making a mental note never again to be formally introduced to someone while naked), was aged around forty, a little younger than Daphne. She had a cloud of dark, shoulder-length hair that not even the steam could flatten. Her face was skeletal, her eyes big and brown, her cheeks so sunken as to make the bones beneath seem visible. When she dressed, it was in flat shoes, tight Capri pants, a close-fitting dark sweater and a black beret.

I liked her. I liked both of them, but granting what they'd asked would put me in a very difficult position.

'Having something that belonged to Stephen or Susan would give such a focus to our work,' said Daphne.

They'd asked me back for supper while we were still in the steam room. Oh, and they'd invited me to live with them. For a couple of weeks, maybe a month or two, until I found somewhere else. I'd rushed back to the station, to check in with Sharples, who gave me the go-ahead to get as close as I could to Daphne and her friends. The sniggering, as I left the room, didn't go unnoticed.

Sharples had been less impressed, though, by my theory that Marlene Labaddee, one of the witches, had phoned the station anonymously the night after we'd found Patsy's body. 'There's dozens of West Indian women in town, Lovelady,' he'd said. 'They all sound the same.'

Avril topped up her own wine glass and then Daphne's. I'd declined all their offers of alcohol. 'When you use police dogs, you have to act quickly, don't you?' she said. 'There's a short period of time when the dogs can pick up a scent?'

'Usually about half an hour,' I agreed. 'After that it gets harder.'

'Well, it's the same with us,' said Avril. 'We found Patsy because the trail was fresh. Susan and Stephen have been missing for longer, so we need extra help.'

I was supposed to be pumping them for information, not the other way round. 'So have you had other successes, with your magic?' I asked. 'I hope that's not a rude question. I never met any witches before.'

They both looked at me and smiled.

'I find it all fascinating,' I said, and felt they could see right through me.

'If you could let us know when a particular search is going on, we could time our meet to coincide with it,' Avril said.

'Yes, give you a bit of a boost,' said Daphne. 'Point you in the right direction. How likely is it that Stephen and Susan are in graveyards like Patsy was? There can only be – what, six of them in town?' She looked at Avril. 'Darling, we could perform a trace ritual in each of them.'

Avril said, 'We avoid graveyards for a reason.'

'Have you healed anyone?' I was trying to remember what I'd read about the Pendle witches. 'Or saved a crop that was blighted by . . .'

They waited, politely.

'Blight?' I wondered if I should quit while I was ahead.

With an air of someone taking pity on a simple child, Daphne said,

'There are three disciplines of witchcraft: healing, divination and magic. I was going to explain in the library, but we got distracted. You'll find all witches are naturally drawn to one of them. Em, whom you met at the baths, is one of our healers. We'd love to have Sally, of course – what a strong team we'd have then – but she's always resisted joining a coven. Some witches prefer to work alone.'

I'd been waiting for the right moment to ask more about Marlene, but this took me completely by surprise.

'Sally? Do you actually mean Sally Glassbrook?'

Sally was a witch? She was a bit odd, granted, and she certainly knew a lot about herbs and plants, but a witch?

'Sally is a very accomplished healing witch,' Daphne said. 'Midwives often are. And Avril has always been drawn to divination. Magic is my thing.'

'Unfortunately, offering a coherent explanation is not,' said Avril. 'Florence, by its very nature, much of our work has to be done alone. Em needs quiet and concentration to study the qualities of plants and to produce the compounds that are most efficacious. I require the same when I'm reading the tarot, or the runes, or the crystals. When we come together as a coven, it is to gain spiritual strength from each other and to perform magic.'

'And if you don't mind my asking, what is it that you're trying to achieve? Apart from find missing children, I mean.'

'Well, when we meet, after the greetings and the opening rituals, we ask if we have any work to do. Someone might say that a friend or relative is ill and we'll work towards getting that person better. Someone might be facing a particularly difficult decision and need guiding in the right way. Someone else might need a bit of luck.'

I thought for a second. 'How about winning the pools?'

'Magic rarely works for that sort of personal gain.' Avril's voice had taken on a disapproving note. 'Nor do we work towards anything negative, anything that might do harm.'

'And the different members of the group have different skills?' I asked. 'Are there more healers than . . . magicians?' I was fishing for more names, and from their polite smiles I could see that they knew that.

'The strongest covens are always the most balanced.' Avril got to her feet. 'Let's take coffee outside.'

'Florence.' Avril put the coffee pot down on the table. 'Are you sure we can't help you? If it's not too rude, your police colleagues don't seem to be getting very far.'

'It's quite apparent there's some dark magic going on,' said Daphne. 'Or at least an attempt at it. The clay effigy, the children disappearing at the new moon. It's obvious you think so too – you're clearly fascinated with the subject.'

'Sorry, what? What do you mean, they disappeared at the new moon?'

The two women looked at each other. 'We thought you knew,' said Avril.

'How can you not know?' said Daphne. 'It's obvious.'

'Not to me. Nobody mentioned new moons. Are you sure? And what does it even mean?'

'You really do have to work on your interview technique.' Avril got to her feet. 'Where will I find the calendar, Daffers?'

'The three teenagers all vanished on or very close to the new moon,' Daphne told me, as Avril disappeared through the back door of the house. 'One could argue it was for purely practical reasons. When there's no moon in the sky, the night will be much darker. Misdeeds go unseen.'

I looked up into the turquoise sky. There was no moon that I could see.

'It will rise at nine thirty-five,' said Daphne. 'One day off full.'

'How do you know that?'

'I'm the supreme witch in a moon coven,' she told me. 'I always know what the moon is up to.'

'She has a calendar.' Avril was back and crossing the patio towards us. 'And you are not the supreme witch. We are a gathering of equals. Here you are, Florence. A lunar calendar.'

The calendar was a colourful affair, its cover filled with animal and plant illustrations. I took it and started flicking through. The new moon in March was on the eighteenth day of the month; Susan had gone missing on the seventeenth. In April, it had happened on the sixteenth, the exact day of Stephen's disappearance. Patsy had gone missing on Sunday, 15 June, again the day of the new moon.

'Why is it relevant?' I looked up to find them both watching me. 'I know you think it is.'

Neither spoke for a moment – at least, not out loud – but their eyes moved quickly, in unison, as though there was some sort of unspoken conversation taking place that I just couldn't tune into.

Eventually, Avril said, 'Witches believe that their work is more likely to be successful if the phase of the moon is advantageous.'

'If we were to perform dark magic,' said Daphne. 'Which we never have, by the way, it would be at the new moon.'

'You think the children are being taken for some sort of dark magic?' I said.

'You found a clay effigy stuck with thirteen pins of blackthorn,' said Avril. 'What more evidence do you need?'

'The original Louvre Doll was part of a love spell,' I said. 'Although, when I read that spell, I thought it sounded more like slavery. A dead slave wouldn't be much use to anyone.'

Daphne's eyes flashed.

'Did you think of something?' I asked her.

'No, dear, I'm far from my best after a drink or two.'

'Or three,' Avril said.

'If someone's performing dark magic, then who?' I asked. 'Is there another coven in Sabden?'

Neither woman spoke.

'Is there?' I repeated.

Avril reached out and put a hand on Daphne's. 'Not that we are aware of,' she said. 'Goodness, is anyone else getting chilly?'

I left Daphne and Avril's house shortly after nine-thirty, promising to think about their offer of staying in the spare bedroom. Before I left, Daphne took hold of my hands and held them up for inspection.

'You have lovely hands, my dear,' she said. 'In fact, you are a very lovely young woman. But you should make a little more of yourself. A bit of lipstick, maybe some nail varnish.' She dug into her pocket and pulled out a small bottle. 'Here,' she went on, as Avril shook her head. 'Cutex Frosted Ice, in Rosehip. If it's men you want to attract, these little superficialities are important.'

'I think Prince Charles is still free,' Avril said.

'I don't,' I said. 'I'm focusing on my career right now.' And then I had a vision of Tom Devine, lounging drunkenly in the passenger seat of his own car. 'Really, I don't. But it's very kind of you. Thank you.'

It was almost a quarter to ten when I got home, and sure enough, the moon had appeared on the horizon, a beautiful almost-full globe of pale gold.

I turned my key slowly, trying to be quiet. I really didn't want another confrontation that day. As it turned out, I was wasting my time. The second I opened the front door, Sally appeared from the kitchen, Larry close on her heels.

'Flossie, thank God,' she said, rushing towards me. 'Luna's missing.'

38

We were in the Glassbrook kitchen. Sally, Larry and Cassie, John Donnelly, whose presence here I didn't understand quite yet, and me. I'd made the others sit down round the table, mainly to stop them rushing around the house and yelling all at once in my face.

They hadn't called the police. They'd been on the point of it when I'd opened the door.

'OK, tell me,' I said to John. 'Make it quick and clear.'

'We had a row,' he said, and from the faces of the other three I knew they'd heard this already.

'What about?' I said.

'Is that important? Sally was even paler than usual, and I could see the effort she was making to stay in her seat.

'Yes,' I said. 'What about?'

'About nothing. It was stupid. But she walked off.' John turned to Sally. 'I shouldn't have let her go. I'm really sorry.'

'Concentrate,' I snapped. 'What time was this, and where?'

He gave his head a tiny shake, as though to clear it. 'Thirty minutes ago,' he said.

It was now nine forty-seven.

'At the bottom of Wraithe Road,' John went on. 'I followed after ten minutes. I thought I'd keep her in sight, but I couldn't catch up with her.' He took a deep breath, as though he'd sprinted some distance. He was holding down panic. They all were. Even Cassie's hands were trembling.

'What time did John arrive here?' I asked.

Larry had lost his usual swagger. Even his hair seemed to have flopped, lying limp and greasy on his forehead. 'Can't say for sure,' he said. 'I saw him in the garden when I got back. He was looking up at Luna's window.'

'He does that a lot,' said Cassie.

'I was throwing pebbles up,' John said. 'Tiny ones, not enough to do any damage. I just wanted to get her attention, make sure she was all right.'

'It would be about nine-thirty,' said Sally. 'I was watching *Mission: Impossible* and the ads were on.'

'Where had you been?' I asked Larry, as Sally gave a whimper of frustration.

'Pub,' Larry said.

I left it at that. We could check later. 'Did you check her room then?' I said to the group in general. 'When John appeared?'

'I did,' said Cassie. 'I went to tell her her boyfriend was outside again, but she wasn't there.'

'Any sign that she'd come back? Her coat? Bed ruffled?'

Cassie shook her head.

I stepped towards the door. 'Right. I'm going to call the police. All of you stay here and think where she might have gone after she left John. Friends, neighbours, secret places. Cassie, get a pen and make a list.'

I used the phone in the hallway to contact the station. I figured it would take fifteen to thirty minutes before the police arrived.

'I need permission to search the house,' I said when I got back to the kitchen. 'Sally, come with me, please. Larry, take a torch and make sure she isn't in your workshop, or the garden shed, or anywhere in the garden. Cassie and John, carry on thinking. I want that list when I come back down.'

Sally and I started in Luna's bedroom. The bed was neatly

made. The window closed, the curtains open.

'I tidied up after she went out,' said Sally. 'She's hopeless about putting clothes away. I don't think she's been back.'

I couldn't disagree: the room looked undisturbed. 'You didn't hear her come in?' I asked.

'No, but the TV was on, and we weren't expecting her back till ten,' Sally said. 'She promised us she wouldn't leave the others.'

From Luna's room we went up, checking the attics, which were full of boxes and possible hiding places, but that was a search I could safely leave to the dogs. We looked in every room on the first floor, including my own, and then the ground floor. When we got to the kitchen, Larry had arrived back before us.

'Nothing.' He put the torch on the table.

At that moment, we heard a car crunching over the gravel and saw the flickering of a blue light in the darkness.

'Tell me what you and Luna argued about,' I said to John Donnelly an hour later, when he and I were in the interview room, together with Tom and the duty solicitor.

'I told you, it was nothing.' In the last hour, the self-assured, rather arrogant boy I knew had become a nervous, jumpy mess. He'd been picking at the loose skin around his thumbnail until he'd made it bleed. He kept sighing, and jiggling about in his seat.

'Nobody argues about nothing,' I said. 'Luna must have thought it important enough if she was prepared to walk home alone. Especially given everything that's been happening lately.'

He looked past me, at the two-way mirror. 'Who's behind that?' he said.

Most people didn't realise the significance of the mirror.

'I'm not sure,' I said, truthfully. 'Maybe no one. We're pretty busy at the moment.'

He ran a hand over his hair, in a gesture that reminded me of

Larry. 'What about Luna's parents? Will they be there?'

I shook my head. 'Definitely not. Mr Glassbrook is out with the search party, and Mrs Glassbrook is at home with Cassie. We wouldn't let other witnesses hear what you had to say anyway.'

'Tell you what.' Tom got to his feet. 'I'll check.' He vanished, reappearing a few seconds later. 'No one,' he said. 'Everyone on duty is out and about, looking for Luna, which is what we should be doing, so why don't you just answer WPC Lovelady's question, John, and then we can move on?'

John dropped his eyes to the table between us. 'She wanted me to have sex with her,' he said.

I didn't look at Tom. 'And that was a problem?' I asked.

John glanced up. 'She's only fifteen. Her dad would kill me.'

'I'm sure he would,' said Tom. 'I'm also sure most lads of fifteen wouldn't let the threat of an angry dad put them off if sex was on offer.'

John glared at Tom. 'She's only fifteen. It's illegal.'

'Very sensible,' I said.

'She's been on at me for a while.' John focused on me now. 'I've been saying we should wait, but then she started going on about how I didn't fancy her. She accused me of wanting to chuck her and go with Tammy instead. And then she wanted to know if I'd had sex with Patsy because—' He stopped.

'Because everybody knew Patsy was keen on you,' I said.

'I never did, I swear.'

'What about Susan Duxbury?' Tom asked. 'Did you have sex with her?'

John's lip curled in distaste. 'I hardly knew her.'

'Same class. You're a good-looking lad. You must have lots of girls interested. Don't tell me you're turning them all down?'

John's eyes went past me again to the mirror. 'Is it still empty through there?'

'As far as I know,' I said. 'What is it you're worried about saying?'

'What I tell you, who else has to know?'

'It depends how relevant it is to the investigation,' I said. 'If it's something about Luna, you really shouldn't keep it to yourself.'

He ran his hands over the lower part of his face. 'It's not about Luna; it's about me. Well, it sort of is about Luna and the other girls. I need you to know there was nothing going on with any of them.'

I had a feeling I knew what John was about to tell us.

'I'm not that sure I'm into girls,' he said. 'Not in that way.'

'What are you trying to say?' Tom said. 'That you're a poofter?'

'Lots of teenagers are unsure about their sexuality.' I wished I could kick Tom without making it obvious. 'I know I was for a long time. It's nothing to worry about.' I tried to smile at John, but his eyes were fixed on his lap. 'Thank you for telling us,' I added.

'Will you tell my dad?' he muttered.

'No,' I spoke firmly. 'And neither will Tom.'

We finished the interview after forty minutes. John went to join his mother in Reception. Tom and I headed back to CID.

'He doesn't know anything, does he?' Tom said.

'I don't think so. But two of his friends have gone missing now. Has he ever been in trouble before?'

We'd reached the stairs.

'Not especially,' Tom said. 'He was given a caution about a year ago for driving his dad's van around the pub car park and clipping another vehicle. No real harm done.'

Rushton was in the CID room when we arrived.

'Right,' he was saying, 'the dog unit have called it a night. No trail at all that they can pick up. Randy's taking charge of the area search. He's lived in that part of town for two years and knows it as well as anyone. He's got fifteen men, and a few of the neighbours have come out too. It's a bit hit and miss, frankly, because she could have been taken anywhere in a vehicle, but we have to be seen doing it. Gusty is leading the house-to-house.'

'We've got officers at the railway and bus stations,' Sharples added. 'They've been there since half an hour after she went missing, thanks to Florence's prompt action. Fortunately, young Elanor is quite distinctive-looking.'

We all turned to the photograph on the noticeboard. A head that seemed a little too big for her thin frame. Huge eyes, long red hair, a pointed chin and over-plucked eyebrows. Sometime tomorrow, that photograph would be on a fresh batch of missing posters.

I'd forgotten that Luna's proper name was Elanor, but remembered Sally telling me shortly after I moved in. Spelled the Tolkien way, she'd said. Not the Jane Austen way and not . . . I couldn't remember the other way. It was all so much harder when the missing child was someone I knew.

The door opened and Brown walked in.

'What have you got, Woodsmoke?' Rushton asked him.

'Got Roy Greenwood out of bed and drove him to the funeral parlour.' Brown pulled cigarettes out of his pocket. 'We checked everything. Three stiffs in the chapel of rest, everything as it should be, no sign of the girl.'

'I want an officer at every funeral parlour in the area first thing on Monday morning,' said Rushton. 'No coffin is nailed shut until we've checked it first. I also want a round-the-clock watch on every graveyard in town. Plain clothes. Discreet. Starting tonight. Not you, Florence – you go home and get a good night's sleep. Some of us need to be fresh in the morning.'

'Sir, I'm very happy to—'

He pointed a finger at me. 'Young women do not work the

night shift while I'm in charge, and they sure as hell don't stake out graveyards.'

Even I knew when to stop arguing.

39

Sally's face looked unnaturally creased, like a crumpled dishcloth that had been left to dry. Without waiting for her to speak, without even closing the front door behind me, I summarised what was happening, what would happen for the rest of the night.

In the darkened hallway, she stepped uncomfortably close. 'Flossie, I'm so sorry about what happened earlier. We didn't mean it. Of course we don't want you to leave. Please don't. At least, not until we've found Luna. And even then, not if you don't want to.'

Well, that was one problem fewer, I suppose. I patted her shoulder. 'I'll stay as long as you need me.'

Sally was hot on my heels as I climbed the stairs. 'Flossie, how can she have vanished?' she said. 'I've been going over and over it in my head. We're more than a mile from where the others disappeared. She had to walk along two streets, both wide, both well lit. Then she was home. If someone snatched her from the garden, I'd have heard.'

I wasn't so sure about that, with the TV on, but nodded.

'And Larry practically came home the same way. Why didn't he see her, or hear her?'

She followed me into my room, pushing the door closed. 'What if they've put her in a coffin? What if she's in the ground, like Patsy? She's claustrophobic. She'll be losing her mind.'

'She isn't.'

I told her about the contact we'd made already with funeral parlours, what we were planning to do the next morning. 'There's no chance of her being put in a coffin, Sally. She won't get anywhere near one.'

'They'll dig a grave up, like they did with Patsy.'

'No, they won't, because every churchyard in the area is being watched. Starting now.'

Sally threw back her head and wailed. I stepped closer and put my arms around her. She clung to me.

'Larry's having an affair,' she wept into my shoulder. 'That's where he was tonight. While our baby was being abducted by a monster, he was screwing that tart.'

What I wouldn't give to be staking out a graveyard right now.

'What tart?' I said, before correcting myself. 'I mean, who?'

She sniffed hard. 'Beryl Donnelly, John's mum.'

As gently as I could, I pulled away. 'I'm really sorry about that, but we need to concentrate on finding Luna right now.'

Sally sniffed again. I took it as agreement.

Shortly after midnight, Randy came in, but only to change into warmer clothes. He shook his head at my raised eyebrows and went out again ten minutes later, heading for the churchyard of St Joseph's, on the far side of town. I persuaded Sally to go up for a bath, and while she was gone, purely to keep my hands occupied, I painted my nails with Daphne's polish. Sally came back down and I sat up with her until Larry got home at nearly two in the morning, but no news arrived and he didn't bring any with him.

While Larry poured himself a drink, Sally's head drooped onto the kitchen table and didn't bounce back up again. Larry put his drink down and scooped her up into his arms. I held the door open as he carried her out.

'Get some sleep, Flossie,' he said, as he turned to climb the stairs. 'We're going to need it. Nice nails, by the way.'

I watched him climb the stairs, his sleeping wife in his arms, and thought how strong he was. And also how handsome, even though he'd been awake half the night and must be out of his mind with worry. And how much I wished Sally was wrong about Beryl from the Black Dog, but knowing she wasn't. What man notices a woman's nail polish when his daughter is missing?

Two hours later, after about an hour's fitful dozing, I gave up trying to sleep.

I parked outside St Wilfred's. The pre-dawn sky was a gun-metal grey, and the few trees in the churchyard stood in stark, dark relief against it.

By a winged statue of an angel I stopped and looked at its shadow, a perfect outline on the ground. Turning round, I saw the almost-full moon, almost directly above me. Daphne and Avril were wrong. The abductions weren't just happening at the new moon.

'WPC Lovelady, as I live and breathe,' grunted Tom, from the dark depths of the children's den.

I held up the flask. 'Brought you coffee,' I said. 'And a cheese sandwich. I wanted to do bacon, but I thought the smell might wake the house.'

'Bloody angel.' He was out of the den, stretching, rubbing his cold hands together. He grabbed the coffee with one hand and held out the other. 'Food,' he said.

I gave him the sandwich.

'How are they?' he asked, with his mouth full.

'As you'd expect.'

Tom finished the coffee and held the cup out, before leaning back against the angel statue. 'Bloody spooky here, isn't it? So did you mean it, what you said at the station? About being a carpet-muncher.'

I sighed. 'No. I was trying to show sympathy with the witness. And what does that even mean, anyway?' I held up a hand. 'No, don't tell me – I really don't want to know. I came here to make sure you got a couple of hours' sleep. Go home. I'll take it from here.'

'You heard what the super said. No young woman will do a stake-out in a graveyard while—'

I pointed east, to where the sky's colour was warming. 'The sun'll be up in ten minutes,' I said. 'Go home.'

He turned to leave and then stopped. 'Word to the wise, Florence?' he said, and I knew he was asking my permission to say something I wouldn't like.

I nodded.

'Drop the Freemasons thing.'

We stared at each other.

'Are you one?' I asked.

He gave a short laugh. 'Do me a favour. I'm not old enough, grand enough or rich enough. And before you ask, I don't know anyone who is, but I will tell you one thing. If they're behind this, we may as well give up and go home now. You can't touch those buggers, Flossie.'

He left. I watched the sun come up alone as tears poured down my face. Something was telling me this would be the last day that Luna Glassbrook saw.

40

When the sun was still low, I heard the church gate and looked up to see Dwane coming towards me with a red-and-white-striped mug in one hand. He had a black eye, and his upper lip looked swollen.

'Made you a brew,' he said, when he'd reached me. 'I put two sugars in it. I didn't know whether you took sugar, so I only put two in.'

'Thank you. What happened to you?'

'Couple of blokes outside pub t'other night. Jumped me. Don't know why. I didn't just take it. I fought back.'

'Did you report it?'

'Don't know 'em.' His eyes left mine for a second.

'How did you know I was here?' I asked.

'Saw you walking around. I don't sleep much. Headaches.'

Dwane's head was substantially larger than most. It hadn't occurred to me before that its unusual size might cause him pain.

'Dwane, I know you'll be busy with it being Sunday and everything, but do you have time to let me see your model of the town again?'

'You like small things?' he asked, when he and I were once more in the shed at the bottom of the Ogilvy yard.

'Could you help me find Nelson Street?'

Dwane leaned over and pointed out the place where Patsy had been seen last.

'Do you have anything I can put down there, just so I can fix the place in my mind?'

Dwane crossed the shed to a small, narrow chest against the far wall and pulled open the top drawer. When he held out his hand, it contained nearly a dozen tiny plastic figures.

'How many different colours do you have?'

'Six,' he said, without needing to check.

'I need four. Can you get me four different colours, at least six of each?' Please,' I added, when he didn't move.

'What colours do you want? I've got black, white, green—'

'It doesn't matter. Green. Give me some green ones.'

'I've got pink too. Do you like pink?'

'Anything.' I put a green figure down at the top of Nelson Street, at the point where Patsy had last been seen.

'Red? Blue? Purple? I changed the curtains. Did you see?'

I was putting green figures where sightings of Patsy had been reported. 'What curtains?'

'At your bedroom window. They were lilac before. I've made them blue. And I've put some flowers in the window. Red roses.'

I froze. 'Dwane, did you leave some flowers for me? A couple of weeks ago?'

His eyes dropped.

'Dwane, those flowers had been left on a grave. The card said, *RIP*.'

He kept his eyes down. 'Not like he's going to miss 'em,' he said, after a moment.

Silence. I was on the verge of laughing. RIP? I'd been so spooked.

'OK, we can deal with that later. Can you see what I'm doing? I'm putting figures where the children were seen. I'll use pink for Susan Duxbury. Blue for Stephen Shorrock.'

'What colour do you want for Luna?' he said.

I carried on putting figures on the model. I knew where most of the sightings of the three children had been. I'd have to double-check a few of them, but I knew I remembered enough to make this work. When I'd finished, I stood back.

Dwane said nothing, his eyes going from the model village to me.

'They all vanished from in and around the town centre,' I said. 'Except for Luna.'

I carried on staring, at nearly twenty tiny figures in green, pink, blue and red, each representing a sighting. I let my eyes drift and, when I came back to the moment, I was staring at a cricket green, towards the northern side of town. Two teams were playing, all the players in white, and in front of the pavilion was a small crowd of people.

Dwane stepped closer. 'Do you like cricket? You can come and watch sometime. Lots of families watch.'

'I do like cricket,' I said, thinking it wasn't a complete lie. I'd watched my brothers play a few times, when there'd been nothing else to do. 'It looks like quite an occasion,' I went on, noticing the table of food and drinks, the deckchairs, even bunting strung round the pavilion.

'Every Saturday afternoon,' he said. 'Lots of women come. And kids, but they're no trouble. They come for the free tea. The wives and girlfriends make it. You wouldn't have to, though, not your first time.'

Oh Lord.

'Thank you,' I said. 'But I'm not sure about my shifts yet. I have to work a lot on Saturdays.'

'When the kids go home, we go to the pub,' Dwane said. 'Black Dog.'

The Black Dog was just a couple of streets from the cricket green 'What's this?' I pointed to two large trapdoors immediately in front of the pub.

'Cellar,' he said.

'Of course. For storing beer. Well, I really must—'

'Dates back yonks,' he said. 'They kept prisoners in there before taking them to Lancaster Gaol. You can still see the chains. I can show you, if you like. Landlord lets me go down when he needs help bringing barrels up.'

'I have to get back,' I told him. 'Thank you, Dwane, and for the tea.'

I tried hard, but I couldn't stop him walking me to the car.

All leave had been cancelled for the day, and every serving officer had been told to report for duty. Constables were walking their beats, knocking on doors, peering into outbuildings and even coal bunkers. Others were out searching the parks and surrounding moorland. Patrol cars were stopping all traffic out of the town.

To my frustration, I'd been assigned to stay with the Glassbrook family. I could see the logic, but I was itching to be doing something more productive than babysitting. So, it turned out, were Larry and Sally. Midway through the morning, as rain started to fall heavily outside, they went to join the search, leaving me alone with Cassie.

She denied having any homework. There was nothing she wanted to watch on television. She wouldn't leave my side, following me from my room to the kitchen, even the lavatory. She checked that the doors, even the windows were locked and started at every unexplained noise. In the kitchen, she wouldn't sit but paced the floor, opening and closing drawers. When she came to the cutlery drawer, she began lifting and dropping the heavy utensils, making a sound like chains rattling.

'Cassie, stop it!'

She jumped and pushed the drawer closed.

'Sorry,' I said. 'I know you're worried. I am too, but we have to keep occupied. Haven't you anything to read? Piano practice?'

'Can we look at your charts?' she said.

'Which charts?' I asked, although I had a feeling I knew.

'The ones in your bedroom.'

I raised my eyebrows. I'd made a point of putting my charts away every day before I left for work, on the top shelf of the wardrobe, under my piles of sweaters. She couldn't have seen them unless she'd been snooping.

'Luna found them,' she said defensively. 'She was always going in my room too.'

It was no time for a lesson in morality. I nodded my agreement and Cassie sprinted from the room to fetch them.

I started with the funeral chart, unrolling it so that we could see all sixty-six rows, one for each of the burials that had taken place in and around Sabden that year. I'd made seven columns headed *Date, Time, Name of Deceased, Gender, Age, Funeral Director, Coffin/Casket* and *Cemetery*.

'Where do you even begin?' Cassie looked dismayed, as though she'd expected the answer to appear magically once she and I looked together.

'Well, the starting point is always what we know for sure,' I said. 'We know that Patsy was found in this grave.' I pointed to the listing on Monday, 16 June, of Douglas Simmonds, in a casket, buried at St Wilfred's, at 10.30 a.m., by Glassbrook & Greenwood. As I did so, I remembered that Cassie was only sixteen. I should not be talking to her about the possibility of her sister being buried alive.

She nodded at me to go on.

'So I looked at other graves in St Wilfred's,' I said. 'But there have been nearly a dozen this year, and only one of them was a casket burial.'

'It has to have been a casket.' Cassie was scanning the rows. 'There wouldn't be room in a coffin.'

'Exactly,' I said. 'So I ruled out all the coffin burials on the chart. 'Unfortunately, that still left over twenty.'

She looked up, as though startled by an idea. 'How would they know? Whoever took Patsy, the same people who've got Luna, how would they know whether it was a coffin or a casket in the grave they were planning to use?'

'Good question,' I said. 'We think they could only have done it by watching funerals, by hanging around outside funeral parlours when the hearses left. That's another reason why we think we have to look in recent graves.'

'Someone hanging around funerals would be noticed,' Cassie said. 'That's weird behaviour. My dad would spot that: he doesn't miss a thing. I think it's someone whose job involves funerals.'

'What do you mean?'

'Someone who works for a funeral parlour would know whether it was a coffin or a casket. The vicar or priest would know. The man who digs the graves would know.'

With an uncomfortable twist in my stomach, I remembered that Dwane was employed to work in other churchyards apart from St Wilfred's. He dug most of the graves in Sabden.

'Twenty caskets.' Cassie was tapping each casket burial as she came to it. 'Why can't you look in them all? Why have you waited this long?'

'The Home Office would never give us permission to open all those graves without something more to go on,' I said. 'We have to narrow it down a bit.'

'So you take out all those places that are closed at night.' Cassie's voice was getting higher and more shrill. 'The cemetery on

Duckworth Street only has one gate and it's locked at sunset. No one can climb over a wall with a dead body.'

My respect for Cassie was growing. 'It's very unlikely but not impossible,' I said. 'If it all happened after interment, then Stephen and Susan almost certainly aren't in the cemetery. They could be in any of the church graveyards, though. None of them are locked at night.'

'If she was put in the casket before the funeral, it couldn't have been a funeral in the afternoon,' said Cassie. 'Caskets aren't sealed until a couple of hours before they leave the parlour. People always want to do last-minute viewings if they can.'

'Good point, but nobody really thinks she was in the casket before the funeral,' I said.

Except Dwane.

'You have to consider it, though, don't you? What do you say, keep an open mind?'

'We do.' I gestured at the chart. 'But there are over twenty funerals that were carried out before midday. Again, too many to exhume without something more.'

'What about those that happened soon after the abductions?' Cassie had spotted three lines of text, more or less evenly spaced. The first said, *Susan Duxbury goes missing, Monday, 17 March*; the second, *Stephen Shorrock goes missing, Wednesday, 16 April*; the third, *Patsy Wood last seen, Sunday, 15 June*. 'A grave would be easier to dig up if the ground was still soft,' she went on.

'I thought of that,' I said. 'On the other hand, the recent graves are the most frequently visited by family members. The sexton and churchwardens will keep an eye on them too. Any disturbance would be spotted.'

'It's hopeless, isn't it?' Cassie's face crumpled.

'No,' I said, with more confidence than I felt. 'It's there. We'll find it.' And then, because giving Cassie something to think about seemed to help keep her calm, I swapped the charts. The one that focused on the missing children was much simpler. Just three columns, one for each child.

'You need a new column,' said Cassie. 'For Luna.'

This didn't feel like a good idea to me, but Cassie was thrusting a pencil into my hand, so I took it and then went down the column, firing questions at her. Luna's birthdate. Her class at school. The subjects she took. The school mates with whom she was friendly.

'There's nothing,' she said, when we'd got to the bottom. 'There's not a single thing all four have in common, except school and age.'

She was right, but I didn't want to agree out loud.

'And they definitely weren't friends. Luna wouldn't have been seen dead with Dumpy Duxbury.'

I thought back to pictures I'd seen of a plump Susan. 'What about Stephen?'

'No, they thought he was a weirdo. And that he had BO.'

'Cassie, how do you know this? How do you know so much about them?'

'I don't. I just saw them at cricket sometimes.'

Cricket? I remembered the frozen game in miniature I'd seen that morning. A crowd of admiring wives and children.

'Your dad plays, doesn't he?' I said. 'Do you go and watch?'

'Mum makes us. She says it's a family occasion and we should support it.'

'On Saturday afternoon, is that right? Cassie, I don't suppose you can tell me who's in your dad's cricket team, can you?'

I had no paper to hand: I'd have to write on the chart.

'Apart from Dad, you mean? Mr Butterworth is, but you'd know about him already. And Mr Greenwood, Dad's partner. I think he's chairman of the club.'

'Eleven players,' I said. 'And possibly some reserves. Can you remember any more of them?'

'John's dad's a good batsman, but he's usually too hungover to run,' she said. 'And that creepy dwarf guy.'

That made six. 'What about Mr Wood, Patsy's dad?'

'Oh yeah, him.' She looked at me. 'Shit,' she said.

'Mr Duxbury?' I asked her. 'Mr Shorrock?'

She nodded, her eyes wide and shining.

'And their wives and children would usually come along too?' I said. 'To support the team, and because there's a good tea afterwards?'

She nodded again. 'Flossie, is this it? Is this what you've been looking for?'

I shushed her, rolled the charts and pulled the elastic band back over them.

'I need to use the phone, Cassie,' I said. 'And we should ask a neighbour to come and sit with you. I have to pop into work.'

41

'OK, Flossie, what's on your mind?' Rushton said.

Outside Sabden Police Station, the rain was still pouring down, beating against windows, turning gutters into fast-flowing streams, causing mini-waterfalls from the corners of buildings. The sky had darkened to a flat grey.

A damp chill had settled over the CID room, in spite of the number of bodies gathered round my charts.

'Cricket,' I said. 'You know I've been saying from the beginning that there'll be something that links these children? And that when we find it, it'll point us in the direction of the killer?'

'And you think it's cricket?' Brown pulled a face. 'Do girls play cricket now? I thought it was netball.'

'Not the kids,' I snapped. 'Their dads. According to Cassandra Glassbrook, who's a pretty smart girl, all four of these children's fathers played in the Sabden Weekend Cricket League at the cricket green on Tythebarn Street.'

I could see scepticism on all the faces around me. Even Tom didn't look convinced.

'The Sabden Weekend Cricket League is a family affair,' I said. 'There's always tea afterwards, which the wives and girlfriends make. The children come along too, for the tea.'

No one spoke. Christ, could they not see it?

'That's where he found them,' I said. 'Cricket matches go on for hours, don't they? The team that's batting spend most of the time in the clubhouse, or sitting outside, watching, waiting for their turn. They'll watch the kids playing, get to know them. I think our killer could be someone on the cricket team or some-one who attends the matches regularly.'

Around me, expressions were changing, opening up, as they thought about it.

'You're sure about this?' Rushton said. 'About Susan's dad, Stephen's dad and so on.'

'Not a hundred per cent,' I said. 'We'll need to check, obviously, but—'

'She's right.' Tom's face had turned an odd shade of grey. 'I play in that league. Shit.' He spun on his heel and walked away. At the window, he leaned his lower arms on the sill and dropped his head.

'Question is, who else?' said Rushton. 'Get back here, Tom. We need you for this.'

'At least eleven,' I said, as Tom straightened up. 'Maybe up to twenty. The point is, our man will be one of them.'

'Who's the secretary?' said Sharples. 'He'll know who's in the league.'

'Beryl,' said Tom. 'Beryl Donnelly. But I know everyone, sir. I can do the list.'

'Better late than never,' Rushton said. 'Florence, sit with him. Keep him on his toes. Make sure he gets them all. Then we can start ruling them out.'

42

Forty minutes later, the blackboard in the CID room listed the names of seventeen men. Those I recognised were Larry Glassbrook, Roy Greenwood, Robert Duxbury, Jim Shorrock, Stanley Wood, Ted Donnelly, John Earnshaw, Reg Bannister and Dwane Ogilvy. Also, I noticed with a start, a Charles Labaddee, who I guessed must be Marlene's husband. Tom Devine and Randall Butterworth were on it because Tom had insisted. In between were five names I didn't know. Interviewing all of them was to take priority that day.

Tom and I were tasked with talking to Roy Greenwood.

We'd thought we already had every crime reporter in the North of England staying in town, but the number seemed to have increased at the news of another missing child. Several cars we didn't recognise were parked outside the station, and men in raincoats and trilby hats were hanging around the front entrance, chatting, smoking, stopping everyone who came out.

Tom and I used the back entrance. While Rushton hadn't said anything in my hearing, I knew he had to be regretting his decision to televise the reconstruction of Patsy's last movements. I said as much to Tom as we climbed into his car.

'We wouldn't have found Patsy if we hadn't done the TV appeal,' he said, in an unusually flat voice. 'Or should I say you wouldn't?'

He drove fast out of the station car park. We tore round the corner and raced along the main road. When we were almost at the market square, we ran a red light.

I sat still and silent, conscious of everything that wasn't being said, and wishing someone else had thought of the cricket connection. Whatever I did, it seemed, I made people dislike me.

We didn't have far to go. Greenwood lived on the main road, not far from the funeral parlour. On the outside, the grime-stained stone house was large but nondescript: two storeys, plus an attic and a cellar. Tall, narrow windows with lace curtains hung in each. The roof was steeply sloping, its black tiles stained by pigeon droppings. The doorbell chimed four times, we waited, and then Roy Greenwood, dressed in his customary dark suit, peered down at us.

'Officers,' he said, not looking at all surprised.

Tom held up his warrant card. I did the same.

'Sorry to disturb you on a Sunday, Roy, but we'd like a word,' Tom said.

Greenwood's haughty expression softened. 'About Elanor, of course. Mother and I were awake long into the night. Please come in.'

'Were you out searching, Mr Greenwood?' I asked, as we followed him down the dark hallway.

'No, I never leave Mother at night. She has bad dreams.'

The room Greenwood led us into was large. Four armchairs were placed round a central hearth, in which a fire blazed. The chairs were upholstered in a dark green fabric, protected by antimacassars. In front of the window was a baby grand piano, as black and shiny as Greenwood's hair. It held at least a dozen silver-framed photographs.

In a chair by the fire sat the tallest, thinnest woman I'd ever seen. Her head and shoulders rose above the high back of the armchair, while her legs stretched out in front of it. Her black dress and cardigan seemed to sag, as though held up by stuffing, rather than by a corporeal person. Her eyebrows had been drawn on, and the left didn't quite match the right. Bright peach lipstick was streaked across where her lips should have been. She looked like a child experimenting with make-up for the first time, except for her deeply lined skin and the endless folds of her neck. Through the soft shade of lavender that was her hair, I could see a scabbed and flaking scalp.

She looked a hundred years old.

'Mother, these are Detective Constable Devine and WPC Lovelady. Officers, my mother, Grace Greenwood.'

Mrs Greenwood extended her trembling right hand and I noticed a small cut-glass tumbler with amber-coloured liquid on a table by her side.

Tom took her hand, and for a weird moment I thought he was going to bend to kiss it. 'I'm very sorry to disturb your Sunday, Mrs Greenwood,' he said. 'But I'm sure you understand we have to do everything we can to find young Elanor.'

Her eyes glistened, and her garishly painted mouth twitched in what I thought was a smile. It was probably a smile. Tom was the sort of man old ladies would naturally warm to. She didn't acknowledge me.

'Dark times,' said Roy Greenwood. 'Please have a seat. We don't serve alcohol in this house, but perhaps I can bring you a glass of cordial?'

I could smell spirits in the air and wondered why he was lying.

'Not for me, thank you,' and, 'No, thank you,' Tom and I spoke in unison.

We sat down carefully. There was something about this room that intimidated movement. Roy and his mother waited, watching us with identical brown eyes. She raised a lace-trimmed handkerchief to wipe away a tear.

'I'm going to come straight out with it because time is of the essence,' Tom began, 'and ask you where you were, Mr Greenwood, yesterday evening between the hours of nine o'clock and midnight.'

Greenwood's eyes closed briefly, as though determined to remain calm in the face of indignity. 'I was here,' he said. 'We listened to the radio. Mother prefers it to the TV. Her eyesight isn't what it was.'

'May I ask what you listened to?' I said.

'*Saturday Night Theatre.*' Mrs Greenwood's voice was low and smooth, without the harsh grate heard so commonly in aged voices. 'Sybil Thorndike and William Ingram in a new production of *Night Must Fall* by Emlyn Williams.'

'Mother loves the theatre. She was an actress before she married.'

I wasn't surprised. There was something about the upright posture, the regal turn of the head that suggested royalty. Or the ability to fake it.

'We switched off when the weather forecast came on at ten o'clock,' said her son. 'We didn't stay up to listen to it. The rain this morning rather took us by surprise.'

'And what did you do at ten o'clock?' asked Tom.

Greenwood looked affronted. 'We went to bed. I'm a church-warden. I have to be up early on Sunday.'

'Just to be clear, you didn't leave the house at all yesterday evening or last night?'

'I think I went into the garden at one point, to see if the cat was anywhere around.'

I turned to look at the radio. 'This is Chopin, isn't it?' I said. 'Do you play, Mrs Greenwood?'

'It's the Prelude in C sharp minor,' she said. 'We've been looking forward to it.'

So much for my charm offensive.

Tom cleared his throat. 'Good game I thought yesterday, Roy. Nice catch for the fourth wicket.'

Greenwood sat forward as though about to get to his feet. 'Are there any more questions?' he said. 'Mother hates to miss a concert.'

Tom said, 'I had to leave early. I don't know if you noticed. My wife had a family thing. I missed tea. I was wondering if Luna was there.'

Greenwood frowned. 'Surely you've asked the Glassbrooks this? Larry was playing yesterday. He'll know whether his family came with him or not.'

'We're asking everyone,' Tom said. 'Do you remember seeing Luna?'

'Yes, I think I do, now you mention it. She arrived with a group of young people at about four o'clock.'

'Did you notice anything unusual about her behaviour?' Tom said.

'In what way?'

'Did she seem troubled at all? Did she speak to anyone in particular other than the friends she arrived with? Did anyone – one of the adults, for example – take a particular interest in her?'

'You surely don't suspect someone at the cricket club?' Greenwood said.

'A lot of people go to watch the matches,' I said, thinking back to the group of spectators on Dwane's model town. 'Did you have the usual crowd yesterday?'

'I'd say so, yes,' Greenwood agreed. 'And for that reason when I wasn't needed on the field, I sat in the changing room.'

I waited for Tom to follow up. He said nothing.

'You don't watch the match?' I asked, when the silence was becoming awkward.

'There are no locks on the changing-room door, and the men tend to be very trusting, leaving wallets and watches in their coat pockets,' Greenwood replied. 'When there are so many people around, I sit quietly in one corner of the changing room, reading a newspaper. So I'm afraid I didn't see much of what Luna was up to.'

Tom got to his feet, suddenly enough to surprise me. 'Well, thanks for your time,' he said. 'Very much appreciated. We'll leave you in peace now.'

As the door closed behind us, Tom pulled out a cigarette and leaned against the car.

'Bit abrupt,' I said.

'"Do you play, Mrs Greenwood?"' he mocked.

'What's wrong with that?'

'Gracie Greenwood couldn't play "Chopsticks",' he said. 'That piano belonged to her late husband, who played in the music halls. It's just for show now. And she wasn't an actress; she was a Bluebell Girl.'

'Wow. Really?'

'I've seen pictures. She was sex on two very long legs.'

'Well, I'm glad you've cheered up. Even if it took Grace Greenwood's very long – if varicosed – legs to do it.'

Tom pulled a face. 'I didn't have the hump with you, Florence. I was annoyed with myself. I should have picked up on the cricket connection.'

He dropped his cigarette and stepped on it. 'Jump in,' he said, holding the door open for me. He'd never done that before. 'Is your A to Z of Sabden funerals back at the ranch?'

I waited until he'd joined me in the car. 'Yes. Why?'

He stared straight ahead. 'I know where Stephen and Susan are.'

43

'How'd you get on?' Rushton, I swear, was in exactly the same position in the CID room. He didn't appear to have moved an inch.

'Well, they're both creepy as bats in the bedroom.' Tom walked straight past the boss, throwing his jacket across his desk. 'Where are they, Florence?'

'And? Anything more concrete to add?' Rushton said, as I crossed to my desk and reached for my rolled-up funeral chart. 'Florence?'

'His mother alibis him,' Tom told Rushton. 'For last night, anyway. And they were quite knowledgeable about the programme they'd listened to. Mind you, a copy of the *Radio Times* would soon tell them what was on.'

'You think they were both lying?' I brought the chart over to the table.

'Come on, let's have a look.' He took the chart and flipped off the band. It shot into the air and vanished. 'Got a sec, boss?' he said, although Rushton was close enough to hug him. 'Anyone else free? Florence and I have had an idea.'

We had? I hadn't a clue what he was about to say, but I found paperweights and a stapler to hold the chart down at the corners. Others gathered round.

'First of all, do we agree that Susan and Stephen are probably in a grave somewhere in Sabden?' Tom said. 'Possibly in a nearby village, but most likely here?'

'Not necessarily,' Sharples said. 'They might be nothing to do with what happened to Patsy'

Tom looked round the table, eyebrows up.

'For what it's worth, I think you're right,' the DI conceded. 'The chances are, they're somewhere on this chart of Flossie's.'

'In that case,' Tom said, 'the biggest problem we've had is not knowing when the children were put in the caskets. Whether before or after burial. Until we know that, we can't begin to narrow it down.'

'I thought we decided it couldn't have happened before,' said Rushton. 'Every funeral director we spoke to said it was impossible, that their security was too tight.'

'Yes, that's what they told us,' Tom said. 'Larry and Roy being particularly adamant on that one, probably because if Patsy was put in the casket before the funeral, one of them had to be in on it.'

'They both have alibis,' said Rushton. 'Not the best, I admit, given that Greenwood's is his mother and Glassbrook's his girlfriend, but without something more to go on, an alibi is an alibi.'

'Yeah, well, I've just remembered something that opens it out,' said Tom. 'Which means if Patsy was already in that casket, as Florence's good friend Dwane has always insisted, it wasn't necessarily Larry or Roy who put her there.'

'When you say you remembered something, is it to do with cricket, by any chance?' Rushton wasn't going to let that one go in a hurry.

Tom faced up to him. 'It certainly is, sir. Specifically the changing rooms.'

'Come again?' Sharples asked.

'Tell 'em, Florence,' Tom said.

Huh?

'Roy Greenwood spends a lot of time in the cricket changing

rooms when he's not playing,' I said, stalling for time, because I had no idea where Tom was going with this. 'He doesn't watch the match, or sit outside enjoying the fresh air, because he's a bit worried about security.' I was waffling and any second now they'd know it.

'Exactly,' said Tom. 'Greenwood is worried about security. All the players leave their stuff in the changing rooms while they're playing and he's concerned that valuables are being left unattended. Such as watches, and wallets, and . . .' He turned to me, nodding at me to fill in the gap, which I was as clueless about— Oh Lord, I should have spotted that.

'And keys,' I said. 'Players keep their keys in the changing rooms. And when Roy Greenwood is playing, no one is watching them.'

'You're saying someone nicked Roy or Larry's funeral parlour keys while Roy was on the pitch?' Sharples said.

'We think that's exactly what happened,' said Tom. 'The season's two months old. That's nearly nine Saturdays when our man has had chance to sneak into the empty changing rooms and nick the keys.'

'They'd notice,' said Rushton. 'They'd report it.'

'Maybe,' I said. 'Although I can see Larry not wanting to admit to Roy that his precious parlour keys had gone missing. I can see him quietly having a new set cut.'

'They might not have been nicked,' said Tom. 'A couple of bars of soap, a clever locksmith, how hard can it be?'

'We can check local locksmiths,' Sharples said.

'So the Saturday-afternoon cricket matches not only gave our guy the opportunity to watch and select his victims, it gave him the means to get into the funeral parlour and dispose of their bodies?' As Rushton spoke, I could see some of the tension seeping out of him. 'Well done, you two.'

I opened my mouth again. I wasn't about to take credit for something I hadn't done. Then a thought occurred to me. 'Being able to access the funeral parlour wouldn't necessarily let him know when a casket burial was planned. I'm not sure we're quite there yet.'

'Roy keeps the bookings in a big black book on his desk,' said Tom. He turned to Sharples. 'He has beautiful handwriting too. We spent a good twenty seconds admiring it, didn't we, boss? Anyone could find out about forthcoming funerals just by looking in the book.'

'What about the additional weight?' Brown asked. 'I thought we'd agreed an extra occupant would be blindingly obvious when the coffin was pick up.'

Silence for a moment.

'I'm not so sure about that,' I said. 'Roy Greenwood claimed it would be noticed, but he never carries the coffins. Neither does Larry. Greenwood walks in front of the procession with a black and silver cane. Larry doesn't usually attend funerals at all. The pall bearers are all big men, and there's six of them. They wouldn't necessarily know who was in the coffin, let alone what it was supposed to weigh.'

More than one head nodded in agreement.

'Sorry to piss on the bonfire, but we still haven't solved the problem of the kids waking up and screaming the place down,' said Rushton. 'They all vanished late evening. Whoever took them would have to let themselves into the funeral parlour while it was still dark, so we're talking early hours at the latest. It's still a fair few hours before they were lowered into the graves. I just don't think alcohol alone would do it.'

'And we know none of the conventional anaesthetics was found in Patsy,' Sharples said.

We all fell quiet while we thought about that.

'OK, let's park that one for a minute,' said Rushton. 'Let's just say you're right, Flossie. Let's say they were in the caskets before the burials. Does it help us find them?'

I looked at Tom. He looked back at me. His eyebrows twitched.

'In your own time, love,' Sharples said.

'Yes,' I said. 'Probably.' I picked up a yellow crayon, dark enough to make a mark but pale enough for writing in ink to be seen through it. 'At the very least it helps us narrow it down.' Leaning across the desk, I drew a long, horizontal line through one of the entries on the chart, the listing of the funeral of Douglas Simmonds on Monday, 16 June, at ten-thirty in the morning at St Wilfred's. It was his grave that I'd dug up in the early hours.

'Patsy,' Tom said, with a tight little smile.

If he didn't help me out soon, there was going to be a fresh grave with his name on it. I looked at the chart, then back at him. He gave me an encouraging nod. I looked at the chart again, willing myself to focus. I found the date when Stephen had gone missing. Oh, for—

I leaned further up the table and drew a second horizontal line.

'*Thursday, 17 April, Ada Wright,*' read Tom, who was closest. '*Casket, St Joseph's Churchyard, 10.30 a.m. funeral, Glassbrook & Greenwood officiating.*'

'Thursday, 17 April was the morning after Stephen disappeared.' I smiled at him. I was still going to kill him, though.

'There were four funerals that day,' Brown said. 'Why that one?'

'One of them was in the afternoon,' I said. 'And there would have been a last-minute viewing, or at least the possibility of one. The other two were coffins rather than caskets. Not enough room.'

I moved higher up the chart and drew the third line.

'*Tuesday, 18 March, Winifred Brown, casket.*' Tom did the honours again. '*Duckworth Street Cemetery, 9.30 a.m., Glassbrook & Greenwood officiating.* The only funeral they did that day. And the morning after Susan Duxbury was last seen.'

I turned to the superintendent. 'Can we do it, sir? Can we exhume these two?'

Silence. Then, 'Possible. Yes, on balance, I think so. I think we can probably make the case. But it'll be tomorrow at the earliest. Maybe Tuesday. I may have to send someone down to London to pick up the order.'

'Luna won't live till Tuesday,' I said.

'It won't help us find her anyway,' Tom said. 'We've already made it clear we're watching every funeral parlour. He can't put her in a Glassbrook casket.'

'Digging up the graves is about Stephen Shorrock and Susan Duxbury,' Rushton said, 'and we're pretty sure they're already dead. A couple of days' delay can't hurt them.'

'In the meantime, we work this list.' Sharples turned round and pointed to the blackboard. 'We can find out where each of them was last night. Check alibis. Start narrowing it down. Take fingerprints. Search properties if we're allowed; get emergency warrants if we're not. Come on, people, get to work.'

44

Several hours later, a blast of cold air hit me and I swayed in the doorway of the Black Dog. I reached in my bag for my keys and set off towards where I'd left the car. Behind me, I heard the pub door open and the sound of Dionne Warwick promising to say lots of little prayers for the man she loved.

'*For ever and ev—*' I sang, and stopped. There was a white van in my way. It had reversed right up to the cellar trapdoors, and its rear doors were open. A male figure was leaning inside, and on hearing my footsteps, he straightened up.

'Evening, Miss Lovelady,' John Donnelly said.

'Evening, John,' I said.

'All right, mate,' said Tom from somewhere behind my shoulder. I didn't look round. I wasn't sure I could rely on my balance. 'You not out searching?'

'I'm on my way now.' John's eyes went from Tom to me. 'Had a few jobs to do for Dad first.'

'Don't stay out too late,' Tom said, as I set off again. 'And make sure you're not on your own.'

My car had gone. I turned on the spot. There were only four cars in the car park, apart from the white van that belonged to the pub. One of the other cars was Tom's.

'Where's my car?' I turned to face him. 'Someone's stolen my car.'

'Your car's parked outside the Glassbrook house,' he told me. 'Randy drove it home.'

I looked down at my hand, at the car ignition key sitting there, and was conscious of John Donnelly, inside the van again but perfectly quiet, as though he were listening.

'We keep spare keys at the station.' Tom kept his voice low. 'The last thing we need right now is you in a car accident.'

'I'm perfectly OK to drive.'

'Keep your voice down,' he said. 'Now, close your eyes and walk in a straight line to my car. If you make it, you can drive me home.'

I closed my eyes and the world began spinning. Noticeably, I mean – I know it does anyway. I opened them again. 'Babycham is disgusting,' I said.

'I told you not to have a fifth.'

I could not have drunk five Babychams. We'd only been in the pub an hour. 'A swift one before we get some kip,' they'd said. 'We all need to unwind.'

I stumbled on the uneven ground. Tom caught me and steered me over to the car, opening the door and gently pushing me inside.

'So tomorrow you will take one of the most crucial tests of being a good copper,' he said. 'Doing a full day's work with a hangover.'

He started the car engine. From the back of the pub van, John watched us leave.

'Where are we going?' I said a couple of minutes later, because even in my not-quite-with-it state, I could tell we weren't heading for the Glassbrook house.

'You need to sober up before I take you home,' he said. 'Sally and Larry will not take kindly to the detective working their daughter's case rolling home drunk and disorderly. There are some mints in the glovebox. I suggest you start chewing them.'

We carried on along the main road, leaving behind the big Victorian buildings, the shops and the terraced housing. Tom turned on the radio, of course. We hit the open moor and still Tom drove on. The radio station started playing the latest Simon & Garfunkel song, 'Scarborough Fair'.

'We're heading for the Hill,' I said, when we came to a crossroads and turned left. I could see it ahead, a dark shape on the horizon. It was a bit like driving into darkness. Then we turned suddenly off the main road, along a track tucked away behind a stone wall. Tom dropped into second gear and we started to rock and pitch up the side of the Hill. I wound down the window.

'Nearly there,' said Tom, to the back of my head.

'Nearly where?' I managed.

'*A true love of mine*,' sang Tom. He turned again, and this time we left the track behind and were driving over rough ground. After a few more yards, he pulled up and switched off the engine. 'Come on,' he said, opening the driver door. 'Got something to show you.'

I pushed open my own door and got unsteadily to my feet. The Hill was very close, but we were on a sloping piece of ground that seemed neither farmer's field nor open moor. There were trees some distance ahead that, in the darkness, looked like evergreens. I turned at the sound of the boot closing and saw that Tom had something under one arm.

'I'm not sure I'm up for a hike,' I said.

'Gentle stroll,' he replied, and then he took my hand. He set off, pulling me along with him, and all I could think was, *Tom is holding my hand*.

We followed a short path, dry and crunchy with pine needles, towards a great expanse of blackness. It was a lake. I heard the scurrying of waterfowl as they took shelter in the reeds and could smell the bitter scent of the air coming off the water. We stopped about five yards from the lake's edge, and Tom unrolled a blanket, laying it on the ground at our feet. He sat down. After a second, I did the same.

'This is the Black Tarn,' he said. 'We used to come here when we were kids, frighten ourselves to death with ghost stories.'

I thought of the monster creeping around the streets of Sabden, of Luna, alone and terrified. 'I don't need ghost stories to be frightened.'

Above us, the moon was full, its reflection shimmering on the water, creating a constantly moving pool of bright silver. Away from the light pollution of the town, the stars seemed unnaturally bright, and they, too, were replicated in the water. The lake was like a black mirror, surrounded by forest.

Black mirrors, I remembered, were used in dark magic.

'There's a legend attached to this place,' Tom said. 'According to which, female babies of Pendle are baptised twice. Once in church, in the way of all good Christian people, so that they are welcomed into the family of Christ, our saviour . . .'

'I didn't know you were religious.'

'. . . and then once in this lake, in the Black Tarn, at the foot of the Hill. At which time they become daughters of a different master entirely. The double baptism is a blessing because it gives them powers beyond those allotted to mortal women, and at the same time a curse because they must spend the rest of their lives coming to terms with the dark side of their nature.'

'That's very poetic,' I said and, in a way, I almost meant it. I didn't think I'd ever heard Tom be quite so serious before.

He turned to look at me. 'So the question is, Florence, do you want to be a woman of Pendle?'

'What?'

'This lake is also famous for skinny-dipping.' He jumped to his feet and shrugged off his jacket. I heard change clinking in his pocket as it dropped to the grass.

'You're not serious?'

He was. Or, at least, he might be. His shirt was halfway off. He didn't bother with all the buttons, simply pulled it over his head, and then his hands dropped to his trouser fastenings.

'I don't believe I'm seeing this.' I wanted to look away, I really did.

He kicked off his shoes, bent and pulled off his socks, and then was walking the last few steps to the water's edge. 'Don't worry about your modesty, Florence – I won't look round until you're in.'

'You're out of your mind. It must be freezing.'

He stood on the edge and rubbed his upper arms. 'Only when you get in. And pretty cold for the first ten minutes, I grant you. After that, you get sort of numb.'

I struggled up. 'Tom, you'll have a heart attack. I won't be able to get you out.'

He pushed his jeans over his hips and bent forward to tug them off. I turned away, so I heard, rather than saw, them fall to the ground. I kept my eyes on the car some distance away, but its surface was reflective, and I saw Tom in miniature, naked, rush forward and leap out of sight. For a split second the night was silent, and then I heard a yell of bravado that I thought must surely wake every sheep for a mile around and an almighty crash as he hit the water.

I turned back then and saw his dark, wet head break the surface.

His shoulders were white against the black of the water, his arms ploughing up and down, one after the other, in a strong front crawl. He was swimming away from me, getting smaller by the second.

I strode to the beach, ready to yell again. He was a good twenty yards out – he had to be way out of his depth, but he trod water and even raised an arm to wave. Then he dived and I held my breath until he appeared again, a few yards further along the shoreline.

'What?' He cupped a hand round his mouth. 'Do posh girls not swim?'

I was still drunk. I have no other excuse for what I did next. Tom whistled as I pulled off my own clothes. Unlike him – I could see his underpants on the grass at my feet – I didn't go the whole hog. I left my bra and pants on.

I remember to this day how cold that water was. I didn't dive straight in – I didn't have the nerve, and besides, I've always had a healthy wariness about clinging pondweed, big fish and what might lie beneath the surface of deep, dark water. So I stepped in, gingerly.

Tom vanished below the surface again, but I was in shock and worrying too much about my own wellbeing to care about his. Then he reappeared a few yards in front of me and started splashing. Each cold drop felt like it was burning.

I turned round and set off back. 'Stop it. I'm getting out.'

'Oh no you're not.'

Two strong, wet arms grabbed hold of me and then I lost all ability to act, or even to think, as I was dragged under and the cold flooded the inside of my head. I was being burned alive by ice. When we broke the surface, I was gasping out loud. Then I wasn't, because Tom's mouth was on mine, and I was holding him tight, feeling his naked body hard against mine and his arms around me, and suddenly it wasn't so cold after all.

Tom and I made love three times that night, on the blanket he'd brought from the car. I'd like to say I remember every kiss, every touch of his hands on my body, but the truth is that much of the detail has fled, the way all sense of caution and common sense left me that night. I remember the cold wind on our still-damp bodies and his hot breath against my neck. I remember the urgency of his kisses but the torturous gentleness when he entered me. I remember a night bird screaming overhead, and the sounds of my own cries echoing around the Hill.

After the second time, the night was growing colder and he pulled me close, drawing the edges of the blanket up around our bodies. After the third, we lay flat on our backs, holding hands, staring up at a moon that I swear was looking right back down at us.

I said, 'We probably shouldn't mention this at work.'

He gave a soft laugh. 'Contrary to popular belief, it's women who kiss and tell, not blokes. And I've got more to lose.'

The moon's light dulled a fraction. 'I don't exactly have mates I can gossip with,' I said. 'I suppose I could tell the bees.'

He turned his head, puzzled for a second. 'Oh, right. Sally keeps bees.'

'Hmnn.'

Silence.

He gave a heavy sigh and said, 'You're going to have to give me some time, my love. I can't walk out on Eileen without some plans in place. And I don't think either of us need any more upheaval while this case is ongoing.'

Half of me was thinking, *Wow, he's making plans for the future and they include me.* The other half, though? *And so begin the excuses. First it was the case. What would it be next?*

I sat up. 'On the subject of the case, I am now completely sober and ready to face the music at home.'

We found our clothes and dressed with difficulty, because we were damp and sticky, then hurried back to the car, seriously cold by this time. We kissed some more, and then he started the engine and drove me home.

He didn't kiss me as we said goodnight in the street outside the Glassbrooks' house, because we had no way of knowing who was watching, but he squeezed my hand and smiled, and that felt like enough.

45

Monday 30 June 1969

I woke in the night, a second before the phone started to ring. Don't ask me how. All I know is one second I was in a deep, deep sleep, the next I was wide awake, sitting upright in my bed.

Then the phone rang.

I was out of bed, on the landing, sliding down the stairs before my thoughts had a chance to catch up, but by the time I reached the phone, I knew this call had to be about Luna, was almost certainly coming from the station and that neither Sally nor Larry could be the first to hear whatever the news was.

When my feet struck the cold tiles of the hall, it occurred to me that it might be Tom, and I dismissed the idea as stupid, even as my heart started thumping at the sheer inappropriate wonderfulness of it.

'Hello.' I spoke softly, although I could hear muffled voices and movement upstairs. 'WPC Lovelady.'

I was so completely prepared for the station officer that for a second I didn't take in what was happening when a voice I didn't know said, 'Flooorrrenssse?'

I'd never heard my name pronounced that way before. I'd always quite liked my name, but not then. Not that way.

'Who is this?' I was still half whispering into the phone.

On the floor above, I heard a door opening, Larry saying, 'What's happening?'

'If you want to save her, you'll have to be quick.'

I cupped my hand round my mouth. 'Do you mean Luna? Where is she?'

'She's walking the corpse road, and we all know where that leads. She's almost at her grave, Florence.' Again that drawn-out, hissing-consonant version of my name.

The line went dead.

Corpse road. My first thought was that it was a figure of speech, but a couple of seconds later, I wasn't so sure. Corpse roads were real: I'd read about them.

Larry, meanwhile, was halfway down the stairs, Sally close behind. Cassie was leaning over the bannisters, and Ron, the third lodger in the house, was standing in the doorway of his bedroom. The only occupant of the house I wanted to see wasn't there. Randy was on the night shift.

'What? What is it?' Larry had grabbed the phone from me, even though the line was long dead.

'Sorry.' I looked up. 'Sorry, everyone. Nothing to do with Luna. I have to go into work, but there's no news. Sorry. Go back to bed.' I pushed past Larry and ran upstairs.

I felt bad about keeping the Glassbrooks in the dark, but getting them involved would achieve nothing and might actually slow us down. Sending a silent prayer of thanks to Tom for getting my car back safely, I drove to the nearest police box and reached the station officer in a couple of seconds.

'Corpse Road?' he said, and I could practically see him scratching his head. 'I've lived and worked here for nearly thirty years and I'm pretty certain there's no road with that name.'

'It's a generic name, not a specific one,' I said. 'There are corpse roads all over the country – they're basically paths to churches – but they're not usually called that. They're called other things, like Coffin Road, Bier Road— Oh Lord, Sarge, I've got it.'

'What?'

'Lych Way. It's a farm track and then a footpath off the Well Head Road.'

'I know it. At the foot of the Hill.'

'Lych Way is a name for a corpse road. Sarge, do you know where it leads to? When I was up the Hill yesterday, I thought I could see a building in some trees.'

'Not any more you can't. There was a church there, ages ago, not now. It's a pile of stones now.'

'What about the churchyard? Will that still be there? Sarge, are there graves there?'

'I'm calling Jack Sharples,' he said. 'And I'll get a car up there. You'd better come in, Flossie.'

'I'm going to drive up,' I said. 'I know where I'm going. I'll stay in the car and wait for back-up.'

'Flossie, I do not want you going up there on your own. Come in, now, and get your orders here.'

'I'll be careful, Sarge, I promise.'

I disconnected. I'd be in trouble for putting the phone down on the sergeant, but arguing would only waste time. I was the one who'd been called. I was the one who'd been told to hurry if I wanted to save her.

It took less than ten minutes, at that hour, to drive to the point on the Well Head Road where the farm track leading off it was signed Lych Way. I turned off the main road and drove slowly, because my car wasn't built for such rough terrain and because the track was narrow. When I reached the stone stile and the hairpin bend that, yesterday, had taken me up the Hill, I could drive no further. Leaving my headlights on, I got out of the car.

There was a great, flat stone at the foot of the stile. In its centre was a small candle in a jam jar; I knew it had been left for me.

She's walking the corpse road.

I knew, from my reading on the occult, that corpse roads dated back to mediaeval times, when new churches were being built all over the country, and when priests in charge of the mother churches were anxious to protect the influence, and the income, that arose from having the rights to bury the dead.

Paths were made, linking the isolated communities to the mother church, often using the new satellite church as a starting point, and it was along these that the coffins were carried.

Lych Way, a path along which the dead had been carried for hundreds of years, stretched ahead of me, disappearing into darkness. At the far end of the field, though, I was pretty certain I could see a light.

I'm not an idiot. Of course I thought *Trap* as soon as I saw it. I stepped away from the car, turning in a big, slow circle in case someone was creeping up on me.

The light in the distance didn't move. It was there to light my way. Or maybe to lure me in.

I looked back to the road, searching for approaching headlights. Nothing that I could see. *Come on, come on.* I had no desire to walk, alone, along the path of the dead.

From somewhere in the distance I heard a scream.

I set off running, telling myself I was an officer of the law and it was my duty to attend the scene of a crime. None of my colleagues would wait at the car having heard screaming; they'd be doing what I was now, racing towards it, being careful, keeping a watch on all sides, alert for anyone springing out, but going on, running towards danger, not away from it, because that was the job.

When I reached the wall at the far side of the field, I stopped. The light I'd been following was another candle in a jam jar, set on a flat stone in the wall. There was another stone stile, and on its far side ran a small stream with stepping stones to allow me to cross. I remembered from the reading I'd done that spirits could neither cross running water nor negotiate stiles with ease. Every step a dead body was carried along the corpse road was designed to ensure the spirit didn't come back. This was a one-way street. I had to hope it wouldn't prove so for Luna.

Or for me.

I set off again, my pace a mixture of fast walk and half-jog, afraid my courage might break, and by the time I was nearing the end of the next field, I thought I could see the ruined outline of the old church among the trees ahead.

I climbed the last stile and moved into the darkness of the woods. Slow steps now, listen carefully, look all around. I was not going to be taken unawares. One last bend.

The tiny churchyard looked as though no one had disturbed it in years. Apart, of course, from whoever had left yet another candle, in a glass jar, directly beneath one of the headstones.

Through the trees I could see the distant road and, at last, headlights. Still a mile or so down the road, but coming.

The porch had long since crumbled and the entrance was guarded only by two large stones. I passed between them, heading for the light, watching out for moving shadows, for anything or anyone that didn't belong.

The path through the graves was overgrown, but I could see where it had once been. I was close enough now to see the name on the headstone, but I wasn't looking at the stone. I was looking at the grave.

Graves flatten over time. Immediately after a burial, there is a mound of soft, loose earth. Even after the sexton has stamped and shaped his mound, after the turf has been replaced, it protrudes above ground level. This isn't only the effect of the coffin, or casket: the sexton will allow for that. It's because the earth has air trapped within it, and it takes time for the air to escape, for the soil to firm up. According to Dwane, it can take up to six months, depending on weather conditions, for a grave to settle.

No one had been buried in this churchyard for decades. The ground in here should be as dense as that covering the rest of the Hill. And it was.

But not where I was standing. This grave was a mound of loose soil. Not smooth and rounded, the way Dwane shaped his graves, but clumsily done, like a child's sandcastle. This grave was fresh.

The mound began to move.

I think I cried out. Who wouldn't? I'm sure I staggered back. I probably closed my eyes and prayed it wasn't happening, but at some point, and I'm sure it only took me a second or two, I opened them to see the earth was still moving.

It seemed to be falling in on itself, as though something beneath the surface was tunnelling upwards, and then mounds of soil began to bubble up, like a stew coming to the boil. I heard the low, muffled sound of terror.

I shut my mind to the horrifying pictures flooding into it and dropped to my knees. I scooped earth into a cup made by both my hands. The ground felt warm and damp, as though absorbing the heat of the body trying to be free. I scooped again, dreading what I might unearth but knowing I had to keep going. I kept plunging my hands into the soil, getting deeper with every attempt.

When I touched warm flesh, I cried out again and pulled away. From beneath the earth came an answering cry. Luna. This was Luna, not some creature from my worst nightmare, and I had to keep going.

I resumed digging, my hands bleeding by this time. I carried on, even when I saw another torch shining from behind, when I heard the cry of the constable from the patrol car, and his running footsteps. By the time he reached me, a hand had appeared from beneath the earth and was grasping tight hold of my arm.

46

I don't like to admit how close I came to tugging free and running at that moment, but the arrival of the other constable gave me the extra bit of courage I needed. The two of us scrabbled around in the dirt like dogs until Luna's head was free of the earth. She gasped for breath and spat out soil, while I told her it was OK, we had her, she was safe now.

At one point, she seemed to stop breathing, but the quick-thinking man at my side stuck a finger in her mouth and scraped it clean. When we were sure she wasn't going to choke, the two of us pulled her clear, and by the time she was out of the ground, other officers were arriving. The first set off back at a run to call an ambulance. We didn't want to wait, though, so we carried her, between us, back along the corpse road.

Luna had been lucky, in many respects. She'd been buried shallowly, not in a coffin or casket at all, but in some rough sacking that she'd managed to tear apart. She smelled of alcohol and, when she could speak, complained of feeling woozy, of having a terrible headache.

Two of us travelled in the ambulance with her as she was rushed to Burnley General. We didn't ask questions, but she wanted to talk. She told us she had no idea who'd abducted her. Her last memory had been of walking the final street before home when she'd heard a vehicle pulling up behind. A small van. Thinking it might be her dad come to find her, she'd waited. A masked figure had leaped from the driver's side and bundled her into the back.

Her next memory was of waking up in a very dark space, blindfolded, with her hands tied behind her back and a sickening smell around her that had reminded her of the dentist.

Chloroform. I glanced at my colleague, saw the same idea reflected in his eyes.

In that short ambulance journey, Luna seemed determined to tell us everything she remembered. After a while – impossible for her to say how long, because she'd lost track of time – she'd been forced to drink something that had burned the back of her throat and made her feel sick and sleepy.

Another look at my colleague. Alcohol?

She claimed to have no memory of being carried from the dark room and put back in the van. Or of being carried again, or of being laid in a hole in the ground. She'd woken to find herself gasping for breath and could only have been in the ground minutes when I arrived. Her rescue could easily have been watched by the man who put her there. The man who'd phoned me.

Why had he done that?

We arrived at Burnley General at the same time as the rest of the Glassbrooks, and for the next half-hour chaos ensued. Only when the doctor insisted on Luna having some quiet did she say that she wanted to speak to me. Just me. She wanted everyone else, even her parents, to leave the room.

I tried to smile down at the pinched face on the white hospital pillow.

'You've been so brave,' I said. The smile wasn't working. You'd have to toss a coin to say which of us was going to cry first.

Her little face seemed to contract further, and her big, scared blue eyes filled up. She reached towards me, her hands still grimy, the skin around her fingernails soaked in blood.

'Can my mum hear us, do you think?'

'I doubt it,' I said, although I wasn't sure. Sally hadn't been pleased at being dismissed and wouldn't be far away.

'I don't want her to know.' The tear pools in Luna's eyes brimmed over and fat droplets began rolling down her cheeks.

'Know what?' I whispered, although I was fairly sure I knew. There is something about that stricken look, the inability to meet people's eyes that women instinctively recognise. I had yet to deal with a rape victim. I was pretty certain I'd found my first.

'He did things to me.' Her eyes were fixed on the ceiling. 'He hurt me.'

It was important to know the details, and so I coaxed them out of her. Her parents would have to know. There was no way we could protect them from that.

'Did you get a look at him, Luna?' I asked.

She shook her head and another tear rolled across her temple and onto the pillowcase.

'Sometimes I thought there might be more than one man,' she told the ceiling light, 'but I only heard one voice.'

'Did you recognise it?'

She shook her head.

'Was he young or old?'

I concentrated on the voice for a while: she thought he was older than her father and definitely from Lancashire. There were no particular mannerisms or pronunciations that she remembered.

I spent over an hour in the hospital room with Luna, conscious of movement outside, of hushed voices and then raised voices, of faces peering in through the small window. Only when a ward sister came in and announced that the child really had to sleep did I give way to her mother, who looked at me as though I were the enemy.

I'd hoped, even expected, that Tom would be in the hospital waiting for me, that he would have volunteered to drive me home, or to the station if a debrief couldn't wait until the morning. It was already gone three o'clock.

Instead, DI Sharples and two uniformed constables stood at the end of the corridor, as though blocking my way out.

'WPC Lovelady,' Sharples said, as I approached. 'Come with us, please. We're taking you in for questioning.'

47

The station was busy. All the staff on duty, and quite a few drafted in for overtime, had been out looking for Luna. Those not needed to process the crime scene up at the old churchyard had gathered in the station awaiting developments.

I was the development.

I was given no praise for being the one to dig Luna Glassbrook out of a premature grave. No one patted me on the back. There was no chorus of three cheers. Instead, they were waiting in the car park as we arrived, or looking out of one of the upper windows, or hanging around in reception. Eyes watched me pass and I knew that something indefinable had changed.

I'd never been popular, but I was tolerated, as something of an oddity maybe, but one of them. Not any more. There was an invisible line, and I'd crossed it without even realising it was there.

By this time, I was shivering. Hours earlier, I'd left the Glassbrook house in a hurry, without a coat. The hospital had been as hot as hospitals usually are, but no sooner had I left it than the shaking began. No one offered me a coat, or a blanket, or even a cup of tea. Looking back, I'm not sure it would have helped much. I'm not sure the uncontrollable trembling was about cold.

I was led to the interview room and told to sit down. Not asked, told. Sharples and Brown sat opposite. I was facing the mirror that was really a window because that was where the suspects always sat.

'Who's watching us?' I asked.

'Couldn't say.' Sharples opened a file. 'What's puzzling me, Lovelady, is why you got a call from the killer, abductor, whatever we want to call him. Why would he phone you and tell you where Luna was in time to save her life?'

It had been puzzling me too.

'I don't think it was the killer,' I said. 'The killer gave no warnings about Patsy or the others. He didn't want them to be found. I think the person who called me tonight was someone else.'

Sharples gave me a long, cold look. 'Interesting theory,' he said. 'That you only now choose to mention.'

'I've been a bit tied up the last few hours, sir.'

'If not the killer, then who?' asked Brown.

'Someone who knows him,' I said. 'Someone who knows what's going on but is too scared to say anything.'

'But why contact you?' Sharples said. 'You're not even a proper detective.'

'I'm the only female officer at the station,' I said. 'I tend to be noticed.'

'And this person who wants to help just happened to know your home telephone number?'

'The Glassbrook house is a guest house,' I said. 'Anyone can find the number.'

In the room next door, something was dropped. I looked directly at the mirror, saw my own reflection and wondered whose eyes I was meeting on the other side.

'Funny how you seem so adept at finding these missing kids,' Brown said. 'First Patsy, now Luna, and you've pointed us in the direction of Stephen and Susan. If that hunch turns out to be right, I think we'll be asking ourselves whether you've a brilliance way beyond your age and experience or . . .' He let the sentence hang in the air.

'I was sent to St Wilfred's after some children reported hearing screaming,' I reminded him. 'It was considered to be a prank call, so I was sent.'

'Did someone point you in the direction of Stephen and Susan, or did you work that one out by yourself?' asked Brown.

'Tom thought of that, not me.' I fixed my eyes on the mirror, searching him out. If he were behind it, he'd damn well know what I was thinking right now.

'Really?' Sharples said. 'Because I remember you talking us through it, all proud of yourself. Tom was his usual gormless self.' He turned to Brown. 'Do you remember it any different, Woodsmoke?'

Brown shook his head.

'The whole house heard the phone this morning,' I said. 'How was I supposed to have phoned myself?'

'Ah, well, that's the thing,' said Sharples. 'We've spoken to Mr and Mrs Glassbrook, and Mr Pickles, even young Cassie, and none of them can definitely remember hearing the phone.'

The sense I'd had since leaving the hospital, that this was an annoyance but one that would soon be cleared up, was fading. A tightening in my stomach told me that something might be going on here that I hadn't quite figured out yet.

'That's ridiculous,' I said, trying to sound calm. 'They were all awake when I took the call.' I thought back to the moment when my caller had disconnected, when I'd looked up to see an audience on the first-floor landing.

'They say they heard you banging your bedroom door and running down the stairs. Then the sound of your voice. None of them are certain, but they don't remember a phone ringing.'

Was that possible? I'd moved quickly, but the phone had still rung three, maybe four times before I'd reached it. The Glass-brooks were waiting for – dreading – a phone call. They wouldn't sleep through three or four rings, would they?

Brown, meanwhile, had been fumbling beneath the table. He straightened up and I saw my clay figures in clear plastic bags. A rabbit, a cat, a fish, a bird and my crude attempt at a human figure.

'I told you I wanted to see how easy it is to make effigies from local clay,' I said. 'I dug the clay out of the Glassbrooks' garden. I told you that too.'

'So you said.'

'We found a lot of books in your room, Florence,' said Brown. 'Books about witchcraft, ghost stories, folklore. It's a wonder you can sleep at night.'

'I was under direct orders to learn as much as I could about witchcraft. I had no interest in the subject until we found the effigy with Patsy.'

'You have to see this from our point of view, Florence,' said Sharples. 'You arrive in February, and not a month later, we have a child go missing. Then a second, a third, a fourth. And you seem to have far more success in working out what's going on than a whole load of officers with twice your experience.'

I had an answer to that, but I had a feeling it wouldn't help my case.

'Luna was raped,' I said, instead. 'I haven't had chance to make a report yet, but she was forced face down onto a flagged floor in a dark room and taken from behind. Twice. Am I supposed to have grown a penis?'

They both looked shocked. It was a word that nice young women didn't use back in 1969.

'You'll be aware of the case of Myra Hindley, Lovelady,' Sharples said.

'I'm familiar with the case of Hindley and Brady,' I agreed.

'So you'll know that Hindley was the lure. The pleasant young woman who was supposed to make the children feel safe about getting into vans and being driven off.'

'She wasn't only a lure, though,' said Brown. 'She played an active part in the torture. Some people believe she was the brains behind the business.'

'I'm not a lure.' I saw no point in pretending I didn't know where this was going. 'I don't have an accomplice, and I had nothing to do with the disappearances.'

Sharples stood up. 'I'm going to call it a night. Lovelady, Mr and Mrs Glassbrook don't want you going back to their house tonight, and I have to see their point. I think it's better if you stay here.'

The twisting thing in my stomach tightened. 'In a cell?'

'We're not running a B and B, love. Be grateful you're not under arrest.'

48

I might not have been under arrest, but when the cell door clanged shut and the footsteps of the duty sergeant faded away down the corridor, I was genuinely frightened for myself.

The cell was small and cold, and the flickering light remained on for the rest of the night. There was one blanket, and the mattress smelled of urine. There was a bucket in the corner. The walls were smoke-stained, and damp in places.

This was worse, far worse than stealing into churchyards in the dark and unearthing missing girls. That had called for bravado and the confidence of youth. This felt as though events had spiralled totally out of my control. How had I gone from a trusted member of the team to suspect? Had suspicions been growing over time and I'd been too self-absorbed to notice?

The books, the charts, the clay models? I'd been trying to get close to the killer, see what he was seeing. Instead, I'd put myself so completely in his shoes as to be almost indistinguishable, and I was no nearer being able to identify him.

I didn't sleep much, and as dawn broke outside the high, barred window, I sat up on the bunk and tried to be calm. By her own admission, Luna had been raped, and I was clearly incapable of such an act. There was no accomplice that they could point to because I had no real friends outside the station.

Precious few on the inside, as I'd learned over the last few hours.

Luna had trusted me, had chosen me to confide all the worst

aspects of her ordeal. The notion that I was an accomplice in her abduction was absurd. They would see that, soon. This would be over, soon.

Prisoners being held under arrest are supposed to be offered food every few hours. In spite of being in the cell for half the night, I was offered no food, not even a cup of tea. At eight in the morning, Detective Sergeant Brown pushed open the door.

'You're wanted upstairs,' he said.

I got up, straightened my clothes as best I could and followed him along the corridor and up to the first floor. Once again, the station seemed unusually busy. Once again, conversations lulled as I approached .

Brown took me through CID to the superintendent's office. Sharples was with him.

'I'm suspending you without pay for the foreseeable future, Lovelady,' Rushton said. 'If you attempt to leave town, to contact the Glassbrooks or to come into the station, I'll put you under arrest.'

'With respect, sir, I have a right to know on what grounds.' My legs were almost buckling beneath me, but I don't think any of them would have known from my voice. I kept it steady. I kept it angry.

'The team have raised questions that need answering.' Rushton was struggling to look me in the eyes. 'You've demonstrated insights into this case that don't add up. You have no alibis for any of the nights the victims went missing—'

'Sir, that's not true,' I said. 'I was with Daphne Reece and Avril Cunningham when Luna was abducted.'

'We spoke to the two ladies,' Sharples said. 'They weren't sure what time you left their house on Saturday evening. There are no clocks in their house, and neither of them possesses a watch. They tell the time by the movements of the sun and the moon, apparently, and neither is reliable to anything more than a half-hour.'

Just my luck.

'Luna Glassbrook has made a statement this morning that contradicts what you told us in the early hours,' Sharples went on. 'She thinks there may well have been a woman involved in the abduction and remembers thinking at one point that you'd come to rescue her, because she distinctly smelled a perfume that reminded her of you.'

'I don't wear perfume,' I said.

'Soap, hairspray, whatever,' said Sharples.

'She's a scared child and someone is planting ideas in her head.'

'Needless to say, the Glassbrooks want you out of their house with immediate effect,' said Brown. 'Your things have been collected and are waiting for you downstairs. We've retrieved the keys of the car you were driving.'

The knots in my stomach were getting tighter. My head was telling me to keep fighting; my instincts were to run and hide.

The phone began to ring.

'That'll be all, Lovelady.' Rushton looked relieved as he grabbed the receiver.

Sharples and Brown ushered me out through the door and all eyes in the room turned to us. On my desk was a cardboard box. Someone had cleared away my personal stuff and I would have to carry it out of here, collect the rest of my worldly goods in Reception and . . .

I had nowhere to go, and no means of getting there. I wasn't even sure I had the money to get home, and in any case, I'd been told not to leave town.

It would take me twenty steps to get from the door of Rushton's office to the one leading out into the corridor and I was going to be watched every second of the way. I had to pass Tom's

desk to get to my own. He was the only person in the room looking down.

I stopped. 'Anything to say?' I asked the top of his head.

He looked up and his eyes were hard as marble. 'Don't make it
worse, Florence,' he said.

If I stayed in this room much longer, there was a danger
I'd be sick. I crossed to my desk and picked up the box. It was
pathetically light, but when I glanced inside, I saw my police-box
paperweight was broken into several pieces.

Brown was holding the door open. I walked through it and felt
the room sighing with relief behind me. Picking up my pace, I
reached the stairs and went down. In Reception, a young woman
in a purple miniskirt and matching high-heeled boots, her hair a
tall, blonde beehive, was sitting, smoking. She stood up when she
saw me. She was maybe a year or two older than I: her make-up
was a little heavy for first thing in the morning, but she was an
attractive woman.

'Eileen,' said the desk sergeant, in a warning voice. From the
back room other constables appeared. The one at the front was
grinning.

She strode up to me and jabbed her cigarette towards my face.
I had to dodge backwards to avoid it.

'You, whore, can stay the hell away from my husband or I will
have you.'

'Eileen.' The sergeant had come out from behind the counter.
'Leave her,' he said. 'She's not worth it.'

My things, two suitcases, another cardboard box and several
plastic carrier bags were piled up by the door. There was no way
I could carry them out of the station by myself, and yet everyone
was determined to watch me doing so. Then a constable in the
doorway was pushed rudely to one side and two newcomers
strode into Reception like players onto a stage.

'There she is,' said Daphne. 'Darling girl, the car's outside. Let me take that.' She pulled the box from my grasp as I stared at her stupidly.

'Are these your things?' Avril looked down at the pile by the door. 'Well, I'm sure the sergeant will help us to the car.' She turned to face him. 'We're blocking the superintendent's car, Bilko, so in your own time.'

The sergeant didn't move, but he nodded to one of the watching constables, who picked up my suitcases. I grabbed the box, Avril took the carriers, and two minutes later, I was in their Triumph Herald, top down, speeding out of town towards their house.

Avril, who had to get to her offices in town, dropped us off at the door and roared away. Daphne, who didn't have to be at the library until ten o'clock, steered me into the kitchen, made tea and flicked on the immersion heater so that I could have a bath.

'They hate me,' I said. 'All of them.'

Daphne's movements around the kitchen were abrupt and noisy. She banged down mugs, clattered spoons onto the work-top. When she pulled open the door of the fridge, I was afraid it might fall off its hinges.

'It's stupid,' I went on, thinking that she hated me too and was just being a bit more civilised about it. 'They have no evidence, but they've all leaped at the idea of my guilt. It's as though they want to believe. As though they've been waiting for the slightest excuse.'

I could see Daphne getting angrier by the second. She'd spilled tea all over the counter because her hands had been shaking when she'd tried to fill the pot.

'I'm so sorry.' I dropped my head into my hands. I couldn't look at another angry, accusing face a second longer. 'I'll go when I've had my tea. I'll call a taxi. Thank you for picking me up.'

With a howl of rage, Daphne raised a milk jug high into the air and then slammed it onto the tiled floor. It shattered. We stared at each other.

'You are going nowhere until that bunch of morons issue you a public apology,' she spat at me. 'Until we find those poor children and string the monster that's hurting them up by his pathetic, shrivelled-up testicles. And that was Avril's favourite jug.'

She pulled out the chair next to mine, sat down and burst into noisy tears.

'To be clear,' I said, in a small voice, 'is it me you're angry with?'

She sniffed, wiped her nose with the back of her cardigan sleeve and reached out a hand. It clasped mine and I had my answer.

'Tell me something,' she said, when her sobs had subsided. 'That rather magnificent blonde baggage at the police station, the one who called you a whore. Was she getting her wires crossed?'

Tom's wife, Eileen. Oh, to turn the clock back twenty-four hours.

'I see.' Daphne gave me a weak smile. 'Well, we all make mistakes, dear, especially when we're young. I hope he was worth it.'

'He wasn't,' I said. 'He's turned on me as well. I don't get it, Daphne. I've tried to be as brave as they are, and as clever as I know how, and to work as hard as I can, and I thought they were starting to like me.'

'My darling, be thankful we're not in the Dark Ages. They'd be building a stake by now and dipping torches into tar.'

I stared at her.

'That's the patriarchy for you. It's what men do when they're afraid and they feel helpless and out of control. They turn on the outsider, usually a woman, and they blame her for everything that's going wrong. You've become the witch, my dear.'

I thought of the Pendle witches. Accused of murder, sentenced and hanged, when they'd almost certainly been guilty of nothing more than a bit of low-key extortion. Up till now, they'd been characters from a storybook. Suddenly, they felt very real.

'They're going to charge me with murder,' I told her.

'Oh, poppycock. You know better than that. Do they have a scrap of evidence?'

I shook my head. They didn't, did they? No, of course they didn't.

'But you may have to be prepared for some ugly rumours flying around town. Superintendent Rushton will be under huge pressure to catch this man. While attention is focused on you, he gets a reprieve.'

'I thought he liked me.'

Daphne gave a bitter laugh. 'I'm sure he does, but he likes himself more. And his livelihood. And the respect of his peers at the golf club. He will throw you to the lions if it means he gets out of this unscathed.'

She got up and looked out of the window into the sky. 'Dear, I have to get to work. Will you be OK for a while?'

I nodded.

'Have a bath, unpack your things, go to bed for a couple of hours and sit in the garden.' She smiled at me and glanced down. 'Do your nails. That varnish is badly chipped. Avril and I will be home shortly after five and we can talk then about what we can do.'

'You can't do anything. I don't want you getting into trouble.'

She leaned down towards me. 'Those dimwits got their knickers in a twist over a smart girl they think is a witch.' She winked at me. 'Wait till they find themselves dealing with some real ones.'

49

For the next couple of hours, I did what my friend the witch had told me to. I had a bath, ate some toast and marmalade, put my clothes away and redid my nails. I lay on lavender-scented sheets and tried to sleep. After half an hour, I gave up. I brushed my hair and left it loose, then found my best dress, an apricot shift with a white Peter Pan collar, for no other reason than I thought Daphne and Avril would approve, and caught the number 18 into town.

Monday was market day in Sabden and the town centre was busy. As I climbed down from the bus and made my way across the terminal and towards the main road, I had the sense of people watching me. I didn't think too much of it at first. When your hair is the brightest shade of ginger imaginable, when it's long and very curly, you get used to being stared at.

My first stop was the Over Sabden Building Society. I'd been suspended without pay and I would have to offer Avril and Daphne something for my keep. I had a little under a hundred pounds saved up. I withdrew half of it. I had to queue for a while, and when I stepped outside, fifteen minutes later, I felt an immediate stab of alarm.

Word of my fall from grace had got round very quickly. At the foot of the steps, leaning against the railings that kept pedestrians from falling into the building's cellar void, even stretching a little way back along the pavement, people were waiting for me. They were mainly women, but quite a few elderly men, and some younger men who weren't on the morning shift at the factories.

They were obviously waiting for me. They were all staring at me.

I knew none of them. A quick glance around told me that. Also that some of those at the back, the men in unnecessary raincoats and garish sports jackets, were press. One of them had a large black camera. He held it loose, pointing down, but his eyes were fixed on me.

Instinct told me to brazen it out, to pretend they weren't there, walk down the steps and out onto the pavement. They weren't exactly blocking my way. But some crabbed curiosity held me back. They seemed to be waiting for something, and oddly, I wanted to see what it was.

A dozen yards away, at the edge of the market, a stallholder was talking to a thin man in a black jacket. A paper bag was passed from one to the other.

Then a woman, middle-aged and heavyset, was walking quickly towards me. Her permed hair gleamed in the sun, and her chins bounced as she strode across the narrow road, over the pavement and up the steps. She was breathing heavily by the time she reached me, and a gleam of sweat was visible on her upper lip.

She pointed a finger in my face, the second time that morning such a thing had happened. 'Do you know where my Susan is?' she demanded.

Tricky one. Technically, I did, if Tom's guess proved right, and I had a feeling it was going to.

'No, I don't,' I said. 'I'm very sorry for your loss.'

'How do you know she's dead?' said a woman holding the handle of a large pram, and the mean, thin smile on her lips said she was taking a spiteful pleasure in getting one over on me.

Mrs Duxbury stabbed a finger at me again, this time hitting

me on the chest. 'If you've hurt my Susan . . .' She left the threat hanging.

I felt something strike my shoulder. Someone had thrown an egg at me. I could see it out of the corner of my eye, yellow and glutinous, running down the front of my dress, but I wasn't going to give them the satisfaction of looking at it.

Not far from the egg stall was someone I recognised. The bobby on the beat, watching while pretending not to.

I raised my voice. 'PC Roberts, get over here now and deal with these people or I will report you to the chief constable.'

I had no idea how to report someone to the chief constable, but the bluff worked. He sauntered over and the crowd began to drift away, even Susan Duxbury's mum.

'If you don't want trouble, stay out of town,' Roberts said in my ear, when he was close enough so that only I would hear him. 'In fact, why not leave it altogether?'

I stood my ground and glared. 'I will remember you,' I told him, and saw with satisfaction the flicker of alarm in his eyes.

So that was what it felt like, to be a witch.

I wanted nothing more than to flee the town centre, but I was giving nobody the satisfaction of seeing me run, so I walked round the market to a stall on the other side, where they might not have seen the confrontation, and at a butcher's stall bought three Barnsley chops. When I turned away from the stall, it was to find Marlene Labaddee standing in my way. For a second her brown eyes glared into mine.

'Stand still,' she ordered, and then she raised her hands towards me. One caught hold of my shoulder; the other began dabbing a damp cloth at the bodice of my dress.

'Why shouldn't we put Patsy back in the ground?' I asked her.

The pressure of her hand increased.

'You called me, two weeks ago, at the station. It was very late and I was the only one left in the building. You said we shouldn't put Patsy's body back in the ground, that she wouldn't rest.'

'That's the worst of it off,' she said.

'I still struggle to understand the Lancashire accent much of the time, so I've got into the habit of listening very carefully, especially on the phone. People round here don't say "burn" the way you do. I realised when we were in the steam room, when you said you had to leave, that you were burning up.'

'Soak it when you get home,' she said. 'Use bicarbonate of soda. Egg can stain.'

'Why do you want us to burn Patsy's body? Why will she not rest?'

Her lips moved soundlessly for a second, and then she turned and walked away.

I went back to the bus terminal. The bus I caught, though, didn't take me back to Avril and Daphne's house, but rather up to St Wilfred's.

'Dwane,' I called, when I found him pushing a lawnmower around the few patches of flat grass in the churchyard. 'Do you have a moment?'

'Heard you'd been sacked,' he said, leaning on the handle.

'Something like that,' I agreed. 'I need to ask you a big favour.'

'Will you be leaving? Going back to . . . wherever it is you come from?'

He looked quite downcast.

'So, about this favour,' I said. 'It would be really helpful if I could spend some time in your shed, looking at your model of the town.'

His eyes gleamed. 'You really like—'

I didn't have time to be coy. Besides, I was a witch now, and witches weren't scrupulous when it came to getting what they wanted. 'Dwane, I do like small things, and I like you. You're clever and talented and helpful. I think your model will help me work something out. Only the thing is, and I know this is a lot to ask, I need to be alone.'

'You want me to let you in and leave you?'

'Yes. I do my best thinking when I'm on my own. I'll be really careful. Do you mind?'

Without another word, he left the mower in the middle of the grass and set off back towards his house.

Dwane's model town was exactly as we'd left it the day before. The coloured plastic figures were all still in place. He was hovering in the doorway and I turned to smile at him.

'Thank you,' I said.

He nodded and left the shed.

I'd misremembered yesterday morning. I thought back to the map at the station and moved three of the figures. Then I pulled over Dwane's work stool and sat on it. It raised me high enough to be able to see the whole town.

Sometimes in order to see a pattern, we need to see what breaks it.

Luna's movements on the night she was taken bore no resemblance at all to those of the other three. They'd all said goodbye to their friends at various points close to the town centre and then headed towards their homes.

Two out of three children had been seen at the railway station. Another had been spotted on the road leading up to the bus depot. And yet I was pretty certain none of them had left town.

Luna, though, had vanished from over a mile away, on the outskirts of town, forced into the back of a white van by a masked figure. And she'd been allowed to live. Someone had made sure she lived.

Luna had vanished during a full moon. The others when the

moon was at its darkest. Luna had been raped, and yet there was no evidence that Patsy had been sexually molested. The only sensible conclusion was that Luna wasn't part of this. Or if she was, that she was serving a different purpose entirely.

It was obvious. Luna wasn't the fourth victim. Luna had never been intended to die. Luna was about throwing us off the scent.

Throwing me off the scent.

Dwane walked me to the bus stop and waited ten minutes until the bus arrived. 'I know you didn't do it,' he said, as the bus pulled up. 'You've still got one friend.'

When I got back to Avril and Daphne's house, it was to see my bike leaning against the frame of the front porch. The last I'd seen of it was outside the back door of the Glassbrook house, at least two miles away on the other side of town.

Maybe I had more than one friend, after all.

That night, after dinner, Daphne spent the evening arranging a meeting of her moon coven. She didn't tell me, but as I came barefoot down the stairs to collect a glass of water, I overheard her on the phone.

'Tomorrow at moonrise,' she was saying. 'We can't leave it any later: we're already two days past full. I'm hoping to get the full thirteen. Goodness knows the poor girl needs all the help she can get.'

As I came down the last flight, where she saw me and ended the conversation in a hurry, I had half a mind to volunteer my services. After all, what did I have to lose?

50

Unlike Avril and Daphne, I couldn't tell the time using the astral elements, so I set an alarm for four o'clock in the morning. I dressed in clothes I'd put out the night before and crept downstairs. As I let myself out of the house, I could hear voices on the first floor. I was sorry to have woken them, not least because of the questions I'd face later, but there was no help for it.

I might be a rookie witch, but I was still a police officer, and this was police business.

The exhumations of Ada Wright and Winifred Brown were to be carried out by the book this time, taking place simultaneously in the early hours of Tuesday, 1 July. I cycled out towards St Joseph's Churchyard, on the south side of town, gambling that Tom, who lived closer to Duckworth Street Cemetery, would be attending the other one.

Rushton's car was parked by the gate.

I left my bike and slipped over the wall into the churchyard to see the exhumation a good hundred yards away. Detective Sergeant Brown was supervising the cordoning of the site and the erection of the tent. Rushton stood a little way distant, smoking. I could make out a man in black whom I assumed to be the priest. I watched council workmen carry in the soil tray, the turf board, the specialist cutting and digging equipment. The men installed lights and then, under the guidance of a man I knew to be a sexton from Burnley Council, they entered the tent. Brown and Rushton left, I guessed to sit in Rushton's car.

I sat on the dew-damp grass, knowing I'd be less visible, and listened to the rhythmic sound of spades striking the earth. I watched cigarette ends like fire-flies light up the darkness and heard mumbles of conversation.

As the first factory whistles started, at a little before six in the morning, one of the workmen went to fetch Rushton and Brown. I waited until they were inside the tent before moving closer.

I couldn't see what was happening in the tent, but I could picture it.

The grave, I knew, would be rectangular, about four feet deep. The box of earth would sit on one side; the other would be left free for the exhumed coffin. Rushton, Brown, all the others would be gathered at the grave's foot and head.

'On you go, then, lads,' said Rushton.

Bulges appeared in the side of the tent. I heard a low-pitched grunt.

'Steady, nice and steady,' said a voice I didn't know, and I pictured the casket slowly rising from the ground, the strained faces of the workmen.

The casket would be dull, its lovely glow tarnished from months in the ground. As it rose, it would brush against the sides of the grave; loose soil would crumble onto its lid.

Silence fell. A rattle. A couple of mumbled curses.

'Let me have a go.'

'Give it a good tug.'

I gave them several more minutes, listening to the sound of fingers sliding along the casket rim, pulling at trimmings, until I couldn't bear it any longer.

'I can do it,' I called.

Silence inside the tent. A second later, Rushton was out, striding towards me.

'What the bloody hell are you doing here, Lovelady?'

He looked as though he might hit me. I took two steps back, not because I was afraid of him but because I was thinking properly and he wasn't. 'Stay where you are, sir. You too, DS Brown.'

To my surprise, they both did. Over their shoulders, I could see the workmen filing out of the tent.

'I told you to stay away,' Rushton snapped, as Brown called over the constable at the gate.

'With respect, sir, you said you'd arrest me if I came into the station, if I attempted to contact the Glassbrooks or if I tried to leave town. I've done none of those things, and this is a public open space. I haven't come anywhere near the crime scene and there is no possibility of my compromising it, but if you touch me, then you might.'

I could see him breathing heavily.

'Do you know how to open this coffin?' Brown asked me.

'There'll be two gold trimmings on the opposite side to the hinge,' I said, conscious that demonstrating a familiarity with caskets would hardly help my case at the moment. 'Slide them along the wood, away from the centre as far as they'll go and then twist. You'll feel the internal mechanism move and you should be able to open the lid.'

Brown looked at Rushton. Rushton nodded and then turned to the constable, who'd reached us.

'Stay with this one,' he told him. 'Don't let her move.'

Rushton and Brown went back into the tent. I waited.

'Jeez,' said one of the men. A second later, the smell of putrefaction and chemicals reached us. The constable at my side inhaled sharply.

'Nothing,' I heard Brown say. 'There's nothing there except—'

'Ada,' said another voice. 'Jeez, I had no idea corpses looked like that.'

'Sir, that smell isn't right.' I was itching to get in the tent. I took a step closer and a hand closed around my arm. 'Sir, that's not how an embalmed corpse is supposed to smell,' I went on. 'I dug up Patsy, remember? You have to check properly.'

'She might have a point,' said Brown, in a voice I probably wasn't supposed to hear. 'That satin fabric doesn't look quite right to me.'

'Move it,' I said. 'Pull it to one side. Check underneath.'

Silence in the tent. Then a ripping sound.

'Oh my good God,' said Rushton.

He came out of the tent and spent a moment looking at the sky, breathing deeply. Then he took me into custody. Again.

51

'Luna's changed her story,' he said to me three hours later. 'Seems she wasn't raped after all.'

I was back in the same interview room, facing the same mirror. Rushton and Brown were interviewing me.

There was something going on in the station, some sort of removal work, because I could hear heavy, solid objects clanging together. Each bang resonated along the corridor outside. Each one made me start, although I think I managed not to let it show. After a while, the din took on the sound of my world falling apart.

'Then she's a liar,' I said. 'She lied to me or she's lying to you. Either way, I'm disappointed you trust her more than one of your own officers.'

From directly outside the door came a shrill, metallic clatter and both men flinched.

Even given the noise, Rushton seemed uncomfortable. He never normally led interviews. Nor, I was discovering, was he particularly good at it. He lacked the quick wit of Sharples, the dogged attention to detail of Brown. He looked sad, too, I thought.

'Or did she make a mistake?' I asked. 'Well, that's easily done. I can see how the act of sexual penetration by a complete stranger can be mistaken for something else entirely.'

He winced. 'This isn't helping.'

'Luna is now saying that she had sex recently, for the first time, with one of her friends,' said Brown. 'She was frightened her parents would find out, or that she'd get pregnant. So she figured if she told us she'd been raped, she wouldn't get the blame. She thought better of it once she'd calmed down a bit and decided to tell us the truth.'

Something banged on the floor above us. Both men looked up. I was thinking about Luna's new story. It was credible, except . . .

'I spoke to John Donnelly,' I said. 'He denied that he and Luna had ever had sex. I believed him.'

'Not John Donnelly,' Rushton said. 'Dale Atherton. Luna was angry with John for not wanting to sleep with her, so she did it with Dale instead. To spite him.'

It was exactly the sort of stupid, reckless thing Luna would do.

'Is she still claiming she could smell my perfume when she was being held prisoner?' I said. 'Perfume that I don't actually own.'

'She was never sure about that,' Brown said. 'She isn't accusing you. No one's accusing you.'

'Not yet,' Rushton said.

We all three of us jumped then. Directly above us, someone had knocked over a filing cabinet.

'What the hell is going on?' Without waiting for the interview to be formally concluded, Rushton got up and stormed from the room.

Six hours later, I was driven back to Avril and Daphne's house, feeling . . . well, more bemused than anything else. Apart from the brief interview with Rushton, I'd spent nearly ten hours in a cell, seeing no one except the duty sergeant, who brought me two meals, five mugs of tea, escorted me to the ladies' on the hour so I wouldn't have to use the bucket and kept me up to date with news of the investiture of Prince Charles as the Prince of Wales at Caernarfon.

Avril's Triumph Herald was parked outside the house when the police car pulled up. My bike, once again, was leaning against the inside of the front porch, as though it had developed a boomerang ability to come home.

'We're in the garden,' Avril called as I made my way into the kitchen, ready to apologise for worrying them. 'Bring a glass.'

There was a wine glass on the kitchen table, and it says something about my mood that I picked it up without question. The two women were on the patio, enjoying the early evening sun in two low garden chairs. Avril wore her sunglasses, Daphne a large, floppy straw hat. A bottle of red wine, half empty, was on the wrought-iron table in front of them. There were only three garden chairs in Avril and Daphne's garden, and I wasn't sure where I was expected to sit, because in the third chair sat Tom Devine.

It didn't seem necessary to speak.

'He brought your bike back,' said Daphne in a small voice.

'Again.' Tom's grin faded within seconds.

Avril rose. 'We should leave them to it,' she told Daphne, who pushed herself up, slightly less gracefully. They both walked past me, their eyes down and the back door closed behind them.

I sat in the seat Avril had vacated and put my glass on the table. 'Give me some of that,' I told Tom.

He poured. I drank. The wine was blood red in colour, leaving grains of a crumbly sediment in the bottom of my glass.

'Talk,' I said. 'Or leave. Make your mind up quickly.'

'I take it you know Stephen was found this morning?' he began.

I fixed my eyes on the moors. 'I guessed as much. They didn't let me see.'

'He was tucked away under that satin the undertakers put in coffins. My group found Susan.'

'You were bang on the money, then.' I watched a large black

bird making slow circles. 'Or do they all still think I deserve the credit for that one?'

'I didn't mean to drop you in it. I was trying to prove to you I don't always act like a pillock.' He picked up the wine and topped up my glass as well as his own. I didn't object.

'Post-mortem?' I said.

'Only initial examinations,' Tom said. 'They were both dressed, on top of the corpses, just under that satin stuff that funeral directors use. We're all agreed now that the kids were put in the coffins before they were buried. Both jobs were too neat, too clean. No way you could achieve that by digging up a grave.'

I leaned back in my chair, still looking at the moor. Knowing that someone had accessed Glassbrook & Greenwood's parlour on the nights before three early morning funerals took us no further forward. We'd already guessed as much.

'Stephen didn't wake up.' I was picturing the dead face of an elderly woman surrounded by undisturbed satin. 'He and Susan might have been dead when they were put in the caskets.'

'They weren't,' Tom said. 'We found vomit and saliva beside Susan. Stephen had wet himself. But you're right: neither woke up. They were lying too neatly, no sign of a struggle or distress.'

'Well, that's something. It would have been hard to look at another like Patsy.'

There was a moment's silence, while I'm sure we were both thinking about the torn satin wrapped round Patsy's bloodstained hands, her cracked lips, the scratch marks on her face.

'Maybe he thought Patsy was dead,' Tom said. 'Maybe she was never intended to go through that.'

'Or maybe with Susan and Stephen he got it wrong. Maybe he had to keep trying until he succeeded.'

I'd spoken without thinking, but it was important. Had the children been meant to wake up and find themselves trapped or not? Did he creep into the churchyard and sit beside the grave, enjoying the sound of their screams? Had he been frustrated with Susan, then Stephen and driven to try again?

'Anything else?' I asked.

Tom reached into an inside jacket pocket. 'I'll be in deep shit if anyone knows I showed you these.' He put two Polaroids on the table.

'Louvre dolls,' I said, bending closer. 'Clay pictures, as they say in these parts. In the caskets?'

'Both very similar to the one we found with Patsy,' Tom said. 'Susan's is a bit tubby, as you see. Stephen's has male genitalia. Blackthorn spikes in all the right places.'

I didn't want to look at them, so I looked at him instead.

'Did they both have all their teeth?'

'Both missing one canine. Recent extraction. We're checking with their dentists. And yes, both teeth appear to have been baked into the effigies. I tell you what, Floss, it's some sick shit.'

'What about Luna?'

He shook his head. 'Nothing. No clay picture, no amateur dentistry.'

'She's different, Tom. She's not a part of the pattern.'

He visibly perked up at my use of his name. 'Throwing us off the scent, you think?'

'Of the seventeen members of the cricket club, who do you think is the last one we'd suspect when Luna went missing?'

Tom shrugged.

I said, 'Luna was taken by someone who cared about her. Who wasn't prepared to let her die and who made sure she didn't by getting me involved.'

Tom leaned back, exhaled, picked up his cigarettes. 'Larry? Jeez. Good luck trying to argue that one, love.'

It was on the tip of my tongue to tell him not to call me 'love', but that was an area I didn't want to stray into. 'I won't be arguing anything,' I said instead. 'I'm suspended without pay, remember?'

'No, you're not.' Tom's face relaxed. 'Bloody Norah, I need a fag. Wilma and Betty wouldn't let me smoke.'

'Good for them – it's a filthy habit. And I am.'

'Rushton can't do that and he knows it. He has to pay you. He just lost his temper. I'll make sure someone drops your wage packet off on Friday.'

Well, that was something.

'He's sending a car to pick me up in the morning. He wants me back for more questioning.'

Tom nodded.

'I spent the whole of today in a cell alone. Rushton spoke to me for ten minutes.'

'So take a book,' Tom said. 'Not one about witchcraft.'

'What's going on? Why does he want me in again if he's got nothing to say to me?'

'Has it occurred to you that he might want to keep you safe?'

It hadn't. But while I was a suspect in the case, there were people in town who were perfectly capable of taking the law into their own hands.

'Personally, though, I'd say he's keeping you out of trouble,' Tom went on. 'Half the blokes at the station are taking bets on what you're going to do next.'

He looked at his watch, drained his glass and got to his feet. 'How long are you staying here?' he asked.

'I can't leave town,' I told him. 'And I don't have anywhere else to go.'

He lowered his voice. 'Just be careful.' His eyes were darting nervously from the house to me and back again. 'Blokes down at the nick have been talking. There's something not quite right about those two.'

'They're lesbians,' I said. 'I'm not. But I shouldn't have to tell you that, should I?'

We stared at each other, and I don't think Avril and Daphne were uppermost on his mind any more.

'Why did you tell your wife about me?' I asked.

He gave a heavy sigh. 'I'd no idea she'd do that. And I didn't tell her anything. I came home late, obviously not myself – I mean, come on, it's not the sort of thing that happens every day – and she found one of your hairs on my jacket.'

'That's it? She raises merry hell because of a hair?'

He shrugged. 'She's had a thing about you for months now. Pretty much since you arrived. She knows I . . .'

'What?'

He held up both hands. 'Floss, we can't do this now. We have to get this case over with. Then we can talk about you and me. I'll be in touch. Please stay out of trouble.'

The back door opened mysteriously before Tom could touch it and he disappeared. I stayed where I was, watching the sun sink lower over the moor, turning the pale grasses a deep gold and sending rosy trails across a turquoise sky. Lancashire was beautiful, I realised. Inhospitable, unpredictable, verging on savage at times, but heartbreakingly, wonderfully beautiful.

There was still a 'you and me'.

It wasn't until later that I wondered whether that might be exactly what I'd been intended to think.

52

'You two are plotting something,' I said when dinner was over, and Avril and Daphne had spent most of it exchanging meaningful looks.

'Nonsense,' said Avril. 'We merely have a lot of non-verbal communication going on. It happens to couples when they've been together for any length of time. Tom seems like a nice young man.'

'Tom is married, and don't try to change the subject. I know you're going out tonight. I've seen the bags by the door. Is it a coven thing?'

'Goodness' – Daphne opened her eyes wide with fake surprise – 'whatever gave you that idea? Oh look, one last mouthful. You have it, Florence, dear. You've got a nice relaxing evening ahead of you.'

She emptied the bottle into my glass. It was more than a mouthful. It was our second bottle of the evening and I'd drunk my fair share.

'What gave me that idea? How about any number of phone calls the last couple of days about getting the gang together and meeting up at moonrise?' I said. 'And there is a blue velvet cloak hanging by the front door. Don't ever apply for a job at MI5, either of you.'

Another shared look.

'So given that I'm a trainee witch these days, can I come?' I asked.

'You're quite mistaken, dear,' said Daphne. 'We're rehearsing tonight. The velvet cloak is for Lady Macbeth. And we'd love to take you, but the director has a strict rule about no audiences until the opening night.'

I didn't see any point arguing, so I helped with the washing-up and then it was time for them to go. I finished my wine and thought I might be getting a taste for it.

'Enjoy the peace and quiet,' Daphne said, as the two of them left. 'I think *Z Cars* is on at eight. We'll be back before ten.'

She patted my shoulder, and then the two of them went out into the evening. I waited a couple of minutes before going upstairs. In a bedroom that I honestly couldn't decide whose influence had decorated – it was such an odd mix of Eastern luxury and spartan minimalism – I found the lunar calendar. Moonrise was at 9.30 p.m.

They wouldn't be back for ten. Why had they said that when I'd so easily catch them out in a lie?

I stumbled on the way downstairs, a sharp reminder that I'd drunk more wine than I was used to. In the kitchen, I swallowed a tumbler of water and felt better. I found some aspirin, because the beginning of a headache was creeping up on me, and felt good to go. At a minute before eight o'clock, I set off down the road on my bike.

It was a wonderful evening, warm and scented, with a light breeze. I rode quickly down towards the town centre. Brakes? Who needed them?

Avril and Daphne couldn't be going straight to the Hill. In Avril's car, they'd be there in a little over fifteen minutes. They were going to collect other members of the coven. I had time to get ahead of them.

The wind cooled my neck, lifting my hair so that it trailed behind me like a flag. I went faster still.

Yes, I knew that spying on people who'd befriended me was a pretty mean thing to do, and I didn't feel good about it. On the other hand, I was a police officer and children were dying. Avril and Daphne knew more than they'd told me. They might believe the information they were holding back wasn't relevant, but they were hardly the best judges. Also, I wanted to see who else was in the coven. And I wanted to see what they did, damn it! To make sure that the magic they were performing really was as benign as they pretended.

A car horn sounded, loud and angry. I swayed and nearly fell, just managing to get my foot off the pedal in time to steady the bike.

Woah! I was in the town centre, in the middle of a junction. A Ford Cortina had braked hard to avoid me and the man in the driver's seat was shaking his head. A bus went past; several heads turned my way. I held up a hand to apologise and pushed the bike to the side of the road.

I had no memory, none at all, of getting from the end of Avril and Daphne's road to the middle of town. And yet here I was, at the main shopping stretch, within sight of the outdoor market and the bus terminal.

The world made an odd swooping motion, almost knocking me off balance.

I got back on the bike, felt my head spin and pushed off, telling myself a bit of light exercise and fresh air were just the thing. I'd be fine in a few minutes.

Superintendent Rushton was standing at the side of the road, smoking a pipe and wearing blue-and-grey-striped pyjamas. He tapped the road sign by his side. *Pendle Road*, it said. I'd been about to go the wrong way. I turned into Pendle Road, and as I peddled away, I was thinking that Superintendent Rushton really shouldn't be smoking in bed. It was dangerous.

I was never drinking alcohol again. My headache came back, making it almost impossible to pedal up even the gentlest of hills. I got off and pushed most of the way out of town; only when I reached Well Head Road did I mount the bike again.

A car went past. Not Avril's Triumph but a car from a circus, bright yellow, with blue bumpers, driven by a clown who held a striped umbrella over his head. I watched him speed away down the road and thought, *He's a fool: it isn't raining.*

I rode on. The golden light faded. The sun sank below the horizon and the sky became the deep purple of pansies mottled with lavender clouds. When I looked at my watch, I saw that it was gone nine. It had taken nearly forty-five minutes to do a journey I'd estimated would last thirty at most.

I was losing time. No sooner did I realise it than a small nugget of panic burst inside me. Something was happening. Something out of my control.

Then my insides turned upside down. I leaped off the bike and almost before I knew it was going to happen, I threw up. My dinner came pouring out, burning my throat.

When I eventually stopped vomiting, I set off walking. Around me, colour faded quickly as the daylight gate opened and beckoned me in. The Hill was casting its shadow over the surrounding moor, increasing its resemblance to a crouching beast. Rocks took on strange forms: curled creatures ready to spring, winged sprites with wild grass hair.

A dawning sense told me that I wasn't alone. Tiny stones tumbled from the wall at my side, as though something small and invisible were scampering along it to keep pace with me. The grasses beyond the wall whistled, as though light footsteps were running through them.

At the point where the Lych Way path left the road, I stopped to rest. The witches would drive this track. I wasn't safe yet. The pale face of a rotting corpse watched me from behind the slender trunk of a sycamore, but he was only trying to get my attention and so I ignored him and started to climb.

The Hill soared, dark and massive, above me.

I would never make it. Each step up threatened to send me spinning back down again. I turned on the spot to find the moon and saw it was high in the sky.

And then I heard the car. It stopped directly below, followed by another and then a third. They were coming. They were less than two hundred yards away, and every step I took drained me.

I left the path and began climbing the Hill, on hands and knees because I could no longer stand upright. I heard voices again, and the low, experimental tapping on a drum as car doors slammed. When I looked back, I could see tiny lights and vague shadows making their way towards me.

I could go no further. I sank down onto cold earth, hoping the darkness and the heather and the bumps and ridges of the Hill would conceal me. I heard Avril's deep contralto voice and Marlene's low-pitched tones. I heard a laugh that I thought was Daphne, and then they were yards away, directly below me on the path.

A man led the way. Roy Greenwood, Larry's undertaker partner, was one of the moon coven. He was dressed in loose, casual clothes, and beneath one arm he carried wood for the fire. Daphne came next, wearing the blue cloak and carrying the drum, then Avril, then two women I didn't know, one of them similarly draped in a long, dark cloak. Marlene Labaddee walked alongside David Milner, the geography teacher from the secondary school. Another two women, then Brenda, who operated the switchboard at the station. I knew the woman behind Brenda, although for a moment I couldn't quite place her. Of course – she was Mrs Ogilvy, Dwane's mother, who worked in the police canteen. Another man and woman who struck me, although I had no idea why, as a married couple. Thirteen. The number of the coven.

They passed me and went on up the Hill. I could not follow them. I wasn't sure I'd ever get up again. I had two thoughts as their lights dwindled in the distance. The first, that maybe Daphne and Avril hadn't been indiscreet after all. Maybe they'd intended me to overhear them planning this meeting, in the full knowledge that I'd follow.

The second, that I wasn't drunk. The lost time? The hallucinations? Alcohol alone wouldn't have this effect. This sense of the world slipping away had been caused by something else entirely. Alcohol and drugs. It was how the victims were subdued.

I'm sure I tried to get to my feet, to flee down the Hill if I could. I don't remember doing so. I don't remember anything else.

53

I woke in complete darkness, face down, my hands tied tight behind my back, my feet strapped together, unable to move.

Coffin! I was in a coffin!

My scream went nowhere. I wasn't just bound but gagged too, with something dry and foul-tasting in my mouth. Instantly terrified, I rolled and kicked out. I had movement. Space. I could feel cold stone beneath me. I was not in a coffin. Not yet.

Panting, sweating, I pushed and struggled to a sitting position, but just the effort of doing so seemed to suck all the breath out of me. There was no air in this place. I was going to suffocate.

I screamed and screamed into the gag, and the darkness wrapped itself around me.

When I came round a second time, my right arm felt like I'd broken it and my head as though something was striking it repeatedly. This time, though, I was ready and could catch the terror before it ran away with me. Breathe in, breathe out. Think about nothing but breathing. Eyes tight shut so the darkness couldn't win. Count the breaths. I counted fifty. Then a hundred. I could breathe. I was ready to try moving. I pushed up and opened my eyes.

The darkness around me was solid, like a black wall that I could almost touch. I had never before understood how bewilderingly terrifying it is to be blind. There could be anything, absolutely anything, inches away and I wouldn't even see it coming.

This was all wrong. Why had he picked me? I wasn't a teenager. I was twenty-two. It wasn't fair.

My breathing was quickening again. I closed my eyes, resumed counting breaths. After ten, I was steady enough to try again. I blinked twice, just to check my eyes really were open.

Turning my head, I couldn't see the faintest chink of light. I leaned forward, to either side, expecting to come up against something solid, but there was nothing there. The space I was in was sizable.

Not beneath the earth. Not yet.

I had to stay calm. I had to keep breathing. I had to think. Whatever had drugged me hours earlier had worn off. They'd taken away my power to think for a while, very successfully, but I was myself again. Frightened out of my wits, but myself.

Think.

I was indoors. The darkest of nights wouldn't produce blackness like this. I was sitting on something cold and hard, a stone floor. At the same time, the heavy, damp air suggested somewhere underground. A cellar.

Keep breathing. Take stock.

My head was hurting. I was thirsty. The pain in my arms and shoulders was fading, being replaced by a nasty attack of pins and needles. I told myself that was a good sign. My arms and legs would still work. I wasn't badly injured.

Keep breathing. Make plans.

My hands and feet were bound tight, but if I could get the gag off, I could breathe properly, even yell for help. I began twisting my head, rubbing my chin against both shoulders, stretching and flexing my jaw. I kept going, even when I felt like I might choke, focusing only on getting my mouth free, shutting my mind to where I was, and what might be in here with me. It took a while, and almost made me throw up, but I got the gag off in the end. I spat out the rag and gulped in several deep breaths to steady myself.

The difference that being able to breathe properly makes. I'd never properly understood that before.

I could breathe. I could scream. Already an improvement. Next up—

Something close to me moved. I froze, waiting to hear it again, praying I wouldn't.

Scratching. Followed by a small sound like that of something being rolled. Rodents. I pictured tiny, bright eyes somewhere close. A twitching tail. Whiskers on alert. That was OK. I was not afraid of rats.

Without realising it, I'd curled into a tight ball to get away from the rat I wasn't afraid of. I took more deep breaths and told myself, several times, that I was not afraid of rats.

It was time to move. Time to find out where I was, to get a feel for the space I was in. How big it was. What might be in here with me.

As I inched my way along the damp floor, I tried to get a sense of time. The last thing I could remember was the coven making its way past me at moonrise, nine-thirty in the evening. I was vaguely hungry, which could mean several hours had passed. I was thirsty, but didn't have the raging thirst that might suggest I'd been here more than a day.

I'd been missing hours, I thought, rather than days. It was still Tuesday night, or early Wednesday morning. This was better. I was making progress. Working things out.

And then the sound came again, and it was louder this time, and very close. It no longer sounded like a rat but something bigger. In my head, I could see claws scraping over stone, the thin, twisted body of something that never saw the light of day. A creature that lived in this subterranean place would be able to see in the dark. It could see me. It was coming for me.

I'm not sure how long I screamed before I realised it wasn't.

Just a rat, then, that I'd scared away. Or something that was biding its time. Something that enjoyed my terror.

Stop it! Keep breathing. Think.

There was no getting away from it. I was in a great deal of trouble. Daphne and Avril had drugged me. Using Marlene's knowledge of herbal medicines, they'd put something in the wine I'd drunk. I hadn't lost my mind when I'd seen Rushton in pyjamas on the main road, or the clown driving along Well Head Road. The drug they'd given me had had hallucinogenic properties.

I inched my way across the floor, feeling it cold and sometimes wet beneath me, and I began to wonder if I was in a cave, and whether I was simply shuffling deeper and deeper underground.

Keep breathing. Keep going. Keep thinking.

I'd been a gullible idiot. Daphne and Avril had been the obvious culprits from the beginning. The case was about witchcraft and they were self-confessed witches. We'd been fooled by their self-assurance, by their alibis and also – in my case, anyway – by the fact that I'd genuinely liked them.

Avril and Daphne. How could I have got it so wrong?

Avril and Daphne would not report me missing. When the constable who came to collect me from their house in the morning didn't find me, my colleagues would assume I'd fled. Avril and Daphne would tell them I'd left with my things to catch a train home. They'd send officers to my parents' house, but the police would assume I'd gone on the run, afraid my guilt was about to be proved.

They wouldn't look for me in Sabden. They wouldn't be checking newly interred caskets for me.

As the cold, hard wall struck me so did the thought that Tom could be in on it. He wasn't one of the coven, but did that prove anything really? Maybe his job had been to seduce me, to get close, find out what I knew, what I was thinking.

Telling me what she is thinking.

Tom hadn't needed a love spell where I was concerned.

Tears are an irritant when your hands are tied and you can't brush them away. They sting the eyes, make the cheeks itch.

I resumed shuffling, edging my way round the wall, feeling for anything sharp. When I reached a corner, I heard someone coming.

Heavy doors being closed. Footsteps. Someone descending a stairway? Moving closer, crossing the next room. A bolt being drawn back on the door. We are eternal optimists, I discovered, as the thought of rescue flashed through my head. I fixed my eyes on where the sound had come from. The faintest line of grey against the black. A pinprick of light, dancing about, illuminating nothing. The sound of a door being opened and footsteps on the stone.

Not rescue, then. Someone looking for me would call my name.

A thin line of light was searching the room, showing me dark walls, gleaming with damp and thick iron chains, hanging down from high on the wall. I pressed tighter into my corner, as though hiding were possible. I kept my eyes open, though, because if there was anything to see, I wanted to see it.

Nothing. A vague shape outlined against charcoal grey in the doorway. The room beyond this one was equally dark.

The light found me, hit the centre of my chest, then rose to my face, effectively blinding me.

'I am an officer of the law and imprisoning me is a very serious offence,' I began. 'Avril? Daphne? If that's you, the police know about you, and they know where I went last night. If you harm me, you will spend the rest of your lives in prison.'

The shape came at me, keeping the torch fixed on my face. My feet were grabbed and I was pulled roughly out of the corner, my head banging the wall as I went down. Then he was on top of me. This wasn't a woman. This was someone big and muscled. He turned me over so that my face was pressed against the stone again and I began to yell. My head was pulled up by my hair and my face banged down hard. I stopped screaming.

He was sitting on my chest. I could hardly breathe. I lay there, trying not to suffocate, and felt him shift round. My hands were grasped and held tight.

Something sharp and cold closed round the stem of my third finger and dread washed through me like a cold flood. I knew what he was going to do a second before he did it. Even so, the pain was extraordinary.

I didn't hear the sound of the metal clipping together, or of my bone splintering. My scream drowned out everything else.

54

There followed a period of darkness and hurting. Each time I came round, it was to a sense that I was still in the same place. It felt the same – cold, damp and hard. It had the same earthy, dank smell. And it still looked as black and empty as the soul that had put me in there.

The pain in my hand was like fire. Had he taken more than one finger? I tried tapping them in turn, but after several attempts, I gave it up. It was too confusing. I had some fingers left, I knew that much.

The creatures that shared my prison had become bolder, no longer scrabbling away every time I moved, and their scurrying and scratching became the soundtrack for my incarceration. More than once I felt something touch me.

As I drifted in and out of the world, I had visions of the rats lapping at my bleeding finger, then getting bolder, nibbling at my flesh. My hand was hurting so much it could be happening and I wouldn't know. And then those bloodsucking creatures were no longer rats but something else, something that wasn't natural. My dreams were bad, but the worst moment of all came when I woke up after a good dream, a dream of being rescued, of waking up in a hospital bed to see Tom smiling down at me.

The thirst was dreadful, as though I'd been wrung out and squeezed dry.

The gag had been replaced, tighter this time, which told me

something else. I could not be allowed to scream. If I screamed here, there was a chance I might be heard. I was not too far from people. I would have found the thought encouraging if I'd had any hope left. I lay on the cold stone, wondering how much longer before he came for me again, and felt myself getting weaker as more and more blood seeped from my open wound.

The sound of the doors woke me for the last time in that dark place. They were pulled open in a hurry, allowed to clang, then banged shut. I heard footsteps coming closer, smelled something all too familiar and knew, finally, who had taken me.

I asked myself if I had the strength to fight and the answer came back, no. I caught a glimmer of light from a torch beam and closed my eyes, an instinctive response to an imminent yet undefined horror, and felt something harsh and rough being tugged over my head.

Sacking.

I was fighting now, bucking and wriggling, because I could picture the rough sacking we'd pulled out of the grave that had briefly held Luna. He was encasing me in sacking. No coffin for me, just a rough shroud, which he would have checked already for its strength. Unlike Luna, I wouldn't be able to claw my way out.

My frantic thrashing about made no difference to him. He pulled the sacking down over my body, lifting me when he had to, holding me down when he didn't. I kicked and hit out, even with both wrists together, even with pain shooting up my arm. I felt my shoe leave my foot and still I kicked. I grabbed and pulled and heard fabric tearing.

He beat me, of course. He was much stronger, uninjured, and I was bound hand and foot. When he finally got my feet inside the sack, he drew the opening together and I sensed knots being pulled tight.

A stillness fell. I could hear him panting, then getting to his feet. I heard banging, scraping sounds that I couldn't interpret, but I felt a faint change in the atmosphere. Even through the sacking I could tell it was marginally cooler, a little fresher. And I could hear sounds of the outside world. The distant roar of a car.

He picked me up. I was carried a few yards, then thrown – there was no other word for it – but I landed almost immediately, as though he'd lifted me from a hole in the ground. He pushed and I rolled, and then I heard the banging again, which I thought, this time, was the sound of heavy doors being closed.

I was lifted again. Put down again. Another hard surface, but metal this time. Doors closed; an engine started. The vehicle I was captive in moved away.

I'd wait for it to stop, I decided, and then roll to the side and hammer against the metal with all my might, or I'd kick the back doors open and roll out. Better to die on the road than what this bastard had in mind.

He didn't stop. Not once. We hadn't been driving for much more than fifteen minutes when he pulled over again. I heard the driver's door open and close, then the rear doors.

I had plenty of fight left in me. My life was about to end in the most horrible way. I fought hard inside that sack, and I screamed as loud as I could, even with the gag half choking me.

He carried me over his shoulder and in no time at all I was on the ground. I squirmed like a worm. I kicked and punched and rolled. I made noises that in my head were as loud as thunder but which probably travelled no more than a few yards. I went on and on until I collapsed from sheer exhaustion. Enough. I could do no more. I waited for him to roll me into the open grave.

He didn't do it. I lay, panting and sobbing, bracing myself for the last blow. It didn't come.

He'd gone.

I knew it as surely as I knew I was still alive. There was no sense of anyone near me. Wherever I was, I was alone.

Then footsteps, running.

I began fighting again. Someone was at my feet, pressing down hard. There was a pulling sound, a slicing sound and then my feet were free. Still tied but free of the sack. I could hear the sacking being torn, someone telling me to keep still – 'For the love of God, keep still' – and then the sack was pulled off my head. I could see the night around me, the stars and the moon. I could see the trees round the edge of the graveyard and the headstones, one of which so nearly became my own. And I could see the large head and small body of the man who was reaching behind me now, untying my gag, pulling the rag from my mouth and staring at me with wide, frightened eyes as though he really had pulled something undead from beneath the earth.

Dwane recovered quickly from his shock. He pulled away and yelled, 'Mam! Dad! Get out here! Someone get an ambulance.'

Speaking was hard, but I had to shut him up.

'Dwane, stop. Please stop shouting.'

I wasn't sure he'd hear me, but he must have done because his lips slapped shut.

'I need a drink,' I croaked. 'Now. And I need to phone Superintendent Rushton. Can you help? Can you help me get up?'

He looked at the ropes round my ankles and wrists, and, practical craftsman that he was, took a penknife from his back pocket. Within seconds I was free and he was pulling me upright. One of my shoes was missing.

I swayed and Dwane caught me, and then we were staggering together, like a drunken, mismatched courting couple, towards the entrance of St Wilfred's Churchyard.

'I need a phone,' I said.

'Heard you t'first time,' Dwane replied.

At the porch, I had to stop, to lean against the gate stone. 'Did you see who left me there?' I asked.

He shook his head. 'Nah. Heard an engine. Odd, this time of night. I looked out t'window and couldn't see anything, but I weren't happy. Not with all the shenanigans going on in grave-yards lately.'

In different circumstances, the word 'shenanigans' might have made me smile. As it was, I was glad Dwane was stronger than he looked, because I was fading fast.

'I got you.' He wrapped an arm around my waist and turned me to face the street.

'Whole bloody town's been looking for you,' he said as we set off again. 'Rushton's had us all combing t'moors.'

The whole town?

'They've got posters up and all. Nice picture. I've got one in my bedroom.'

'How?' I managed. 'How did they know I was gone?'

'Them two lezzers you live with now reported it. Camping out at station, according to my mam. Making right bloody nuis-ances of themselves. Insisting you can't have run off, because your handbag and all your stuff is still at their house. I agreed with 'em. I said you wouldn't run.'

Oh, Avril, Daphne, I'm so sorry.

'And then they found your bike up on top road. It didn't look good.'

We'd stopped at the house at the end of the terrace, not a stone's throw from the church. Dwane rattled hard on the door knocker.

'What time is it?' I asked, and knew I should really be asking what day it was.

'Gone three,' he told me. 'She won't be best pleased.'

Above us, a window opened. 'What the bugger?' someone called down.

'Lady needs help,' Dwane called up. 'Police business. Look sharp.'

While we waited, he told me it was the early hours of Friday morning. I'd been missing two full days.

'Dwane,' I said, a couple of minutes later, when the door opened and he barged our way inside, past a startled woman in her dressing gown. 'I need to speak to Superintendent Rushton. I don't trust anyone else. It won't be easy for you, because the sergeant at the station will want to take your call himself, and he'll want to get a patrol car out here, but it's really important that I talk to the superintendent before anyone else knows you've found me. Can you try, please?'

He gave me another of his completely unfathomable stares and picked up the phone. He dialled four numbers.

'Uncle Stan,' he said, after a few seconds. 'It's Dwane. I'm at Auntie Janet's. Get thee sen round here. There's a reet to-do.'

55

Friday 4 July 1969

While we waited for the superintendent to arrive, I learned that Dwane's mother and the super were cousins, and that Rushton was Dwane's godfather. His Aunt Janet, an honorary title because she was no blood relative, was a quiet, sensible woman. She brought me a glass of water, then a mug of tea, thick with sugar, and then aspirin. By the time the super's car arrived, I was feeling a little better.

'Florence, what the bloody hell—' Rushton was saying as he walked through the door without knocking. Then he saw me, sitting on a chair in the hallway, a blanket around my shoulders, my hand on a clean tea towel on the hall table. Aunt Janet was trying to clean my wound with warm water and cotton wool, while Dwane stood guard at my right shoulder. 'Jesus.' His face drained. 'Ambulance on its way?'

'There isn't time,' I said. 'Sir, I know who did this. If we can find him quickly, we can prove it.' For the first time, I opened my clutched right hand and let him see the small triangle of apricot fabric and the tiny button that I held there. 'I tore this off his shirt,' I said. 'It will be covered in blood too. If we can find him quickly—'

'Who?' he said.

'Larry Glassbrook,' I replied. 'I smelled his aftershave.'

★

Rushton drove me in his car to the Glassbrook house. Dwane sat immediately behind me in the back seat. Rushton had tried, briefly, to send him home, but the little guy was standing tall. He wasn't leaving me. A panda car followed us, lights and sirens off, and two more joined our convoy along the way. Rushton was taking no chances.

It hadn't been easy persuading him to go straight for the arrest rather than get me to hospital. Especially as Aunt Janet kept pointing to the red streaks running up my hand, and talking about infection, and predicting the loss of my entire arm if I didn't get it seen to soon.

Eventually, when I pointed out that I wasn't going to stop arguing, he agreed to give me an hour.

'Them two daft old bats drugged you,' he said to me as we pulled away from the church. 'Bloody well admitted as much. Said they wanted to make sure you had a good night's sleep and that you didn't follow them up the Hill. We realised what must have happened when we found your bike on the top road. Spent bloody hours looking up there. Dogs and all.'

'Larry found me,' I said. 'He must have followed me from the house and carried me to the van while the coven was on the Hill.'

'If someone had told me when I joined up that I'd be arresting witches and warlocks . . .' He shook his head. 'Why you, Flossie? No offence but you're no teenager.'

'He knew I was getting close,' I said. 'I've kept my charts and my notes in my bedroom and it didn't have a lock. I know the girls were looking at them, so he must have been too. That's why he wanted me to leave. He thought I'd spot something, work out that it was him. When we homed in on the cricket club, he knew he didn't have much time left.'

'Luna, though? The lass is his own daughter.'

'I don't think Luna was ever in any real danger. She was only in the grave for a few minutes. He knew I was on my way up there.'

'Now, see, that's what I don't get.' Dwane leaned forward. 'If it was him, how did he phone you, Florence, that night to tell you where Luna was? How did he do that if he was in bed, upstairs?'

Rushton practically stepped on the brakes. 'How the bloody Norah do you know about that?' he demanded of the face in the rear-view mirror.

Dwane looked offended. 'Mam serves breakfast, dinner and tea to your lot three days a week,' he said. 'You think she's deaf?'

Rushton sighed as I turned back to Dwane. 'I'm guessing his girlfriend, Beryl, made that call,' I said. 'She must have given him false alibis too.'

We turned into the Glassbrooks' road. I recognised several cars parked some way down from their house, and as Rushton pulled over, I saw their drivers getting out. Sharples, Brown, Green, Butterworth. And Tom. I wrapped the tea towel more firmly round my hand – it was already soaked in blood – and tried to unlock the car door, but Dwane had jumped out and beaten me to it. He wrapped an arm around my waist to help me walk and I didn't have the heart to stop him. The others had gathered on the opposite pavement and they waited for us to cross.

'Good to see you, Florence,' said Sharples in a low voice. Tom looked as though he wanted to stamp on Dwane.

'I want the place surrounded,' Rushton said. 'I'm going in with Florence and Jack. Randy, Tom, you're back-up. Dwane, stay in the bloody car.'

Rushton, Sharples and I led the way up the drive, Tom and Randy following, Dwane tagging along at the rear. The others spread out round the property.

The house seemed to be in darkness. 'We should go round the back,' I said.

We left the drive and made our way through the garden. As we neared the back door, I could see a low light in the kitchen. Rushton stepped in front of me and tried the back door. It opened.

Larry was sitting at the kitchen table, a bottle of brandy and a glass in front of him. His shirt was apricot-coloured, and there were bloodstains near the buttons. His head was in his hands and he didn't look up as we came in. I followed Rushton; Sharples came next, then Tom and Randy. We moved around the table, but I was in the middle. The one closest.

'On your feet, please, Larry,' Rushton said. 'I need to have a look at your shirt.'

Larry tossed back the remainder of the brandy and, finally, looked at me.

'How you doing, Flossie?' he said, with a grin that struck me, at the time, as pure evil.

'Up,' said Sharples, and Larry stood up. His shirt was untucked and we could see very plainly the torn bottom corner with the missing button.

'Do you want to do the honours, WPC Lovelady?' said Rushton.

I did. I really did. I just couldn't remember quite how 'the honours' went. I'd dreamed of making my first arrest; I'd practised it many times in front of the mirror, but when it came down to it, the words escaped me.

'You're going to die in prison, you vile man,' was what I said to him.

Rushton did it properly, and then Tom and Randy patted him down and searched his discarded jacket, looking for hidden weapons. In his jacket pocket Tom found something that I knew would haunt him for ever.

My finger.

Part Three

'... Make thick my blood.
Stop up the access and passage to remorse,
That no compunctious visitings of nature
Shake my fell purpose ...'

Macbeth, William Shakespeare

56

Tuesday, 10 August 1999

'We need to find Sally,' I say.

'You said we were going home.'

'Larry knew I'd come back here for his funeral. He knew I'd find the clay picture. He practically told me where to look. And that means Sally must have put it there.'

'I don't see how.' Ben wrinkles his brow, an old, babyish habit that to this day tugs at my heartstrings.

'It couldn't have been Mary. I saw her face. She was frightened. She and Sally were the only ones with keys.'

'Hello? Beehives? No key needed. If Larry had told Sally to hide a witch's doll on the off-chance of you pitching up, it would have been in the house. Mum, this is pointless.'

I'm not really listening to Ben. 'Sally was the only one who visited him apart from me. Besides, I have her keys. I need to get them back to her.'

I stand up. He stays where he is. 'It's not a good idea, Mum.'

Ben is wise beyond his years, but he is still a child, and I've had decades of telling other people what to do. We find the car and head out. Once we leave the town and its new traffic systems behind, familiarity steals over me like a worn but warm cloak. The narrow road is unchanged. Its walls are still blackened with grime, and their state of repair seems the same as the last time I drove this way. I expect to see escaping sheep round every corner.

The farmhouses and agricultural buildings we pass are the same eclectic collections of old stone, rotting wood and corrugated iron.

I brake hard once, to let the inevitable ewe scuttle out of the road.

As we climb higher, the moors spread out around us, their colours glowing in the bright sunlight. The grass is shamrock green, and the heather is starting to cast swathes of bruised colour across the landscape. Dominating it all, treeless, thin-soiled, watchful, stands the Hill.

Ben is mostly silent on the journey, looking out of the window, only once turning to me. 'It's all a bit *Wuthering Heights*, isn't it?' he says, and I don't disagree. Neither do I say that he's seeing the Pendle Forest at its best. In the cold months, the beauty around us turns grim.

Northdean Nursing Home is large: three storeys, stone-built – of course – with gabled windows and multiple chimneys. It is not dissimilar to the Glassbrook house and I wonder if its style and proximity to the Hill was chosen to make Sally feel at home.

In the reception area – clean and functional, smelling of chemically produced rose essence – Ben and I wait for attention. When a woman in blue overalls arrives, I give our names and ask if we can see Sally. She says, 'Of course. Come this way,' and would we like tea in a half-hour when the residents have theirs?

'I haven't seen Sally for many years.' We follow the woman down a corridor and up the stairs to the first floor. 'What can I expect?'

She glances back over her shoulder. 'Early onset dementia. She may not know you, I'm afraid. But it's nice for her to have visitors. Do you know her well?' She smiles at Ben, even though she is older than I am, and I realise that female attention is something my son, and I, will have to get used to.

'I'm an old friend,' I say. 'Do her family visit much?'

She says nothing, and by the slightly different rhythm her foot-steps make along the upper corridor, I know that she is aware of Sally's history and her connection to the man we buried today. She raps on a door at the end of the corridor and opens it without waiting to be invited. I think I hear voices in the room beyond, but when Ben and I follow her in, we see a single figure, sitting in an armchair at the window.

'Hello, Sally,' I say, as the door closes behind me. 'It's Florence. Do you remember me?'

There is no reply, and so I approach the chair, catching her re-flection in the glass of the window before I see her properly. The beautiful woman I remember has gone. Sally was always thin, but in her late sixties, her skin seems loose on her bones, as though at some point she lost weight suddenly and quickly. There are deep grooves around her mouth, and her eyes seem almost to have dis-appeared beneath a brow that has grown more prominent with age. Or maybe it's an illusion created by her lack of hair.

I can see large patches of reddened, scabbed scalp. I watch a thin, trembling hand reach up and take hold of her hair, and then I notice that clinging to her clothes, lying scattered around her chair on the carpet, are dozens of stray fair hairs. Sally is pulling out her own hair.

The sight of her has blown away the conviction that brought me here. She doesn't look capable of leaving the room by herself, never mind carrying out malicious errands for Larry. Sally cannot have left the effigy for me to find.

'We're not alone, Mum.'

I spin round and see what Ben has already spotted.

There is a woman in the corner, by a bookcase, frozen in the act of returning a book. For a second I think I've made a mistake, that this is Sally and that she has barely changed at all. She is still slim as a young willow tree, and her hair gleams silver blonde, although it's much shorter than I remember. She's wearing make-up, though, which I never saw Sally do, and her clothes don't seem quite right. I never saw Sally in jeans and high-heeled boots.

'Hello, Flossie,' she says. 'What a surprise. And who is this gorgeous young man?'

'My son,' I say. 'Ben, this is Cassandra Glassbrook. You might have heard of her. Cassie Glass, the songwriter?'

'He's too young.' Cassie smiles from me to Ben, like a fox wondering which chicken's throat it's going to rip out first. 'I haven't released anything in years.'

'A lot of people believe that Cassie, not Bryan Ferry, wrote "Slave to Love".' As I speak, I'm hoping Ben won't say he's never heard of 'Slave to Love' or Bryan Ferry, that for once in his life he will be tactful.

'Did you sue?' he says.

'We reached an agreement.' Cassie gives that small, smug smile I remember so well.

'Good song. Mum and Dad play it when they think I'm in bed.'

'We didn't know you were here,' I say. 'The woman who showed us in didn't mention it. If you and your mother want some privacy . . .' I leave the offer hanging.

Cassie steps away from the bookshelf. 'It's been years since Mum and I had a conversation. Stay for a few minutes. She seems to like people talking around her. Although it's impossible to know how much she takes in.'

We sit, moving chairs so that Cassie, Sally and I form a little group in the window, and it feels as though the Hill is the fourth member of our party, not Ben, because he takes a chair a little out of the circle and opens his book.

'I don't announce myself at reception,' Cassie says. 'There's a side door that's not locked during the day. I just slip in.'

I remember Cassie's old habit of moving around silently, of sneaking up on people when they had no idea she was close.

'I didn't see you at the funeral,' I say. 'I looked for you.'

She shrugs. 'I wore sunglasses, sat upstairs. I figured Luna would enjoy having the attention to herself.'

Luna. She'd vanished after the service into a waiting car, seemingly unmoved by the hostility of the townsfolk. She'll be miles away by now, speeding back to her affluent life. Last time I checked, she was London-based. Cassie, on the other hand, lives in a converted loft in nearby Salford.

'Cassie, when did you last go to the old house?' I ask her.

'Why?' she counters.

I remind myself that I cannot demand information from Cassie Glassbrook. I will have to tease it out of her.

'I found something there today. It might be relevant to your father's case and I have to report it to the police. If you—'

'How thrilling. What?'

I allow a second or two to pass and hold her stare.

Her smile fades. 'Get over yourself, Flossie. What do I have to gain from winning your approval? Or lose by being myself?'

I say nothing.

'You saw Dad in prison,' Cassie says. 'I know you did. Mum told me. What did he talk about?'

Sally's face starts a strange, twitching motion, as though an insect is bothering her and she's trying to shake it off.

Cassie did this too, back in the old days, said whatever came into her head without considering its impact. I remind myself that she has never married, never had children and that she achieved financial success early in life. She has probably never, properly, grown up.

'He talked about the three of you,' I say. 'You and Luna and your mum.' I glance at Sally, but her face has fallen into stillness again. 'Cassie, if you went to the house today, or recently, if your father asked you to leave something there, it would be very helpful if you told me.'

'I'll tell you if you tell me what it was.'

'You know I can't do that.'

She twists abruptly at the waist, a movement that seems a little unnatural. 'Why don't I ask this gorgeous boy of yours?'

She smiles again at Ben, and the predatory look on her face makes me want to scratch her. I imagine my fingernails raking down from her eyes, tearing apart the skin, causing blood to run like tears down her face.

My breathing is quickening again; I can feel my face glowing hot. Ben was right: I was a fool to come here.

'I was in the car,' says Ben. 'I can't tell you anything.'

Cassie exhales loudly and seems to deflate in her chair as she turns back to me. 'I haven't been to the house of horrors for over a decade,' she says. 'I'm never going back.'

Cassie's face is entirely serious now, the mocking sneer gone completely. I believe her. I try to take deep breaths without letting it show. Even so, I see Ben glance sharply at me.

'Why did you never leave town, Cassie? Surely it would have been easier for the three of you?'

Cassie's eyes glance towards her mother. For a second their eyes seem to meet, and then Sally's glass over again. 'Mum refused,' she says. 'She gave various excuses over the years, didn't you, Mum?' She leans over and unwinds the hair from Sally's finger, gently pushes her mother's hand back to her lap.

'Dad wouldn't agree to selling the house, was one excuse. Another was that nobody would buy a place with such a gruesome history. After a few years, Luna and I both went to university and it was less of an issue. At least there we could pretend to be normal people. Tell me something, Flossie, did he ever tell you why he did it?'

'Many times,' I say. 'He said he did it out of love.'

She pulls a face. 'That's twisted.'

'Yes, I always thought so.'

Her eyes narrow and then settle on my left hand. 'Still missing,' she says, and I swear there is a tiny smile tickling the corners of her mouth.

'Fingers don't grow back,' snaps Ben, surprising us both.

'No,' Cassie says, and I know that she is unruffled by my son's annoyance, possibly even entertained by it. 'But you know, prosthetic limbs and stuff.'

'A finger isn't a limb, it's a digit, and Mum doesn't model nail varnish, she catches criminals.'

Ben does not have my hair colour, but he has the classic redhead temper. 'Are you still in touch with Luna?' I say, to change the subject, because I don't want these two spatting. Ben is smarter, but he also has a strong sense of fair play. If they fight, Cassie will win.

She turns back to me. 'Not since she went to university. I don't think Mum's seen her for years either.'

We both glance at Sally. It's probably coincidence, but her eyes seem to be holding more water than a few minutes ago.

'What you went through was a major trauma,' I say. 'It affects people in different ways.'

Cassie pulls a face. 'It wasn't only about Dad. Luna was pissed off about John. He dumped her a few weeks after Dad was convicted.'

'Well, that's not entirely surprising,' I say. 'And in any event, John had issues back then. I'm not sure he was ready for a serious girlfriend.'

'He dumped her for me.'

What? I don't say this. I say, 'Really?' as though it's no big deal. Even though it is a big deal.

'It was always me he was interested in,' Cassie says. 'I wasn't sure about dating someone younger. Pretending to be keen on Luna gave him an excuse to hang around.' Her eyes drift away and she laughs. 'Remember that time you found a dog in your bedroom? It was John's. His dad's pub always had black dogs, to make some sense of the pub name, I suppose. He was with me in the house. We didn't know where it had gone.' She laughs again, and it feels as though she's laughing at me. 'We nearly died when you raised blue murder and Dad came charging upstairs.'

I find myself shaking my head and not really sure why. John, interested in Cassie, secretly dating Cassie, while telling Tom and me he thought he might be gay? What boy of fifteen, back in the 1960s, would claim to be gay if he wasn't?

I get up to go. Being here has reminded me of why I never liked Cassandra Glassbrook. I feel sorry for Sally, but there is nothing I can do for her. I simply have to hope she is being kindly treated. I bend to pat her hand and wish her goodbye, but her eyes are fixed on the Hill and I don't think she has even realised I'm in the room.

Cassie watches us go, her eyes on Ben, but her last words are for me. 'Did you ever think, Flossie, that Larry was keeping you close for a reason?'

57

The sun is still strong when we step outside, but the breezes dance around our heads, lifting my hair, cooling the beads of sweat on Ben's temples. Neither of us head back to the car. We both seem to need the fresh air, although there had been nothing unpleasant about the atmosphere in the nursing home.

Nothing we could put a finger on, anyway.

We walk to the edge of the car park and look out over the moors.

'You've still got the keys to their house, Mum.'

I glance down at my bag. 'Oh, so I have. I forgot.'

'No, you didn't. I saw you look at your bag three times.'

A flock of birds flies past. Small, black rooks. The only bird I ever saw on or around the Hill.

'You had your head in that book all the time we were in there,' I say. 'You didn't see a thing.'

'I saw that old woman watch you both talking every time she thought you were looking the other way. She hasn't got dementia, Mum – she's faking it.'

I turn away from the view to face him. 'Nonsense,' I say, but the look on his face doesn't falter.

'When you said he did it out of love, she reacted. Her face screwed up, like she was in pain. And then again when you talked about the dog.'

'She had her back to you. You couldn't see her face.'

'I could see her reflection.'

What he is telling me seems absurd. And yet Ben's intelligence has been surprising me for fifteen years. 'Sally isn't even seventy yet. Why would she fake dementia and lock herself away in a nursing home?'

'If people think she's a spanner short of a toolbox, they'll leave her alone. Not hassle her with questions. There are lots of ways of running away, Mum.'

I think about this. No. 'She could have sold the house. Moved the girls away. Made a new life.'

'You're assuming she could. What if she couldn't?'

There is a knot tightening in my stomach. Thirty years ago, we thought we had the answers. Not all of them maybe, but enough. I've been back hours and I'm realising how little I know.

Ben and I walk, by unspoken agreement, out of the car park and onto the road.

'I've been thinking about that letter,' Ben says. 'About Larry writing to you a lot. Any number of people could have known that, and that you visited him. They would have expected you to come back for the funeral. Any one of them could have left that thing for you.'

'They couldn't know I'd go to the hives, though.'

I remember my hairbrush, left behind in the Glassbrook house. *They have my hair. They have my hair.*

What if they have my finger too? What if they somehow managed to get hold of it, all those years ago? What if they have my bone, the most powerful essence of all?

'Mum!'

I make myself focus on Ben. I am being ridiculous. There is no 'they'. Larry, the child killer, the man who planned to kill me, made the clay picture thirty years ago, and it got overlooked somehow.

'Was he guilty?' Ben asks.

And there it is. The question I have never allowed myself to ask. When I wake in the night, and it seems I am the only person alive in the world, still that question will not form itself in my head.

'There was a lot of evidence,' I say.

'What evidence, exactly?'

I take a deep breath. 'Partly circumstantial. He had access to the caskets directly before burial. He had transport to ferry the unconscious kids around. He knew them all, via the cricket club, so they wouldn't be afraid of him. He was a good-looking man, so people were more inclined to trust him.'

'And he was found with your dismembered finger in his jacket pocket.'

'That too,' I agree. 'And my blood on his shirt and in his wood store. He claimed that's where he kept me the two days I was missing. Gagged, so none of the family would hear me screaming.'

Ben starts. I let my hand touch his briefly.

'The police found an unfinished clay effigy in his workshop, and some belongings of the three earlier victims,' I say. 'Enough to convict him even without his confession.'

'So was he guilty?' Ben repeats.

'He never said he wasn't,' I say.

'Er . . .'

'He pleaded guilty. But he said the minimum he could get away with in court. There wasn't a trial, so to some extent he didn't have to say much.'

'But you must have interviewed him?'

'I didn't. I wouldn't have been allowed to, but yes, he was interviewed at length, and I read the transcripts.'

'And?'

'They were vague at times. There were things he refused to

answer, or claimed not to remember. He insisted it wasn't Beryl, for example, who'd made the phone call to me that night about Luna's whereabouts, but he wouldn't say who.'

Ben gives me a pitying look. 'And you all just accepted this?'

'You have no idea of the pressure we were under to get a conviction,' I tell him. 'Larry was a gift horse.'

'So was he guilty?' Ben asks again.

When his mind is on something, Ben will not let it go.

'Ben, I honestly don't know.' I turn round. 'Come on, we have to get back. I want to catch someone senior at the station before they all go home for the day.'

He follows, unable or unwilling to see the dread that's creeping over me. 'Now we're getting somewhere. Why would Larry, why would anyone plead guilty to a crime they didn't commit?'

'You tell me,' I snap. The Glassbrook case made my career. It made me famous. Even now I see young officers nudging each other when they look my way. *That's her. That's Florence Lovelady.*

It changed me, too, in ways it took me years to fully realise. I have demons, of course I have. No one could go through what I did and emerge unscathed. There are times when the dark places seem just round the corner, and God knows they feel a whole lot closer now that I'm back in the North.

But I lived. I brought the killer to justice. I won, and that knowledge made me more confident, less inclined to step back and let others have the limelight. It gave me a sense of the importance of life, of the need to reach out and grab opportunities with both hands. It taught me never to waste time, because time is precious. Larry's conviction made me who I am.

'Who was he protecting?' Ben says.

We get back to the car and sit, doors open, because it's too hot to close them.

If Larry's conviction is unsafe, what does that make the woman who was born out of it?

'Is it possible Larry knew who the real killer was and took the blame anyway?' Ben asks.

I say, 'Why would he?'

'It would have to be someone he cared about a lot.'

I shake my head. 'That only leaves his family. The two girls were kids. Sally wasn't a big woman.'

'None of the victims were big. And Sally, in fact everyone in the house, had access to some weird and wonderful drugs. Sally's midwifery drugs, not to mention all her herbal stuff.'

I had no idea Ben knew so much about the case. I'd been forgetting the increasing potential of the Internet, and the determination of fifteen-year-old boys.

'Sally?' I say. 'It isn't possible.'

'She hasn't got dementia, Mum. I'm sure of it. But great way of avoiding awkward questions – pretend you can't remember your own name. Who's going to take her in for questioning?'

'The killings stopped.'

Ben thinks about this. 'Well, maybe that was the deal. He'd take the blame if they behaved themselves. Maybe he had an insurance policy. Something hidden in that old house. Maybe that's why he wouldn't let them sell it.'

Ben cannot be right. The house was searched. Thoroughly. Anything that was there to be found would have been found. I've stopped arguing, I realise. I'm actually thinking about it.

'Or maybe they didn't stop.' Ben is on a roll. 'Maybe they chose their victims better. Teenage runaways. Homeless kids. Who'd miss them?'

'You have a very warped mind, you know that?'

'What can I say? You taught me everything I know.'

I force myself to smile, although it's the last thing I feel like doing. 'But not everything I know,' I say. 'Come on, it's getting late.'

He makes no move to close his door. 'We're not going home, are we?' he says, and he looks so worried that for a moment I'm tempted to head straight for the M6.

'One night,' I say, instead. 'What's the worst that can happen?'

58

Sabden Police Station is in the same building, but I'd barely have recognised it. A new extension has been added to the front, all glass walls and revolving doors. The fluorescent lights glow softly, and not even those in the corner of my eye flicker. The scuffed tiles have been replaced by a spotless blue carpet. Huge, professionally taken photographs of the police in action hang around the walls: men in high-vis jackets helping pensioners from flooded homes, a pretty young constable visiting a primary school, a young black copper chatting to some kids on the street.

The desk sergeant and his team live in a glass box in the corner. The uniformed officer behind the glass looks up without interest until I hold up my warrant card. Then he practically jumps to his feet.

'Good afternoon, ma'am. Do you have an appointment?'

I explain that no, I don't, but I have new information about the Glassbrook case and I'd like to speak to a senior officer about it.

He disappears for two minutes, and when he comes back, Ben and I are escorted through to an interview room on the ground floor.

'The cells used to be on this corridor.' I speak to Ben, but am conscious of our escort listening too. 'I was kept here overnight once. Cell next to this one, I think.' I smile at the sergeant, as though to show there are no hard feelings, even though he is far too young to have been on duty back then.

'Before my time,' he confirms. 'Can I get you a coffee?'

I decline. Ben asks for black with three sugars.

'What?' he says, at the look on my face, when the door closes. 'Since when do you take sugar? Or drink coffee?'

He gives me his full-tooth grin. 'I know. It just seemed like a bad-ass cop thing to do.'

The coffee appears, faster than expected, and a glass of water for me, which I didn't ask for but appreciate. And then, in the corridor behind the attending constable, he appears.

He isn't in uniform but in a dark suit with a black tie, which he's pulled loose. He waits for the constable to vanish, then steps inside and lets the door close. He looks Ben up and down, and I'm proud as punch that Ben gets to his feet, and then he turns to me.

'Florence Lovelady, as I live and breathe,' says Tom Devine.

I'd seen the odd photograph in thirty years. I'd read reports of cases he'd been involved with. Stalking old flames has become a whole lot easier with the dawn of the Internet. Nothing, though, could have prepared me for the smell of Tom. For the way that while his skin has aged, and his dark hair assumed a silver sheen, his eyes are still that same deep blue.

Shorter hair and a clean-shaven face suit him, making it easier to see the shape of his head and his jawline. I hadn't realised before what a perfect face he has. He is bigger than I remember, but solid with muscle rather than running to fat.

Neither of us seems to know what to do. Old friends kiss and hug when they meet, but the idea of Tom and I doing that seems absurd. Then he turns to my son. 'I'm Tom.' He holds out his hand and they shake. 'Your mother and I worked together years ago.'

By unspoken agreement we all sit. I put my bag on my lap like a nervous middle-aged woman. Which I am, I guess.

'I'd heard you were in town,' Tom says.

I say, 'I thought I might see you in church.'

'Events.' He gives a little shrug. *You know how it is.*

Ben has his book, but it sits unopened on the table. His eyes are flicking from Tom to me. Tom is staring at me across the table.

'Well, didn't you do well?' Tom says.

'Likewise,' I counter, although I far outrank Tom. I am currently the most senior serving policewoman in Britain. The nature of my role at the Met keeps me out of the public eye, but few in the force won't have heard of me.

'How's the family?' I ask.

He nods his head. 'Good, thanks. Kent teaches at Lancaster University. Charlene's a nurse.'

I wait.

'Eileen and I divorced ten years ago. Job hazard, as you know. She's fine, according to the kids.'

I don't know how I feel about Tom's marriage breaking up. Thirty years ago, barely any time at all after Larry Glassbrook's arrest, Eileen announced that she was pregnant. I'd never seen Tom so uncertain, totally thrown by a decision he didn't feel remotely able to make. So I'd made it for him.

People assume I left Lancashire because I was traumatised by the Glassbrook case, and I've always been happy to let them. The truth is, I left because I couldn't bear to be around Tom.

'So what can I do for you?' he says, and I realise Ben is looking puzzled, and that I might have drifted away for a few seconds.

I reach into my bag and find the effigy. When I pull the wrapping off, I watch Tom's face. I see the shine leave it, his eyes lose their spark.

'Where did that come from?' he asks, and all the joy has gone from his voice.

'I found it in the house this morning,' I tell him. 'Or rather, in the garden.' I reach out and, without touching it with my bare hand, turn it. 'It's me,' I add. 'And somehow it doesn't look thirty years old.'

'Can I ask why you thought it necessary to visit the house?' Tom's face twists, his eyebrows shoot up, and for a second the old Tom is staring right back at me. 'Oh Christ, you didn't break in, did you? Tell me you didn't break in.'

'I went out of curiosity,' I say. 'And no, I didn't break in. Sally's old housekeeper was there.'

'So what do you think?' Ben says, and for a moment we are both surprised, almost as though we'd forgotten he was with us. 'Was Larry Glassbrook guilty?'

'Of course he was.' Tom's eyes drop to my hand on the table. My left hand.

'So how do you explain a clay picture of my mother in a garden that he hasn't set foot in for thirty years?'

'I can't, Son,' Tom says, and I know that Ben won't like that. 'But if you ask me to guess, I'd say practical joke. There are a lot of journalists in town. Maybe it was a ruse to get a comment from her.'

He looks at me again. 'Anyone who's done a bit of digging over the years will know you were in touch with Larry. You're the obvious one to go after for a story.'

That makes sense. It seems odd, I know, but simply being in the same room as Tom is making me feel calmer.

'It was hidden in a beehive. How could anyone have known Mum would look there? She couldn't have been supposed to find it.'

Tom lifts his head, like a hound picking up a scent, but his eyes catch mine. '"Tell it to the bees,"' he says, and we smile at each other.

Ben pushes his chair back noisily.

'If you leave it with me, I'll have it checked for prints,' Tom says. 'See if anything crops up. Maybe have someone compare it to the originals. Although God knows where they are now. We'll have to use photographs.' He bends closer. 'It doesn't look that similar to me. Darker clay.'

He's right. I'd have spotted that myself if I hadn't been so spooked. 'Thank you,' I say.

Picking up on my improving mood, he smiles. 'How long are you staying?'

'We're booked into the Black Dog for two nights.'

'Do you have a free evening for dinner?'

Ben says, 'I'm too young to be left on my own. And she's married. To my dad. Who will be joining us as soon as he can get a flight.'

Tom's eyebrows are high with amusement. 'You were invited too,' he says.

I stand up. 'It's probably not a good idea. But it's been great to see you. And I'm sure I can leave this in your capable hands.'

Tom starts to get up too. Ben stays exactly where he is. 'You're going to leave it here?' he says to me.

I shrug. 'Not my case, angel. Not my patch.'

'Mum, it's a voodoo doll. If someone damages it, they damage you too. You can't just leave it with this lot.'

I've never seen my son quite so anxious. Even Tom looks surprised.

'We'll take good care of it,' he says. 'Nobody hurts your mother on my watch.'

Tom walks us to the door.

In Reception, I say, 'I was talking to Cassie Glassbrook earlier, up at the nursing home where Sally lives now.'

Tom gives an exaggerated sigh. 'You're not going to make me put a tail on you, are you?'

'She and John Donnelly were dating back then. When he told us he thought he was gay.'

'Lots of kids are confused about their sexuality. You said so yourself.'

'He wasn't confused. He was lying.'

We've reached the exit. Tom gives another heavy sigh. 'Florence, it's over. Let it go.' He holds the door open, and as I step past him, I hear him mutter, 'I let you go.'

When I see Ben's face, I know he heard it too.

'Did you shag him?' he says.

We stare at each other from one side of the station entrance to the other, and I know anyone passing will think, *Mother collecting her wayward son after a police caution.*

'What happened fifteen years before you were born is none of your business,' I tell him.

'I'll take that as a yes.'

I wait. We continue to stare.

I ask, 'What's wrong with you?'

His face goes from angry to sad in a split second. 'I don't like this place. It's giving me the creeps. I want to go home.'

'First thing in the morning.'

I see his leg twitch, as though he might actually be about to stamp his foot.

'No, now. I don't like the way people are looking at us. I don't like the way you were conned into coming here, and I don't like that smooth twat in there.'

I set off, leaving him behind, but he is only fifteen and of course he follows. As I beep open the car, he says, 'Sorry, Mum.'

He looks it, so I let it go. Ben rarely gives me any real grief. I'm about to start the engine when he speaks.

'You've still got those keys, Mum.'

This time, I don't even pretend to be annoyed with myself.

'It was thirty years ago. I don't care if he was guilty or not. Please, Mum, let it go.'

59

John Donnelly is waiting in the bar when we get back. He offers us both a drink, on the house, and because I want to talk to him, I accept a Diet Coke. So does Ben, although he's fallen uncharacteristically silent.

John is forty-five now, still good-looking, but with an odd, sly manner. He has a way of looking at people sideways, of smiling to himself when they speak, as though entertained by some mean private joke. Maybe he was always like this. Maybe I see more now.

Like the wedding ring on his left hand. 'Did you marry a local girl?'

'Yes, he did,' says the barmaid, and I turn to look properly at her. She is plumper, especially around the face, and her hair is dyed dark brown now. I know that because I can see a half-inch of grey roots close to her scalp.

'Hello, Tammy.' I let my eyes drift back to John. 'What a surprise.'

'Why?' she asks, stepping forward.

'I wasn't sure you were the marrying type, John,' I say, knowing there is a limit to how far I can go with this. 'But if you were, I thought you'd marry one of the Glassbrook girls. I was never sure which one.'

He smiles to himself as he polishes a glass. Tammy glares.

'I saw Cassandra earlier,' I say. 'She was unusually talkative. I learned a lot.'

At that very moment, a black whippet appears from the back room. In that delicate, light-footed way they have of moving around, it steals behind John and makes for the hatch. John turns to see what I'm looking at. When he looks up again, he's grinning.

'Some dogs live a long time,' he says.

No dog lives for thirty years. Even so, this one looks eerily similar.

'Who's the potter?' says Ben.

I turn, to see what he has seen. A set of shelves to one side of the fireplace holds a collection of pottery. Each piece has been turned with some skill, and the similarity of style suggests a single craftsman.

'I am,' says a voice behind me.

The man who has come into the lounge is in his late fifties. His coarse skin is lined, and his thick hair grey as dust. He is much better dressed, though, than I remember, and gold rings gleam on his fingers.

'They told me you were back,' he says, as I step towards him, drop to my knees and hold out my arms. 'I came as soon as I heard.'

'Oh, Dwane,' I say. 'I'm so pleased to see you.'

The hug goes on, longer than it possibly should.

'My knees aren't really up to this,' I mutter, and at last he lets me go.

'This is my son, Ben.' I get to my feet awkwardly. 'Darling, this is Dwane. Do you remember? I told you about him.'

I've told Ben that I was once good friends with a dwarf, and I'm really hoping my son will be tactful enough not to mention that.

Ben holds his hand out to Dwane. 'Good to meet you. Will you join us?'

Dwane looks pleased, and picks up his pint glass from the bar. As we find a table, I wonder at my son's sudden social maturity, but as he opens his mouth, I suspect a motive other than friendliness.

'So you're into pottery now, Mr Ogilvy? As well as making model villages?'

Dwane speaks to me. 'I started after you went. After all that fuss. You know, with the kids and that. I wanted to see how it was done. I wasn't bad at it, so I took a course at night school.'

'You're very good,' I say, 'but you were always very talented.'

'I did a sculpture of you,' Dwane says. 'From memory. And that poster from the time you went missing.'

Ben and I stare at each other.

'A sculpture of me?' I say. 'Dwane, why would you—'

'We found it,' says Ben. 'Up at the Glassbrook house.'

Dwane's face clouds over as he nods up at the shelf. 'No, you didn't. It's up there.'

He stands up, but doesn't move. 'I can't reach it,' he says. 'You'll have to get it. John won't mind. They're still mine unless he sells them. I put yours at the back, Florence, so it won't get sold. I used to have it at home, but the wife didn't like it.'

Ben is already up, standing on tiptoe, peering towards the back of the shelf.

'Careful,' I say.

He comes back with the clay sculpture of a head. About ten inches high, it is of me as a young woman. My hair flows over my shoulders, and I'm smiling, in a way I never see myself smile.

'It's great.' Ben has cheered up visibly. 'It really looks like you, Mum.' He turns to Dwane. 'Can we buy it? Dad would like it.'

'It's not for sale,' says Dwane.

'No,' I say, 'it belongs here. I was that woman here.' I smile at Dwane.

Ben coughs under his breath. 'The one we saw today was different,' he says, and when I frown at him, he ignores me. 'We found one at the Glassbrooks' old house. Stuck with wooden pins. Know anything about that one?'

Dwane stares at Ben, then looks at me for confirmation. I nod.

'Like the ones found with the kids?' he says.

I nod again.

'That's not good,' he says.

'Did you do that one too?' asks Ben.

'Hell, no,' says Dwane. 'Florence, when are you going home?'

'I just got here,' I say. 'Are you trying to get rid of me already?'

'Yes.' He gets up, leaving his half-finished pint. 'You should go home, lass. There's nowt for you here.'

He walks away and leaves the pub.

'He seems nice,' says Ben.

We look at each other and try to smile. We can't.

60

After dinner, surprisingly good given what I remember of Lancashire food in the 1960s, I tell Ben I have to pop out. He knows where I'm going. He knows me better than to try and persuade me otherwise. He makes sure I have my mobile and tells me to drive carefully and to let him know if I'm running late.

The gravel of the drive crunches beneath my feet, and the windows of the house stand dark and empty before me. It is an unwelcoming house, especially as the sun fades, but I do not feel like a trespasser. I have a sense that the house has been expecting me. Even looking forward to my coming back.

It is a little after nine o'clock and light is fading. Overhead is the deep turquoise of summer twilight, and the remains of the day's sunshine run across the horizon like the flimsiest shawl of gold and pink. In another hour, it will be fully dark.

Daylight gate.

There will be no moon tonight. Wherever the invisible astral body is, it is setting. It won't rise again until early tomorrow morning. This will be a dark night. A time for dark magic.

I'm almost at the house now.

I have never performed dark magic, but there is a darkness in this house that I will lift if I can. Thirty years ago, I took away the evil at the heart of it, but the energy that Larry and his deeds left behind is still here. I felt it earlier today. I can feel it now as

I walk up the drive. This house needs help, and so do all those bound to it. Cassie, Sally, Luna – wherever she is – even Mary. And me. Finding the clay picture has spooked me more than I care to admit. I had no choice but to hand it over to Tom, for all that my giving it up freaked Ben, but I'm not going to wait calmly for whatever is brewing.

And something is brewing. I've felt it all day.

I open my bag when I'm within arm's reach of the house and take out the salt. White salt, sea salt preferably, is used for most house-blessing spells, but for the rare occasions when a house has a particular negative energy, black salt can absorb and remove it. I pour the black grains into my hand and let them trickle to the ground as I walk round the house's perimeter.

A magic circle is the starting point of most spells, creating the 'sacred' space that contains and focuses the spell's energy. At the same time, it serves as a protection.

Creating the circle makes me feel better for a moment or two, but then I approach the back door and my misgivings return. The negative energy that Larry left behind has intensified in the years since he left. It frightened me today. It will be stronger now that night is falling.

I slip the key into the lock – how well Ben knows me – I never had any intention of returning the keys until I'd had chance to visit one last time.

Immediately something moves within. I hear a panicked scurrying, maybe even the slam of an internal door and my heart leaps forward like a trapped animal trying to squeeze free of its bars.

'Have courage, Florence. Nothing here can harm you.'

I speak aloud, because words have power and I cannot perform a blessing spell if I am afraid. I will have disturbed rodents, nothing more.

I move through the kitchen and into the dark hallway. Kneeling, I take out five short candles, place them in a circle and light them.

More movement in the house. Rats, I tell myself, again. Maybe squirrels.

My chalice, a solid silver bowl, goes into the centre of the candle circle, and in it I put a compound of dried herbs and plants. Holly for protection, rosemary for cleansing, sandalwood for exorcism, pine to reverse negative energies and rose to return calm.

You've brought some weird stuff, Mum.

The dried herbs catch fire quickly. Smoke will fill the tiniest corners of the house, reaching where even my voice cannot. I open my mouth to begin, and from somewhere above me comes sound so unexpected that it takes me a second or two to realise its significance. A short, rhythmic burst of drums, the whine of a guitar and the rich, deep voice of Elvis crooning about heartbreak.

The temptation to get up and run is overwhelming. My hands are spread on the floor, ready to push me up. The music stops.

It's not real. It's not real.

The house is silent, but my breathing is fast and my heart pounding. I have a powerful imagination, so much so that at times the line between what I know to be real and what I know cannot be becomes blurred.

That music, though. Never have I imagined anything so vividly.

I don't run, much as I want to. I count down from ten, picturing Ben holding my hands, counting with me. Love will combat most negative energy, but it's hard to throw off the creeping feeling that I'm not alone in the house.

'I'm not afraid,' I say, although I am. My back is to the family drawing room and I'm wishing I checked it before kneeling down.

The dark hallway seems to have closed in, the shadows grown deeper. I shut the back door, but there is a draught running through the house, chilling it. My candles are fighting to stay alive. Their shadows dance on the walls and their movement is unnerving as I get to my feet.

'Touch the hearth and touch the wall; blessings on this house befall.'

Reciting the words of an old blessing spell, I move around the hall, touching each door as I pass.

'Bless the chair that stands by itself. Bless the food on the pantry shelf.'

I have performed blessing spells before – they are a sweet and simple form of magic – but this one is hard, as I knew it would be. I struggle to remember words and feel drained as I climb the stairs. The burning herbs have none of their usual sweetness, as though something in the house is turning them rotten.

To do the spell properly, I should go into each room, but as I climb, I'm picturing the sleepwalking Cassie with her vacant, wide-eyed stare and flowing silver hair, the evil-smelling black dog curled on my bed with malevolent intent, and Larry, leaning against a wall, eyelids lowered, as though his wandering eyes might be less noticeable if they are half closed. I can't help feeling that they're all still here, waiting for me behind the closed doors.

As I reach the first floor, the sense of being watched is stronger. I turn, looking for movement where all should be still, for a shadow that doesn't belong, but the feeble light from my candles can't reach up here.

The house is darker than it should be. Outside, some fading light still lingers in the sky, but in here, there might almost be a force that is keeping it away, as effectively as blinds on the windows.

The door to my old room is open, although I'm sure I closed it when I left earlier. I push it further open and step inside. The spell is mainly for my own benefit, and it is in this room that any essence of me will remain.

'Friends who leave here, let them bear; luck and hope, wherever they fare.'

I touch the walls, try to send calm and happy thoughts into them, but the words I'm reciting sound trite and foolish in my ears. I feel like a child in my mother's high heels, and when I open my eyes, I'm looking out of my window, at the shadow that is the Hill, and at Larry's workshop where he kept me prisoner, bound, gagged, terrified, for nearly three days. Down there is the place where I was maimed and changed for ever, the place where I lost part of myself, and I'm not now talking about my missing finger, which to this day burns me with a phantom pain.

I leave the room and walk quickly downstairs. With a quick, last prayer, I blow out the candles, gather the ashes of the herbs, still warm in my hand, and scatter them around the hall in the traditional dispersal of energy. Gathering my detritus, and the keys that are hanging in the kitchen, I leave the house.

It is thirty years since I set foot in Larry's workshop. The space has been cleared. The heavy power tools I remember have gone, possibly sold. There are no coffins or caskets, either complete or in a half-finished state, and I guess Roy Greenwood, who ran the business until his early death, removed them.

In his testimony, Larry claimed he kept me in the smaller wood store at the back. I walk past workbenches and clamps, and feel the trace of wood shavings underfoot, as though no one has swept here in thirty years. The door sticks and I have to push it hard. As I do so, I remember heavy doors banging shut.

Doors, I remember, not a door.

But it was all so long ago, and I've buried those memories, far deeper than Larry buried his victims. After I gave evidence, I never again consciously tried to think about those few days. I never spoke of them. When I woke in the night after dreams of being trapped, immobile, in the dark – and those dreams lasted for many years – I switched on the reading lamp or the radio, read a book, anything to draw my mind back to the light.

So my memories are vague and elusive but, even so, this room I'm standing in now feels smaller than it should. In my head, it was a large, cold space that felt damp and very old. This utilitarian building is neither old nor damp.

'Hey!' I listen for the echo that doesn't come.

There is one way to know for sure. I get to my knees and lower myself to the floor, already knowing that there isn't room in here for any scuttling about. I lie flat, my cheek pressed against the hard floor, and I know for certain then. This floor is rough concrete. When I was Larry's prisoner, I lay on smooth stone. He lied.

I was kept in a large, stone space. There were wooden doors, and when I left that place, I was thrown upwards, as though from underground. A cellar. The drive to the churchyard was a short one. It was somewhere in town.

I leave the wood store, slamming the door behind me, telling myself that it is not my problem. Larry confessed. The killings stopped, and I should let sleeping dogs lie.

And then I stand in his workshop and remember him dancing to Elvis as he showed me how he made his beloved caskets. I never felt comfortable with Larry, but was he really a killer?

We can never predict who will be killers, or recognise those who have become so. If I've learned one thing in thirty years, it's that.

Outside, the absence of the moon unnerves me. I feel a sudden urge to get back to the Black Dog, to my son. At the same time, there are stars above me in the dark sky, and not too far from here, they'll be shining down on a black lake, as still and clear as a mirror. It was on a night like this that I swam with the man I loved and became a woman of the Pendle Forest.

A woman who will forever be trying to come to terms with her dual nature.

A feeling steals over me that I haven't known in years, a sense of wild and twisted possibilities. I can't help thinking that if I were to drive to the Black Tarn now, Tom would be waiting, and that my life, even so late in the day, might take a very different turn.

I love my husband. I adore my son. But Tom.

Tom . . .

They are powerful, these primitive, unsought urges, and I actually set off for the drive, and my car, when I catch sight of the face in my old bedroom window, staring down at me like one of the ghosts of the house.

This is no ghost, though. I've found Luna.

61

She is waiting in the hallway, staring down at the remains of the burned herbs.

'I kept hearing noises,' I say. 'Even music. You scared me.'

She doesn't apologise. 'I found his old record player in the attic. I'd forgotten how much I hate Elvis.'

She looks down again at the burned herbs. 'Thank you,' she says. 'It was good of you to try. We did lots over the years. Mum mainly, but Cassie and I pitched in sometimes. It won't work, though.'

Spells never work in the face of doubt, but I don't say this. Instead, I take in the woman she has become. Some women only really grow into their beauty in their forties and Luna is one of them. Her nose, chin, cheekbones fall a fraction short of being sharp, and her skin is tight and smooth. Her eyes are still huge, but the make-up she wears seems to soften them, to make them inviting rather than challenging. Her lipstick is perfect, even so late in the day, even here, and it strikes me that this is a woman constantly maintaining her make-up like a mask.

She is wearing the same tailored black dress and smart shoes that she wore to the funeral. I know she is a corporate lawyer in London and that her clothes will be expensive. Over her shoulder, though, is a large bag that is utilitarian rather than beautiful.

She is breathing heavily, too heavily for someone who has been doing nothing more than meandering about an empty house.

'You look well, Luna,' I say, although actually think she looks like a polished but empty vessel. I think something may have gone from Luna and I'm starting to feel nervous in this dark hallway.

'Elanor,' she corrects me. 'Luna was his name for me.'

She stares at me for too long. To break the tension, I walk back to the kitchen and hear her heels clipping behind me.

'Sit down,' she says, and it sounds like an order.

I'm unsettled and want to leave, back to the Black Dog now and my son – all thoughts of searching out lost chances have fled – but at the same time, I'm starting to accept that I came back to Lancashire for answers and this woman may have them.

She waits for me to do what she says and so I pull out a chair slowly and take my time sitting in it. We are playing a game, dancing in the dusty, dark kitchen, and I hope she knows the rules, because I'm not sure I do.

'My father was a monster.'

I don't argue.

She is still standing over me. 'I came to burn this house down.' She pulls her bag up from the floor and takes out a plastic petrol can. I hear liquid sloshing inside as she puts it on the table. The can is small but, if full, would provide enough accelerant to ensure the house goes up quickly.

'I'm glad you changed your mind.' Mentally, I'm measuring the distance between me and the back door. I'm closer than she is, but I'm sitting down. 'It wouldn't have been wise.'

She looks at the can, then at something I can't see in her bag. Matches, I think.

'Were you here earlier?' I ask, and I'm thinking about the effigy in the beehive.

She shakes her head. 'I didn't want to bump into Mary. I doubt she comes here after dark. I doubt anyone does. You're braver than most, Flossie. But then you always were.'

'Did you suspect?' I ask her. 'When it was happening, when you were all living here? When you were taken, did you never once think that perhaps you knew who was holding you prisoner?'

I'd known. In the first few hours, maybe days, I hadn't, but when Larry came to take me out of that place, it had been obvious. The smell of him, the feel of him. I'd known Larry. How could Luna not have known her own father?

'I would have defended him to my last breath.' Her big eyes are glistening in the dark kitchen, and her lip is trembling, but the Luna I remember was a great dissembler.

'Once,' she says. 'Just once, I thought, *Oh, that's not right.* You know when something hardens in your stomach, Flossie, as though you've eaten clay and it's setting and tightening, and drawing everything in so that you can hardly breathe?'

'Yes,' I agree. 'I know that feeling. It's called dread.'

She nods, sharply, with a tiny smile, as though pleased by the word. Then she crosses to the window and leans over the sink.

'He was out there, one night. Oh, we can't see it from here. Come upstairs.'

She turns and walks from the room. I hear her heels echoing along the parquet floor of the hall, and her muttered 'Come on.'

The petrol can is still on the table; her bag is at my feet. It seems safe enough, so I follow her up. She is in my old room, kneeling on the bed so that she can see out of the window. She beckons me to join her.

'You were in my room?' I say, because I can't resist.

'You'd been missing nearly three days,' she replies. 'Cassie and I were doing a protection spell for you. We looked it up in one of Mum's books. Cassie said it would work best in your room.'

'Thank you,' I say, oddly touched. 'Maybe it worked.'

347

'Cassie got called downstairs and left me to tidy up. Typical. But I'd just finished when I saw someone in the garden outside.'

I climb onto the bed and inch my way to her side. There is still some light in the sky and we can make out the outlines of the garden: the orchard trees, the line of box hedging round Sally's herb garden, the old beehives.

'In front of the hives,' Luna says. 'It was Dad. He had a spade and he was digging.'

'It's a garden,' I say.

'It was dark,' Luna counters. 'And did you ever once see Dad gardening, in all the time you lived here?'

I hadn't. Sally worked in the garden, with Mary's husband to help her with the heavy stuff. I'd never seen Larry dig.

'It gave me shivers, watching him,' Luna says. 'It wasn't right. No one digs at night unless they have something to hide, do they?'

'Were you tempted to find out what it was?'

'I didn't dare,' she says. 'And then within hours you'd been found and he was under arrest. We heard he'd confessed. I suppose I thought he was hiding evidence, and it wasn't as though you needed any more of that. It seemed best to keep quiet. Whatever it was, I didn't want to know.'

'You never told anyone?'

'No.'

I would have to tell Tom. Or get a message to him somehow. Seeing him again probably wasn't the wisest idea. It was good, though, potentially, that there was fresh evidence to be found. Reassurance that we'd charged the right man after all was what we – I – needed.

'I have to get back.' I think it better not to mention where I'm staying. 'Where are you spending the night?'

'Here. I don't like hotels. Especially not in this town.'

'Then you should probably rethink your plan to burn it down.'

She gives me a glum smile. 'The morning will do.'

As I walk downstairs, I can hear her following me, but I don't look back until I'm at the kitchen door.

'Do you think he was guilty, Elanor?' I say.

'Of course,' she tells me. 'He confessed.'

As I walk down the drive, I'm conscious of a lightness in my step that has been missing all day. Luna's certainty in the face of her father's guilt has cheered me. She knew him. She has no doubts. Earlier today, Cassie expressed no doubts. We caught him and now he is dead. Finally it is over.

Traffic is light on the way back to the hotel and I make good time. I catch a glimpse of the public bar as I head through reception and see the head and shoulders of someone who might be Tom, but I don't stop. It is my son I need to be with now. My son, who has been my rock today, centring and grounding me, just as he's done since the day he squeezed and yelled his way into the world.

I swear that darling child was cursing as he pushed his way out of me. I feel a sudden, twisted desire to hear him swear.

His door is unlocked and his room empty. I knock on the bathroom door and getting no grunt in response, push it open. Empty. For a second I wonder if he is hiding, but it is years since he and I played hide and seek and I know that he wouldn't. Not here. Not now.

He will be in my room, messing up the covers on my bed, having munched his way through the biscuits in his own. I close his door, spotting his phone on the floor beneath a chair but not giving it much thought.

My own door is locked, and as I pull out my keys, my breathing is quickening. The room beyond is in darkness, and exactly as I left it. There is no sign that Ben has been in here, but I check the bathroom all the same.

My son has gone.

62

I only panic on the inside. On the outside, I step calmly around the room, checking the wardrobe, beneath the bed, behind the shower curtain, in case he is playing a sick practical joke, although I know he is not. I will be expected to have checked the rooms thoroughly and so I do.

I run downstairs and out through the back door to the car park. There is no reason to think I might find him here, but I check all the same, and I peer over the low, black wall to the river that runs through the centre of town, mostly underground.

The water is low, the banks rising steeply towards me, thick with summer vegetation. He cannot be down there. I cannot think of my son in relation to this nasty, creeping river. And so I go back indoors, and I'm only panicking on the inside. I push my way behind the bar, ignoring the protests of the barmaid, and find John Donnelly in the kitchen.

'Ben is missing,' I tell him. 'I can't find my son. Is there a games room or a lounge I don't know about? Anywhere he might be watching television?'

Tammy appears, wide-eyed and taut of face.

'No,' John says. 'Children aren't allowed in the public rooms. When did you last see him?'

I don't answer John's question. I have too many of my own. 'Did you see him at all this evening? After I left?'

'I haven't seen him since dinner,' Tammy says. 'Over

an hour ago. He went upstairs with you.'

John lifts his hands in a gesture that says he has nothing to add. They should be annoyed, at my barging my way into their private rooms, throwing questions at them, but they aren't. They get it.

'Has he been talking to anyone else in the hotel?' I think of Dwane and wonder if he's still here. Dwane might have invited Ben up to see his model town. Please God, let Ben be with my old friend.

Tammy shakes her head.

'Do you want me to call the police?' John says.

'Give me a sec.' I leave them and head out to the public bar. I'm still not panicking on the outside. I push open the door and see that I was right: Tom is here. He has his back to me, but I recognise his jacket from earlier, and his voice as he laughs.

'Tom,' I call to him as I cross the room.

'Hey.' He feigns surprise, but the warmth in his eyes tells me he was hoping to see me, that he came here to engineer a meeting. Then he looks properly at my face. 'What?'

'I need to talk to you. Now.'

He follows me to the corridor, which is deserted, apart from John and Tammy, hovering by the kitchen door.

'Ben is missing.' Because I don't want to waste time waiting for him to ask questions, I tell him everything that he will need. 'He was here when I left ninety minutes ago. I've searched our rooms, the car park and the public rooms. He hasn't taken his coat, his phone or his wallet. Tammy and John haven't seen him. He said nothing about going out, and he knows no one in town. Going out without leaving me a message would be very out of character.'

Then, because I know it's coming, I add, 'I went up to the Glassbrook house. I have a set of keys. He knew I was going.'

Tom's eyes narrow. 'Could he have followed you up there?'

'Not impossible,' I say.

'Do you have a photograph?'

'Upstairs. It's a couple of years old, but—' I stop, because panic is fighting its way out. That is a scream in the back of my throat and—

'Florence!' Tom says.

I meet his eyes.

'Get it. Quick. I'll see you back down here. Two minutes. Go.'

I go, pushing someone aside on the stairs, running into my room. I pick up my bag and from Ben's room grab his phone and look for his room key. I don't see it.

The hall downstairs is empty when I get back. Ben's key isn't hanging behind Reception, and its absence suggests to me he didn't plan to leave the hotel.

'Florence.'

Tom is back. 'Let me tell you what I've done.' He beckons me closer. 'I'm taking it seriously,' he says. 'Not because I'm worried – I'm not. I'm sure he's fine and not far away – but I'm pulling out all the stops because it's you.' He gives me a tiny smile. 'And because it's us. And it's here.'

I manage a similar smile back to thank him. Tom knows I'll demand everything he can throw at the search for my son and that I'll raise hell if I don't get it. He knows that because of what the two of us went through we will always take seriously the disappearance of a child. And he knows that here, in the North-West, we will always assume the worst.

'I'm listing him as a vulnerable missing person and I'll get his picture sent round,' he goes on. 'There'll be a dog team here in ten minutes.'

A dog team will only find a trail if Ben left on foot.

'I've got Uniform coming to do a search of the hotel. Tammy and John will cooperate. Another team will start combing the town, the public parks, the pubs that we know are tolerant of underage drinkers.'

I nod. I know Ben is not in any of those places but that Tom has to follow procedure.

'You and I are going up to the Glassbrook house now, to make sure he's not there. Then I'm going to bring you back and you will wait here for him, checking with his dad, and any friends at home he might have been in touch with.'

His dad. Oh God, his dad.

'Right, then.' Tom pulls me along the corridor and out of the hotel as a wave of déjà vu washes over me. He and I did this so many times back then. But never when I was feeling this sick. This helpless.

'You're doing great.' Tom opens the car door for me.

'I need to get onto the system,' I say, as we head out of town. 'I'll come in after I've made those phone calls. I need to check other teenage disappearances in the North-West. I'll speak to Yorkshire too.'

Tom says nothing.

'Cumbria,' I say. 'Merseyside,' and I'm conscious I'm half talking to myself. 'He wouldn't take them from here. Not without throwing suspicion on himself. He'd go further afield, but not too far. He must be based here. How the hell did he know I'd come back? And how did he persuade Ben to leave the hotel? Ben's smart.'

'Florence, get a grip.' When Tom snaps at me, I see the fear he's trying to hide for my sake. 'There is no "he",' he goes on. 'There is no child predator on the loose around Sabden. Larry Glassbrook killed those kids, and he's dead.'

Tom has switched on his blue light and we speed through the quiet streets. Half of me wants to yell at him to slow down, so that I can check each dark street and corner we pass; the other half needs him to go faster. We reach the Glassbrook house and Tom sweeps into the drive without checking his speed, pulling up beside the front door. From the boot he takes a torch and two pairs of disposable gloves and I thank God he's still thinking clearly, functioning as a police officer and not a close-to-panicking parent.

He bangs on the door to raise Luna as I run round the garden, checking behind trees, under shrubs. When there is no response from the house, I hand over the keys and we go inside. We check it from top to bottom and then Larry's workshop, the wood store at the back, the garden shed. We find nothing. Luna isn't here. Neither is Ben.

'Tom.' We are standing directly outside the back door, wondering what to do next. 'I know what you think, and I know I'd be the same in your shoes, but will you humour me, please?'

'Go on.'

I tell him what I heard from Luna earlier. That one night, while I was missing, she saw Larry digging in the garden after dark. That it had creeped her out, partly because gardening was out of character for her father, and partly because who digs in the dark unless they have something to hide?

'Where in the garden?' he says.

'By the hives.'

Tom says nothing.

'"Tell it to the bees,"' I say. 'The last time I saw Larry, there was something on his mind. He said he'd told it to the bees. I thought it was the effigy I was supposed to find. What if it wasn't? What if Larry knew nothing about that but hid something near the hives?'

Tom sighs. 'Your call,' he says. 'We could spend half an hour looking for the remains of Larry's pet cat, and I think that time could be better spent. But we've got a torch, and there are spades in the shed, so your call.'

I make the call. I find a spade and lead Tom over to the bee-hives. He shines the torch on the ground and we see nothing but smooth lawn, the grass overly long, and a few common weeds. We could dig for hours and not find what Larry left here. I step closer to the hives and feel something hard beneath my foot.

I grab Tom's hand and shine his torch down. A small stone, which means nothing, except that there are more than one. A line of them. Six stones in a straight line, then a line of four stones, at right angles. The letter 'L'.

'This is it,' I say. 'It's here.'

I hold the torch. Tom digs quickly.

'L' for Larry? 'L' for Luna? 'L' for Lovelady? 'L' for love?

'Hello,' Tom mutters, and I hold the torch still. In the deepening hole is a canvas bag with a drawstring top, old and very dirty.

'Inside,' Tom says.

At the kitchen table, Tom pulls apart the string tie. What falls out of the bag is a large brown envelope without stamp or postmark, addressed to *Larry Glassbrook, Esq.* in neat, old-fashioned writing. Tom upends it and we see several black-and-white photographs and one scrap of stained tissue. Tom turns all the pictures so that they lie face up, and I know the sight of the first hits him as hard as it does me. It is a photograph of the two of us.

The picture is thirty years old, taken when I lived and worked here. I am a young woman of twenty-two in this picture and I am drunk. The Tom I remember from those days is leading me out of the Black Dog.

In the second photograph, we are a few feet from the pub, and I can see Tom's car in the background. In a third, I see the pub van, and John Donnelly loading something from the pub cellar. These photographs were taken the night Tom and I made love at the Black Tarn, the night I pulled Luna from a premature grave.

The fourth is not of Tom and me but of Luna herself, and she is climbing into the back of the Black Dog's van. Standing ready to close the doors behind her is John. The last picture is of the van leaving the pub car park. John can be seen at the wheel. He was too young to drive legally back then, but I think I can remember Tom telling me he'd been pulled over once and given a caution for driving without a licence.

'I don't get it,' Tom says. 'Who took these?'

'It's the same night,' I say. 'In every photograph John is wearing the same clothes.'

'He always wore the same clothes. The poor bastard didn't have any clothes apart from his dad's hand-me-downs.'

I point to the photograph of Luna getting into the back of the van. 'Those are the clothes we found her in,' I say. 'This is the night we found her.'

Tom doesn't reply.

'Look at the moon.' My finger hovers over the bright white ball in the sky and moves from one photograph to the next. It had been a nearly full moon the night Luna was taken, full when she was found.

'Not in the same position,' Tom says, but there is doubt in his voice.

'It wouldn't be. The moon moves across the sky. I'd say the pictures of John and Luna were taken about an hour after we left.'

'Who?' he says. 'Who took them? Who on earth was waiting outside the Black Dog for hours on the off-chance?'

I don't know, and that's not what's uppermost in my head right now. 'These pictures prove that Luna was not abducted. Not by her father, not by anyone. Does she look as though John is forcing her into that van? They faked it. I said all along Luna's abduction was different.'

Tom seems to sway on the spot. 'Hang on, Florence – you found her in a shallow grave.'

I reach out to touch his arm, but he flinches away. 'Yes, a very different burial to the one the others got. She wasn't in a coffin. She was miles out of town. And I was tipped off. I was told where to find her. Luna was never in any danger.'

He steps back, as though to get a better look at me. 'So where was she, all the time she was missing? And why? Why the hell would anyone fake an abduction? What was the point?'

Suddenly I am so sure of my ground. In time, I will be angry, furious with myself for not seeing it before, for ignoring the nagging doubts I'd always had about Larry's guilt, but for now, acknowledging what I know to be the truth will be enough.

'To draw attention away from the real killers,' I say. 'Them. John and Luna killed Stephen and Susan and Patsy. The others, Tammy, Dale, Unique, they were probably in on it too. Tom, remember at the time we said Luna's abduction was a ruse, a way for Larry to draw attention away from himself, because what man would kill his own daughter? Well, we were right about the ruse bit, just not about who was responsible.'

He shakes his head, but I know Tom. He's thinking about it.

'They knew we were getting close,' I say. 'They knew I was getting close. Luna found my charts, knew I was interested in the kids at school, that I was gathering information about them. She and John saw me visiting school. God, they even tried to pump me for information here in the garden one day. Remember John telling us he was gay? Luna trying to throw suspicion on me? They are manipulative liars. They were dangerous when they were teenagers, they are doubly dangerous now, and they have Ben.'

I think back to John and Tammy's concerned faces at the Black Dog earlier and feel how easy it would be to rip people apart with my bare hands. I feel my nails digging into my palms and my breathing spiralling. I am burning with rage. These people have no idea, no idea at all, what they unleashed when they went after my son.

'Elanor Glassbrook hasn't lived in Sabden for years,' Tom says, and his voice sounds as though it is a long way away.

I have to force myself back to him, to speak in a calm voice when all I want to do is howl. 'John Donnelly and Tammy own the pub we're staying in. Ben would trust them. If they knocked on his door and said, "Something's happened to your mum. She's downstairs. Come quickly," he'd do it.'

Tom turns from me and leans over the sink. For a second I think he's about to vomit. 'Why did Larry confess?' he asks the taps. 'If Larry was innocent, why did he serve thirty years in prison?'

'Out of love,' I say. 'He knew Luna had done it. He took the rap for her.'

He talks to his reflection. 'She let her dad go to prison?'

I move to stand behind him. 'She was a teenage psychopath. She'd have seen her father hang.'

Tom exhales another long, slow breath. I feel myself on the verge of losing patience, but I need Tom with me.

'Someone sent him proof,' I say. 'Someone sent these pictures to Larry.' I reach out and nudge the scrap of tissue. Were I not wearing gloves, I'd still have no fear of contaminating it with my DNA. My DNA is already on it. This tissue wrapped my severed finger.

'Someone sent him my finger,' I say. 'He would have known it was mine: he complimented me on my nail varnish. He knew his daughter was a monster, but he acted to protect her.'

Tom turns and I can't read the expression in his eyes. 'The killings stopped,' he says. 'I've been here for thirty years plus and there have been no more unexplained disappearances of Sabden children.'

'That would be the deal,' I say. 'He takes the blame; they have to behave themselves. He buried proof to make sure they kept their word. All this time he wouldn't let Sally sell the house because the pictures were buried in the garden.'

'Oh crap,' Tom says.

'And maybe they didn't stop,' I say. 'Maybe they got cleverer. Which is why I need to do that search of missing children cases. After we bring in John and Tammy.'

We speed back through town. For much of the journey I'm clutching my seat, because Tom's driving hasn't improved in thirty years and I'm not about to ask him to take it easy. When he's forced to brake for traffic, I say, 'I wasn't kept in Larry's wood store those two days. He made that up. I went in earlier. It isn't the same place.'

This time he doesn't argue. 'Where, then?'

'I'm guessing the Black Dog,' I say. 'That place will have big cellars. And those double doors we saw will allow easy access to the car park. I think that's where they kept Luna and where they kept me too. Maybe the others for a time.'

'We searched the Black Dog.'

'Maybe there's a hidden cellar nobody knows about.' I wonder if I'm clutching at straws, that my need to find Ben is so strong I'm imagining hiding places that don't exist. 'Dwane told me about something once. A very old cellar, still with chains, used to keep prisoners on their way to Lancaster Gaol. Did you ever hear about that?'

He lifts his shoulders in a brief shrug. 'Maybe.'

'And Luna at least will have been a willing captive. She'd have been prepared to hide.'

'You weren't, though. We looked for you in the Black Dog cellars. We looked everywhere. None of us slept for three nights.'

His voice breaks and I reach out to pat his hand. I can't allow either of us to give in to panic. Ben is my son. My life will end if his does.

We reach the pub quickly. There are patrol cars in the car park, their lights flashing.

Tom switches off the engine and turns to me. 'You're staying here,' he says.

I reach for the handle and he grabs my arm. 'Don't be a fool, Floss. I can't involve you in this. I am going in, alone, and I will have John and Tammy Donnelly driven to the station for questioning. If they won't go willingly, I'll arrest them. Then we'll search the cellars. You will stay here till the Donnellys have left, and then you will go to your room. Do I make myself clear?'

I can't argue. I can't do anything that might delay the search for Ben.

I watch Tom disappear inside the pub and stare at the door for a second. I catch sight of the canvas bag, now carefully wrapped in evidence bags, that is lying on the back seat. And then I panic on the outside too.

Tammy and John are driven away in separate cars. Tom reappears; a smartly dressed man is following him. I think I must know this tall man in the expensive suit, but can't quite place him. He is in his early forties, with dark hair, heavy eyebrows and narrow, slate-coloured eyes, and something about his bearing tells me that he is police, a senior detective. I get out of the car to meet them. Both see that I've been crying and neither can meet my eyes.

'I'm going in to lead the questioning,' Tom says. 'It will take a while because we may have to wait for solicitors and—'

'I know how it works,' I say. 'I want to watch.'

He shakes his head. 'Can't be done, Florence. I'm leaving you with DI Brian Rushton. Stan's son. He's heard all about you. He'll look after you.'

I nod at the man I remember only from photographs, a stocky child in a policeman's helmet. It is his resemblance to his father that I recognise and I warm to his presence. Behind us, I hear Tom getting into his car and driving away.

'We're going to check the cellars, ma'am,' Rushton says to me in his father's voice. 'You can come, if you do exactly what I say.'

The cellars are vast. The walls are stone, painted white in places, but the paintwork is old and peeling. The floors are flagged, except where stained and curling sheets of linoleum have been laid. The rooms we walk through are cold and smell of spilled beer and damp towels. I see gleams of lichen on some of the walls.

The kegs are down here, of course, gleaming silver barrels in neat lines, connected to the walls by a labyrinth of tubes. There are boxes of crisps, nuts and pork scratchings, crates of bottled beer, of cans and soft drinks. There are rooms where trestle tables are stacked against walls, and towers of gilt chairs stretch to the ceilings; others where bedroom furniture and bathroom fittings are kept.

We don't find Ben. We check everywhere possible. I even insist that empty barrels are checked, but he isn't here. When we reach the room where the great double trapdoors allow access to the car park above, I pause. These could be the doors I heard, the doors through which my limp and hurting body was thrown, but I cannot be certain.

'There's another room through there,' the barman who is our guide tells us, and we follow his gaze towards a stone wall, with barrels stacked against it. Behind the barrels, I can see a sheet of reformed wood.

'What sort of room?' Rushton says.

'It's old,' the barman says. 'We don't use it.'

The barrels are heavy and it takes four men – Rushton, the

barman and the two constables who have accompanied us – to tip and roll them away but, after a few minutes, they slide aside the wood to reveal a low archway, stone-lined, gleaming with damp from the nearby river and containing the husks of old wooden barrels. None of us will be able to stand upright in it.

Claustrophobia grabs hold of me as we step beneath the low, uneven roof and watch Rushton's torch pick out a narrow, crumbling staircase at the far end. It is so old and worn the stone seems to have melted into its surroundings, and it gleams with a liquid sheen that makes me think it won't be solid enough to hold our weight.

'Mind yourself,' the barman says, and slips up the staircase like a squirrel.

'You don't have to come,' Rushton tells me, but I do, and a few uncomfortable seconds later, he and I have scaled the slippery steps and are standing in the furthest part of the Black Dog's cellars. The two constables wait below.

This is the room Dwane told me of long ago. The place where miscreants and villains were kept on their way to Lancaster Gaol.

The stone is crumbling in places and the earth breaking through. It is small, not big enough to stand upright, and feels crowded even with three of us. I guess it to be twelve feet by eight. There is an iron grille above our heads, through which plant life trails. I guess this grille is on the riverbank and that at times of high water the cellar floods.

There are the remains of chains around the walls, and iron clamps – fetters or manacles, I think they'd be called. Iron rings are set low in the walls.

'Have you been in here before, ma'am?' Rushton asks me, in a low voice.

I take my time. The flagged stone beneath our feet, the sense of being underground, the damp and the cold all feel right. The space does not, though. The prison in my memory was bigger than this.

'I don't think so,' I say.

'It wasn't searched before,' Rushton says. 'I know that old case. I've looked through the files many times. This part of the cellar was blocked off and not searched. So you could have been here. Luna Glassbrook and the others could have been kept here.'

'Ben isn't here,' I say. 'That's all that's important now.'

63

I make my phone calls. I phone my husband, who is still in Paris, and lie to him, telling him I'm not worried, that I'm only check-ing in with him to make sure all boxes are ticked. I phone Ben's grandparents and lie to them too. I phone my son's best friend, and his second-best friends, and the girl I know he'd like to be his girlfriend but hasn't dared ask yet. None of them has heard from him, and despite my lies, I sense tiny darts of my own panic speeding across the country, lodging in hearts and nerves.

Naming fears gives them power. Ben's abduction – I can no longer say 'disappearance' – is becoming more serious with every passing minute. I want to run out into the night, yelling his name. I want to bang on every door in the hotel and make people tell me what they saw and heard. I want to go to his room, to find something of his that still carries his scent and hold it to me. I do none of these things. The first would achieve nothing, the second would get in the way of the police investigation, and as for the third, I've seen enough cases of missing kids to know that to be the action of a parent who has given up. I will not give up.

I'm thinking whether there is anyone else I need to phone when there is a knock on the door. Ben wouldn't knock, so I quell the leap of hope and open it to see Brian Rushton.

'Have you got a minute, ma'am?' he says, as though I might have other, more urgent tasks on hand. Tucked beneath his left arm are a stack of old cardboard files, the sort we only see these days when we have to dig into archives that haven't yet been computerised. He sits on the bed. I take the chair.

'My dad talked a lot about the old days,' he says. 'Especially the Glassbrook case. It bothered him, right up until the end.'

Not just me, then. I hadn't been the only one who couldn't quieten those nagging doubts. 'Your father was a fine officer,' I say.

He half smiles. 'There's stuff I'm betting you don't know about,' he says. 'Stuff in the files, going back years. It was investigated but kept quiet. Almost as though someone didn't want any boats rocking.'

Boats rocking? I have heard this before.

That someone could only have been his father, but I don't say this. I say, 'What sort of stuff?'

He glances down at the files. 'Four months after her funeral, her real funeral I'm talking about now, Patsy Wood's body was stolen.'

Whatever I'd been expecting him to say, it wasn't that.

'Someone got into the cemetery one night and dug her up,' he continues. 'They replaced the coffin, filled in the grave, put it all to rights, but the groundsman saw it next morning and knew something was up. He reported it and there was a low-key investigation. The coffin was empty.'

It is as though the room has suddenly grown hotter. 'How could I not know about that?' I ask.

'It was kept quiet.' Rushton shrugs. 'I'm guessing Dad figured enough damage had been done. It wasn't as though the girl could be hurt any more. The family could, though. Maybe he didn't want to cause them more distress.'

I look at the window. It is already open, but there is no air in this room. 'He hushed it up?'

Brian Rushton inclines his head. 'I wouldn't have mentioned

it – you've got enough on your plate – but there was something else.'

'What?'

He gives a deep sigh. 'They couldn't match DNA in those days, so don't read too much into it, but human remains were found among the ashes of a bonfire on the Hill.'

She will not rest . . . You have to burn her.

'Why are you telling me this?'

He looks down at the files on his lap.

'Why do you think this is relevant to Ben's disappearance?'

He looks up. 'I don't know that it is. I just know people weren't happy about Larry Glassbrook's conviction, even though they never voiced their concerns out loud. It preyed on minds. I sensed it in Dad.'

He gets to his feet. 'Tom told me what you found at the Glassbrook house, about your new theory, that it might have been the kids after all. If you're right, there's a hell of a lot we've missed.'

I stand up too.

'I just got a call from the boss,' Rushton says. 'John and Tammy's solicitors have arrived and the interviews are about to start. He says you can come in and watch, if you want.'

'He wants to keep an eye on me, doesn't he?' I say, as we head down the stairs.

Rushton says, 'He also tells me you've stolen evidence and that if you don't hand it in now, he'll have you arrested.' He half smiles, to show he only half means it, or maybe that Tom only half means it. Whatever. It's a fair cop. I hold open my bag to show the envelope I took from the canvas bag while I was left alone with it in Tom's car.

'Not compromised in any way,' I say. 'I wore gloves the whole time, and it's bagged separately.'

He holds my stare.

'I couldn't just sit there waiting for you to take Tammy and John in. I was going out of my mind. I thought if I looked at the photographs again, something might occur to me.'

'Did it?'

I shake my head.

'Hand them over.'

64

'Not the same evening,' John Donnelly is saying, as we arrive. He is leaning back in his chair, but his hands on the chair arms are clenched. 'What do clothes prove? Back then we wore the same things till they stank.'

'Same moon.' I can't see the face of the detective sergeant interviewing him, just her shoulder-length brown hair.

'Far as I know, the same moon has been coming up every night for millions of years,' John says. He lifts one hand to his mouth to nibble at his nails, but the hand is shaking.

An officer next to me says, 'He's insisting the photos were taken before Luna disappeared.'

'Any sign of Luna?' I ask, and he shakes his head. Luna has vanished as effectively as Ben has.

Tammy and John are being interviewed in separate rooms. There are close-circuit television cameras in both that relay footage to the waiting offices. We can step from one screen to the next, keeping track of both interviews.

On the other screen, Tammy isn't even pretending not to be scared, but her story is the same, that none of the teenage gang knew anything about the other children's disappearances.

'Luna believed her dad was guilty,' she is saying. 'She was never the same after he was arrested. Never got over it. Larry must have taken those pictures.'

'Why would Larry send pictures to himself?' Tom asks her. 'Why would he even take them in the first place?'

She doesn't answer him. 'John was going with Luna in them days,' she says instead. 'He was always nicking his dad's van to drive us around. It doesn't mean nothing.'

Tom leans back in his seat and scratches his head. 'Now, you see, I interviewed John the night Luna vanished and I distinctly remember him telling us he was gay. Which is odd, when you think he's been married for over twenty years and the two of you have three grown-up kids. Why would he say he was gay, Tammy?'

'Being gay wouldn't make him a murderer,' she says.

'Not being gay makes him a liar,' Tom counters.

'I wonder who's going to tell the truth first, you or your wife,' says the detective sergeant to John. 'I hope it's your wife. I don't think she could cope with a long prison sentence.'

John's face is pale.

'I can see how it would have worked,' she says. 'Who would kids trust more than other kids? Especially the cool kids, the gang everyone wanted to be part of. You probably sold it as some sort of prank: "Let's break into the funeral parlour, see a few dead bodies. Meet you there at ten o'clock. Can you sneak out without your mum seeing?"'

'For the benefit of the tape, Mr Donnelly is shaking his head,' says the accompanying constable.

'You wouldn't even have to break in. Luna could have sneaked the spare set of keys from home. Her mum's bag would have all the sedative drugs you needed. Easy.'

'My client has no comment,' says his solicitor.

'You had the cellar to keep Luna in while she was missing,' the sergeant says. 'So you see, John, we know how you did it. We just don't know why.'

★

'Why did you kill your friends, Tammy?' says Tom. 'What had Susan, Stephen and Patsy ever done except want to be part of your gang?'

We hear the door to the interview room open and a uniformed sergeant pokes his head into shot. 'She's ready for you, sir,' he says. 'She's signed the immunity-from-prosecution form.'

Tammy's solicitor, whose eyelids have been drooping, sits up. 'What's that?' she says, and rubs her face.

The door closes behind the sergeant.

'Going to have to leave you for a while, Tammy.' Tom gets to his feet. 'Someone else needs my attention. I hope she'll be more cooperative.'

'Who?' Tammy says. 'Who's here?'

'Tammy, keep quiet,' her solicitor says. 'I've never heard of an immunity-from . . . What was it again?'

'Oh, ignore Mack — he's always getting his forms mixed up,' Tom says.

'Is it Luna? Is Luna here?'

'Luna was threatening to burn down the Glassbrook house earlier this evening,' says Tom. 'I'd say that's a woman with a lot on her mind.' He pauses at the door. 'I might be a while. I'll have someone bring you both a brew.'

'Wait,' Tammy calls.

Tom frowns as he turns back.

'Tammy, I don't think—' her solicitor begins.

'You can't trust Luna,' Tammy says. 'No one could ever trust Luna. She's not right.'

Tom sighs. 'Tammy, do you actually have anything to say, because I—'

'It was her idea.'

In the office, we all take a breath and hold it.

Tom lets the door go. 'What was?' he says.

An hour later, seven of us gather in a meeting room.

Tom kicks off. 'According to both John and Tammy, and their stories seem to agree, Luna's abduction was faked by the kids themselves. They cooked it up between them. She hid in the Black Dog cellars for a couple of nights, and then John drove her up to that old graveyard. She'd only been in the grave a few minutes when Florence arrived.'

'Why?' I ask. 'Why would they do something so stupid and irresponsible?'

'For a bit of a laugh, John claims.' The female sergeant pulls a sympathetic face at me. 'I know, I know, but I can see it,' she says. 'Those kids had been on television. Attention's a funny thing. The more you get, the more you want.'

Tom says, 'According to Tammy, it was entirely John and Luna's idea and she was bullied into going along with it. She does admit, though, to making the phone call to you that night, Florence, the one that told you where to find Luna.'

It could have been Tammy I heard that night. I remember it being high-pitched and sexless, the sound of someone trying to disguise his or her voice.

'It would explain why Luna's disappearance differed from the others in some crucial ways,' Brian says.

I'd argued that myself. Oh God.

The female sergeant says, 'Where John and Tammy differ is in John's view that Luna's real reason for suggesting the prank was that she already suspected her dad, or saw that other people suspected him, and wanted to draw attention away. She figured that no one would suspect Larry if his own daughter was one of the victims. The story about being raped, the accusations about you, ma'am, were all about getting attention away from her dad. She was trying to protect him.'

'Luna hates her dad,' I say. 'She called him a "monster".'

'She might still have wanted to shield him,' the sergeant says. 'For as long as she could.'

More than one head gives an almost imperceptible nod and I sense a relaxing of tension around the room. I know that feeling. It steals over police teams when they see the end in sight. It has never terrified me before.

Tom says, 'So if they are telling the truth, we're back to Larry Glassbrook being the rightfully convicted perpetrator of the three murders and the abduction of WPC Lovelady in 1969.'

'What about the photographs taken in the Black Dog car park that night?' I say. 'It makes no sense for Larry to have taken those and sent them to himself.'

'It doesn't make sense for the kids to have done it either,' says Tom.

Nobody speaks. He's right. It doesn't.

'John and Tammy Donnelly are liars,' I say. 'They lied to us years ago and they're lying now.'

Suddenly no one can look at me.

'We can find no indication that either Tammy or John left the Black Dog tonight,' says a young male constable. 'On the contrary, they were unusually busy. Tammy was in the kitchen; John was running between kitchen and bar, helping out with the serving. If either of them had vanished for any length of time, one of the staff would have noticed.'

'There were three others in that gang,' I say. 'Dale Atherton, Richie Haworth and Unique Labaddee.'

'Dale Atherton died,' someone says. 'Years ago. Heart attack.'

'And I'm pretty certain Richie Haworth emigrated,' someone else says. 'New Zealand, I think.'

'There is something else,' Tom says. 'We've had a report in from the railway station. The ticket office isn't manned after six o'clock, but we have a witness who claims they saw a boy answering Ben's description buying a ticket from the machine. About five minutes before the train to Manchester.' He leans back in his chair. 'Florence, I know you said you didn't have a row, but is it possible there may be something going on that you don't know about? Some reason why Ben suddenly had to get back South?'

I can only stare at him.

'West Coast Trains run south every hour from Manchester,' someone else says. 'There'll be CCTV at Victoria Station, and at Piccadilly. I can get on to Greater Manchester, sir, request someone go through footage.'

Tom nods and the idiot who thinks my son caught a train to Manchester tonight gets up and leaves the room.

'They did this before,' I say. 'After every child vanished, we had sightings at the bus station, at the railway station. They tried to make us think the children had run away, had left the area; then we wouldn't look for them here.'

'Who did?' someone says. 'Who is "they"?'

I ignore him.

'The dogs picked up a trail,' the uniformed officer at Tom's side says. 'Leaving the Black Dog.'

I raise my voice. 'Why am I only hearing this now?'

'The trail left the Black Dog, turned right along the main road and followed it for two hundred yards,' Tom tells me. 'Then it turned right again along Old Sabden Road. They lost it towards the end of that.'

At the end of Old Sabden Road is Station Road. The trail the dogs supposedly picked up was heading towards the station.

I get to my feet.

'Florence, sit down,' Tom says.

I ignore him.

'Brian, go with her.' Tom raises his voice. 'We'll keep looking, Florence. We'll look all night. We'll find him.'

They will keep looking. I believe that, at least. But they will not find him.

65

I let Brian Rushton drive me back to the hotel and then I tell him to leave me. I tell him I will be fine, and that the best thing he can do for me now is join the hunt for my son. I remind him that he still has the envelope with the photographs.

When he is gone, I go in through the front door and out at the back. No one sees me as I climb into my car.

My first stop is the Glassbrook house, where I let myself into Larry's workshop. It takes me five minutes to find what I need, and there is an old rucksack that will help me carry everything. Before I leave, I take one last look at the hives. Thirty years ago, they were alive and buzzing, full of tiny creatures, and Sally attended to them regularly. Larry could not have put the effigy of me in the hives before his arrest. Which means someone else did, within the last few days, knowing there was a chance that I'd find it. The question is who.

Maybe easier to answer why.

To intrigue me. Frighten me. Anger me. Possibly all of these, but most of all to keep me here, to make sure I don't leave town. No officer involved in the Glassbrook case would walk away from a discovery of fresh evidence. Someone knew that. Someone has deliberately manipulated me into staying in town. I planned to anyway, but they wouldn't know that.

John and Tammy would have known. I booked into the Black Dog for two nights. They would have no need to lure me with effigies. According to the police, John and Tammy almost certain-ly didn't leave the pub tonight. The police don't believe that John and Tammy abducted Ben, and I may be starting to agree.

Luna? The family can access the house. If Luna had left the effigy for me, I'd have found it sitting on the pillow of my old bed, not in the garden. Dale Atherton is dead. Richie Haworth emigrated. My certainty that the children were responsible for the deaths of their friends seems to be leaving me as quickly as it came.

Leaving me with nothing.

I get back in the car, reach open countryside and keep driving. The Hill looms in front of me and I carry on. I drive to the fur-thest point I can and park. I am about to get out when the worst thought of all hits me.

Why do they want me here? Why do they want to keep me in town?

I am the last person they should want reopening the old case. And why on earth go after my son when they know I will stop at nothing to find him? Why, of all the police officers in the country, would they throw down the gauntlet in front of me?

I can think of no reason but revenge and, if I am right, Ben will be dead already.

No, I cannot give up.

There is no moon tonight, but there is an astral energy on my side that is keeping the sky cloud-free, and the starlight seems extra bright as I leave the car and start to climb. I am thirty years older than when I last climbed Pendle Hill, and anxiety is robbing me of breath, but I press on. Half an hour is all it should take me. I think it takes me less.

I will not give up.

At the small plateau where the witches used to meet, I stop. There is a ring of stone, ash and even some charred wood where they last had their fire, and I am encouraged by the knowledge that this is still a sacred site.

This may or may not be the site of Malkin Tower, but it hardly matters. It is the place where for decades my sisters have practised their craft. There are energies here that I can harness.

I use the wood I stole from Larry's workshop and build a fire. It need not be large, but it must burn brightly and for some time. When I think I have enough, I take matches from my bag and light it.

Long ago, Daphne and Avril taught me that witchcraft has three disciplines: healing, divination and magic. I have studied all three, and I practise all three, but they spoke the truth when they said that witches are always drawn to one in particular. I am a diviner, one who practises the art of foreseeing future events and discovering hidden knowledge through omens. I have tarot cards, Viking runes and hanging crystals, but scrying has always worked best for me, and my favourite method is fire.

The kindling catches quickly and within minutes there are golden flames licking the wood and embers forming. When I'm confident the fire has taken, I scatter the herbs. Lavender, sage, mint and rose petals have powerful protective qualities. The yarrow and the camphor enhance psychic abilities. The anise will help me sink into a trance. I settle down and let my mind drift towards the empty, receptive condition that I need.

'My son is here. My son is alive. My son is in danger.'

I watch the smoke spiral up and the heart of the fire grow hotter. I see Ben's face but know it to be nothing more than a manifestation of my fear. I need to go deeper. I lean forward and inhale the smell of the burning herbs. After a few moments, I can feel the calm settling over me. When I reach the stage of being aware of my surroundings but feeling quite separate from them, I will start to see.

The wind builds. The Hill begins to moan and sigh, and the scented smoke wraps itself around me.

I see chains. I see my son lying on darkness and darkness surrounding him. I see a small, scurrying creature that is predatory and afraid at the same time.

My son is underground, but he can move and breathe. I see thick, strong walls around him. I see flashes of locked doors.

I cannot see him moving. He lies perfectly still, like a—

A fresh scent comes to me then, not the bitter smell of burning herbs but one sickeningly sweet. It is the smell of buddleia. I can't remember if there is a bush here, and I don't want to break out of my trance to look. I see heads of men, angry men. A crowd. High walls. Bright lights.

Am I seeing where my son is being held or just remembering where I was? It hardly matters. Either way will take me to him.

Talk to me, Ben. Tell me where you are.

A piece of wood shifts in the fire, sparks fly up, and the picture shifts. The shapes I can see form themselves into upright spikes, a high tower, a soaring bird.

I can't hold the vision. It breaks apart before my eyes and I have no choice but to look away. Staring up at the star-speckled sky, I come back to the present. I am high on the ancient hill and no longer alone. Dark figures surround me. My scorched and strained eyes struggle to make them out, but after a second or two, I can count twelve people. Some young, some old. All women. The witches have come for me.

I get to my feet, unsteady at first, and Avril Cunningham catches me.

'Take it easy,' she says. 'Step away from the fire. Deep breath.'

In the starlight, she seems hardly to have aged. Her hair is still black, although possibly a little thinner. She is still tall and angular, her eyes huge in the darkness. Only when she smiles do I see the deep wrinkles around her eyes and mouth.

'Darling girl,' she says. I turn to the others, recognising Marlene Labaddee and a younger, very similar-looking woman, whom I assume must be Unique. At the sight of her something clenches inside me. Unique was one of the gang.

'One of us.' The warning is clear in Avril's voice. 'You must trust somewhere, Florence.'

Unique stares at me with big, chocolate-brown eyes. She is as lovely as I remember her mother being.

'Did you steal Patsy Wood's body?' I demand of Marlene. 'Did you burn her?'

'We all did,' says Avril. 'Florence, you must be calm. You must trust us.'

I spin back to face her. 'Daphne?' I say.

'In the car,' says Avril. 'She wanted to come up, but I told her to save her energy for the important stuff.'

I step away and look down the hill. I cannot see the cars in the darkness, but I think I can make out a glow that might be an interior light. I lift my hand in greeting.

'We don't have much time,' Avril says behind me.

'How did you know I was here?' I ask her.

'We went to the Black Dog when we heard you'd left the police station,' she says. 'You weren't there, so we tried the Glassbrook house, and the churchyard at St Wilfred's. Then we saw your fire.'

One of the women I don't know has brought more wood and she builds up the fire.

'This is Jenny Ogilvy.' Avril gently pushes forward a very small, slim woman of about my age. 'Dwane's wife. And did you ever meet Lorraine his sister?'

'My husband's been in love with you for thirty years,' Jenny tells me.

I am in no mood for apologies. 'I love him too,' I say. 'He is my very dear friend.'

She nods at me without smiling, as Avril introduces the others. I remember Brenda, who operated the switchboard at the police station, but most of the names go into my head and leave it without so much as an echo. Last of all steps forward Mary, the Glassbrooks' housekeeper, who has been hovering at the back. She greets me with an unsmiling nod.

'Did you see anything?' Avril indicates the now roaring fire. I tell her what I saw, but when I add that I might just be remembering the place where I was kept, she inclines her head.

'The police think Ben left town,' I say. 'They're blinkered, like we all were thirty years ago. They still think Larry killed those children. He didn't. The real killer's still out there.'

'We know,' she says. 'But the important thing now is to find your son.'

'We're going to do a search spell,' Jenny says. 'We'll split up and go to the four corners. We know he's somewhere in town.'

The four corners are simply the most northerly, southerly, easterly and westerly points of town. The coven will have worked them out years ago, will know exactly where they are heading and what to do when they get there. They will work with smoke, or possibly dust, watching the way it drifts as they say the words of the spell. Then they'll compare results, try to pinpoint the area of town where Ben might be.

Avril lifts a chain from round her neck. In the fire's light, I see a teardrop-shaped crystal. She passes it over my head and I feel its cool smoothness against my neck. 'Marlene is going to stay here with you,' she says. 'She has much to tell you.'

I shake my head. 'I'm done here. I need to be back in town, looking for my son.'

Avril holds up both hands, as though she might physically stop me leaving. 'Florence, you must stay. You need to know about the Craftsmen.'

66

The others leave us. As though we have agreed in advance how it must be, Marlene and I take our places on the hard ground and look at each other through the flames. My anxious body is demanding movement, and sitting feels like a form of torture, but I wait.

Marlene stares into the fire as though she too is scrying and I know I will have to work hard for whatever she has to tell me. She doesn't want to be here any more than I do.

If I have to be calm for Ben, I will be calm.

'The Craftsmen?' I say. I have never heard of such a group, and yet something about the name feels oddly familiar. As though I have been waiting many years to learn about them. 'Who are they?'

'We don't know,' Marlene tells the flames. 'That is the first thing. We do not even know for certain that they exist. But there was always talk, over the years, about another group in town.'

'Another coven?'

I see her head bounce gently through the smoke. 'Yes. But different. Very different to ours.'

'In what way?' Already this is feeling agonisingly slow.

She picks up a stick and pokes the fire. 'There were signs, through the years, signs we couldn't ignore. Graves disturbed, but the damage blamed on foxes. Churches vandalised. Animals stolen or maimed.'

What she is describing are classic signs of dark magic. They are also things that happen, from time to time, with nothing sinister behind them at all.

'There is power in this town, concentrated upon a few people,' Marlene says. 'Men on the town council, officers of the law, factory owners, rich businessmen. They do what they like and the law cannot touch them.'

'Sounds more like Freemasonry than witchcraft,' I say, and even as I speak, I'm remembering Larry's warnings from long ago.

'Maybe the two are not so very far apart. Or maybe one is a cover for the other.'

'You're saying all Freemasons are witches? That's impossible. There were so many of them, around here especially.'

'No, not all. Of course not all. Maybe an inner circle. Maybe the wider brotherhood protects them, even if only by not questioning, not challenging.'

She stabs at the fire again. Sparks shoot upwards and piled wood at its heart collapses. 'Years ago,' she says, 'when the children started vanishing, we feared it might be the work of the Craftsmen. We did what we could: protection spells, trace spells. It was a relief when Larry was arrested, when he confessed. A sick, twisted killer? We told ourselves that's not so bad.'

She keeps her eyes shielded, and I wonder if there was anyone in town who really, deep down, believed in Larry's guilt.

'Was Larry a Craftsman?' I ask.

She shakes her head. 'Impossible. They would have protected him. Larry was alone. Whatever else he was, he was alone.'

'Tell me what you know,' I say.

She takes a deep breath. 'They were men,' she says. 'No women ever joined this group. We only spoke about them among women because you never knew whether the man you were talking to was one of them.'

'There were men in your coven,' I say. 'I remember seeing them.'

She nods. 'Not any more. A long time ago, we stopped trusting men who were interested in the craft. Men who would join us to learn our skills, then use them for the wrong ends.'

I remember Roy Greenwood, Larry's partner. David Milner, the teacher from school.

'What else?' I say, because she has given me nothing so far.

'They needed us. They needed me. Men never make good healers. Every so often I would be asked about cordials. Asked to supply them. But always through messengers. Never directly.'

'You were a herbalist – of course you were asked about cordials.'

She shakes her head. 'Not these kind of cordials.'

There is something fearful in her face.

'Did these cordials send people to sleep?' I ask, knowing there are many herbs and plants with soporific qualities. The common poppy, for one.

'No,' she tells me. 'They were interested in a cordial that keeps people awake but completely immobile. These people can see and hear, but they can't move.'

I feel something tight grabbing hold of my chest. She is talking about an induced state of paralysed wakefulness. Possibly the most frighteningly vulnerable position anyone could find themselves in.

'If you believe the Craftsmen were responsible for the children's disappearances,' I say, 'what did you think was behind it? Why did they want to bury children alive? Were they sadists?'

'No, I don't think it was for pleasure. I think it was about power. A very bad power.'

'What do you mean?'

Her face twists, looks ugly for a second. 'My people have a way of making slaves from the dead.'

I look at her gleaming black skin, her bright eyes and say, 'Zombies?'

She lifts her upper lip in a sneer. 'No. Zombies are slaves in body only, their minds dead and gone. My people made other slaves from dark magic. Slaves in which the body is dead, but the mind still lives. Only in chains.'

I'm not following. A mind in chains?

'I have no knowledge of this, you understand,' she says. 'It is just stories I heard.'

Marlene is starting to protest too much, but I cannot challenge her. I need her. 'I understand,' I say. 'I understand that this is speculation on your part.'

Marlene says, 'If you take a person, a living soul, and trap them in a place of death, and the rituals are performed, so that as they are dying, the energy is leaving them and coming into you, if you do all this, the body dies, but the soul does not.'

I say to her, 'Many people believe that anyway. Christians talk about the immortal soul.'

'But these souls do not move on,' Marlene says. 'They are trapped, the slaves of those who performed the binding spell.'

I am puzzled by her continual use of the word 'slave'.

'What use can a slave without corporeal form be to anyone?' I ask.

'Every use in the world if you are a dark magician. An unfettered soul can slip through walls, can fly through air, can frighten enemies to death. A slave that is not bound by earthly laws would make its owner powerful beyond imagining.'

I hold up my hands. 'Marlene, you're losing me. I believe there are natural energies to be harnessed, but what you're talking about now—'

'It is not the worst of it.'

'It's not?'

'The chained soul has no rest. When he is not doing his master's bidding, he returns to his grave, to rejoin his rotting body. Only he does not know that his flesh is being eaten by worms. He thinks he is still alive. When this magic is performed, the one who is trapped below ground will remain so for all time.'

'No spell can keep a body alive without air.'

She leans forward, almost forgetting there is a fire between us. 'You don't get it, do you? The body dies, but the soul doesn't know it. It is the worst of all deaths because it never ends. It is worse, far worse than being buried alive, because if you are only buried alive, you will die after a few hours. The Craftsmen were trying to make a soul slave when you were here before. The first two were killed by the cordial. Patsy Wood was enslaved, but we set her free when we burned her body. When Larry was in prison, they could not act, because they feared he would retract his confession if more children started disappearing, but they have always yearned to make a soul slave and they are trying again now. With your son.'

She looks down at my left hand. 'They will have his bone, which is your bone. They have made the effigy. That figure you found will no longer be at the station. Somewhere there will be a coffin, a place of death. They will have planned to use you when they knew you were coming back. Your boy was a bonus.'

This woman is mad. What she is talking about is impossible. Unspeakable. I push myself up.

'An effigy of you will work for him too because he is flesh of your flesh.'

'Why children?' I ask. 'Apart from me, the early victims were all children.'

She gets to her feet too. 'Not children. Teenagers. Because they are almost grown but still small and cannot fight well. Adults would be best, but adults are harder to entrap.'

'Why didn't you tell us this before?' I say. 'When the children vanished, you must have known this then. You burned Patsy's body.'

She turns and spits. 'You think the police would have believed stories about black magic? Would you?'

'We would have dismissed stories of black magic,' I admit, 'but we might have been prepared to accept that others believed in it. You should have told us.'

She looks away. 'We didn't know anything.'

'Rubbish. You know more than you're admitting,' I say. 'It may have been speculation and rumour for Avril and the others, but you are too well informed.'

She looks down.

'Your husband is one of them, isn't he? Charles Labaddee is a Craftsman.'

'He is no longer my husband.'

She has given me the answer I need.

'Who else?' I step round the fire to get closer to her. 'Who else is a Craftsman? Where do they meet? Where are they keeping Ben? And when do they plan to perform this sick ritual? Tonight?'

I remember that this is the night of the dark moon and panic surges inside me.

'I don't know.' She shakes her head. She will not turn from me, makes no attempt to walk away, but I sense that she is broken. And that she has told me all she knows.

'If my son dies tonight, I will make sure that you are charged with obstructing the course of justice and being an accessory to murder,' I tell her. 'Your husband will rot in prison and—'

Her scream stops me in my tracks.

'You think any of that matters?' She grabs hold of my shoulder and hisses into my face, 'Listen to me. Your son will not die. Dying would be a blessing compared to what he will suffer. He will be trapped in that box to the end of time, gasping for breath and banging on the wood until he thinks his fingers are broken and screaming to be set free. He will be crying for you to save him long after you are dead and turned to dust.'

The ground beneath me shifts and I feel myself falling. All the stars have been extinguished and the darkness is closing in on me. Then something slaps hard against my face.

Marlene has hit me. I see her hand raised, ready to strike again. 'You must find your boy's body and then you must burn him,' she snarls at me. 'If you don't do that, he will never know peace. It is the last thing you can do for him. Find him and burn him.'

67

I can't remember getting back down the Hill to my car, but I am here, switching on the engine, about to drive away. There are cuts on my hands, and my knees are grazed, but I don't recall falling. I don't remember heading back towards town, but suddenly I am in the police-station car park. I switch off my engine, knowing my car will have been spotted by the desk sergeant, that already people in the building will know I'm back. I take a second to sit in the car, breathing deeply, counting to ten, plastering on the façade of calm, of sanity.

Marlene thinks I've lost. She thinks Ben is already dead, that the Craftsmen have taken their revenge on me and that all I can do now is to save his immortal soul. I will not accept this. I am looking for my son, not his body.

Larry was not the killer. I know this now. Larry confessed because he believed his daughter, Luna, had killed three of her friends and he took the blame to protect her. His secreting away of the photographs was an insurance policy: as long as she stayed out of trouble, he'd keep quiet.

I've kept them safe for thirty years, he wrote to me. *Over to you . . .* I thought he meant his family. He didn't. He meant the children of the town.

But Larry was wrong too. Luna and her friends were no more responsible for the deaths of Susan, Stephen and Patsy than he was. Larry was misled by the people who sent him photographs and my finger. I think of my hair and shoe, of the combs and handkerchiefs and keys of the other victims that were found in Larry's workshop and wonder whether they were planted, sent to him like the photographs and my finger, or whether he picked them up himself when he rescued me.

Larry rescued me. Although I think I've known this for some time, the realisation hits me hard. I owe my life to the man who for thirty years I called a monster.

I must trust someone, Avril said, and she is right. I trust the coven, even Marlene. I believe that in the end she told me everything she knows. Avril and the others understand what is going on here, but most of them are elderly women, women with neither power nor influence, and there is a limit to what they can do. There always was.

I trust Tom. I believe in the collective power and integrity of the British Police Force, but Tom and his team are blinkered. Faced with different possibilities, they will pick the one that is easiest to manage, just as we did thirty years ago. Tom and his team are looking for Ben, but in the wrong places.

And so now I have a choice to make. I can join the coven, put my faith in the power of collective thought and the ancient forces of the world to guide me to my son, casting protection spells and finding spells. I have been a witch for thirty years, almost as long as I've been a police officer.

But I was WPC Lovelady first.

When I go inside, I ask for Brian Rushton, not Tom. I trust Tom, of course, and deep down, I realise, part of me still loves him, but Tom is tainted by what happened thirty years ago. He is still clinging to the belief that we got it right back then. On some level, Brian knows that we didn't.

Finding him, I explain quickly what I want. That I know there was another group of witches in town thirty years ago and that I believe they may have been responsible for sending Larry the photographs.

'They need to be fingerprinted,' I said. 'Can you do that here?'

'Witches?' he says in response.

'You don't have to believe it,' I say. 'Just accept that they do. Can you find fingerprints here?'

'Very crudely.' He is still frowning at the mention of witches. 'We can't pick up partials or find anything difficult, but obvious, clear prints we can usually find.'

'Can we try?'

He sets off, gesturing that I should go too. 'Already in hand. Come on, we'll see if they've found anything.'

I follow him along the corridor and down into the basement.

'Found three more or less complete prints.' The officer in the fingerprint room has deep furrows between his brows. 'But to be honest, this might be contaminated evidence.'

'What do you mean?' Brian asks.

The officer pushes an enlarged image of a fingerprint at us. I look at the arches and whorls, surrounded by black dust. 'This is the boss's,' he says, an embarrassed grimace on his face. 'Easily done,' he goes on. 'Especially when emotions are running high.' He looks at me. 'We'll probably find yours on here as well.'

It takes me a few seconds to find my voice. 'I guess we weren't thinking properly. We were both so excited to find something.'

Brian swears beneath his breath but is too respectful to criticise me or Tom out loud. 'Any luck on the others?' he asks.

The officer shakes his head. 'Not yet.'

'We should leave him to it,' I say. 'Brian, I'm not feeling well. Do you think I can sit down somewhere?'

I knew when I said it that there was a risk Brian Rushton would take me to Reception, or one of the interview rooms, but he takes one look at my face and realises I really am not well. He daren't leave me alone. So he takes me up to the CID room and sits me at his own desk. He makes tea and speaks quietly to a woman in the corner before he leaves, glancing often in my direction. It is clear she has been told to keep an eye on me.

I am not well. I have never in my whole life been less well. I am fighting an urge to run screaming from the room. I can feel the world spinning away from me, leaving me in vast, inescapable darkness, but I know I have to cling on somehow. I close my eyes, drop my head onto Brian Rushton's desk and pray for calm, for strength, for clarity of thought. I try to connect with my sisters at the four corners to draw in some of their power.

My head is leaning on the files that Brian brought into my hotel room. The old Glassbrook files.

When I lift my head, I am not being observed. There are three people in the room, but they are being sympathetic, giving me privacy, so it isn't difficult to slide the files off the desk and into the bag that is waiting on my lap.

'I'm going to the ladies',' I say, to the woman who has been tasked with looking out for me.

She half gets to her feet. 'Can I help at all? Do you know where you're going?'

'End of the corridor,' I say. 'Look for me if I'm not back in ten minutes.' I give her what I hope is a brave smile.

The ladies' toilets have improved considerably since my day. There are six cubicles, all of them empty, and I lock myself in the one furthest from the door.

Thirty years ago, the people who murdered the children, the people I must learn to call the Craftsmen, saw a chance to frame

Larry for the murders when they realised what his daughter and her friends had done. Quite why they would want to I don't know. Maybe they felt vulnerable, saw the police search closing in. Maybe we were close with the cricket connection and they felt the need to close the case down quickly.

Having decided to frame Larry, they sent him the incriminating photographs, and evidence that he would have believed entirely convincing – my amputated finger – and let him reach the only possible conclusion. They gambled on him rescuing me and taking the blame for the crimes.

Which means they must have told him where to find me. There must have been something else sent to Larry in that brown envelope. Something I haven't seen yet but have a chance of finding now, if it wasn't destroyed or lost thirty years ago.

I sit on the lavatory lid and make my way through the file. I see photographs that I remember and handwritten notes, many of them mine. I flick through witness statements and file notes, and thank heaven for the computerised databases that make our jobs so much easier now. I keep going, with one eye on the time, because I know that sooner or later someone will look for me.

At last, three-quarters of the way through the file, I find the list of clothes that Larry was wearing on the night he was arrested. As I read through, I'm remembering the straight-legged jeans, the light brown jacket edged in lilac, the apricot-coloured shirt, the pointed-toe suede shoes. Winkle-pickers. The name comes back to me after all these years.

The list goes on to detail the contents of his jeans' pockets: *One set of three keys, one black leather wallet, containing a five-pound note and three one-pound notes. Loose change, including six shillings and ten pennies. A blue-and-white-striped handkerchief. A brown, plastic, fine-toothed comb.*

And then the contents of his jacket pockets: *One amputated finger (believed to be third finger of the left hand of WPC Florence Love-lady), one bloodstained tissue, wrapped round said finger, one cutting taken from the* Sabden Gazette, *dated 18 June 1969.*

I can think of no reason why Larry would have a cutting from the *Sabden Gazette* in his shirt pocket, that night of all nights. Two minutes later, I find it, shrunken, faded, its ink rubbing off on surrounding papers but legible enough.

It is the story of the riot at the Perseverance Mill. I'd had no idea there was even a photographer there that night, but there must have been, because the photograph that accompanies the story was taken from the back of the crowd. It shows dozens of men, many in the flat caps worn in those days, staring at the doors of the mill, while six officers – Detective Inspector Sharples, Detective Sergeants Brown and Green, Constables Butterworth, Devine and Lovelady – face them off.

Great metal doors. An underground space. A place within a short drive of St Wilfred's Churchyard, where I was found. This is it. Thirty years ago, Larry Glassbrook rescued me from the Perseverance Mill. My son is in the Perseverance Mill.

68

I trust no one.

I leave the station seeing only the desk sergeant and I tell him that I'm going back to my hotel. He nods, hardly able to meet my eyes, but that is a good thing. He does not see the spark that I know I won't be able to hide.

I drive as fast as I dare, keeping a constant lookout for headlights tailing me. Once again I go via the Glassbrook house. Taking only a few minutes, I find the tools I will need in Larry's shed. A very sharp knife, heavy-duty metal cutters, a large iron hammer and a carbon-steel rod shaped at both ends, which in the US is called a crowbar, in England a jemmy. I wrap them in a piece of canvas and I'm ready. In my car I have a torch and the CS gas canister that Ben teased me about this morning.

Only on the two-mile drive back to the mill does my resolve waver. Thirty years have gone by. The mill was empty in 1969 and I'm being stupid to imagine it is even still there. It will have been demolished long ago. I will arrive in Jubilee Street to see a block of residential flats. Despair washes over me and I almost pull over, but something keeps me driving, along the main road and into Jubilee Street.

It is there. I see the tall, dark-brick walls in the pale glow of security lights as I draw closer. The surrounding wall is still standing. The gates have been renewed and look stronger and more forbidding than ever. Somehow the mill survived long enough for a preservation order to be put on the building.

To one side of the gates is an illuminated sign, and as I park at the kerb, squeezing in between a Citroën and a Honda, I read, *Perseverance Mill. Offices, light industrial premises and workshops to let.*

The Craftsmen that Marlene told me about are powerful men. Rich men. They may own this building, may have owned it for over thirty years. Maybe John Earnshaw, who owned it in 1969, is one of them. Unable to keep it empty, in defiance of all urban-development regulations and compulsory-purchase orders, they may have developed it, let it out, keeping some parts of it for themselves.

Am I clutching at straws? I don't think so. Something about this place has always felt very wrong, and that tells me I'm right.

I don't have much time. The Craftsmen will have been watching me since I arrived in town; they may already know that I left the police station. If they realise I've seen the file, they might know I'm coming here. I have no time to waste, but I will not disappear without trace.

I reach for my phone. Avril answers on the first ring.

'Florence, darling, we're pretty certain he's somewhere in the town centre. Not too far from the main road, closer to Padiham than the Hill, not as far as the Hinton Street bridge. I'm sorry we can't be more—'

She is describing an area of roughly half a square mile.

'It's OK,' I tell her. 'And you're right. He's in the Perseverance Mill. I'm there now.'

'Oh my goodness. Wait for us. We're on our way.'

'No, Avril. I need you to stay where you are, you and the others. Stay at the four corners. I need you to send me protection. And strength. For me and Ben. Right now. Can you do it?'

'Florence, please tell me you're not—'

'Avril, I have to go. Can I rely on you?'

A short pause. Then, 'Always.' The line goes dead.

I look around carefully when I get out of the car. The parked cars – so many of them now – are empty. No one is watching me from the surrounding houses. I touch car bonnets. None of them is warm.

The mill pond is still here, but transformed now into a garden where office workers can enjoy their lunch. As I peer over the wall, I catch the sickly scent of buddleia blossoms. Back on the Hill, I didn't check for a buddleia bush and so have no means of knowing whether what I smelled there was real, a memory or clairvoyance. It hardly matters.

I remember a second set of gates at the rear of the building, and memory serves. They are smaller, less forbidding than the front gates, and it is darker at the back. Women of my age are not natural climbers, but I am worried about neither dignity nor clothing. I push my tools and bag through the bars and in less than a minute I am in the yard.

There are no vehicles parked here. No lights in the building.

I make my way round the walls, keeping to the shadows, watching out for surveillance devices, knowing that if Ben is here, he is likely to be guarded. At the same time, I am going as quickly as I can because they are coming. The metal trapdoors are at the side of the building, just as I remember them, but there is no way to access them from the yard. They will be bolted from beneath.

Thirty years ago, Larry found his way into this building. Back then, though, it was derelict, and my captors wanted him to find me, could even have left the door unlocked. I wonder how scared he was, making his way through the dark mill, whether at any time he was tempted to give up.

Larry was acting to save his child, as I am. I stop moving for a second, when the thought occurs that Larry may also have been acting to save me.

I keep going, looking for the entrance Larry may have used. There is a side door round the next corner, but it's locked. I carry on, and the smart office windows at the front and side give way to more utilitarian ones at the back. This will be where the maintenance rooms and kitchens are. I spot patterned glass, which probably indicates a bathroom.

I left the station twenty minutes ago. They are coming.

Back at the bathroom windows, I roll a metal bin until it can get me up high enough and use the jemmy to smash the glass. No alarm sounds, but I feel a stinging pain in my right hand, and when I reach down, touch the sticky warmth of blood. Cursing my own clumsiness, I pull my sleeve down round the wound and scrape the rest of the glass from the window ledge before scrambling through. Still no alarm. I am in a male bathroom, about to climb down into a washbasin. It holds my weight and I land on the tiled floor.

Instantly my head starts to throb. I give myself a second, breathing deeply, but the room has been cleaned recently and the smell of bleach seems to burn its way into my throat. When I turn back to the basin, I see the scarlet splashes of my own blood and suddenly I feel deeply unwell, as though I might faint.

From the first cubicle I pull a length of toilet tissue, twisting it into a rope and wrapping it tightly round my hand, but the pain in my head is getting worse.

Already this is going badly.

And then I realise I'm not alone. Someone is standing behind me. I can feel his breath on my neck, actually hear the rattle in his lungs. I spin round, already cringing back against the cubicle wall, and see nothing but a central heating vent on the opposite wall.

I have to get out of this bathroom.

The door opens onto a corridor that is dimly lit by security lights. I turn left, heading towards the trapdoors, through an interior that has changed completely. There are glass-walled offices to my right, and beyond them an atrium, which will let in light when the sun comes up. On its far side are more offices and the outer wall of the mill. There is no light coming in now.

People in the glass-fronted offices! I see several figures, dark shapes, moving with me, speeding up as I do, racing for the doors to cut me off in the corridor. I turn, head back the other way, and they turn too. My head is pounding and I think I am about to be sick.

As I pull open the bathroom door again, a gust of fresh air hits me from outside. I smell grass and woodsmoke and it clears my head a little. A thought occurs to me and I turn once more.

The figures in the offices are stationary, watching me. I lift my right arm. They copy. I step forward. They do the same, so that the distance between us narrows, and so convincing are my doppelgängers that I almost turn and run again. But I know them now for what they are. Shadows and reflections, given a grim power by my own fear.

I am wasting too much time, jumping at ghosts. Outside, I think I hear a car engine.

I set off again, ignoring the odd noises that the building produces. The sibilant sound is internal plumbing, not the hiss of lurking snakes. The flickering shadow high on the wall is made by a night bird passing by outside. It is not a bat.

I reach the end of the corridor and turn. In the old days, there was a narrow doorway here that opened onto stairs, leading down to the subterranean floor below. My headache is fading, but in its place is the weariness that might be the result of several hours of frantic worry. I need adrenaline right now, nervous energy, but that most basic of instincts seems to have deserted me.

The air in here is hot and stale.

The rotting wooden door I remember is gone, but in its place are larger, steel-slatted doors. Doors like that always lead into maintenance rooms, or boiler rooms, or basements. I reach the doors and stop to catch my breath. Still no alarm has sounded.

The door is locked, but it is no match for Larry's jemmy and my desperation. The lock breaks on my fifth attempt. Were I myself, it might only have taken three, but at last the door swings open. I am no longer expecting alarms. For whatever reason, this place isn't protected by the normal security installations. The staircase in front of me leads down into darkness, and diviner or not, I have no way of knowing what I will find at the bottom.

I have been here before. *Hello, Florence*, the darkness says. *Welcome home.*

I give myself a second. The locked door suggests Ben might not be guarded. I may have to do nothing more than descend this staircase, free my son and help him out of the building. But there is dark magic at work here. I sensed it the second I broke in. Even now, staring down into blackness, I can almost see it moving, as though there is a presence lurking below.

I switch on the torch and shine it down. I see bare plaster walls, a metal handrail and concrete stairs that go on forever. There is no end to these stairs; they are leading the way straight down to hell. At that moment, the top step, the one I am standing on, gives away and I fall. As I reach out and grab the safety rail, the torch leaves my hand and goes clattering down the steps. My arm is wrenched; my head hits the wall, but I don't tumble. Not daring to let go of the rail, I look back at the top step. It is intact. I lost my balance, that is all.

At the bottom of the steps, and there is a bottom, I see now, not twenty steps below me, my torch beam shines out, illuminating the damp-stained stone floor, the dust of years. It is pointing the way to my son.

If ever I needed to be brave, it is now.

At the four corners of town, my sisters are sending every bit of strength and courage that they can. They've had no time for complex preparations, so will have to fall back on the simplest of rituals, a time-honoured spell. Basically, they are praying for me, and I will take that.

On the third step down, I hear mewling.

I freeze. There is an injured animal below that is bleating out its pain. I picture it crawling towards me, dragging a skeletal body across the cellar floor, wrapping itself round my foot and sinking its starving teeth into my flesh.

For God's sake! I have to get a grip. It is my son that I can hear below.

'Ben!'

The whimpering stops.

'Ben, it's me. I'm coming.' I carry on down the steps. I get half-way before the torch goes out.

I keep going, stepping down into complete blackness now, but I am afraid that if I stop, I will never move again. I think I remember at least nine more steps. On the seventh, I tread carefully and can tell when I've reached the bottom by the different feel of the cellar floor.

I look back up at the open door, but the corridor was very dimly lit and none of its sparse light can reach me here. I bend down, feel for the torch and try to switch it back on again, but the fall has broken it. I must find Ben in complete blackness.

If they come now, we are both trapped, defenceless in the dark.

'Ben,' I try. 'I'm here, but I can't see you. Can you hear me, baby?'

That noise again. The high-pitched puling that I can't associate with my tall, strong son. I force myself to turn in its direction and take a step forward, then another, but it is so hard to keep moving when every second I could come up against a brick wall, or a sheer drop, or a snarling face.

Above me, the cellar door slams shut.

Now I am whimpering and I have to force myself to be calm. Ben is in here somewhere and he needs me to be strong. But the mewling sound has started up again and now it's coming from somewhere completely different. I turn towards it and take a step, but I've lost all sense of direction. I don't know where the stairs are, where I thought the sound was coming from before.

'Ben?'

The hideous noise he is making, if it is he and not the vile crawling thing of my nightmares, seems to be coming from all around me, as though the cellar has an echo. I'm no longer sure whether my eyes are open or shut, but I can see pictures in my head and they are of creeping things, scraping their claws along the floor, their huge, milky eyes able to see in this blackness. I can hear them. I can hear the sounds as their fleshless bodies drag over the rough floor.

They are winning. The Craftsmen are beating me.

My hand goes to my throat in an instinctive, protective gesture and my fingers curl round the crystal Avril gave me. I think of them, those thirteen women on the town's edges, and picture their thoughts streaming towards me like moonlight.

Above me, I hear noises and shut my mind to them.

'Ben!' I find my voice. 'Ben, listen to me. I need you to do something and it's very important. Remember when you were little? When we played hide-and-seek? You'd pretend to be a mouse, remember? And you'd squeak like a mouse and I'd come and find you? I need you to do that now. Squeak like a mouse, Ben. Like you did when you were tiny.'

For a second, then more, there is silence.

And then, 'Eeek!'

Got him! I spin in the right direction and wait to make sure. It comes again.

'Eeek!'

Yes. I take a step, then another.

'I'm coming, baby,' I say.

'Eeek!'

The squeak is wrong, but I remember how I was gagged when I was down here. He is doing his best. He squeaks and I take a step forward, and I am thinking back to the days when the only thing that mattered in life was the tiny human who'd been given into my care. We were everything to each other then, Ben and I. The world existed just for the two of us, and most days, from as soon as he could walk until he went to school, we played hide-and-seek.

'Keep going,' I say. 'I'm almost there,' and I know that I am because the sounds he is making are getting louder and closer. And then my foot pushes up against something soft and I drop to my knees and grab hold of his leg. I run my hands down to his feet and find his ankles taped together, then back up his body to his arms, which are taped behind his back. He is sitting up. I find his face and clutch it tight, cup his head with my hand. I take my hands off him for a second to find the knife.

I cut the tape on his legs first so that he can run, and then the tape round his wrists so that he can fight. Finally, I help him peel away the tape from his mouth so that he can speak.

He gives a soft moan and leans into me. He's alive. I've got him, but the Craftsmen are still out there.

'Ben, can you stand up? We have to get out of here.'

I wrap my arm around him and try to drag him upright. I had no idea how heavy my son has become, but after a few attempts, when his legs buckle beneath him like a newborn colt, he gets to his feet and can lean against me.

We are surrounded by blackness and I have no idea of the way out.

'Avril, help me!'

I don't mean to cry out. I so desperately want to be strong for my baby, but I can't help it. To have got this far and be stuck here with him, to die together after everything he's been through.

'Madness,' he croaks at my side.

I'm trying not to cry. He's right. I've been fighting off madness all these years. I lost part of my soul in this cellar, and now that I'm back in it, I'm sinking.

'Madness,' he says again, except it doesn't sound so much like 'madness' this time, more like—

'Matches,' he says, clear as a crystal bell. 'Mum, you've got matches.'

He's right. There are matches in my bag. Even candles. Telling him to keep hold of me, I rummage in my bag till I find the matches. I strike one and in its tiny, clear light I see the stairs, not fifteen feet away. We are halfway to them when the match burns my fingers and goes out. A second match gets us to the bottom step and then we climb.

The door has only blown shut. We can get out. We stumble along the corridor, holding each other up, and burst out through the fire exit. I drag him to the main gates so that we can look through the bars and see the world again.

Only then, when I know that we are safe and beyond their reach, do I call the police.

69

Ben is taken straight to Burnley General. In the ambulance, there is enough light for me to see his grey, clenched face and trembling limbs. My first act is to take up both of his hands and count the fingers. Ten, thank God. He pulls them away from me and tucks them beneath his upper arms.

I want him to cry, because crying has always felt like the action of a sane person, but he doesn't.

As we are rushed into Accident and Emergency, Brian Rushton appears, and I explain about seeing the picture of the mill in the old file and working it out. I tell him I saw no one there, that I have no idea who kidnapped my son. He tells me the entire mill has been closed off and has become a major crime scene. They will want to talk to Ben, he says, but it can wait until the morning.

Ben has cuts and bruises, and a suspected concussion, but nothing that I need worry about long term, according to the staff who attend him. Nothing physical, anyway. They talk about counselling and offer contacts, but I tell them I am taking him away as soon as he can be moved.

'Don't underestimate the impact something like this will have on a young mind,' the doctor says, as though I, of all people, need to be told about the long-term impact of trauma. When I think about Ben going through what I did, both in that basement and in the years following, I am taken aback by how much rage I am capable of feeling.

It is two o'clock in the morning by this time, and I think the hospital staff are surprised by the crowd heading our way when the doctor and I leave the private room where Ben has finally fallen asleep.

Daphne, smaller and fatter but unmistakably Daphne, walks towards us on Avril's arm, the other women following behind. At the back, in between his wife and sister, is Dwane. Daphne takes me into her arms, and the others gather round, pressing close and sharing what little strength they have left. I feel their life forces flowing into me, as though they know how much more I have to do tonight.

'I don't want to leave Ben,' I tell Avril and Daphne. 'I'm scared to leave him.'

Avril touches my upper arm. It is a gesture of solidarity not comfort. 'My dear,' she says. 'We will be here till you get back. However long it takes.'

Dwane breaks from our little huddle and takes up his stance at Ben's door. His feet are planted wide, his arms folded. He stares into the middle distance like a Lilliputian president's security guard and I know he will die before he lets the wrong person into that room. The women settle themselves in the corridor, dragging chairs closer. They take up positions around the door and my sleeping son is safe.

'Are you sure, Florence?' whispers Avril, and I know that in spite of everything, she wants me to change my mind.

As I walk away down the hospital corridor, I take out my phone and type a quick text message.

Fancy a swim?

70

I reach the Black Tarn first, as I expected to. As I am counting on.
The police have a lot to do tonight and he will not be able to get
away quickly. I take the rug from my car, and the wine and plastic
glasses I bought in a twenty-four-hour petrol station. I sit by the
water while I'm waiting, scooping up the thick clay mud from the
lake's edge, smoothing it and shaping it, adding drier earth from
the bank when I feel it needs more solidity. I am no craftsman, but
the picture I am making need not be recognisable. It is my intent
that is important. I have to mean it.

I mean it.

I have been here nearly half an hour when I hear another car
engine. I put the picture among some reeds and lean down to the
lake to wash my hands. I am shaking them dry when Tom's car
appears.

For several seconds I am caught in the headlights. They feel like
searchlights and my heart starts to beat faster. I cannot see who
is driving that car. Then the lights go out, and as I blink my eyes
back to normal, I see the tall outline of Tom getting out of the
car. He's had music playing, of course he has, and he leaves the
radio on. I'm not surprised to hear that it's Simon & Garfunkel's
'Scarborough Fair'. He walks the last few yards towards me, stops
when he is three feet away.

'How is he?' he asks.

'Sleeping,' I say. 'Surrounded by an armed guard.'

'Armed?'

'With love, courage and the very best of intentions.' I watch his puzzled frown melt into a smile.

'You are amazing, you know that? Thirty years on and you still run rings round us.'

'Want a drink?' I say.

He nods and we sit. I pour the wine. He tells me what's happening at the Perseverance Mill, about some fresh leads they've found, witness statements that they can follow up in the morning, although of course they're hoping that Ben's testimony will help a lot.

I tell him that I haven't allowed Ben to be interviewed yet and he seems to relax. I check the lines of his jacket for hidden weapons but see nothing. Nevertheless, there is an energy building within him. I check that my bag is within reach.

'Do you believe the old story,' I say, as we watch the still, black lake, 'that women baptised in this water serve two masters?'

'Do you?' I hear an edge in his voice that tells me to be very careful.

'I believe women who are baptised in this lake change,' I say.

His blue eyes look black. 'If you changed, it was down to a very bad case and nearly being killed by a maniac.' His face softens and he smiles. 'But right now, Floss, I swear you haven't changed in thirty years. It must be the moonlight.'

'There is no moon.'

'I hadn't noticed.'

He leans forward and kisses me. I let him because some part of me has always loved Tom and always will. I let him because the last time Tom and I were here, like this, I was a woman whole and undamaged, a woman for whom the world was full of wonderful and exciting possibilities. For a second or two I want to be that girl again.

We break apart. He smiles. I smile back. He reaches out and I know that this time his hands are aiming for my throat. Not in a friendly way.

I gas him.

CS gas works surprisingly well.

I aim at his chest, as I was taught years ago, when I still came into regular contact with the unpredictable public. The spurt of liquid hits its target and evaporates instantly into a gas that will cause Tom almost unbearable pain for the next few minutes. I jump to my feet because I cannot afford to be caught by it too. He falls forward, clutching at his eyes, although he probably knows it is the worst thing he can do. I have to act fast. I push him face down and cuff his hands behind his back. Then, before he can re-cover and start kicking, I tie nylon rope from Larry's shed round his ankles. I take hold of his collar to drag him back to the car.

It isn't easy to get a man of Tom's size and weight into the boot of a car, but I have faced bigger obstacles than this tonight and I am determined to manage it. He fights me, of course, but he is still weak and shaky from the gas.

'What the fuck are you doing? Are you insane?' he spits out when he can speak again.

'I'm the woman you made me,' I say. 'When you locked me in that basement and cut off my finger and drove me out of my mind with terror.'

His face screws up incredulously, but I see the fear in his eyes. 'Floss, you've got it wrong.'

'We found your fingerprints on the photographs from the Glassbrook house,' I say. 'You sent those pictures to Larry Glass-brook. You knew he'd assume Luna was guilty. You planted the evidence that framed him.'

He shakes his head. His eyes are red and streaming.

'You and I wore gloves all the time we were in the house tonight,'

I say. 'There is no way your fingerprints could have been on those pictures unless you touched them thirty years ago. You're a much more careful officer now than you were back then.'

He bucks, tries to sit upright. I push him back with Larry's jemmy.

'You have one chance to make me change my mind.' I'm lying. He has no chance of living beyond the next few minutes, but I still want information from him. 'Tell me who the other Craftsmen are.'

'I don't know what you're talking about.'

'I'm guessing Roy Greenwood and David Milner, back then,' I say. 'Greenwood had access to the funeral parlour. Milner was interested in pottery, and both were members of Daphne and Avril's coven. Greenwood's dead now, of course, so someone would have replaced him. Charles Labaddee I know about. John Earnshaw maybe. How many more?'

He surges up again and I have no choice but to whack him hard with the jemmy. I aim for his shoulder because I want to keep him conscious. He falls back down.

'I'd say seven in total,' I say, knowing that covens are typically thirteen in number, but thirteen is a lot of people to trust, especially when dark magic is your thing. Seven is the next most propitious number. 'You, Charles, Milner, if he's still alive. Who else? I want four more names.'

He sneers. 'They will kill you.'

I bend lower. 'They can try.'

And because all pretence between us has been dropped, I take out Larry's knife and make a small cut above his cheekbone. He swears and starts to buck in the car boot. My heart is leaping in fear. If he gets loose, our positions will be reversed in seconds, but I'm almost done. I step back to the lake, find the clay picture, still damp and pliable, and smear Tom's blood over it. When

I get back to the car, he is half out of the boot, so I gas him again.

When he can see, I show him the effigy of himself, see the horror in his eyes and know that he believes. He starts to scream as I put the effigy in the boot with him, but we both know that no one will hear him here. I get into the driver's seat, start the engine and drive to the edge of the water before getting out.

'Last chance,' I lie again.

He spits at me. 'I will haunt you,' he says.

'Oh, I'm counting on it.' Pushing him down, I close the boot. Then I start the engine again and release the handbrake. The car rolls forward. Tom bangs and kicks against the inside of the boot. I think I can see the metal buckling.

The front of the car hits the water and it rolls on, sending black waves up the muddy shore towards me. Soon the water will kill the engine, but gravity will take over. This lake is very deep.

When a third of the car is beneath the water, I begin speaking. I have never performed a binding spell, but the actual words don't matter so much as the intent. I am surprised, though, by how readily the words of the very first binding spell I ever heard come back to me.

'Lead Thomas, whom Mary bore, the son of Harold, to me,' I say.

The car slips further into the water and begins to float. Bubbles of air burst up from all around it, and I can still hear Tom banging and yelling to be free. If what Marlene told me is correct, he will be doing that for all eternity.

'Drag him by his hair, by his guts, until he does not stand aloof from me,' I say, 'and until I hold him obedient for the whole time of my life, loving me, desiring me and telling me what he is thinking.'

The car is sinking, the bubbles becoming less frequent. There is one last slick of silver on the lake's surface and then it too vanishes. I stay until the water is still again, and then I gather up my things and leave.

71

Wednesday 11 August 1999

The sky is overcast when we gather round Larry Glassbrook's grave for the second time. We don't call it a second funeral, of course. Even in Sabden, we prefer to bury our dead only once. So we call it private prayers for the family, and this time Sally and her daughters stand at the graveside and weep together.

A sharp breeze from the moor wraps itself around us as the vicar begins to speak feel the need to press closer to someone for warmth, but no one is near enough. I'm standing alone.

Apart from the tall man a few inches behind me. I can feel his breath, cold against the side of my neck. There is no warmth to be had from him.

'We thank you now for all his life,' says the vicar. 'For every memory of love and joy, for every good deed done by him.'

On the other side of the grave, a little removed from the group, I catch Dwane's eye. For some reason, he has dressed today in his old sexton's clothes, and he leans against a spade.

In my ear, I hear a heavy sigh.

This time there are flowers. The coven came with arms laden, many from their own gardens, others they've gathered from the summer fields and hedgerows. Mugwort, meadowsweet, guelder rose and mallow, flowers that ease pain, take away anxiety, give restful sleep. My friends, the thirteen witches, stand in a circle round the grave now, and when I look at their faces, I see many expressions: sadness, shame, guilt, but most of all fear. They know how powerless they are. How powerless women such as they have always been.

Above us, the clouds shift and the sun shines through, flooding the churchyard with light. Still quite early in the day, the sun is behind us and shadows appear, smooth-lined from the head-stones, spiky and swaying from the trees, human-shaped and still from the congregation.

There are twenty-two of us gathered round the grave. I count twenty-three shadows.

As soon as I allowed him to be interviewed, Ben named Superin-tendent Tom Devine as the man who called my son's hotel room shortly after I left, coaxed him down to the car park under the pretence of my needing help with the car and stood by while someone else grabbed him from behind. A search for Tom Devine is underway and he is generally assumed to have left the area. Whether he will ever be linked to the three murders thirty years ago is a moot point. In a whispered aside as we were waiting for the vicar to arrive, Brian Rushton told me that the photographs we found at the Glassbrook house, the ones with Tom's finger-print, have vanished. As has the effigy of me.

Tom didn't act alone.

I will haunt you. Tom's voice is so clear in my head that for a moment I'm sure I actually hear it again. I find myself mouthing back my answer and see Daphne on the other side of the circle watching me. I clamp my lips shut and tell myself to focus.

The other man that I love – the good man that I love – my hus-band, Nick, arrived early this morning, hurtling over the moors from Manchester Airport in a rattling hire car, and he and Ben haven't been apart since. The two of them look at me strangely, almost as though they think I might be leaving them. In a way, I already have. I crossed a line last night. I will never completely cross back again.

'We thank you for the glory we shall share together. Hear our prayers through Jesus Christ our Lord.'

I doubt there is a Christian at the graveside, except perhaps Brian Rushton, but we dutifully mutter our 'Amen's, and then people start to walk away. Sally and the girls leave first, then Ben and Nick, then the witches. Brian follows and my little friend and I are alone.

Almost alone.

'If anything happens,' I say, 'call me. I'll come back.'

Dwane doesn't reply. Nor will he look at me.

'I can help,' I say. 'I know about the Craftsmen now.'

Dwane's eyes go beyond me to the church gate. 'Family's waiting.' He turns his back and smooths the already perfect mound of earth.

At the outer corner of the churchyard, movement catches my eye. I look round to see the three dead teenagers sitting on the wall, kicking their heels against the stones in the way bored kids do, and I remember how close my son came to being one of them.

I regret nothing.

I raise my hand in a wave that anyone watching will think is aimed at Dwane and turn to leave. Two shadows, my own and the one that will haunt me for the rest of my life, go ahead, reaching the path before I do and bouncing along the gravel to where my husband and son are waiting. I thought I might dread this moment but, actually, I find myself interested. Curious to see what comes next.

'I'm glad you're with me,' I say.

'Always,' Tom replies.

Author Note

Sabden, at the foot of Pendle Hill in Lancashire, is a real place that bears little resemblance to the town called Sabden in this book. For my story to work, I needed a town, not a village; I needed dozens of streets, shops, pubs and factories, a well-stocked public library and an equally well-staffed police station. I needed municipal parks, grand Victorian buildings and lots of graveyards.

My Sabden is based on the town of Darwen, a few miles away, where I was born and grew up. Darreners will probably recognise many of the landmarks and streets that found their way into the book. My apologies, as required, to the residents of both Sabden and Darwen.

The historical facts about the 1612 witch trials are correct to the best of my belief.

Acknowledgements

Sam Eades and the teams at Trapeze and Orion for their confidence and support.

Anne Marie Doulton and her colleagues at the Ampersand and Buckman agencies for their wise counsel and tireless efforts; my old friend John Wilcock who helped me understand what witches do; my slightly newer friend Adrian Summons, for casting his mind back to how policing was done in the 1960s; the Killer Women, for letting me join the coolest club in town; those who loiter around the scene of the crime; and finally my family, who help more than they will ever know.